W9-CUG-079

EDITH HOLLER

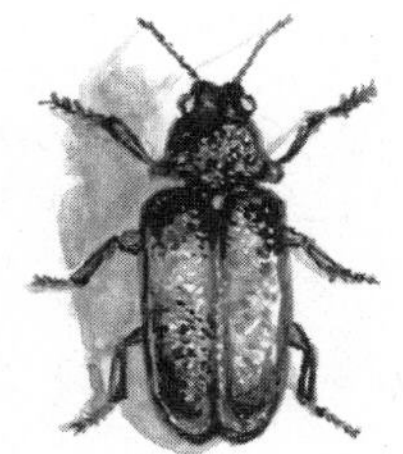

ALSO BY EDWARD CAREY

Plagues and Pencils: A Year of Pandemic Sketches

The Swallowed Man

Little

Alva & Irva, The Twins Who Saved a City

Observatory Mansions

THE IREMONGER TRILOGY

Heap House

Foulsham

Lungdon

EDITH HOLLER

Being her story; and containing numerous illustrations drawn from the life, private albums, and extensive card theatre collection of Edith Holler, authoress

Edward Carey

RIVERHEAD BOOKS
NEW YORK
2023

RIVERHEAD BOOKS
An imprint of Penguin Random House LLC
penguinrandomhouse.com

Copyright © 2023 by Edward Carey
Penguin Random House supports copyright. Copyright fuels creativity, encourages diverse voices, promotes free speech, and creates a vibrant culture. Thank you for buying an authorized edition of this book and for complying with copyright laws by not reproducing, scanning, or distributing any part of it in any form without permission. You are supporting writers and allowing Penguin Random House to continue to publish books for every reader.

Riverhead and the R colophon are registered trademarks of Penguin Random House LLC.

Illustrations by the author

Library of Congress Cataloging-in-Publication Data

Names: Carey, Edward, 1970– author, illustrator.
Title: Edith Holler : containing numerous illustrations drawn from the life, private albums, and extensive card theatre collection of Edith Holler, authoress / Edward Carey.
Description: New York : Riverhead Books, 2023.
Identifiers: LCCN 2023003812 (print) | LCCN 2023003813 (ebook) | ISBN 9780593188903 (hardcover) | ISBN 9780593188927 (ebook)
Subjects: LCGFT: Gothic fiction. | Novels.
Classification: LCC PR6053.A6813 E35 2023 (print) | LCC PR6053.A6813 (ebook) | DDC 823/.914—dc23/eng/20230421
LC record available at https://lccn.loc.gov/2023003812
LC ebook record available at https://lccn.loc.gov/2023003813

Printed in the United States of America
1st Printing

BOOK DESIGN BY MEIGHAN CAVANAUGH

This is a work of fiction. Names, characters, places, and incidents either are the product of the author's imagination or are used fictitiously, and any resemblance to actual persons, living or dead, businesses, companies, events, or locales is entirely coincidental.

For Oliver

That, if I then had waked after long sleep
Will make me sleep again; and then, in dreaming
The clouds methought would open and show riches
Ready to drop upon me, that, when I waked
I cried to dream again.

William Shakespeare, *The Tempest*
Act III, Scene ii

And sometimes sent my ships in fleets
All up and down among the sheets;
Or brought my trees and houses out,
And planted cities all about.

Robert Louis Stevenson,
The Land of Counterpane

The Harlots cry from Street to Street
Shall weave Old Englands winding Sheet
The Winners Shout the Losers Curse
Dance before dead Englands Hearse
Every Night & every Morn
Some to Misery are Born
Every Morn and every Night
Some are Born to sweet delight
Some are Born to sweet delight
Some are Born to Endless Night

William Blake,
Auguries of Innocence

Persons Represented

EDGAR HOLLER, an actor manager

JEROME HOLLER, front of house manager

WILFRED HOLLER, stage manager

GREGORY HOLLER, an actor

THOMAS HOLLER, an actor

(Jerome, Wilfred, Gregory and Thomas Holler:) brothers to Edgar Holler

CLARENCE UTTING, a businessman

OLIVER MEALING, a playwright

MR. PENK, chief cloakroom attendant

MR. PEAT, stage door keeper

MASTER CREE, assistant stage door keeper

MR. LEADHAM, in charge of theatre donkeys

MR. COLLIN, an understudy

MR. JET, a fireman

JOHN HAWTHORNE, an assistant to the stage manager

AUBREY UNTHANK, a boy in a suit

MARGARET UNTHANK, a businesswoman

AGNESIA UNTHANK, her daughter

NORA HOLLER, wardrobe mistress

BELINDA HOLLER, backstage cleaner, sister to Edgar Holler

JENNY GARNER, an actress

FLORA BIGNELL, wig curler

MISS TEBBY, prompt mistress

MRS. STEAD, puppet mistress

EDITH HOLLER, playwright, daughter to Edgar Holler

Other actors and workers of the Holler Theatre,
also insects and spirits found therein

SCENE. The Holler Theatre, Theatre Street, Norwich, 1901

I

A tour of my theatre.

1.

At home.

In Great Britain, in England, on the bump on the right that is about halfway down the country, by which I mean the rounded bit that has a pleasant and generous look to it, something like the handle of a favorite teacup, or the curve of a lovely ear, is East Anglia. The top of that bump is the county of Norfolk. A little to the right of the center of Norfolk is a city called Norwich. Norwich, seen upon a map, is roughly the shape of a leg of mutton. In the centermost point of Norwich, around the tip of the shank, is a castle called Norwich Castle. It was built by the Normans and is the type of castle called a keep. Ten minutes' walk from the castle is the Holler Theatre. I have lived here, upon Theatre Street, my whole life. There are side streets around the building, they are called Chapelfield East and Chantry Road, and there is our neighbor the Assembly House and a little beyond that the church of St. Stephen, and that is the whole box around the theatre. I was born here and have not been anywhere else since, not even once.

The city of Norwich is visible to me from the theatre roof. The cathedral spire I can see, for example, and the castle on its high mound.

Under the mound there is supposed to be a king called Gurgunt. Some say he founded the city, and that he waits in the deep with a whole army ready to rescue Norwich should it come to great peril. It is just a tale certainly, but a wonder tale nevertheless—it makes you feel that magic is local. Finally, I can see the back of the Bethel Hospital, founded in 1725 for curable lunatics.

I see all these buildings because they are tall and large and declare themselves well. But I have never once stepped inside any of them. I don't go out at all, but stay in perpetual. For a better understanding of my life, you may buy a miniature Holler Theatre in card form, from Jarrold & Sons, the stationer, 1–11 London Street, which can be assembled at home. It is a beautiful toy and with it you may mount your own in-house performances; Price 6d. But I live in the actual building.

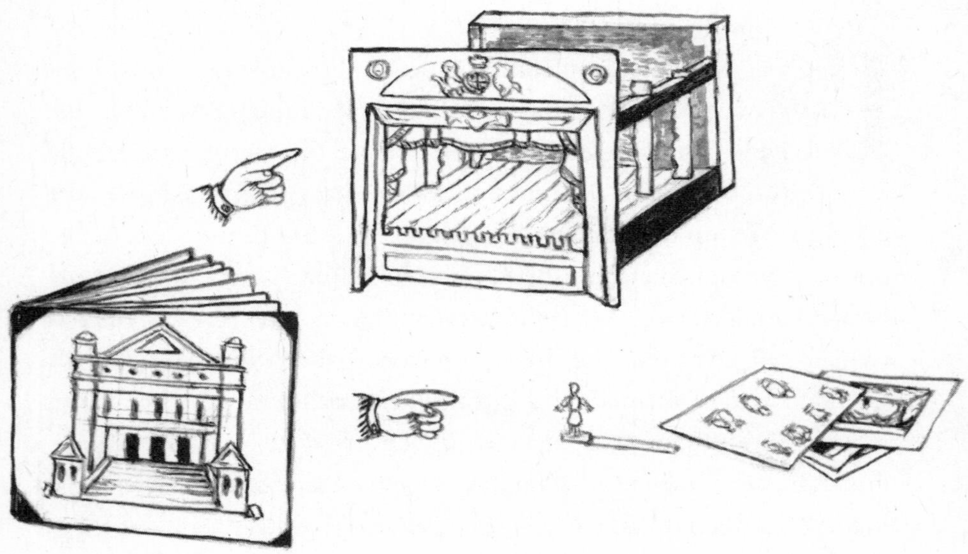

There is a sign outside the theatre, the real theatre, that stays there day and night. No matter what play we are playing, still this sign stays the same; even when the theatre is dark, it remains. The sign says THE HOLLER THEATRE, HOME OF THE CHILD WHO MAY NEVER LEAVE. Just next to the sign is a large plate glass window, and through the window can be seen a little room where the child who may never leave sits and is observed.

It is in this room that I have often performed my one-person dumb shows for the people of Norwich. I get into costume and act out all the parts. The people of Norwich come and watch me, and on a good day I may raise a crowd of fifty or more. Here have I been the mangy ghost dog of Norfolk mythology, Black Shuck, who roams the desolate coastline and the graveyards filled with Norfolk dead; indeed, the sight of the hound is a warning of imminent death. As Shuck, I growl and howl (without making a sound) at the people. Or else I am Boudicca, queen of the Iceni tribe, holding in my hand the head of a Roman soldier (got from the props room); or else, more quietly yet, I am Julian of Norwich, who was a woman who lived not ten minutes' walk from here, long ago, back in the fourteenth century, and was an anchorite, voluntarily walled up inside the church of St. Julian, on St. Julian's Alley in the district of Richmond on the Hill. She was the first woman to write a book in English, the very first. (We are both writers, Julian and I. I always keep a notebook and pencil about me.) She had visions, she did, and I act them out for Norwich, Norfolk.

I have visions, too, of a kind, when I let my imagination go as wild as Black Shuck. I have stories and tales for every day of the week. But most of all I am the discoverer of terrible secrets, I am Norwich's detective, and I have uncovered something dark and wicked—which I shall come to by and by, and for which afterward I may be blessed or cursed.

Figures for a card theatre.

When I am done with my performance I draw the curtains, so that Norwich may know I am no longer

available, and that the spectacle is done with—and then it may seem to them that I have died, or that perhaps I was never truly there. Sometimes, fairly often, when I am not at my post, a doll of me, the hard face made by the theatre's puppet mistress, Mrs. Stead, the cloth body by the wardrobe mistress, Aunt Nora, sits there in my place. (When the doll of me needs to be replaced, if I have outgrown it or it has been accidentally damaged, its material is always taken apart and used elsewhere—nothing does go to waste in this theatre and all must be useful.) (On occasions I pretend to be the doll.) (And sometimes the doll and I sit together and we are twins. I make the doll move more than me, just to confuse.) (It must seem to Norwich that I don't really exist at all, that I am only a person-sized puppet or doll. And perhaps I am, I think that sometimes. Father says it's good they are not certain, it is an excellent device.)

I am Edith Holler. I am twelve years old. I am famous.

The year is 1901. The month is March, by which you'll understand that the Christmas decorations have long been put away and that the pantomime season is quite ended. And what is most nationally pertinent is that the old queen is fresh dead. And the new king, Edward, looks like he has only a little life left himself.

My confinement is for my own safety. I cannot go out, for to go out would kill me.

I have been ill much of my childhood, laid often in my sickbed. They thought I should not last. It was diphtheria and it was meningitis and it was pneumonia; one woe, as they say, did follow on another's heals. I was ill at my birth, and my own dear mother did die then—and so death is never far away. I should have died, I lay lost to the world in my bedroom, and they fussed over me. I have always been frail, Father is terrified for my life, and so I must keep indoors, and so I do.

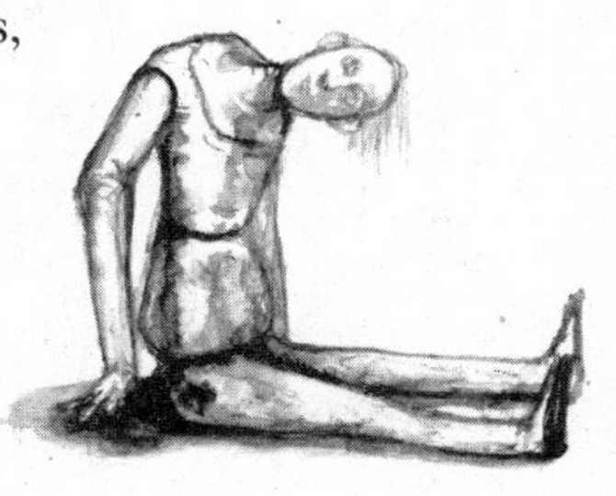

And, which is even more: not only do my illnesses keep me inside, but there is also in addition a nasty curse from an unhappy old actress, which was given to me at my christening. But, though I do not travel, yet there is much to wonder over from my confinement, both within and without. From the walls of the Bethel Hospital, I do hear the dismayed inhabitants often enough. The hospital is just across Theatre Street, and from time to time I watch as the inmates in their courtyard act out their own strange one-man shows. Sometimes some of our actors suffer from a persistent confusion and they have need of the Bethel Hospital. I have known actresses to go across the road, as we call it, and never come back again. Never once.

Though naturally I cannot go out to school, from the roof I can see two gloomy factories of learning. Crooks Place Boarding School, very close to the theatre, is where some two hundred boys are educated and live and, like me, don't get out much. I have watched the boys in their uniform when they come to their exercise yard, have seen them fight one another and play with conkers on a string. After that, I had Mrs. Cudden, one of the seamstresses, bring me in some conkers, and for a little while everything was conkers with me. I felt I was closer to the boys of Crooks Place then, and I found clothes like theirs in the wardrobe and went about for a while as a young fellow and I insisted they called me Bartholomew. But the distant boys never returned my waves—perhaps after all I was too far away; I did spy them only with my old opera glasses—and at last I said stuff them and their dull education. Not for me the conker, after all. It is not natural to me.

Another neighboring property is the Assembly House. This was built as a place of entertainment and dancing, but in 1876 they took away all the entertainment and dancing—said no to the people falling in love, no to the married couples come for music, no to laughter and to cake, no to gaiety and to passion. Instead, they filled the beautiful place with learning and tore out all the light. They threw away all the young males and said, Don't you dare come again, no, you must never. Instead they have there only girls. The girls go in, all uniformed, of a morning, to be taught how to come out proper Norwich ladies. They never wave back at me in their dull lines but look only downward, for I, they seem to say, am not an upright specimen. They think me like Peter the Wild Boy, a famous feral person who came from a woodland outside of the town of Hamelin, in Germany, and once lived in our city. But I cry for the occupants of the Norwich School for Girls. That wasn't the point of that building, I have called to them from our roof. No, no, you have ruined it with your learning, with all the strict women come to suffocate love inside. You have killed the Assembly House, now it is merely another manufacturing shop and the soot that comes from the chimneys is all Latin and deportment.

I take a different school.

For a long time Mr. Lent, one of the old actors, was my teacher. He would make me speak the proper English and not slide into the Broad Norfolk that we have hereabouts. It never did for the daughter of my father, the great actor, to have a child that blurted *ollust* for always or *squit* for nonsense or *muckwash* for sweat. Shakespeare must not be spoken with a Norfolk accent.

But I never speak onstage, I protested.

Even so, said Mr. Lent, it hurts the ears and we'll have none of it. Mr. Lent is gone now, but his lessons have not died with him. And since his passing I have greater study.

In my bedroom do I consider the history of Norwich. For, though twelve, I wonder if I am perhaps also ancient. In my bedroom, where I sit, I have about me all my toys, but also maps of Norwich throughout the ages. For Father had said to me, one day as I lay abed: You must not go out, but Norwich may come in. Ever after, I have made Norwich my great subject. Norwich is outside the dark interior of the theatre, and so to me Norwich represents life and space, and so as I ailed I had the idea that Norwich itself might save me. I demanded proof of Norwich, proof of it in all its different centuries. I clung to the city as I clung to life. I was given all manner of books and papers upon Norwich, Norfolk, for its study was all that would comfort me, and the more I studied the better I felt.

Norwich was my medicine. Norwich is my life. I think, though twelve, I must know Norwich better than anyone.

At first, I got all my information regarding Norwich from the stacks of shelves of the Norfolk and Norwich Subscription Library, which is on Guildhall Street. Norwich is the first city in Britain to have a public library. I eat it all up and remember much of it and it sustains me. Medie-

Backdrop for a card theatre.

val Norwich, I may tell you, for example, had fifty-seven churches, which is very many. One of my uncles or aunts would fetch the books for me, but it was not long before I had read all the library had to tell me, and then I began to get sicker again, and my father in his desperation knew not what to do. It was Mrs. Stead, the puppet mistress, who understood the remedy and proclaimed it simply, "Yet more Norwich." And she, being an ancient and sensible and practical woman, was able to encourage the librarians on my behalf and new material was found. So I came by the Assize Rolls and the Assembly Rolls, the Quarter Sessions books, the Mayor's Court books. Mrs. Stead set out in the morning with her empty basket, walked the short journey to Guildhall Street, and would return with new volumes. She would plump my pillows and sit me up in bed and say to me, "What have we here? Ah, I see Leet Jurisdiction in the City of Norwich. And what else? Here then the Book of Pleas. And here we have the Norwich Census of the poor. There, Edith, that should keep you quiet for a while."

Those brave and clever librarians who, finding this need of mine an interest and a challenge, sought out their colleagues around the city, and so came papers from the Guildhall library, from the Cathedral library, from the library at City Hall. And thus I read on, my pale, long fingers upon Norwich, and I came to learn so much. I saw volumes from the poorhouse, from the Norfolk and Norwich Hospital, I read bastardy records, settlement certificates and removal notices, and many a load of old newspapers and worn-out bill stickers. It was a pleasure for them in the library, I think, to seek out these obscure pages and have them delivered, ever by Mrs. Stead, to a child that they had never met but had merely seen through a plate glass window—made, incidentally, on Wensum Street by the Norwich Glass Company.

As I read on—for I had time where others did not, and I spent patience upon so much communication that had been left lonely for many years—I began at first to have suspicions, and then to grow a terrible certainty, that something abominable was hiding in the pages of Norwich's history. In the annals of the Surveyors, in the pages of reports from the Overseers of the Poor, in the statements of the Vestry and Parochial Church Council, I would find, almost always in single lines, disturbing reports: *Child of Thomas Pelling wanting, Lakenham, last seen Fybridge; ward of Norwich, Carrow, missing at evensong; Mary White, child, & Richard Loftus, child, Colegate, not seen these past 100 days.* A terrible secret began to grow in me, and the discovery of it sent me back into my sickbed and seemed to call me unto death. Indeed, I thought the secret would kill me, until at last I understood that it was the secret that was keeping me alive—and that I must tell it, I must spill my secret of Norwich upon the streets of Norwich, for I knew Norwich, though I have never gone out into it, better than Norwich knew herself.

Norwich steals life. Norwich murders.

Norwich has lost lives in so many ways over centuries, through fire and flood, through cruelty and negligence. Yes, yes, you will say, no doubt: but this is true of many a place. And you would surely be right. But here in this city of mine I have discovered something else, something unexplainable, something terrible that has been going on for centuries, that I rush to set it down: So many children have gone missing, there are lost children everywhere. From all corners of Norwich, from Conesford and Wymer, from Mancroft and Over the Water. Nor were they ever found. Not a one.

Norwich, I must own, is famous for missing children. In 1144 a tanner's apprentice named William disappeared and they blamed the Norwich Jewry, housed between Haymarket and Oxford Street, saying they had murdered the boy for their rituals. And afterward many Jews were murdered in retaliation. It is the first record of medieval blood libel to be found in all of Europe, here in our Norwich city. Now they acknowledge it wasn't the Jews after all, but who then did murder young William, whose poor stabbed body was found in Thorpe Wood? No one can say, and though this murder did certainly happen before all the other children went missing, yet it seems to me a kind of precursor or warning.

Where do they go to, these missing children of Norwich? A single child missing will command the attention of an entire city, especially if that child is from a prosperous family: then everyone will look everywhere in suspicion, then the city will hold that missing face secure in its imagination. But what if there were a hundred and more missing, and all at a time—a hundred a year, say—then missing children will be a commonplace thing, and so seeing the bill posters with lists of the missing will become ordinary, and ordinary means invisible. It has gone on for centuries, I have found it out: Children go missing in Norwich at a terrible number. Some five hundred over the years from Pockthorpe alone. True, sometimes in quiet seasons, maybe only four or five are lost, but this quietness is generally followed by a deluge of fifty or more suddenly absented.

Ah, you will say, let us call this missing of yours instead Small Pox and all is mended. Perhaps—but where then are the bodies? Why are their names in no death registers? Are these *poor* children? you will ask then. And I must say yes, mostly, but not always. Can you prove it, that these children were lost? you will ask. And so then I can show you the years—and centuries—of notices of children lost. It is a very incautious city, you will say. Yes, yes, but I will say: Who takes the children and where do they go? And then you will say—for you have had a moment to consider, and you do not wish to descend with me into dark knowledge, lest it threaten the very foundations of history and governance—No, no, it is all too much, I cannot believe it. And in response I will say, You *choose* not to believe, because it is too terrible a thing, and so you ignore it—and thus it goes on.

You will be in a bad mood with me by then, and irritated that a child, a girl, could so arraign you, and you will not acknowledge your ignorance, you will decide to refuse it. You will say to me, What a horrible child you are. Why cause this dark trouble? You have imagined it all. And have I?

Sometimes I doubt myself, and yet again and again I see in the ancient ledgers: child lost, children missing, boy twelve absent, girl seven unaccounted for, twins nine misplaced. What happened, I ask you, to Lolly Bowes? How did the life of George Kellet end? Who saw Nathaniel Bradshaw at his last, or Millie Bolton or Alfred Waltham? And for those lost children I do call out. How many children have you lost, O Norwich? Where, where is Polly Stimpson? Whatever happened to Martha Higg? Simon Pottergate? I begin to suspect that only people who keep very still may catch the truth that is there before us, for everyone else is too busy. Only I, in illness, with my time and study, in the gaslight in my bedroom, with books as my playfellows—only I might hear such truth in the small hours of the day, like the little tapping of a deathwatch beetle that can only be heard when all else is silent. It is a terrible thing, this knowledge of Norwich. I sit beside my secret day and night—a whole legion of lost children shut out in darkness—and it has made me ill. And I cannot unlearn it.

It was last summer when I came into my horrible knowledge, when I concluded at last that there was no doubting it anymore. Then I called out the names, that they might be heard again: Good morning, someone might say to me, and in response I would reply, *Molly Cruickshank!* In the afternoon, at teatime, I would wonder aloud, *Edwin Bagshot?* And when they tucked me in at night I would challenge them to know *Samuel Carter, never seen again.*

In response to so many names, my aunts and uncles made me sit out on the roof, looking at Norwich. There I stretched out my hands and wondered over my terrible discovery, I shivered over it, it made me vomit. Yet I own I did feel a little better being on the roof, up there standing beside the statue up at that height at the tip of the building's façade. The statue is a Greek-looking lady and some say that she is Euterpe (the muse of lyric poetry) and others that she is Melpomene (the muse of tragedy) and some have wondered if she is Boudicca because she is holding a spear, yet that spear I think was actually only a support that once held a mask or a harp which the poor stone lady has long since dropped. Most people though forget she's there at all, and fail to notice her atop the building. I lean beside the stained statue and look out at Norwich and am calmed, for there is so much to see there, and from my view I saw no children being forcibly lost. So I pretended, when I could, that all might be well. Look there, after all: At a right angle to the Bethel Hospital are the Chapelfield Gardens, which I can peer into and thus see a little nature and people walking about, and in the summer sometimes I can spy, upon the park benches, small scenes of love—for love may be found in my Norwich too. In the park I can see the Chapelfield Pagoda, a great iron pavilion. It looks Japanese but it was made by one of the sons of Norwich, or at least from nearby Wymondham, a man called Jeckyll did it. The pagoda is famous here, like me. But poor Mr. Jeckyll went mad and he was taken to the Bethel Hospital, across the street from both the theatre and the park. They never cured him, he died there under lock and key. I wonder if, like me, he looked out from a high window into Chapelfield Gardens at his rusting construction, and if that was a blessing or a sadness.

I wonder who will believe the truth of my terrible secret, or will they one day, as they did with Mr. Jeckyll, take me to the place that says it cures, though it doesn't always. And then, if I am cured, will I cease to believe my secret? Will the cure let my hair thicken, make my long face rounder, my skin pinker? Will the cure let me travel? And I wonder, would I care to be cured? Could I trust in it?

I do think I'd like to step out, if I could. Father says I mustn't, though, and I shouldn't like to worry Father, he can become very excitable if worried. He is as protective of me as many a parent found in fairy tales. And so I go up to the roof and look out all around at Norwich and feel a little calmed.

What I can't see of Norwich, I can sometimes smell into. The fish market is close by, and the Market Place is hard by that, and these businesses have many things to sniff at. Sometimes I smell flowers and sometimes meat, but usually the fish beats out all the others. And yet, when the wind is right, even the fish will be outdone by the thick air of Beetle Spread.

Ah, now, it is most pertinent that I talk of the beetle. There's generally, in the air of our city, a slight tang of Beetle Spread; we of Norwich have it in our lungs always. Beetle Spread is known of course throughout the country and even beyond. It comes in small 2 oz. jars, filled at the factory in Norwich, which is larger even than the cathedral. The symbol on the labels of Beetle Spread is a deathwatch beetle. Ah, you will say, here is a second mention of a deathwatch beetle!, and it is true I do often have these creatures in my mind. Our city has its most famous tale connected to Beetle Spread. You will probably know this tale already, but I'll mention it here quickly just in case, because the missing children of Norwich are very connected to this ancient story—indeed, they are truly tangled up in it.

Perhaps you are not from Norwich. Perhaps you have never come here yet. We that live on the eastern side of the country are often forgot, I think, and so strange things may happen here and not be noticed far beyond—in London, say, or in Edinburgh. You may turn your back on us, but we do likewise upon you. We exist without you, we have no need of you. And yet perhaps we do, for we have lived alone in our deep east for so long that children go missing and ancient tales do have modern life. All that follows below—all my terrible understanding, all my study, all the black secrets—will not be comprehended without knowing the Norwich folktale connected to Beetle Spread, for it is upon that tale that my discovery is centered.

Sometime in the fourteenth century (during the time of Julian the anchorite), Norwich was overcome by a great plague of beetles. The beetles, which are especially common in the flat, damp lands of East

Anglia, are larger in this part of the world. An ordinary deathwatch beetle grows up to a half inch in length, but here East Anglian deathwatches have been known to reach near two inches. And these beetles threatened to devour the city, which was then mostly made of wood. All was nearly lost, it is said, and would have been entirely, were it not for a woman named Meg Utting.

She had ever been strange and obscure, this Meg; some said she was mad, others that she was evil, but most of all people said she was very hungry. A poor, unmarried woman, and such people can be especially unlucky. Only her sister would speak to her, and that sister would give her half her meager victuals and so kept them both alive. But now she was about to become our city's savior, for Meg Utting had contrived a way of collecting the beetles. One afternoon, in her despair, knocking her head against the oak beam of her hearth, she noticed beetles come rushing out; she crushed them underfoot. In her curiosity, she banged her head once more, and yet more beetles came. By this action, unbeknownst to her, she was simulating the reverberations of some primal beetle mating call, and thereby she brought beetles in swarms to her house. The more she banged her head against the beam, creating a rhythmic thump, the more the beetles rushed toward her. The streets around her home, Fishergate Street, Peacock Street, and Cowgate Street, became so thick with beetles that it was as though a strange muddy river were flowing toward her in a terrible hurry, until the waves broke at the house of Meg Utting.

The best way of demolishing the pest, Meg discovered, was to cook it. She had a great pot on her stove, and when it filled with beetles—by now they were dropping from the ceiling—she let them simmer and boil. What I find most extraordinary about this story, however, is what happened next: somehow, Meg discovered that the cooked beetles, all mixed together, had a taste that was quite marvelous.

Meg Utting began to sell her beetle jam, as she called it then, and soon all of Norwich came to eat it. She made a small fortune from it, in time, and even married a man much younger than herself, a freeman of the city. She had a sister, Meg did, as already mentioned, but it is said that she never helped her sister when she came asking, and the sister died in poverty and of starvation. But that sister's last words, it is said, were to curse Meg, and to proclaim that one day a child would come into her life and that child would be the death of her. "Maybe today, maybe tomorrow, maybe not for many a year, but the child shall come, and that shall mean your end."

Eventually—it may have been from all the knocking of the head against the beam, or perhaps some of the beetles had got inside her head—Meg Utting went mad. She was seen about the streets, crying out, threatening the children. She came to be mockingly called Mawther Meg, *mawther* being our local, mostly ill-meant word for girl or woman; also, our Norfolk word for scarecrow is *mawkin*, and I have often felt these words and their meanings—the beetle woman and the bird scarer—must be related. This name was often reduced, further, to Maw Meg.

It was around this time that the children of Norwich first started disappearing. Some people muttered that Mawther Meg had eaten them or drowned them in the Beetle Spread. That people were eating their own children now on buttered bread. Some mused that she was an ancient, evil spirit come up from hell; others that she had mated with a great beetle devil that lived in the nearby Thorpe marshes. Whatever the truth, Meg Utting grew thinner and thinner, despite all the Beetle Spread, until she appeared the physical embodiment of Hunger itself.

It is certain that from this date the children of Norwich started to be lost in large numbers.

When a child disappeared, the reason given for it was the legend of Maw Meg. Crowds of Norwich hid behind the terrible story. Be careful or Maw Meg will get you, they warned, and it was a great game—but also, you see, a child *did* go missing and was never found.

Who the real Maw Meg was cannot now be known. But what is certain is that she gave us the Spread, and the making of it became a great business, and we have had it here with us ever since. Every jar of Beetle Spread, even now, is said to contain at least one deathwatch beetle. There is a statue of Meg near the Erpingham Gate of Norwich Cathedral (named after Sir Thomas Erpingham, who led the archers at the Battle of Agincourt), and beside her is a statue of our other great Norfolk hero, Horatio Nelson, who went to the Norwich School nearby. People who come to Norwich, I am told, most often head to see the statue of Maw Meg Utting; indeed it is a custom to touch one or two of the bronze beetles at the statue's feet. Touching these beetles is supposed to bring you good health (likewise the Spread), and so the statue of Meg Utting is much more touched than the one of Horatio Nelson, for touching Horatio Nelson is not supposed to do you any good at all, and may even diminish your person—the admiral's statue having but one arm.

In my bedroom is my typewriter table and upon it is my seaweed-colored typewriter. It is like a building, this machine. Like a parliament or opera house upon my table. Father gave it to me. It is very modern. It came up from London in its own crate and says in golden letters THE ENGLISH STANDARD TYPEWRITER, 2 LEADENHALL ST., LONDON EC. It is not a children's object, but beside it I have a toy model of HMS *Victory*. Like many a Norwich child, I also keep close at hand the toy variously called the Beetle Rattle or the Deathwatch Dummy or the Beetle Clacker, sometimes just called the Meg Peg. It is, as you probably know, two wooden spoons bound together with leather straps, bowl against bowl; you pull back one spoon from the other, stretching the leather, and then let it go so that it makes a loud clack that is supposed to replicate the noise of a deathwatch beetle. The toy is supposed to summon beetles. I myself have never had much luck with it and consider it a dull enough project. But I do hear, sometimes, the noise of the Meg Pegs as the Norwich children play in the park.

Forgive me: I was talking of the Spread. Every one of the jars says UTTING'S BEETLE SPREAD and in slightly smaller letters OF NORWICH. People of Norwich (and many who are not) eat Beetle Spread on toast or cheese or fruit or chicken or ham or bacon, or place a spoon of it in a mug of hot water and drink it in the winter. It is a most versatile substance, said to be beneficial against most ailments. In the summer, also, if spread on strips of paper, it can catch flies.

We of Norwich are very proud of Beetle Spread. Here, where the Spread is made, the air itself is often spread with it. Sometimes the city may fall under a dark and ruddy fog, caused by an accident at the factory, when some quantity of Spread has become airborne. On such occasions we all go inside (I don't mean me of course, for I've never left) and wait for the cloud to pass. Afterward, we wipe our windows with newspapers (I don't mean me of course), and the newspapers always come away red. Have I mentioned that Beetle Spread is red? Oh, but surely you'll know that. It has been red for centuries, though originally it was black or brown. It is red now because at some point, no one can say exactly when, madder root was added to the ingredients. We have much madder root in our Norfolk and have for a long time used it in our dyeing of clothes—hence the famous red Norwich shawl—and hence the square of the city called the Maddermarket, which is where they sell the root. At one time our River Wensum ran red because of the dyeing of materials, and today it runs red on account of excess Beetle Spread as it flows from the factory. I cannot see the River Wensum, I have indeed never seen it, but I know it is there, for I have been told about it often enough, and I do believe it is a truth that if I got into the Wensum and swum (I cannot swim), getting very red I suppose at first but then less and less so, I would arrive at last to a place called Great Yarmouth. But I don't go swimming to any (Yare) mouth great or small, I stay here inside the bounds of Theatre Street, Chapelfield East, Chantry Road, and Assembly House.

Here in the theatre, if we are low on pins or spirit gum, we have often been known to fix our wigs or beards with a little Beetle Spread. One of the disadvantages of the Spread is that people can roll a small ball of it and pop it in their mouths and then chew it for hours (making their teeth red—oh, the red teeth of Norwich!) and then, inevitably, after a time, after the taste has gone or jaw ache has set in, they often spit it out, on the street or even upon our front-of-house carpets (which are red in color because of the Spread, in the hopes of disguising it). Cleaning up after Beetle Spread gum is a time-consuming business. The smell of the Spread is hard to explain to the uninitiated. It is like a concentrate of meats. It is like a new animal not yet named. It is like a strange and uninvited intimacy.

Something else about Beetle Spread: I think the missing children are inside it.

I know this was alluded to before, but then it was said in jest and to frit the Norwich slums. But I think it is true. I came to this one morning as I sat propped up by pillows in my sickbed, studying the Norwich lost. A piece of toast beside me with butter and Spread. I read about the lost children, I took a bite of toast. Ernest Ridings I read, and I took a bite of toast. Bess Tollymash I read, and I took a bite of toast. Susie Headley I read, and I took a bite of toast. And then I stopped. I dropped the toast, it fell Spread-side down upon my sheets, a great red mark there.

Oh!

I no longer eat the Beetle Spread. I will not have it near me.

2.

Birth of a playwright.

Perhaps I should describe myself. How to turn my eyes upon my very own self? To give you the correct idea of me?

I am more bony than bonny, I admit, and just a little taller than average. I am flat of breast and likewise of feet. My hands and feet, though narrow, are rather large, so I may grow long in time, and one day I may fill out and thus become a woman.

I look a bit washed out, a bit rag doll you might say. My skin is very pale, almost all white. My own hair is a sort of greyish red, somewhat fair but a dull color, and sometimes seems as ashy as my flesh, and so it may be said I am only one color altogether. Except my eyes, which, like Father's, are a very pale blue. "You look like you've seen a ghost" is a common enough observation. "You look like a ghost" is not unheard-of either.

Well, then, if I am monochrome, I do embrace it. I clothe myself in greys and whites. I am perhaps a little moldy, a touch mildewed, slightly foxed, I am an old book, a little yellowed, mothlike. I do need, probably, a little airing out. Also I have become crooked, perhaps, being so shut up for so long. My body grows awkwardly on account of my illnesses and does not mature. My voice is generally rather raspy.

What else must I say, or else my life be misunderstood?

I have told one story from Norwich; it is necessary that I balance it with one from within the theatre. How I have relied on stories in my sickbed. They have saved me certainly. For we are made of stories, surely, and some are true and some are not, and some are part truth and part lie—well, and perhaps that can be said of all stories. But there is a particular story of this theatre that I am told a great deal, everyone here knows a version of it, but it is Father who is the most regular teller and indeed he does narrate it very dramatically. It is dear to him, because the story is about me. It is the story of my curse.

It happened at my christening—which was upon the stage, this was a family custom, we always had the Bishop of Norwich come in for it, the stage set up for the cathedral in which Thomas à Becket was murdered—and chiefly concerns one of my old aunts. Everyone here to me is uncle or aunt, you see, or, if they are younger, cousins—though we are related not necessarily by blood but by profession. This particular aunt was no longer allowed to perform on account of her failure to remember her lines, though she insisted she could. She was not my real aunt, but a woman named Lorena Bignell, and came originally from Lowestoft in Suffolk. There are always several retired actors about; they are looked after here and find small jobs about the theatre—Father keeps them useful for as long as is possible, and they do on the whole prefer to be around the theatre than in some kennel for old people or in the workhouse or in the Bethel Hospital.

Since her banishment, Lorena Bignell had kept herself miserable in the wardrobe until she delivered her last, and most magnificent, performance. She appeared in one of the theatre's grand boxes attired in a yellowed and ripped wedding dress, and in front of my family and all the actors, all the stagehands and crew, the orchestra, the puppeteers

and the laundresses and wigpeople and carpenters and candlemen (this was shortly before the gas was put in), and even the prompter, Lorena Bignell spat and cried and placed a curse upon me. She was very fine and exact in everything she delivered, not a word was garbled; all was crystal clear and unforgettable. If I ever should set foot upon Norwich streets, she proclaimed, I would die. Then, as if this itself were insufficient, she added—after a grating moan—not only that I would die, but that the entire theatre would come tumbling down.

Ah, I see now that I must clarify.

Do not please think that this whole business was prompted by my father not inviting my aunt to the christening—that I'm simply reviving the story of *Sleeping Beauty*, performed often upon our stage. No, Lorena Bignell had been invited. In her day, she had been a most moving tragedian. The trouble was that she had been abused and murdered, haunted and despised, so many times onstage that the plays had leaked into her mind, and unlike the greasepaint it could no longer be washed off. She had become a woman much given to howling, very angry and uncertain, twitchy and confused. Yes, the poor woman had been ill-used—and it was my father, playing, as he so often did, the villain, who had done it all to her. And so, to get at him, Bignell cursed me. But it was more than that. Oh, she was a good one, and thorough. It was a performance so distinguished that it is still spoken of today. Some argue that she cheated, that her methods were not to be found in the script, that strictly speaking her performance was not theatre at all but something more rightly called a "demonstration." (Norwich, may I say, is a famous city for rioting; much town property was destroyed in one of our worst riots, in 1766, and for their part in the uprising two men, John Hall and David Long, were hanged at Norwich Castle.) Others say that Lorena Bignell did in fact work from the script but rewrote it to serve her own ends. And that last I would agree with, because this extraordinary gesture of hers, within a playhouse, in front of a sizable audience, rewrote my entire life.

So then. Here it is, as it has been told to me: Aunt Lorena Bignell died in an explosion of blood.

My aunt spurted from the balcony onto the stage and everywhere in between. She was afterward to be found, in fact, everywhere—all over the stalls, for example, and the balcony was most spoiled. A good portion of her had reached the stage itself, which no doubt would have made her very happy. For days thereafter there was much mopping and scrubbing—the remaining Bignell was worse than even Beetle Spread—and it took a time, I am told, for the smell to surrender.

To this day, no one is quite sure how my aunt Lorena exploded. It was the most marvelous effect. Several members of my family, myself included—using dummies, you understand—have tried to re-create her extraordinary exit, but the result has always been a disappointment. She had burst into a hundred thousand bits, she had spread herself all over the auditorium. I was baptized twice, once in blessed holy water and once also—there were drops dotted about my gown—in blood, in ruddy flecks provided by my very recently expired so-called relative. This same christening gown is now framed and hung front of house, so that all may see the old blood upon it and remember my curse. Thus was I marked on my first day of life. The many people who had come to witness my christening were given also an Aunt Lorena bath; thereafter, thus besmirched, they walked Aunt Lorena severally all about our city, to the portions called Tombland (it is called this not because of tombs but from an old Scandinavian word meaning "empty space") and Heigham, Millgate and Hellesdon, Lakenham and Pockthorpe, Old Catton and Sprowston, and even into their homes, because she was there upon their clothes and skin.

In consequence of this event, unlike my aunt Lorena in so many bits, I am not allowed out. My aunt's explosion had sealed the severity of her curse. Without it, an exception might perhaps have been made, some way found to circumvent her fury. But Aunt had gone out in a large red puff, a crimson explosion, and that had sealed me, forevermore, inside. There is even a small bronze plaque affixed to the railing of the box:

UPON THIS SPOT EXPLODED
LORENA AUGUSTA BIGNELL

And thus began my father's worrying. Not only had Mother died, but I was ill and cursed right from the start. The actors shook their heads. The doctors shook their heads. There was death all about me. I had not much time, Oh, the poor child. And so I was born to stay inside.

I should include a very small addendum here. It is possible that this story is an exaggeration; it is quite possible that my poor aunt did not explode as such, indeed she had been coughing a good deal I have been told, and it is very possible that in fact my aunt, as a result of a severe lung infection, hemorrhaged, and that a little blood did indeed come from her mouth, perhaps even a quantity. It is difficult, at this distance, to know exactly. Certainly she died, and probably she bled. We who live in the theatre here have some belief in magical things. Rules that apply to other buildings do not apply here. In the theatre we strive to make the impossible possible, to believe in and convince our public of fantastical personages and happenings. Very frequently, for example, we bring back old dead kings (not Gurgunt under Norwich Castle, but the ones often called Henry or Richard) and have them alive here upon our stage. All this makes it seem possible, then, that Lorena did explode, but also that she merely leaked. I cannot say which is the truth. But in either case she did deliver her curse. In either case she did die very shortly afterward, perhaps even instantly. And so, as we are a very suspicious people—we believe in curses and in dying curses particularly—and so here I am and ever likely to remain.

It is well known that ravens must be kept at the Tower of London, or else the Crown will fall and Britain too. That is a London belief. We in the east of England have our own thinking: it is lucky to have a bent sixpence in your pocket; if you shiver, someone is walking over your future grave; if you break two things, you will surely break a third; if you put a broom in the corner, you are sure to receive strangers; if you stumble upstairs, you will marry before the year ends; if you eat pork marrow, you will go mad; you must never look at a new moon through glass; a horse has the power to see ghosts; you must always burn a tooth after it has been drawn, otherwise, if said tooth should be eaten by a dog, you will grow a dog's tooth; a child cursed indoors will die outdoors.

Well, then, I am one of those.

My prison. My palace. My home. Every day and only.

It is a very old building, our theatre, and it has been rebuilt and added to over centuries. Its foundations, so they say, are in part Roman stones moved over from the city of Colchester after Boudicca had destroyed it, but I cannot say if this is true or only another story. When the Saxons conquered Norwich, the spot was made into a great beer hall; thus it stood a long time, and was the place where revelers would come and perform. In the sixteenth century our site was the White Swann Inn, and it was here that the Norwich Company of Comedians did gather and play. At first our theatre was religious, but then it shoved God off and became more and more secular. Increasingly it was about us mortal people and how we rise and fall and how sad we are and how happy and how brief.

In 1754 our neighbor, the Assembly House, was built. Here the well shod of Norwich came to dance and fall in love and have concerts and proper entertainment. At length that uprightness did spread out from the Assembly House until it infected the White Swann, and so at last, three years later, we became an actual theatre. The New Theatre we were called then, and our first show was *The Way of the World* by Mr. Congreve. A small place we were and we had no real license to perform, because only London had permission to have plays put on, and elsewhere went legally playless—until at last, on 17 March 1768, we who were out of the capital were given a royal assent to put on plays. Then we were called the Theatre Royal Norwich, though no royal of Britain has yet warmed our royal box.

Our theatre, greatly loved, was soon too small to fit Norwich in it. In 1801, keeping its old foundations and some of its timbers, it was built all over again in its present wonder. And so here we are—not so fresh as 1801, now that we've grown to 1901, and our decorations are fading and we do crumble in places. Our Norwich ground, after all, is chalk from the bones of thousands of deceased sea creatures that died many millions of years ago, and sometimes that bone does crack. Yes, Georgian are our walls, though our soul is Saxon and dead sea beast, and lately we were Victorian. We had our latest great overhaul near the beginning of her reign, but she did reign for so long that by the time she died, our decorations had lost a little of their shine. And so here we are today, 20 March 1901, the queen is dead, and the seventh Edward has taken his seat.

I can't feel any difference, personally, between the old woman and her son the old man. We have lots of mourning crape front of house, and everywhere public wears the gloom, and my aunts appear in bombazine and my uncles wear black armbands made in our own wardrobe.

Norwich is famous for its mourning cloth, Norwich Black Crape it is called, it is a great business with us. All the nation does wear it when in grief, as it is now. No one knows how to mourn like the people of Norwich.

Otherwise, all is business as usual.

So then I must come to it. For no matter what I say, there is always that other thing behind it, like a creeping shadow. Even when I talk of the theatre, there it is, beside the theatre and within it: my discovery, the lost children of Norwich. I talk of the Spread and there, in the thick red, it does form itself: the lost children. I am riddled with my secret, and in order for me to go on I must let a little out at a time, like the doctors used to with their bleeding—drip my burden onto the page. But how does a twelve-year-old go about telling such a thing, how to make those that are twice twelve and more comprehend my learning?

I have never conquered my suspicion that many of the lost children are to be found inside the Beetle Spread. But I cannot prove it. I have wondered this to my aunts and uncles, yet they give it no creed. How did they get in there? they ask. Why, by murder, I say. Ha, they say, what nonsense. Of course they believe in kings under a hill, and fairy folk in the woods and at the bottom of a garden; they believe in Black Shuck; they believe all Norfolk tales to be purely true. But lost children and murder they will not trust. Whenever I do mention my secret to some

BOX
OFFICE

adult, they do shove me off and tell me about imagination and its dangers and that I should go back onto the roof, and thus let the tale-telling weaken in the fresh air. "What you are saying is not truth." I cannot tell it to the Norwich people, for whenever I go front of house when the public is within, Father insists for my own safety that I remain mute, that I keep a proper distance between myself and my city. "Leave the poor people of Norwich alone, my ailing Edith."

But it doesn't go away, my secret.

And yet, despite all this, I found a way.

I am twelve, as previously advertised, and when we come thirteen in this theatre then do we come of age. There is a sort of ceremony; if we are actors, it is during this time that we are first given a significant part and made much fuss of. And thirteen does come soon for me, as it does for so many of us—though not all, as I have hinted. I could never hope for a great acting role, for I am silent, at Father's insistence, whenever I do tread upon the stage. How then may I make myself heard? There is a way. Oh, it came to me very quick one afternoon as I sat with my discovery beside me, almost tangible, amid all my maps and papers of Norwich, the long lists of children's names, pages and pages of them. Many times have I gone up to the roof, folded these pages of names into paper birds, and launched them into Norwich—though in the main they do tumble unhappily onto Theatre Street. Among my borrowed literature was an etching of a skull upon a gravestone, and this skull turned the thoughts in my head to my own skull, and I whispered aloud: "So many skulls do I learn of, and so many immature." *The skull*—I slapped my own at the realization. How many times had I seen my father dressed in black, holding up a skull in his hand upon the stage? Very well then, I cried.

Clack, clack, clackety clack clack. The machine from Leadenhall Street grew very hot. The knock of my typewriter was very much like the knock of a deathwatch beetle.

I wrote my secret into a play.

I gave my secret voice.

It came out so easily!

I assembled my cast, I ordered my scenes. This must happen and then this and then this, I proclaimed. The cathedral, the castle, older even than Maw Meg, would give witness. All those forgotten children would speak at last, I gave them words with my typewriter. I must give the facts and let the story grow more and more urgent, until at last all bursts out. Part One the introduction, Part Two things are going wrong, Part Three it only gets worse, Part Four all seems lost, Part Five the great calamity.

Every name that I had found now found its way into my play. I should have the Mawther, too, upon the stage, dark and dangerous. Have they been frightened before now of Richard III, of the ogre in "Puss in Boots," of Frankenstein's creature? Ah, but they were nothing yet. Here is new villainy. The adults will sit there in their seats, before my play, those men and women of Norwich, and see what had been happening all along as they slept in their beds. I would wake them up at last! I saw it all coming, all the letters obeying my command, all the keys of Leadenhall Street, one after the other, stamped onto the page, the pages mounting up. Here and here and here. So dizzy with the letting out of it.

I knew, by how easily it came, that I must be right to undertake it, as if my secret were writing the play for me. This, I declared to myself, must be performed for my thirteenth birthday. I would finally speak to Norwich and at last they would hear me. Two months only it took, hammering away at Leadenhall, and then I presented the manuscript to Father, leaving him alone with the pages as I closed his door behind me. How it terrified me to be so separated from my work. What if there were an accident and the manuscript be set alight? What if he should take it out into Norwich and leave it upon a park bench, only to retrace his steps and find it gone? What if he left it upon a tram, one of those new metal dragons in which the common people of Norwich are moved about the city? I did fear for it so, you see, my child of ink, that truth on paper.

But Father, being Father, never took it out of his study. He stayed with it there, the two of them the only company. At last he called for me and I quickly came, my heart yearning to take flight over Norwich like one of my paper messages.

"Edith, Edith. What is this?" Father had been crying, though he tried not to show it.

"It is a play, Father."

"Edith, what strangeness. Has it made you ill, the writing of this . . . business?"

"In truth, Father, I have never felt better nor more myself."

"It is a wonder you found the strength. A full five acts here."

"Yes, Father."

"It is an outrage, I think you know that."

"Is it?"

"So many disappearances, so many deaths. Must there be?"

"Yes, Father, that is essential."

"I do wonder over the darkness of it."

"It must be so."

"But do you mean it?"

"Completely, every word. I can only say it in the play. I couldn't say it to you, Father, not like this. I wouldn't know how. But I could with the typewriter. The words lead me on, I can do it with the words."

"Such a quiet girl, I thought."

"I am an explosion!"

"And it is very bold—indeed, *you* are grown so bold."

"I am. I am!"

"But you are not serious?"

"Am I not?"

"What will Norwich make of it, to have itself as such an outrageous subject?"

"I cannot say, Father."

"You will offend people, I fear. Uttings in particular are unlikely to be happy."

"I cannot help that."

"Of course we may pass it off as nonsense. As fairy tale."

"Are fairy tales nonsense?"

"No, no. And yet, Edith, the play is a story, surely, a tale of Norwich. Children missing, yes, this is very good. But . . ." And here he paused. "Just—not the Spread, I think, Edith. Something else, perhaps, without losing its drama. Children missing is enough; missing is good. Yes, then it might be done."

"But I meant what I wrote."

"Ah yes. No doubt. But we may preserve your intention without being quite so . . . direct. Even improve it. *Subtext*, my darling. But otherwise, what an extraordinary sensation we might cause! A Norwich play! Why indeed not have Norwich upon the stage? For we are Norwich and everyone about us. To have ourselves on a stage! To see ourselves the better! It shall certainly draw attention. People will be very curious. They will come pouring in!"

I saw Father's growing excitement, and imagined with him the reaction of Norwich. We have had, over the years, a horse or two upon our stage, and how the audience did gasp at it—strange that a horse on the street causes the people no reaction, but to have the animal onstage is a thing of great wonder, even if it is the same horse. As if we, my family, had invented the animal. It is all about the context.

I looked at Father; he held the manuscript to him.

"I think perhaps after all we might perform it. A version of it."

"My play! Really? My *play*!"

"There will be adjustments, of course. Changes. You lose your way often enough, and there is much repetition, the accusations must be withdrawn and merely suggested, and we must most of all be certain it connects to us here today, that it speaks properly to the people of Norwich."

"There is much Norwich in it, is there not, Father?"

"Yes, indeed, you have studied well. But there needs to be love, there should be romance. People of Norwich like that. Some sort of love, Edith, even if it is only for a piece of cloth."

"Must we?"

"To hook them, Edith."

"If only for a piece of cloth. Yes, Father. Some love indeed. Of course I can do love."

"Can you?"

"Certainly, Father."

"What knowledge do you have of it?"

"I have seen it often, upon the stage."

"Very well. We shall begin rehearsals in a month."

"A month! A month!"

"I shall make an announcement for it, alongside the next season. Not a full run, mind you, Edith. We must see how it goes down. A Monday performance, say. In case it fails. A play may fail, Edith—you know that, I think."

"I understand."

"And, Edith?"

"Yes, Father."

"You are so clever! My own daughter!"

In the following weeks, an advertisement appeared in the newspaper, and soon after it was on the bill posters for the coming season:

THE TRUE HISTORY OF MAWTHER MEG

by Edith M. Holler, the child who may not leave the theatre

I have the bill posters on the wall of my room, two of them glued there like any other on an outside Norwich street wall, the kind where missing children notices have long been posted. I am a playwright. I tell the stories. Father has proclaimed it and thus it is.

"Now, Edith," said Father, very serious, "your characters have come into life. Now they have independent living. I read your play, and so it exists doubly, and more and more people shall read it. They are abroad, your characters. Your play exists without you now. There is no putting it back." And it was so. Others, beyond the theatre walls, took notice. Said the *Eastern Daily Press*: THE SILENT CHILD ON THEATRE STREET SPEAKS AT LAST! EDITH HOLLER HAS WRITTEN A PLAY.

At around this time, Mr. Shrubsole from Davey Place came to the theatre, with his long-legged companion that is a tripod. I was instructed to get dressed into my best outfit; my hair was tidied up and pinned at the back. The fuss they made, taming me into a smart gown, constricted beneath it by a corset and with a bustle tied around my waist. They were to take a picture of me with my manuscript: Edith Holler, authoress.

I have seen the picture. Is it me? I suppose it must be, yet it is not quite how I picture myself. How smart she is. In the picture she is touching the manuscript that has been to Jarrold & Sons and copied many times over, so that the play duplicated many times must be safe now. The photograph has a cardboard mount that says PATRONS H. M. THE QUEEN AND THEIR R.H.s THE PRINCE & PRINCESS OF WALES—which is wrong of course, but Mr. Shrubsole is still using his old stock because the cardboard thinks the queen is still alive, and no one has told it. Still, to see that photograph is to feel almost attached to royalty myself, to sense that the monarch is just around the corner.

Yet all that was weeks ago. I have not seen Father since Mr. Shrubsole. He is often busy, but lately he has spent more time away from the theatre, out there in Norwich. His top hat is absent, and his best jacket. He'll call for me again soon no doubt, he does love me so. And in his absence I have felt myself drawn to our stage, have heard it calling me, and so on this evening, 20 March 1901, the stage empty between seasons, the old brick wall at its back now fully exposed, I have visited it.

Back wall of a card theatre.

What space it is, our stage. I had lived my life in its proximity, yet now that I was to see my own words take life upon it, I felt we must

Stage floor of a card theatre.

know one another even better. And so, to try to gain a feeling of it, to test what personality it had when not wearing the character of one play or another—to know it as it really is, that great open space, that contained field, that everywhere—I took myself to it, and I undressed myself. After a minute, stood barefoot in the center, I seemed to learn something of it. Cold at first, biting cold, but my own heat soon warmed the wood a little. As I stood and stood, it seemed to tremble beneath me. What a thing it was, what a greed it had. I could feel myself sinking into it. My skin on its surface going down. Very slowly it was taking me in, I was becoming stage myself. Soon I was up to my ankles in it, then my calves and then my waist, falling ever farther into the stage. I was drowning in it. It had taken all of me, until I was nothing at all, nothing left to show of me, as if I had never been.

Yet, very fortunately for me, Aunt Jenny Garner (she isn't really my aunt, but I call her so) happened to be in the wings, and she had a lanthorn with her, and soon was pulling me back with her light and I was myself again and shivering. She wrapped me in her shawl and we sat together and I held on to her like my life depended upon it.

"I felt it alive!"

"It is, my darling. Of course it is."

"It nearly had me."

"It will do that."

"I'm frightened of it now."

"No harm in being a little frightened, no harm at all, Edith. Everyone is frightened of something, and a little fear can be a good thing. Can sharpen the performance, see? But too much is a disaster. Why do you think Mr. Fenwick no longer goes on?"

"Is it the stage fright?"

"Oh, to see him weeping in the wings, taking hold of some rope or flat as if it might save him from drowning! Like Gloucester, he feels the cliff edge, even if many do tell him it is not there, and he horrors at the approaching tumble. Even he, Mr. Herbert Fenwick, who made himself famous as Cinna the poet in *Julius Caesar*, who was so alarmingly bitter as Thersites in *Troilus and Cressida* and so sad and moving as John of Gaunt in *Richard II*. Even he, poor Fenwick, has been bitten so badly by the stage that he can no longer step upon it, for fear that if he did he shall be drowned dead."

Uncle Wilfred and the carpenters had solved Mr. Fenwick's problem by building a ramp on the stage from the stalls, so that, while playing the ghost of Old Hamlet, he might walk through the audience and stand upon the ramp. It was a wonderful effect. And thus he managed, so long as he never needed to tread upon the actual stage.

"What do I do now, Aunt? Now that I am a playwright and almost grown up?"

"This is what you do, and you do it from now on. Perhaps every day for the rest of your life. You stand on the stage and you tell it your name."

And so I did. And, back in my old smock and boots, I said the words that I shall spill upon the stage daily:

"It is Edith here. Hello. I am Edith May Holler, the theatre's daughter, the playwright. This is my world, and I am in charge of it."

3.

I am called to my father.

On the first day of the great change upon my life, I awoke at ten o'clock. I did not yet know of the change, but nevertheless it was coming swiftly. It was Aunt Bleachy who woke me. The sharp smell came first, every bit as vinegar as the words that followed.

"Your father!" she barked. And then: "The Mourning Room!"

I sat up in bed, already in a worry. "The Mourning Room? It cannot be good news if it is the Mourning Room. What is wrong, Aunt Bleachy?"

"Here's your dress. Enter it."

There was never any getting around my aunt Bleachy. She is tough and raw-skinned. Her real name is Belinda, but we all call her Bleachy. She is the aunt who mops the stage side of the theatre. She does never go front of house, but is in charge of the cleanliness this side, the backstage side. She is a monster woman and curses everyone. But in her day she was the very best Helena that ever was, everyone says so, the most beautiful Viola, the most wonderful of actresses, her voice a most exquisite instrument, capable of inducing tears with just a sentence. She was in love once, it is said, with a handsome actor, and they were to marry, but he fell for Hermia instead and so my aunt Bleachy went toward bleach and drank some and nearly died, and ever since she has been with the bleach. She curses the stage, she scrubs it, she slaps it about and kicks it, she pours bleach on everything, and at every stage of the process she is a fearful unhappy person. She hates the theatre, but does live here, in order to give it, one scrape at a time, the full attention of her hatred. Sometimes, in her thoroughness, small pieces of the stage come loose and tumble to the floor below, and then Bleachy is known to laugh.

Aunty Bleachy has a small army of Norwich girls and women who come in to help her, and she makes them all unhappy, for she has only unhappiness about her and nothing else to offer.

"Come along, will you?"

Aunt Bleachy had me out of my bedroom and downstairs. She stopped me at the step just before the Mourning Room.

"Wait here," said the Bleach.

"Is Father inside?" I asked.

"Wait," said the Bleach.

"Why has he summoned me? Is my play canceled?" I asked.

"No special treatment," said the Bleach.

Exit the Bleach.

I sat upon the step waiting for Father, who was just beyond. My father who is big and strange and all living. My father who is tall and dark and strong weather. Thunder and lightning and thick fog. He may be lovely and he may be horrible, but whichever he is, it is always a spectacle. When he keeps still and does nothing, how we wonder over it. Everything he does is fascinating. When he enters a room, it is his utterly; people look only to him. When he blows his nose, it is more exciting than another man's whole Macbeth.

Father had to take on the responsibility of the theatre as a very young man, and that is what has made him great. His own father, my grandfather Richard, was broken by the stage. Unlike Victor Holler, my great-grandfather, Richard had no talent for it, he mismanaged everything, and in revenge the theatre bullied him until he could bear it no longer. By the end, it is said, everything frightened him, and he was taken across Theatre Street to the Bethel Hospital. It was supposed to be only for a week or two, but the weeks spread to months and thence to years and he never came back out again. The theatre nearly went bankrupt—until Father, only eighteen years old, stood up and swore to his grandfather, who was dying by then, that he would save the theatre. I never knew either man, great-grandfather or grandfather. It was for Father alone to save all. (Of my grandmothers I have nothing to tell, for they never figured in anyone's stories. I have often worried over that.)

I have been the cause of sadness as well as delight for my father. My mother, as in a comedy perhaps, went out as I came in. Or one might say that, like the Fool and Cordelia, we may not be onstage at the same time. My father loved her terribly. The doctor was called to her in the theatre, so sudden did she take ill, and soon after came her death and then the curse that quickly followed. Ever since then, Father has walked with death. Carrying me in his arms—blue grey and scrawny as I was, in a soiled christening gown—he made an apartment of the upstairs offices, and we moved into the theatre permanently.

In Father's drawing room, there is a likeness of my mother. She is playing Joan of Arc in the picture, Joan on her way to the burning, just as they used to hang witches here (and also the persecuted Protestants known as Lollards), over in the old chalk pit behind the Bridge Inn—O Norwich you are bathed in blood. Mother looks like she is very with God. I cannot tell how much of the picture reveals my mother and how much it reveals Joan of Arc. Somewhere certainly under Joan is my mother; my mother is still herself to an extent, I suppose, even when she is Joan. Perhaps I go about this a little backwardly. I was talking of my father and my mother's limited likeness came into my eyes at once and Father, for a brief moment, receded. And that was only right perhaps, for Father was everyone and, sometimes, no one at all.

My father could be any body.

He was the greatest actor of his generation; some people say perhaps the greatest who ever lived. (Norwich was very lucky to have him, people often said, I am told, he should have been in London all this time.) But how does that tell you anything useful? If only you could see him physically. He was tall, of course, and broad-shouldered—yet may make himself seem thin and weedy and stooped over.

But if he was caught sleeping—ah, then some greater truth may be discovered.

This I have often practiced: To sneak into his bedroom to observe the human body of Father as it lay there purely itself, without any pretense. Who was it there? That body at rest, at ease with itself, being nothing more than a body sleeping. I would open the curtains of his bed and see a man older than when he was upright, paler of skin and wrinkled, balder than I remembered, and creased. It was always dangerous, this prying, for there was the real worry that he would wake, that the eyelids would spring open and I should be trapped under the beam of his pale blue eyes. On the occasions when it happened, then would come his panic:

"Are you ill, child? What is the matter? Indeed, are you dead, Edith?"

"No, Father, no, I do assure you. Quite well."

"You are so pale."

"Quite well indeed."

Sometimes, too, he would come to check on me when I was asleep. If he could not see the sheets' rise and fall, he would pull back the coverings in a panic and I would wake.

"Oh! Edith! Just checking, only checking. Such little lungs."

And he would weep for joy that I was still living. Oh, he does cry such a deal, he does. On such nights there were only me and him in all the world. But then something other would come along. When a production was nearing its first performance, for example, all was fraught and anxious until the opening night. He was such a nervous man, my father; he lived on his nerves, I think. So little rest. He was always busy flinging himself from role to role, marshaling the actors in rehearsal. To them, his behavior could be cruel; he would scream if they failed to understand some small part of his direction. He does care so. Later I might see an offending actor weeping alone in a dressing room, chewing at his knuckles, pale and shivering and suffering from a despair that might take seasons to be over or may never leave at all.

Often Father would be absent from me altogether, on account of his great labors. He is too busy, I was told then. He is too tired. He has too much to do. Such a great man, do not worry him. Do not exhaust your father, Edith. My aunts and uncles would keep him from me. Sometimes, when I was younger, when I had been forbidden him for a long stretch, I would slip out of my sickroom to listen to him on the stage. His voice would travel up through the heating pipes on the landing, and I would hear him then in all varieties of distress: my father murdering, my father being murdered, my father screaming to his death, his body falling upon the stage. It is one of the natures of this theatre that you may sit by a pipe and hear the work on the stage. The pipes' noise is not always distinct; often it amounts to a general kind of wailing, which may serve for many a production—for how we do wail and wail, we people. What a lot of wind and woe there is. We count ourselves in sadness. So many human lives must wait and wait for their dramatic moments—months and years between events, and sometimes they never come at all. A life may rise and fall and when distilled will prove to have involved scarcely an instant of worthwhile theatre. In the playhouse, however, we get to it right quick. By the end of the first act, which is mostly exposition, we are at full horror and people are being dangerous with one another. We cut and slash lives to their essence. We do exaggerate. We must. We distill. We ladle out sadness to our audience in precise amounts, we feed them tablespoons full of sorrow. Sorrow is our business, after all. We supply it to the people of Norwich for a fee: that, seeing some great sadness, they will feel they have lived a little themselves and feel the more human besides. We are here to remind the human what the human may be, what he is capable of, both the good and the terrible. We teach the humans, in short, about the human.

We have *real* sorrow about us, too. Father, for example, keeps his dead wives in the Mourning Room. It is where he goes when he needs to be alone. Everyone is forbidden him then.

"Sometimes your father may become a little melancholy, Edith, and so then I take myself to this chamber to be sad alone. And then when I step out, see how happy I am again. And so I come and find you."

It was in that place of sorrow, just beyond the step, that I waited, in terror, to hear whether my play had been canceled.

It cannot be good news if it is the Mourning Room. A tour of that chamber is given to me whenever Father wishes to have one of his particular talks. They sit, the dead wives, beside each other—tailor's dummies, one and all, requisitioned from the wardrobe. Rough shapes of womankind, each wearing the dress of a dead spouse, so they have an aura of authenticity about them.

"Here, Edith. Here they are. These were their dresses. These were their shapes."

My mother and the first wife, or the dummies of them, sit together at one side of a table, and on the other side are wives three and four, as if at a tea party.

All those wives were younger than Father, always getting younger, and Father aging, ever older. Sometimes, now, poor Father suffers from a little rheumatism and he aches rather and his hands won't always move in the way he wants them to, especially in the winter months. No more Hamlet for Father, he has outgrown the unhappy prince; now Mr. Emerson plays him and father is the murdering uncle. Father is older than he was when he had his wives several.

"People die, Edith. Death is catching. Keep you safe inside. Are you well?"

"Yes, Father, I am."

"Keep inside."

"Yes, Father, I do."

"People die, they died. Don't die, Edith."

"No, Father."

"You're a good girl."

Number One was Charlotte, before my time, I never knew her. To me she doesn't count, she was only a rehearsal. Father caught death fully only when Mother died. Number Three was Geraldine, an actress in our company, who never liked me very much and would smack me from time to time in private. She walked one night into the Wensum, no one knows why exactly, but the lady was given much to gin and was often confused. Number Four was another actress much younger than Father whose name was Ada. Ada was sometimes very nice and used to play with me on occasions. But sometimes she could be wicked.

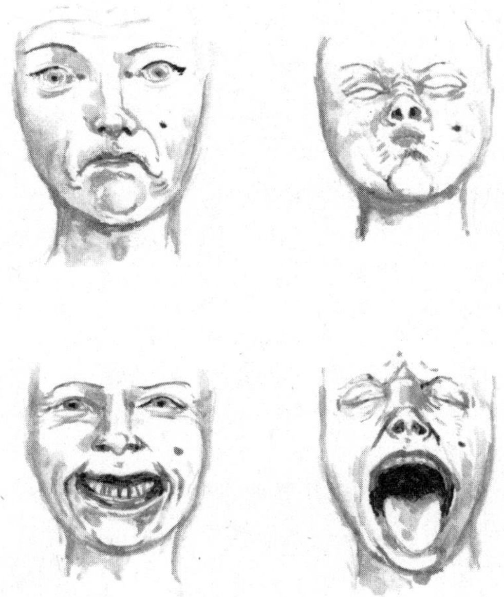

She **would gurn** at me on the stage when I was well enough to play some small and silent part—when her back was to the audience—and these pulled faces of hers would make me laugh, and I would publicly make sound then, because she had made me *corpse*, as we theatre people call it (corpsing is so named after an actor who was unable to stop himself laughing onstage whilst playing a dead person). Corpsing is a very great sin, and afterward Father would be unhappy with me. "You must keep silent," he said. And yet, some weeks later, Ada would do it again—I think she could not stop herself—and I would laugh and Father would be disappointed and I would be devastated. Otherwise, Ada was often lovely. She brought me presents and would fuss over me at Christmastime. But she went and hanged herself one night in a dressing room, number 12, after a terrible review from the newspaper—and not just our local but THE TIMES OF LONDON, which had sent an unhappy critic all the way from the capital, a rather unkempt man as I recall. Perhaps the journey to our eastern address had been so long and uncomfortable that he was discontented before the performance began. Ada should not have taken much notice of that rare insertion of London into our lives, but she did, she paid it very strict attention, and afterward Father put away the wifeing forever.

I have often imagined new mothers and how they might be—a great throng of them lined up to dandle and to chide, all shapes of women come to fuss over me. Yet all of them were so much dreaming—for there never was another.

"Edith, may I remind you," my father would say with great gentleness, "that there is not a single happy marriage in all Shakespeare. And why is that, my child?"

"Because that would be dull, Father."

"Yes, yes indeed! The things you understand!"

When Father was not visiting this small chamber of his cloth wives, it would remain locked. Only Father had the key. And every summer, in the lifeless season, we are closed because so many of the Norwich people are on their holidays—and we are supposed to be on holiday, too, and indeed many of the actors go off, yet I haunt the theatre waiting for their return. During that stale season Father takes his wives out for a parade around Norwich. They all sit in an open carriage together and people bow to him and cheer as he passes. There he goes, Father showing off his grief. How they all love him for it, the people of Norwich. Yet many are frightened of him, too, and of his terrible history: For one man to have so many wives, how did it all happen, was the story all sorrow, or is there something else, something untoward? Are there bloody secrets? They call him in the paper sometimes NORFOLK'S BLUEBEARD. And Father does nothing to stop it; rather, he encourages it. For the more the people think and talk about him, the more they come to the theatre.

Indeed, the people of Norwich find us a fascinating and brutal lot and we often stage fake fights with each other and smash and whip and yell in the streets (not me of course) to tickle the local populace. Then there is blood, but it is not real blood, only our usual imitation. We have at any time two vasty barrels of fake blood just near the stage, we do use it often and paint each other with it freely. (Stage blood is made from vegetable glycerine and water and madder root.) Father is happy for our company to go about the streets of Norwich with stage blood about them, it helps the cause of our theatre. It keeps us in their thoughts.

And there Father was now, inside with his ersatz women, and I outside upon the step. I feared his calling. I feared the reason for it. Of all the Fathers, which Father would I find inside when he called to me?

When I was younger, I used to spend time sitting among my father's false noses. I would try them on, one by one, to feel a little closer to him. I would play with his makeup in his dressing room, with his greasepaints. I knew them all. No. 1, light skin color; 1½ is darker; 2 is pale; 2½, of medium hue; 3 is slightly darker yet; 3½, as if you'd been sunburned; 4 is the ruddy flesh of a drunkard; 5, bright yellow for a sickly look; 6, darker yellow for more sickly; 7, the brown Father uses for Othello; 8, Armenian bole; 9, dark sunburn; 10, brown of a darker hue; 11, burnt umber; 12, black for lines; 13, reddish brown for highlights; 14, chocolate for shading; 15, brick red for lines; 16, dark brown for lines; 20, white for highlighting; carmine 1, 2, and 3 for the best dramatic lines. So much armor had Father.

Underneath, when all was taken away, I thought poor, dear Father might actually be rather a plain man, but so lovely. And he kept his ordinary, commonplace face for me, that was how I saw him: in the role of father, as if he might be any other person of Norwich without his makeup. But he could never be as plain or yet as blank as poor Mr. Collin.

Ah, Mr. Collin. Poor, dear, darling Mr. Collin.

When Father was deep into the darkness of rehearsal and was becoming a character, he would try very hard to lose the Father of him. He would speak in his character all day long and never leave it, he would eat in that character and try to sleep in it besides. He would, in those days, hide Father away as much as he could. In those days of his metamorphosis, when my Father was a pupa, then may Mr. Collin come to me instead, and sometimes wearing Father's clothes. He would appear in a wig of Father's often as not, or with Father's spare set of reading glasses upon his nose—he meant to comfort me by his behavior. I don't think I was ever really convinced by Mr. Collin's performance, for I knew Father better than anyone. Like the stage scenery, it was best seen from a distance. Though Mr. Collin was technically very accomplished, there was always something lacking. You might call it spirit; you might call it soul. I think Mr. Collin was ever in search of a soul, the dear man; the problem was, he was looking for *Father's* soul and not his own.

Mr. Collin, to be clear, was the understudy.

It hadn't meant to be like that. Mr. Collin had had a happy childhood in Broadstairs, Kent (I know nothing about it), and was a wonderfully precocious child, memorizing great speeches and poems and performing them whether asked to or not. He won many a school prize and was particularly good as Juliet (there were only male pupils) in a school production. Many are called to the stage but few are chosen, so they do say. Those were the golden days of Collin. But a shadow was coming.

Twelve years ago Mr. Collin became Father's understudy, and he has lived at that appointment ever since. For twelve years he has been ready, at a moment's notice, to leap upon the stage in Father's place. Never once, in all that time, has it happened. And yet it might happen tonight. And if not tonight, then tomorrow. The readiness is all.

I did love Mr. Collin. He was my surrogate father. Sometimes he brought me a white paper bag filled with chocolates, made by the Caley's factory here in Norwich, from the sweetshop on Elm Hill. Unlike Father, he would often pat my hand; that was one way I may know that it was not my father wearing my father's clothes, for Father would always kiss my hand.

"Enter, Edith." I opened the Mourning Room door. There was Father at the table, his unlovely wives all about him. I could tell instantly despite my anxiety that it was Father himself, and not Mr. Collin. Father sighed deeply, such a noise like great buildings demolishing, a whole city under earthquake. (My father's sighs are such heavy sighs that they can be heard in the balcony.)

"Dear Father! And here you are after all this time!" I said, putting my arms around him and kissing him on the neck.

"Edith, my own child. Do close the door."

I did. "Are you well, Father?"

"I am indeed, how like you to ask. And you, my Edith, chick?"

"Oh yes, excellent!"

"And strong?"

"Like a lioness!"

"So brave."

"Father, we are still to perform my play, aren't we? I have the bill posters upstairs, the newspaper cutting, there should be no going back."

"Edith . . ." He paused. He would always pause after saying my name, always a gap there, filled with anxiety and hope, to see which side Father's news may fall. "Edith, it is certain the play will proceed."

"Oh, that is a relief! I had gotten myself in such a worry over it. Why did you call for me then, Father? Is it to discuss the changes? I do think Aunt Jenny will do very well as the sister, and Uncle Thomas as the mayor of Norwich. The only trouble is the casting of Mawther Meg herself, I cannot see who would be best. Who is it that has that authority and that danger, who may terrify and fascinate? I consider her, of course, a great symbol of all things cruel in Norwich. I wondered whether it might be better not to have an actual person at all, in fact, perhaps a large puppet. To keep her mysterious."

"Edith."

"And as for the young girl, the child who escapes and is not lost—perhaps I may read the part in rehearsals, just to begin with, so that people understand what I mean by it exactly."

"Edith, be still. I have something to tell you."

"I am a statue."

"Edith, I must inform you that I am in love."

"Yes, Father. Of course, Father."

"Edith, my darling, do you attend me?"

"I am, I do!"

"What then did I say?"

"You said . . . you are in *love*!" I exclaimed, catching the meat of his meaning.

"I am, yes. Do you think it strange? Am I so very old?"

"Oh, Father!"

"You are to meet her tomorrow morning."

"Oh, Father!"

"And you are to be dressed like a young lady and to be most polite and welcoming. Nor, Edith dear, are you to talk too much, not at first. Nor, my essential Edith, do we need to hear any of your tales, at least not at first. You are not to attempt to frighten the lady who shall be—it has been decided upon—my wife. Edith? Edith, do you yet attend?"

I was in a confusion at this approaching newness, at this stranger to come into my life. A new woman, a fifth wife. A new Mrs. Holler.

"Edith, you do tremble so."

"No, indeed, Father, not at all. It is a big thing, is it not, this news of yours."

"It is indeed, and I think it shall be a wonderful progression."

"Yes, Father, I am sure."

Then the something new came upon me, creeping fast.

"Will she, this woman, this wife, will she be a mother to me?"

A pause.

"If you let her, I am sure she shall."

"I shall have a mother then after all this time?"

"Well, surely, if you do let her."

"What is my new mother's name?"

"It is Margaret."

Oh, Margaret is it then? What was in the name Margaret? What clue there? (Henry VI should never have married Margaret of Anjou, but he would not listen.) And yet I knew of no Margaret.

"There's no Margaret in the company," I said.

"No, she is not from the theatre."

"Not from the theatre? What strangeness!"

"Yes, Edith."

"Margaret the mother," I whispered.

"Margaret the marriage," he said. "Edith, I want us to be happy. To be a happy family."

"There are no happy families in Shakespeare, Father."

Ah, must we be dull, then?

"Her name is Margaret Unthank."

"Is it then, I've never heard of her."

"She is a widow."

"Poor lady."

"And a businesswoman. And, Edith, I have written to her family about your play."

"My play, Father? Whatever for?"

"And she invited me to visit. She is an Utting by birth, you see. Of the Beetle Spread family."

My world stopped, a wailing in my bones.

"Oh, don't say it's true!"

"And we became friendly, a very nice lady. It is your play that did it, that brought us together."

"So dangerous! My play!"

And then I saw it. The small line on the bridge of the nose. Like a hair, like a small crack on a piece of porcelain. I had been taken in. I, Edith Theatre, had been fooled! And yet I could not stop a glow of admiration—happy admiration, and relief besides. It was all a game!

"You bluff! Ha ha, now I see it! It is all make-believe!"

"Edith, you must be calm."

"I see you, Mr. Collin."

"Edith, steady!"

"Oh, Mr. Collin! Mr. Collin, you were wonderful!"

"I am your father, child."

"Mr. Collin, you have never been so masterful. An extraordinary performance. Your very best yet." A small silence, and then one eye came peeping through. The eye of Collin.

"Truly? Was I? You liked it, you believed it?"

"You were magnificent!"

And there before me was Mr. Collin, crying for pride. In a little voice, grateful but uncertain, he murmured, "Would that others had seen it."

"But, Mr. Collin," I said. "It's not true, is it? There is no new wife. No Utting woman."

"Yes, my dear, it is certain," he said, with kindness. "And you are to meet her tomorrow."

"An Utting? That family shall hate me so. Oh, what is she like?"

"I cannot say. I have very slender information."

"Mr. Collin, why did Father not tell me himself?"

"He is very busy, Edith."

"But such particular news. An Utting!"

"So busy, you see."

"Thank you, Mr. Collin."

"You are to run straight to your aunt Nora now, Edith. She is waiting to fit you for a new dress."

"Let her wait then."

"You must go now. As if your father, Edith, had commanded it and not I. You must not fall into one of your misadventures, Edith. And, Edith, you are not to panic."

"I go, I go!"

Flora Bignell—who would like me to call her aunt, though I find it trying—was waiting outside the door to the Mourning Room. Flora Bignell, old and spongy, who curled wigs for her living, lived with us and ours; she floated like a moth around the clothing of the theatre, nibbling at little bits here and there. She needed very little and was given as much. And, like the moth, she was always somewhere near the stage when the light was upon it.

Flora, once upon a time, had used to work at Utting's. She was one of those who put the lids on the 2 oz. jars of Spread. She had moved to this part of the world from Lowestoft (Suffolk) when her sister Lorena came to our theatre as an actress, but after her sister exploded she lost her nerve and shortly afterward her appointment at Utting's (though she yet retains a dull stain on her palms from the madder root). But employment was found for her here. A smile upon the Bignell face that morning. "She is coming! I have seen her!"

"Oh, what is she like?"

"You shall see!"

Flora was a kind enough soul, perhaps, but she did blame me in some portion for her sister's demise. Though she told me often that was not the case, as she did now.

"Not your fault, of course, that my own dear sister did burst all over your family's property. Not to blame that she was here one day and everywhere the next. Not to blame for that great red cloud of sibling. She could have had no idea that this is what you would grow into."

"Good-bye, Great-Aunt Flora."

"You are to come to the wardrobe. I am here to escort you."

"I go where I please. I am playwright now, and shall be treated accordingly."

"To the wardrobe, child."

"I have business to attend to on behalf of my production."

"We do *Titus* next, you can't fool me. To the wardrobe with you."

The wardrobe was where Aunt Nora measured all the populace and endeavored to disguise them and cut them up with her scissors to make them ready, just as I used to cut all my card people out of the card booklets for my card theatre, before I became a proper playwright. Nora the Needle's wardrobe was down the stairs and on the floor below me. "Good-bye, good-bye," I said. "Leave me alone."

"You are to come with me straight!"

But, despite my long illnesses, I was so much faster than old Flora Bignell. I went down the stairs and then down and down and down beyond her, all in a worry.

4.

Backstage.

All about the back stage, down and down, ran Edith in her grey gown. I am Edith Theatre, I told myself. I know all monsters. I know the truth of goblins, I eat specters for dinner, I am fire and plague, I am the spell caster, the story maker. I am the spider, I am the fly. I am dark and deep and hell all over. Days go by and my hair is unbrushed. Where I go, I leave a trail of blood. I bite my nails. I am the playwright.

Yet no matter how I reassured myself, still I felt so uncertain. A new mother, a new mother and an Utting—what could that mean? Was I to be ignored or worried over? Unstitched or stitched up? How would Father behave toward me, with a new woman busying him? A woman from out there, from beyond the theatre. We never let people from out there come in here, not without permission. And yet, without my knowledge, permission had been granted.

I stood for a while at the stage door, looking out into Chantry Road as if it might provide some answers. Mr. Peat was in his little office, which guards the outside door. Mr. Peat is the Cerberus of the back stage. He always knows who is in and who is out. None may enter or exit, save through him. He swears like a sailor and smokes like a chimney and sits in his box with all his keys, watching all, coughing and swearing and tugging at his forelock, and though he insists the theatre is a childish business, still he loves it well, and guards it with great seriousness. Beyond him is the world.

Mr. Peat taught me all the worst words I know, schooled me in them as if they were precious: *bugger* and *shiteabed* and *quim* and *gonads*. He taught me, too, of Norfolk places, of the watery Broads and the long beach of Holkham, of the holy place of Great Walsingham, where long ago an Anglo-Saxon woman called Richeldis de Faverches dreamed that the Virgin Mary came to her and told her to build a replica of her holy house in Nazareth, and she did and somehow she knew exactly how it looked. It was a miracle. And there in Walsingham they also have a vial of the Virgin's milk. It is an old story like the Norwich tale of Maw Meg. But Mr. Peat was not in the story vein that early afternoon.

"Should you be here alonga me, Edith Holler?"

"I may be if I choose it."

"And not with your aunt in wardrobe?"

"I am getting ready for my play."

"That's not due yet. About yer play, Edith Holler, truly is it set in Norwich?" (*Narridge*, he says.)

"It is, Mr. Peat."

"A play in Norwich! Never known the like. Is it right, do you think?"

"Nothing is righter!"

"Plays are on London, on Paris, on Italian foreign places. No play as ever I heard was set in Norwich."

"Then it is high time."

"Norwich. It don't seem right. Makes me uncertain."

"Father is to marry, I am told."

"Heard the same myself. I am sorry, gearte."

"Oh, Mr. Peat, have you seen this new woman?"

"Might of."

"What's she like?"

"You'll larn soon, I reckon."

"I'm that worried, Mr. Peat."

"Run along to your aunt now. But here first, chidder, afore you go take this then. Have a coshie. Suck on that. Do you good, that will." He gave me a piece of candy-striped Cromer rock, which he hands out now and then on special occasions. "You may, when she has taken her place, if you need it, come alonga me of an afternoon and sit here beside Old Peat and we'll talk of things and that may be a help to you. In the coming times."

"Oh, Mr. Peat."

"Get you gone, gearte."

I did not ascend to my aunt Nora, rather I went to the scenery dock, to visit a certain canvas. But there was no progress since I had last come, which was only the day before, still what a sight.

Here was Norwich, where we make our scene. Norwich in the fourteenth century. Gone are all the Georgian places, gone are the Victorian ones. No streetlamps and certainly no trams, nor any Beetle Spread factory neither. "We are going backward in time, pull up the ghosts, let the past leak out at last. And see that you are now upon ancient Norwich land."

Look closer, though. You know this place. There is the castle and there the cathedral. You know your way around by those ancient beacons, though it is so very long ago.

On the back is painted *Act 1, Sc. 1, True Hist M Meg.*

And that is proof enough. It is a great good thing.

"Hello!" I called.

But no one was there. Where were they all gone? As if Norwich were deserted.

I felt as if I were saying good-bye. Good-bye to everyone. I ran all about, not settling in any one place, but in a fidget everyroom. Upsetting uncles and aunts and disturbing some acting cousins, who were practicing their fencing scenes with Mr. Atkins the fight master. I watched them awhile but ran along again. Ignoring their calls that Miss Edith must to the wardrobe.

I called in on Miss Tebby, who sat dependably in her room of paper. Miss Tebby is the theatre prompt, and her little office is a nest of playscripts. She has them all, and all are up to date.

"Miss Edith, up again!"

"Can I hide here?"

"Yes, my dear girl, come in. Make yourself at home."

"I thank you!"

"In truth, I am glad you are here. I've been wanting to ask, is all well with your family?"

"Well enough I suppose, Miss Tebby."

"And your father? I worry about him. I have of late had to feed him several lines, it's not like him at all. Have you noticed anything different?"

"Yes Miss Tebby, he is to marry!"

"He is? Indeed! Ah well, perhaps that is his distraction then." She knows the news well enough, I can tell. Miss Tebby is a terrible actress. "And *you*, are you well?" Her voice is ever quiet, always a whisper. Miss Tebby, of course, has never in life been heard to her raise her voice. She needs a quiet voice, so that when the actors forget their lines, she from her little trap at the front of the stage just behind the footlights may peek out and pass on to the actors the words they have temporarily misplaced, in a voice so perfectly quiet that the actors may hear it but the audience may not.

"Quite well, I thank you."

"Why then do you shake so, girl?"

"In truth, dear Miss Tebby, I'm supposed to be being fitted for a dress to meet Father's new wife, and I am afraid—for the woman is an Utting you see, Prompt." Miss Tebby, owllike, prompts us all, if we call her, very quietly, by the name Prompt.

"I am a girl of twelve," prompts the prompt, feeding me lines, brushing my hair. "I am not an adult yet, though sometimes I pretend to be. I am the sheltered daughter of a difficult man. I have no power here, and so I will do the best if I observe what small rules are given me. I should keep to my own floor and my own rooms—up where it is lighter and the air is better. I have written a play, a good play some say, especially for my age, drawing upon folklore and history. I am doing well and should walk carefully now. I am better again after a long decline. I should be good to the new mother, and give her every chance. Let us hope she will be a blessing to me and let me welcome her properly."

"Who are you to tell me such things?"

"Prompt mistress."

"You don't have any lines at all."

"I have all the lines, every single one of them. Now go as directed. Arrive at your station. Get back in the script. Where are you meant to be, Miss Edith?"

"In the wardrobe."

"Then find your place."

"I'm leaving."

"Yet wait a little moment, my Edith child. May I tell you, though it is not proper for such as I to have opinions: I love the play. My favorite is the line: 'You look at me, you people of Tombland, as if I had six legs, as if I scuttle in blackness, you see me not as the woman that I am, but as a shadow in rough human shape, a creature of darkness, yet I am a woman still, I am one of yours, though you shun me so!' It makes me think of myself, of the actors when they take me for granted. Oh, Edith, that is very grand. It will be a big success, I think."

"Oh thank you, Miss Tebby! I think so too."

"To the wardrobe, then, clever Edith. Be strong."

But I did not go to the wardrobe that uncertain afternoon. Instead, I found me wandering the dressing rooms, taking the east stairway down as the west stairway is currently forbidden on account of it not being safe. The dressing rooms were where all our bodies are wont to loll when they are not required upon the stage. Ah, I love them so—all the actors I mean, our people, who rush to pat Edith upon the head, to hug and stroke, to pet me and lift me up in a whirl, or to come straight out and kiss me hard upon the lips, to dandle and to fuss over me and also to chivvy me along. Such a tactile nation. All our people in their undergarments, slouchy and smoking, in their peace before performance time, before their hearts start beating faster. Yet how fast mine thrashed as I weaved myself in among the pretending people, all very busy with a costume call for *Titus Andronicus*, in and out of their dressing gowns, so free in their skins.

Aunt Agatha Wilson, in her own skin, came to me direct.

"Miss Edith, I have read the play, I think it quite beastly. Properly beastly, you understand me. I think, especially, that there is a part for me here. The one called Mawther Meg. I've been looking for a part like this. See me now, observe me, darling." She stood up as tall as she might and put on a ghastly visage, and proclaimed: "'Who is it that comes knocking at my door? Who is it that disturbs Lone Meg? No one visits me. I live in silence, yet is there a sound now? There it is again! The knocking! It is the noise of company!'"

She was quoting words by Edith Holler.

"It is lovely, Aunt Agatha. And well done. I must along now."

"You will consider me," she said, offended. "It's all I ask."

"Of course."

"I'm glad to see you up again, my darling."

I am so fond of Agatha, but I'm not certain she has that about her that says Maw Meg. She retreated to her dressing room, closing her door behind her.

I wandered the passageways and followed the noise of men talking loudly. My lesser acting uncles—that is, my actual uncles, who may as well be called Polonius or Albany, Trinculo, Lepidus, Hastings, or Leonato, but were christened Gregory and Thomas—were together in the greenroom, drinking. Father's two acting brothers believe most of all in payday and beer and hot suppers.

"Edith, up again! Edith Holler the playwright!"

"I have read your play," said Uncle Gregory. "Can't say I understand it entirely. Is it right for a woman to be writing plays, and a child at that?

It feels an indulgence. Edgar certainly has gone too far this time. Children missing, Edith? You'll start a panic. And lord knows what Edgar's new woman shall say! Quite the scandal."

"By which he means, Edith, he doesn't like his part."

"I am an old building, wattle and daub!" said Gregory. "Seventeen lines. 'I am thin timbers and leaking roof, holes there are in and out of my walls, by beetles have I been gnawed and gnawn.' A building! A ruin!"

"I am quite happy with my role. Robert Baxter, the mayor of Norwich."

"Thank you, Uncle Thomas."

"There may be room, perhaps, for another scene between him and Mawther Meg. I can see it clearly. I wonder if you've quite considered all the possibilities of this part. A romance, or, alternatively, a murder. We could talk about it. Perhaps the mayor might disappear a child or two himself."

"Oh, Edith," said Uncle Gregory, lifting up my chin, "you look like you've seen a ghost."

"Yes, Uncle."

"And there are other looks to be had."

"Yes, Uncle."

"Edith, you know you must go to your cloth aunt," said Gregory. My aunt Nora was his wife, but they were not on speaking terms, not since Gregory got too close to an actress from Bungay (Norfolk-Suffolk border) and was found in her dressing room without any cloth upon him. Ever since, my uncle Gregory seems to have come unstitched rather himself. Nora has forbidden him her presence, and how neglected his clothing is now, it droops and has patches, there are always loose threads. Even when some third party presents him with a new costume, it is always a disappointment, always shoddy and awkward. How threadbare his performances have been of late. His daughter, my cousin Claire—who might be called a very fine pair of scissors in her late twenties—

keeps her father up to date. She snaps at him all the latest news from the wardrobe department.

"Go now, Edith. New days are coming."

"Yes, Uncle, I have heard. What's she like, Uncle?"

"You shall see quite soon enough. Time to grow up, Edith. Be a Holler, won't you?"

"I try."

"Up you go, then, don't make a fuss." Uncle Thomas pushed me gently from the greenroom and closed the door.

"Miss Edith!"—someone calling me along the passageway. I knew that voice and it signified misery for me. "Miss Edith! Miss Edith, dear Miss Edith out in the world!"

Mr. Mealing on the hunt. I called him Mealy on account of his skin like cold pork and all the small blasts of redness thereabout. He slinked and slurked about the theatre and made his small sounds. He called himself playwright, but what little dramas he wrote were all bland things about drawing rooms in London—though he had never been in such environs—and with not a hint of magic about them. I avoided him at all times. He liked me, Mr. Mealing did. He used to pinch my cheeks, but more recently he had taken to pinching my thigh. I detested the man and fled him always.

"Is it Miss Edith there? Holloah, Edith! Do come and read my new play, shan't you? I have read your play, too, and I have some advice for you. Let me escort you to the wardrobe, shan't you? You and I?"

No, I bloody shan't. On I ran. And down, down and down, where there is ever less light.

There are so few private places in a theatre, when you think about it. You may say the dressing rooms, but they are mostly shared and a stage manager may burst in any moment without knocking and call it business. But I have a little place, down underneath the dressing rooms it is, in the quiet bowels of the theatre, a place I call my own.

Down I went—I held on to the rope banisters, down and down, into the bowels. A new sign there:

DANGER

NO MORE THAN 2 PERSONS

ON THE STAIRS AT ANY TIME

It may be helpful, for those who are not acquainted with the theatre as I am, to think of the backstage side as a great ship. All that wood, all those ropes. And to think of the stage, ever scrubbed, as the deck, and below deck is the understage, which goes down many floors. Unlike the ship, however, there are no portholes, so all gets darker and darker the deeper you dare go.

To get to my private place I must first go to the furnace room, and within the furnace room is the backup furnace, which is never used and so is always private. It is there "just in case," like an understudy, and it has laid cold ever since it was put in, so I have taken it for myself. I climb in there and close the metal door and light a candle and then I have my peace. No one knows I come here; Father would be horrified and forbid it. I can almost hear him: "Suppose it was lit, Edith. And you inside?"

Here I keep my own cardboard theatres; here I play God with the people of card. It is proper to call them *toy* theatres, but that never sounds right to me. They are more than toy, the word *toy* condemns them, it disapproves, it trivializes. They are very dear to me, they are essential.

No one else knows of my visits here, not anymore, not since my friend Elsie Mardle left us. I play here alone, when I am well enough, with all the card booklets I have, and Father often orders me new ones, which are sent all the way from London, from Pollock's Toy Theatres Ltd., 11 Kendal Place, London W1. Though I am twelve, still I love them yet. Here is my great populace when the theatre above me is too busy. I have everyone here: I have witches and trolls and soldiers, I have even Napoleon (who was an emperor and died on an obscure island, though he was more famous than anyone in the world). Sometimes I go about with Napoleon in my pocket, and then I do feel a bit emperor myself.

But the playing no longer comes right since my friend Elsie Mardle left. Elsie worked with Aunt Bleachy and scrubbed herself raw, but at the end of the day we would find each other and then we were together and that was always enough for us. She had a short-tempered father who worked at Utting's and a mother, quite stained red, who washed clothes in the Wensum, but was in with the gin to keep herself warm. I found her that first time, my Elsie girl, shivering by the working furnace, ill like me, and I gave her cake—pocket cake I call it, the food I stuff in my pockets when I set about exploring—and she took it and she ate it. And I kept finding her here and I kept getting her some food.

Most of all we would play for hours at my card theatres, right here in the second furnace, lolling together, our feet touching. There we would perform the whole of *The Corsican Brothers* or *The Children in the Wood* or else *Daughter of the Regiment*, also *Harlequinade*, all of these actual toy theatre plays with cardboard figures and changing scenery. We followed the instructions in the booklet and read the lines that were pro-

vided there and gave card much voice. How we have wept, we two, at the death of Louis de Franchi in *The Corsican Brothers*, though he was only ever a piece of colored card, and how we both agreed that the most moving of all the cardboard populace was the figure of the shade of Louis de Franchi, his face as white as paper and with a devastating red wound upon his chest. For to die in cardboard is still to die.

But one evening we lost time as we enacted the cardboard life of *Blackbeard the Pirate*, and by the time the dreadful end was reached and Blackbeard fell into the angry ocean, we opened the furnace door and heard that the evening's business on the stage had begun, and it was much later than we thought. Elsie's terror now was real as she went miserable into the night, and no matter that I put a sunny country landscape in the little theatre slot, outside it remained stubbornly dark.

She was so badly scolded for being home late that she missed two days of work and was nervous to play with me afterward, so bruised she was. "It goes different with me, Edith. You may have your tales but what use are they to me? Look what they done to me!"

A short time later, Elsie was taken from me. She was given new work in the Beetle Spread factory, and I must let her go. Will you write, Elsie?

"Surely, Edith. When I have the mind for it."

I could not wait to get that letter. What a thing to have a letter.

Yet no letter came.

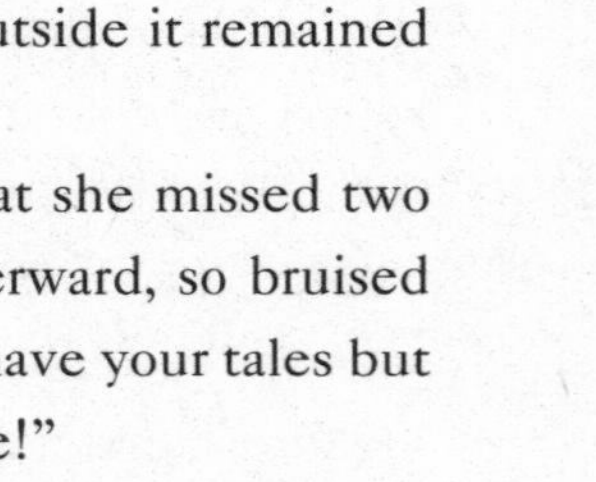

And that day I found that I had no patience for cardboard people, for they gave no hint at the new mother, nor did they show me my play which had grown greater than cardboard and was now canvas and would soon be made flesh. I put them down. I am different now. I have stood naked upon the stage. I am a new Edith without time for card. I am not flat, I am full and solid and real. I blew out the candle. Black went everything. And it was the end of the world and I was dead and buried. And yet. Breathe, Edith, breathe. Count to ten and open the latch. I did, so quietly. Back in the furnace room. Me and the warmth—but then the outside door opened and I wasn't alone anymore.

"Miss Edith! Miss Edith, here you are at last. Whyever do you hide in such a sooty chamber?"

Mealy in my private place, spoiling everything.

"I must get out, you are in my way," I cried.

"Miss Edith, Miss Edith," he says to me coming very close indeed, he always makes the first vowel of my name very long, *Eeeeeeeeeeeeeedif*, he says, like he's breathing all over me with it, or like he's stroking it or taking possession.

"Yes, Mr. Mealing."

"Do, dear Miss Edith, call me Oliver."

I would rather die.

"You say nothing, Miss Edith."

I did not indeed.

"Nothing will come of nothing, Miss Edith. You know that, I think."

"Unhappy that I am, I cannot heave my heart into my mouth," I said, my thanks to Cordelia.

"I do not want your heart in your mouth, Miss Edith. That would be a strange sight indeed. I want you, rather, in an elegant summer dress that I have seen in a shop on Rampant Horse Street. Very light material."

Go away, go away, Mealing. I don't want you here.

"Miss Edith? Miss Edith!" I heard Great-Aunt Flora calling me outside.

"I must go, you see." And I shoved past him. Out into the understage. I shut the door on him, too.

• • •

A very short play

Enter Mealing.

Exit Mealing.

Finis.

"Miss Edith! There you are!" huffed Flora. "You run me ragged. Come here at last!"

Flora, it's Flora. Ignore her, ignore her. Run, Edith. Run.

Across the understage to the puppet workshop and dear Mrs. Stead. Mrs. Stead would surely hide me.

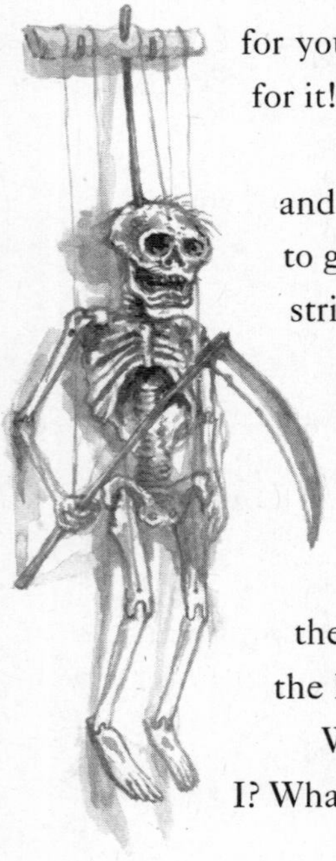

"Miss Edith!" shouted Flora. "You only make it worse for yourself! You'll do yourself an injury and I'll be blamed for it! If you are sick tomorrow it's hardly my fault."

But there was a puppet hanging on the workshop door, and that puppet was Death, which meant that no one was to go in right then. I should have to wait until some other stringfellow was put up there, Pantalone, say, or Columbina or Mr. Punch, and only then could I make a cautious hallo, may I come by? Death means: keep out, Edith. And so I do.

"Miss Edith, come back." Flora yet. "Where are you going? Don't go down deep, I'll not follow you there. You may not descend further. It is expressly against the law of theatre."

Well, that was an idea then. I had no care for signs, had I? What could it matter a grey weight like me?

NO ENTRY, ACCESS FORBIDDEN

"No you don't." Mealy again. Mealy had sudden hold of me, just for a moment.

"Don't touch!" I screamed. And pushed him away.

"Calm, Miss Edith. You must calm, none of your histrionics. There is nowhere for you to go, nowhere but Oliver Mealing."

Yet there were other addresses, at least there was one close by. Inching away from Mealing, I hit against a wall, my back banged into a handle. A door handle. To the trap room. The trap room has two doors so that you may get from it right across the other side of backstage. The trap room is where the actors fall when the trapdoors in the stage are opened. It is a room of mattresses. A quiet place usually, but of a sudden its ceiling opens in certain places and people hurtle from the sky into it. That's the place I went rushing into. I felt Mealy's hand on me, but he was frightened, and he stumbled in the trap room's darkness. Quickly I was behind one of the stacks of mattresses.

"Miss Edith? Miss Edith, where are you? Don't be shy."

Getting yet closer now. I changed my spot, hid behind the next stack.

"Meeees Eeeediiifff, ah you make it a game. I do seek you!" And the next.

"Meeees Eeediii . . . ah!"

Mealing had run into something, and that was what I needed. I'd worked my way round, and as quietly as I may, I was out again and on the other side of the understage. Left behind: Mealing, in the trap room, hurting.

STRICTLY NO ENTRY

THIS AREA OUT OF BOUNDS

Now I could climb down farther yet, to the damp, dark land where the donkeys are kept and blind Mr. Leadham too. The donkeys pull the great wooden wheel that revolves the stage, or sometimes tugs great ships across it. I'd be safe in the deep dark so long as I was quiet. I could hear the donkeys, shifting in the ground, a little unsettled perhaps; no doubt they had heard me. I could barely see them in the deep distance, touched by the shyest puddle of light. Mr. Leadham keeps a lanthorn lit to calm the beasts, even though he cannot see himself. He gives them a little light from his particular small lanthorn, which always has a lucifer connected to it, attached by an old shoelace, so that he may never lose it.

"Who's thar?" It was Mr. Leadham calling.

I kept very still.

"All right, my dickeys," he said at last, "all right, Judy; down, Olive; steady, Old Alice. All is well, stop yer grizzling," and the donkeys calmed.

I'd be good here, so long as I was still and quiet, so long as those upstairs ones didn't come poking. I'd be fine now. Well done, Edith.

A flash of light, a match struck, and through darkness the face of Uncle Wilfred suddenly appeared before me, lighting his pipe. I let out a small scream. Uncle Wilfred is not generally to be screamed at; he is my practical uncle and since his childhood he has always been the maker of things. He has ever found a way of rendering Father's ideas. If Father says *a dragon*, then Wilfred says *twelve sheets of ply, some glass, dry ice, vermillion paint* (at such a cost). He knows things better than anyone and can shape them into dreams.

"Who's thar agin?" called Mr. Leadham.

"Is only me," said Wilfred. "Me and Edgar Holler's daughter."

"Why's the ickeny child down here? Not her place."

"I shall see to it, old bor. Calm and quiet and all is well."

Wilfred took me by the elbow and led me up the stairs.

"There's going to be a new wife," I said.

"I have heard but not seen."

"How long have you known?"

"A week or two."

"And you didn't tell me."

"Was asked to keep it dark. Besides which, I have not seen you."

"She's not from the theatre, she's not one of us."

"I do know it."

"She's an Utting!"

"I have heard that."

"I should have been told. It's not right."

"You've been told now at least so be of good cheer. You're to go along, Nora is waiting. Don't cause grief. Is a celebration."

"Is it?"

"It is and you have written a play, too, niece, and that is a celebration and all."

"Did you like it, Uncle?"

"Not for me to say. But we shall do it, shan't we."

"Can I have everything that is in the script? Can I have all the ghosts?"

"You may have whatever you wish. Whatever is written, we'll find a way."

"How will you do them, Uncle Wilfred?"

"I was thinking, having read the pages, dirty clothes and rubbish. Can easily pick the clothes up from Norwich market, at the rag shop, tuppence a pound. Quite within budget. There, you see, is easily done. Is no great bother."

"And they are very lonely, those orphaned clothes, and would not complain of the attention. They were hoping for a good home. Don't you think so, Uncle?"

But he never answered, because a stagehand, a pleasant young fellow name of Hawthorne, came calling down the wooden stairs, not venturing deeper himself. "Mr. Wilfred, are you there below?"

"I am here, lad."

"It's Mr. Holler. He's asking for you."

"Thank you, Hawthorne."

Wilfred obeyed Father's call, he always did.

"Come on then, Edith. Up the stairs with you, hold on careful now. Watch your step, step over that one, that's good. Do not come down here, Edith, it is not solid and you know it. And, Edith, good my niece, don't cause strife."

"Yes, Uncle."

"Let me see you go along to Nora."

There were the stairs up to the wardrobe, and there was the door with the baize over it to muffle the sounds. That is the door that leads onto the stage. I turned, I took the first two steps upward, but then I stopped. Wilfred went toward the stage and was gone. I took one more step, then turned and followed Wilfred through the door, and I was in the dark of the wings of backstage left. Slipping between the two giant barrels of stage blood, I banged into one and heard the deep liquid lapping inside. From there I could see Wilfred joining the actors. I could even see the vast back of Father. Normally I would run to him, though my uncles and aunts would try to prevent it. But not today, not with this news. Better to leave him. Better to consider the news all alone.

The door had shut silently behind me. Safe. Yet in a moment it opened again. There was Flora and Mealing beside her, and Miss Tebby. Mr. Collin there too.

"Miss Edith? Miss Edith? Have you got Edith Holler there onstage with you?"

"No, no, she's not here."

"She's gone up to Nora," said Uncle Wilfred.

"I've just come down from Nora," said Mr. Collin. "She's not there."

"She'll make herself sick again," said Flora, "and it won't be my fault."

So then there was only one place left for me to go. To the other land of theatre. Every theatre is a house divided in two, the private side and the public side, and the two are separated by a great guillotine: The iron it is called, a thick iron curtain that closes the stage off from the public side. It is there for safety, to stop fire spreading. If there is a fire—and how awful a thing that would be—the whole of one side would burn to a crisp and yet the other would be safe, shielded by the fireproof iron. I often wondered how that would be, to be on the safe side but listening to the great burning of the other, the screams and the terror. I fear a fire most particularly, for if the theatre burns, what am I to do? I who must never leave the theatre or die of it.

The iron was down as I came trip-trap close to it.

I crept by the stage manager's desk and through the pass door—and suddenly I was in a different land, with different rules.

S.

Front of house.

This is where the public knows.

I took my shoes and stockings off so that my naked feet might feel the carpet. Lush, it is. All so grand and so expensive. Such space now! How to do it all justice? Seats for seven hundred and fifty-two people at a time. That may help you picture a size, but it cannot complete the portrait. When fully packed, as the theatre most often is, it feels as if all those people were a great wave that might crash upon the stage.

What drama has occurred front of house:

Once someone swallowed their tongue.

Heart attacks: three.

Twice, our dramas have broken women's waters.

A gentleman's false leg fell from the upper circle into the stalls, causing a concussion.

A woman got locked in an upstairs lavatory and screamed and screamed.

A young man, in the balcony, slashed his lover's face.

Proscenium arch of a card theatre.

An old and ill man came here to die and did die. (How the actors hovered around the body, to look for clues to improve their own performances.)

I ran fast and silent away from the safety curtain. Oh, it is all so threadbare on the stage side! There are no carpets, there is no thick red wallpaper, there is no gold paint; the mirrors lack great frames; there are no cherubs on the ceiling, no golden masks of comedy and tragedy like those out front. (Painted plaster, these last, but most convincing—

except where cracked or flaked.) All is plain, all is working space, but in this other land, just a few steps away, all is luxury—though the cheaper the seats, the farther from the stage, the less of luxury there is. It is indeed quite plain up high in the balcony—so high you are almost in the heavens, and indeed we call it "the gods" there. The rake of those lofty seats does terrify many a person; some will watch a whole show clinging to the metal handrail, for fear that they should go tumbling down into the maw of the stalls.

The whole of it—from the stalls to the royal circle, to the upper circle, to the balcony—is kept upright by scaffolding supports and by my uncle Jerome. He is the front-of-house manager, the master of this half. He opens the doors and lets the people in, he takes all the money. Jerome is a very fine-looking gentleman, and when the theatre is closed, his region is all about tidiness and order. Then all his cleaners come

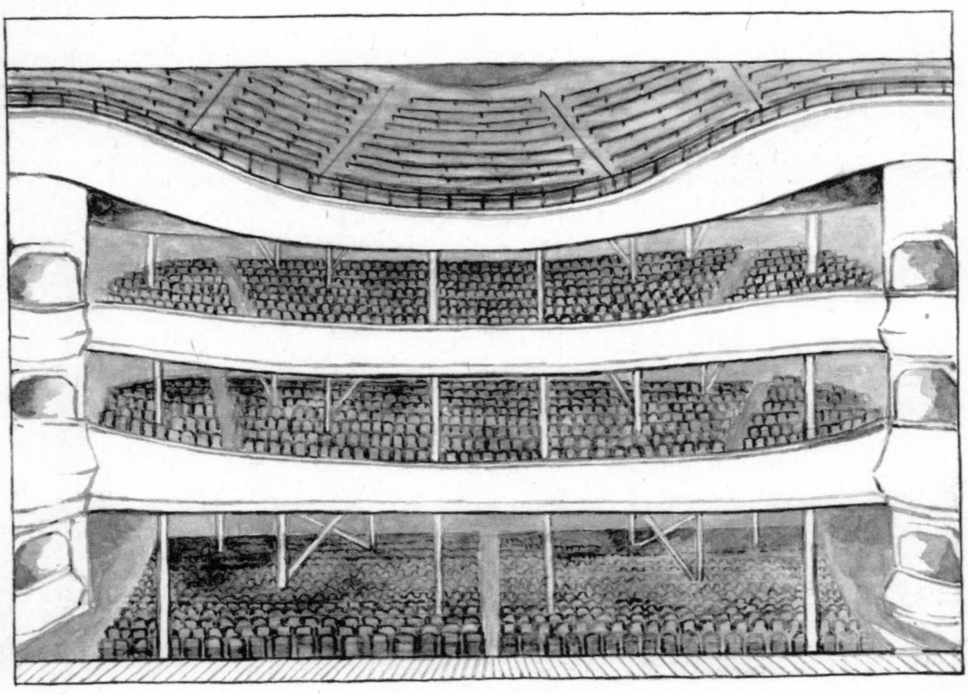

in and brush and polish and sweep and wipe and clean to a sparkle. Jerome is the great enemy of dust and smear. He is very like a theatre man: He wears the face of tragedy in the morning, but by evening, when the public comes in—whether we are playing sad or not—he always becomes comedy. He puts on such a smile for the public.

That is where I fled, to Uncle Jerome's land, that great country of red velvet. It is true, some of the plaster molding is no longer present, and in places the velvet is a little worn and some of the seats are loose at the seams, and some of the old hinges do scream horribly when you unfold them; and it is true, in some places the red wallpaper is stained and scratched, and there are many darker marks that talk of Beetle Spread. And it is true as well that some of the mirrors have lost a portion of their mercury, leaving black blotches upon the glass, so that anyone looking into them will think themselves beset by the bubonic. Norwich is no stranger to pestilence; in 1579 we lost a third of our population to plague. And it is true that when it rains hard upon Norwich it sometimes rains a little inside the Holler Theatre, and then will Uncle Jerome be in a panic and come rushing with a pail. Up he'll go, trying to find where the new leak is coming from, trying desperately to stop rain before the audience is let in. There are indeed water marks here and there. But I don't notice these things, they are small pocks on an otherwise beautiful face.

It is quite the grandest place in all the world, and I do come here often when I feel an urge majestic.

The best of it all are the two huge oil paintings. One is of my ancestor Victor Holler, my great-grandfather, in the role of Hamlet. He is holding a human skull, of course: indeed, the skull in the painting is the likeness of a real skull, which

once belonged to the seventeenth-century Norwich doctor called Sir Thomas Browne who wrote a great deal about death. We rent the skull from the Norfolk and Norwich Hospital when we do the Danish play; it was my great-grandfather who started this, and it is a wonderful piece of local business for the people of Norwich.

The other painting is of my father playing King Lear.

(There is no painting of my unhappy grandfather Richard Holler.)

The portrait of Father describes a man so much older than the portrait of his grandfather. An odd thing, that the young one is long dead and the old one is still full of living. Whatever their age, these are the most dramatic and wonderful artworks in all of East Anglia.

My great-grandfather Victor Holler began, according to family legend, as a street performer in Norwich's Market Place. He recited small one-speech tragedies and comedies, and he did it so well that he was hired as a juvenile performer at what was then called the Theatre Royal. By his thirteenth birthday, Victor was playing Osric, then Laertes by his sixteenth, and when he came eighteen Hamlet himself. Once he'd got his teeth into Hamlet, there was no stopping him. He became such a Norwich spectacle that soon the Royal was forgot and the theatre became the Holler Theatre. In time Victor grew so successful that he bought the theatre.

The painting of Victor has death all about it (I say so), and the one of my father has always upset me, for it shows him howling at the storm, full of distress. When I was younger I would stand before the painting for as long as I could, but after a time I would always run away from it in a terror, imagining that something awful had happened to Father. Between the two paintings are our three busts. The largest one is of Mr. Shakespeare, and that I damaged once when I climbed up upon it in my early childhood. If you know where to look, and I do know where to look, you may see a crack or two, even a few glue marks.

All three are now draped in black tulle, black silk, black cotton, and most of all Norwich Black Crape. The bust of the dead old queen has a veil over it, as if she were a magic trick, so that when we take the veil away I wonder if the buried queen's likeness will quite disappear. Beside her is our newest bust: Edward VII he is, like his mother before him heavy with royalty. We are very modern and up to date. Poor Edward was the understudy for so long that when he was finally allowed to put on the costume, he was no longer looked upon as Hal but tended rather toward Falstaff.

On the opposite wall, you may observe my stained christening gown in its frame.

There is a saying here, a code known to all who work front of house. All are taught it, and on their very first day of employment. One must never call, "Fire!" they learn, even when there is a fire, because then the public are wont to panic and there shall be screams and havoc and what is already bad will grow much, much worse. People will panic and get trapped, and there may be a stampede and consequently people trampled upon, and then death will be in the theatre—and we encourage only fake deaths, not the real ones. The public likes to feel safe when they come to see the terrible things on the stage, because the terrible things must only ever happen to us on the stage, not to them in the seats. So then, never say "Fire!"

If there is a fire, this is what you say to your fellow front-half people before carefully and calmly ushering the public to the twelve exits:

"Mr. Jet is in the house."

I remember, as a child, being so thrilled and terrified by that sentence. *Mr. Jet is in the house,* I would say to my cardboard theatre folk, *Mr. Jet is in the house.* Once my front-of-house uncle heard me say it when the theatre was closed—but Mr. Jet was *not* in the house—and, though I whispered it so quietly, and to a brass fire extinguisher in my make-believe, still he was in such a fury with me over it. You are *never*, Edith Holler, said Uncle Jerome, to use that particular sentence. Not unless—and only if—Mr. Jet is indeed in the house. Nor would my uncle allow me to enter the locked chamber called the Fire Room, which is where his fire extinguishers and buckets of sand are kept.

You might suppose that Mr. Jet is merely a code word for fire.

And yet: There is an actual individual called Mr. Jet.

I have seen him. Once.

I was about seven at the time. I had gone front of house to watch the show, and was darting in among the public, to be seen with them as Father had instructed me. One winter evening, I was wearing my greyest and shabbiest outfit, with ash upon my face that I get from the first furnace and wipe all over me—this Father has always encouraged, and it is a great favorite with the public. I don't mind it, no indeed it is wonderful, to walk among the Norwich populace, but Father reminds me that I must keep silent or the spell will be broken. How I make them scream oftentimes as I walk greyly about them! Well done, Father always tells me afterward, to fright the people of Norwich.

As everyone was being seated, and the last bell had been rung to warn the public that the performance was about to begin, I was under the rotunda, looking down the great stairs, when I suddenly heard a whooshing sound. The gaslights trembled and dimmed—this in itself was not unusual, as the lights are always dimmed and then fully illuminated as a final warning that the doors will be closing—but this time the lights didn't come up, they stayed down. It was dark and there was no one else beside me, though there had been so many very recently. And yet then there *was* someone: I could just see him, a latecomer ascending the stairs. A tall and dark figure, in a long black cloak and with a great black top hat. He made no sound as he came rushing up the stairs—which seemed most strange to me, a man of that size not making noise. (The stairs do creak, you see.) And there was, I detected now, a certain fog that came with him, his own greyness emerging it seemed from under his great coat, and spreading all about until it seemed to me that everything was growing so very foggy, as if the bad weather had been let inside. I was suddenly aware of how hot it was; even my feet felt strangely warm, as if the carpet itself were smoldering. I let out a gasp then, and so doing inhaled some of the fog, and in the taste I knew it was smoke, that there was fire in the theatre. And still the tall figure was moving up the stairs, and was just ascending to the level where I stood, when I let out my gasp. He heard me, the tall and thin man did, and he turned and then, oh then I saw his face. Such a long strange face, with two black holes for eyes and a shriveled twist for a nose and a wide-open hole for a mouth, and the dark figure was floating now toward me, the smoke about it growing more and more thick.

Suddenly there was my uncle, come running from a different place, and with him some five or six ushers, each holding a heavy fire extinguisher, and they were pointing the hoses at the tall man with his

mouth agape. He seemed to dance then, the tall thin man, to waltz and swerve away. But so many hoses were at him now that he could not avoid the spray, and was caught in it, and as the water touched him so the figure thinned and spindled, reduced, became smaller and weaker, though the great mouth was still open wide as if in a scream.

Then the light seemed to come back to the theatre, and the fog to reduce, and other ushers opened the windows and out into the night flew the long tall man in his black coat and top hat. Like a black kite he was, lost up in the air outside, an umbrella swept away . . . and then gone, and we were ourselves again back in the theatre, with our own air to breathe once more.

"Who was that?" I stammered.

"Mr. Jet," said my uncle Jerome. Or did I make it up? Uncle Jerome will not admit to it now, but did he not say, as I recall: "Mr. Jet was just now in the house. But we have chased him off, and may he not hurry back again. Someone, of course, let him in. We must discover who, and that person must be punished. But now let us dry the carpets, make all well again. Come, my lads, stir yourselves. Be quick! Let there be no traces of our recent visitor!"

By the time the interval applause was heard, the carpets were dry. All evidence of Mr. Jet erased.

After the performance, when the unsuspecting public had all returned to the street, Jerome called everyone—ushers, barmen, ticket tearers, sellers of ices, cloakroom attendants—into the hall. Who had let Mr. Jet into the house? he demanded. Someone must know, someone must say. There shall be no going home until the person steps forward.

The answer was soon given. It was a poor young man from Trowse Millgate, on his first evening there. Believing that all the public had entered, he had just stepped out to have a little woodbine on the sly. The moment he struck his lucifer, he looked up and there before him stood a tall fellow in a topper. The boy, not knowing otherwise, bowed, dropping his smoldering woodbine, and opened the theatre door—to Mr. Jet himself.

The boy was instantly dismissed.

Norwich is no stranger to fire. It has been our constant companion, and many have perished by it. In 1004 Sweyn, king of Denmark, murdered Norwich completely by fire. In 1507 the fires took seven hundred houses away. The whole city nearly fell again in 1751, as a fire destroyed the Bridewell to ash. Our Norwich hair is wicks, I do say. And of late our heads have suffered from many a rushing redness. There have been calamities in flames, whole houses have been burned quite to nothing. And how many of our missing children have been lost through fire?

There is no fire today perhaps, but tomorrow one is surely coming. I have seen buildings destroyed from my vantage up on the roof. Whole churches have been consumed, whole streets of houses with Norwich lives still in them. Even our neighbor the Assembly House caught fire once, smoke pouring from its windows, though they got to it quickly and no great harm was done. Theatres, too, have died of flame, all those stories burned to dust. The Grand Theatre on St. Giles Street went up in flames just two Augusts ago. I watched it up on top, screaming, *Come not here! Come not here!* We received many actors afterward, let them on board as though they were being pulled from a sinking ocean liner.

As of now, we are the last working theatre in all of Norwich. Though Mr. Jet has called, he has never yet been allowed to stay. For this reason, I am terrified of Mr. Jet. I know he is real. He may make himself very tall and thin and stretch himself up to high windows and tap a little on the glass and sometimes through a small gap he may find a way in. O Mr. Jet! And yet whenever I ask Uncle Jerome, he tells me that to speak of it is bad luck, that we'll have the place up in flames if I go on about it so.

For this reason, my uncle disagrees with my father: he does not approve of me dressed in ashes. Now that I am playwright, he says, I must put away my childish wonderings. That I must acknowledge *A Doll's*

House was written by Mr. Ibsen and not only *Peer Gynt*. I must not get confused between what is actual and what is merely pretend. Yet I was fed on fancy as a baby and have thrived on it, it has made me what I am; my profit on't is, I know how to dream.

"Edith, you are twelve now, and must be sensible. Be wary, my dear, of letting the strange and the fanciful, the tales of dread and terror, the world of imagination grab you and infect your blood. Many a member of this family has drowned because they have let some unwanted fairy get into their lungs or a goblin to their livers. Don't go that way. Be sensible."

"But I am sure, when I was younger, that I saw Mr. J . . ."

"No, Edith! We'll have none of that here!"

"Do you believe in nothing at all, Uncle?"

"I believe in pound and shilling and pence, for I have met them often enough and they are substantial. Go dream on your side if you must, but not on my carpet!"

That first day of the great change come upon my life, I took refuge in the cloakroom. It is a large and capacious room, of course it is—ours is a great and grand theatre, probably the greatest for hundreds of miles around—and when the expensive people come to our theatre, they come in all their finery. I have often wondered, during the cold months, how it might be to be out in the weather, to feel the wind gallop down the street—to find an actual fog that is not dry ice, for dry ice is just the solid form of carbon dioxide, like people's breathing trapped into bricks.

I was allowed in the cloakroom when old Mr. Turner was in charge of coats and hats, but then poor Mr. Turner died and Mr. Penk took over, and Mr. Penk does not love the coats and the hats as Mr. Turner did. He has opinions, does Mr. Penk, he judges a person; he will, I think, curse the poor man with the much-repaired overcoat, and will purse his lips when a tip is too small or is not at all. After a year of an object not being picked up, the kindly Mr. Turner would allow me to have it. (It is how I come by my fanchon bonnet with its lace ties, my pearl drop hatpin, my top hat, and my black silk mourning parasol.) Not so Mr. Penk, who sells off all unretrieved objects after two weeks. He tells no one this, but I have seen him running out into Theatre Street with a paisley shawl that was never his tucked up under his arm, and come back a little later with a smile and a thin cigar within it.

Mr. Turner took all as it came, and was always grateful.

"For this is life, Miss Edith. And we get to witness it from the cloakroom and it is our privilege to see all the life, and all of life's coats and hats."

It was safe there in the cloakroom that no-matinee afternoon. I felt finally alone. I thought I could be calm now, calm enough to consider the coming mother. And yet that was not to happen, for when I turned around in that room of hooks I saw the unexpected: someone else in the cloakroom. An unknown boy sitting on one of the benches. Like a piece of property someone had neglected to retrieve.

Gave me quite the shock.

"Who are you?" I asked. "Whatever are you doing there?"

It shifted, this boy, terror in his face. I think he had been crying. Hair all ruffed up and coming out at all angles, like a cat when it is alarmed. (We did have a cat here once—an excellent ratter—but the dear creature was run over by a horse-drawn omnibus on the Prince of Wales Road, one of Norwich's busiest streets.)

"You can't be here," I said. "This is not the place for sad boys to be. You must not, you know. And I do know, for I was born here. Miss Edith Holler, the author of *The True History of Mawther Meg*, even now going into production. What are you then? Come on, pipe up. Are you all right? Are you unhappy, gentleman?"

But the boy just sat there staring, a little snivel.

"Poor fellow, whatever is the matter?"

Still silent, still sitting, but the eyes big and afeared and weeping.

"Are you a coat? I don't think you are. This is the place for coats, you see, not unhappy boys. I ask again: Are you a coat?"

He shakes his head. That's good.

"So then, what are you? Come closer at last."

He slowly rises.

"Speak!" I whispered, very gentle. "Are you a goblin damned?"

He put a finger to his lips.

I saw his eyes shine a little in the light, and then his whole face covered over, like a curtain had come before it. His eyes closed; his lids like two folds of cloth. And then I could see the face no more and he looked less and less like a boy at all and more like a piece of old worsted—until the boy collapsed into a pile, nothing but a small heap of old material.

"Where are you? Where have you gone? What have you done with yourself?"

I touched the worsted. He wasn't in there, the boy wasn't. As if he never had been. The material was ever so slightly damp; that discomforted me, as if the tears had wetted it. I dropped it again, it fell in a pile.

"Where are you now?" I called. "Come out. I shall not hurt you."

I looked around the cloakroom. Everything as it should have been. Yet then I spied some hurried movement on the ground, something rushing by in the shadows. A rat maybe? We do have some rats here. I went chasing around after it and just managed to catch a glimpse of the worsted thing rushing down through a gap in the wall, where the skirting had come loose. I leaped at it and caught just the smallest corner of cloth end. I had it in my grasp, but one tight tug and something scratched my fingers, something like a cat's claws, and in my surprise I loosened my grip and it was gone. No, not there anymore. Spirit of worsted.

"Oh!" I said to myself. "You've found yourself a ghost! A ghost!" I cried. Was it so?

I saw it. I did, I did.

There is a ghost in Hamlet. It is not just Hamlet that sees his father, no, no, Francisco and Ernesto and Marcellus start the play with the ghost; even Horatio, who is about the most rational of characters, even he sees the ghost plain enough. So then. There are shifting, danking, creeping ones, hiding in the theatre corners, not just in the plays but emerged, perhaps, to live among us. Whistling in the pipes. Stalking the understudies. Indeed, dear Mr. Leadham, our donkey keeper, has often said that in his blindness he can feel the ghosts of donkeys past all about him.

I opened the cloakroom door. "Ghost! Ghost!" I cried.

"Edith!" called Uncle Jerome.

"Miss Edith, there you are!" Mealing, running.

"How ill she looks." Collin with him.

"I saw a ghost!"

"Miss Edith, come here at once." Flora too.

Exit Edith.

II

She comes.

6.

The new mother.

My aunt Nora, the wardrobe mistress, lived only to stitch and cut. She was always busy about her tailoring, she feared I think ever to stop, but must always be bullying the material, cutting into it, piercing it with her needle until it surrendered. She is of true Norwich stock-in-trade, for what else was Norwich but a city of looms? Our great history is built on wool, we are a weaving people. Or perhaps I should say we *were* a weaving people, but we came to the machinery too late, we mechanized our spindles too long after everyone else, and so we lost to Manchester and Leeds and other places which had so much coal on their doorsteps. They took our clothing from us, and we were left naked and hungry. Down fell Norwich, once the second greatest city in the country, down the list it tumbled, until at last we picked ourselves up again, quite literally by our bootstraps. Where we used to be all clothing, now we do shoes and boots;

Norwich worsted.

we have fallen, you see, much closer to the ground. A little half inch of sole protects us from the unforgiving street.

Yet once we were the greatest city in all the world for worsted, though perhaps only my aunt Nora chooses to believe it still today. (And it is surely Aunt Nora who remembers that the material is properly Norfolk, originating from the village of Worstead, which is but twelve miles away.) Aunt Nora has clothed everyone. She orders her little army of assistants like a great general, and all obey and go to battle over worsted or velvet or calico or silk or cotton. And in her hands, perhaps as much as any actor, she has made characters: she made all the Hamlets and Othellos, all the Changelings, all the Volpones and Alcestes, all the Cinderellas and witches, too, also all the fairy godmothers and every one of the fairies. Without her help they would all be naked, half-thought-out, shocking things. She had rolls of roles upon her shelf, bolts and bolts of them, just waiting for her scissors and needles to cut and prick them into life. And now, a pin in her mouth, she was stitching me up.

"Aunt Nora, the ghost I saw yesterday . . ."

"Not that again, that was yesterday's tale."

"If you see a ghost, does it mean you're going to die?"

"What rot."

"Do you believe in ghosts?"

"Of course I do: ghost of Banquo, for example."

"I mean real ghosts."

"Do keep still. Look front."

"Norwich has many ghosts."

"And here we go."

"There is the ghost of Lord Sheffield who haunts the Adam and Eve pub, he who was killed in Robert Kett's rebellion. There is a monk that comes to the Maddermarket and he is a ghost. There's a woman on fire in the castle moat, and a head that floats inside the castle. And there's the Grey Lady who was a girl like me locked in her home, sealed up during the Black Death—they thought her dead and closed the house up, but she was alive still, and she ate a little of her dead family but still she starved to death!"

"Edith, enough!"

"The Grey Lady, she is called, and she walks Tombland. There she is now!"

"Edith! Stop it at once! Face forward, I do make you a lady in white. Be silent, be still."

No one ever argued with Aunt Nora. When she gave you your costume you took it gratefully and left, and if that costume fitted you strangely, made one shoulder higher than the other for example, or added a paunch when you had not been expecting one, it was because Aunt Nora in her great wisdom had declared it so, and now the actor must alter his performance to match Aunt Nora's chosen dimensions. What seemed at first a strange decision on her part, a terrible artistic dictatorship from the wardrobe, soon became the key to an exacting performance. The actors rarely thanked Nora for her great wisdom, and indeed Nora did not expect them to: she cared less and less for people. When Uncle Gregory betrayed her with the woman from Bungay, her hands afterward felt love only in clothing, never in the wearer. To Aunt Nora, most people were merely coat hangers.

That morning, I tried to understand the significance of the white personality that Aunt Nora was stitching me into. Was I supposed by it to look pure and innocent, or to appear a blank upon which my new mother might feel free to write? To give the impression of a dumb doll, or—like my mother, one of her predecessors—a Saint Joan on her way to execution? Or was I merely a table napkin, or a bit of lavatory roll? Was Aunt Nora disguising me so that my new mother would not be able to get at the real Edith, hidden behind so much blazing whiteness? I could not say. All I knew with certainty was that it was not comfortable.

"I don't like it."

"That's scarcely relevant."

"I feel like someone else."

"You must look perfect."

"Why must I look perfect?"

"Because today she is coming."

"I feel like I'm being readied for my coffin."

"Edith, keep still. It's from an old nativity, one of the angels."

"I'm not an angel."

"You're not an angel."

"What's she like?"

"You'll see."

A bell was ringing. Father's bell.

"It is time, Edith."

"Why am I frightened?"

"You must run along now. Best manners, remember."

"I do try, Aunt Nora."

"And look here quickly, Edith," said my aunt, drawing me to the other end of the wardrobe workshop. "What is this, do you suppose?"

"I don't know, Aunt . . . yet can it be?"

It was a new costume, beggars' clothing, strips of patched-together linen making a hunched spider in form, a poor neglected creature.

"Is it," I whispered, "is it for Mawther Meg?"

"It is, Edith. It is my tryout, to get the spirit of her in rags. What do you think?"

"Oh, it is perfect, Aunt Nora!" I cried, and I hugged her, and in so doing hugged likewise the wretched clothing of Mawther Meg.

"You did this, Edith. Is all your doing," said Nora, gently putting me aside.

The bell sounded again.

"Go child, go."

Mr. Collin was waiting on the landing. He was dressed as Father, just in case I suppose, but was holding Father's nose in a handkerchief.

"Godspeed, dear Edith."

"Once more into the breeches," I said.

"A plague on both your trousers," he replied in good spirit.

At the bottom of the stairs I saw a sullen child in a tattered dress—one of the carpenter's girls, I supposed, or one of Bleachy's. She saw me and scurried away.

Down I went, step by step, communing with Norwich's famous anchorite.

"All shall be well," I chanted.

Step.

"And all shall be well."

Step.

"And all manner of things shall be well."

No more steps, but a door. And then another.

Into Father's drawing room—another room I am not supposed to enter without invitation, but which I sometimes invite myself to visit when Father is long absent. Father was standing at the mantel looking upright. Actual Father, the greatest of all mannequins, the tall master, the shapeshifter, the actor, the boss, the middle-aged man, and the love. He was propped up this morning by one of his most delightful smiles:

a special smile, one he enlists rarely, sometimes there are whole years between appearances. But he had found it this morning, and there he was at last, my darling father. So much love in the morning. I forgave him immediately, of course I did.

"Father, I saw a ghost!"

"*Did* you?" Then, clearing his throat, "Good morning, Edith."

And where was she then, the Margaret Mother?

An armchair, I saw. Father's chair, I saw. She was in Father's chair, I saw. A seizing of property! I came close to Father and put out my arms to hug him, but Father—with more restraint than was usual between us—took me gently by the shoulders and turned me round to face the armchair and the one that was using it.

"Here, Margaret, is Edith. Edith daughter, this is Mrs. Margaret Unthank. Formerly Miss Margaret Utting."

It was true, then. A descendant of Mawther Meg was before me. Maw Meg, from my very own play. And so I saw her. Or faced her, at least. But already a storm of shyness had descended, and I was looking instead at the carpet. An Utting!

"So this is Edith."

No, no, it's the bloody pope, I thought. Head of the Catholic Church.

I'll not look at her, I refuse. I'll never see her face.

Yet I admit, after all, I was curious. And I couldn't wait forever. So, then, I looked up. The neat, sensible shoes; the pretty dress of raw silk; the motherly waist; the necklace with a pendant of a golden beetle hanging from it. It was a deathwatch beetle, confirming outright that she belonged to that family. The great Spread people.

There was Margaret. Margaret upon the land of theatre. Here she is in a hurry: tall, really quite tall, taller than Father surely. A plain face perhaps, rather large, somewhat ruddy. Early forties. Full of bosom. Dark hair. She is an amazon. She is Norwich's Hippolyta.

Will she stroke my hair? I wonder.

She looks so *lovely*. Like a painting, a different creature to the ones here in the theatre. She is so natural. Here is nature! The world beyond the theatre! Here in this person.

I think, for a moment, I might even love her already.

So then why did I go and do it? Why then, when all seemed so good? Why did I? The truth is, I could not stop myself. The idea was suddenly there, and it was so strong and powerful that I could not help but act upon it. I had no choice, not really.

As I stepped forward to greet her, my foot got somehow twisted in the carpet. And next: the modest tower of Edith, more of a tenement I suppose, came tumbling down.

My body collapsed. I fell not unto the hearthrug, nor backward into the huge hands of my able Father. No, I toppled forward, collapsed fully upon Margaret. I launched myself at her. I went Margaret fishing and caught myself a whopper.

There was a slight scream from Margaret, and a gasp, which must have come from Father. But there I was upon her, learning her properly with my senses, my cheek on her, my nose learning her particular smells, my ear learning her heart muscle. I had her. It was the quickest way I could imagine of catching her proper: not by little conversations and nicenesses, but by physical touch, by feeling her body.

The Margaret went stiff as I landed and then her hands were about me patting me, touching my forehead, stroking my hair. She was touching me.

Of course there were cries of "EDITH! EDITH!" as when are there not?

"Is she all right? Is she quite all right?" This from Margaret. "Has she fainted?"

And when she opened her mouth, I smelled her deep within.

There was something under the rose water on her skin—what was it, now? I'll tell thee: it was bacon fat. No, no it was more than that: IT WAS DEATH.

Margaret stunk of many dead things.

And then I saw it for a brief moment: her teeth. Margaret had sharp teeth, like a cat or a vampyre or an ogre or a serpent or a monster. Sharp, pointed teeth. I saw them just for a moment, and she, Margaret, saw my slight look—I'm sure she did, for a second later, as if in a flinch, she was digging her perfect fingernails into my arm and shaking me.

Father was letting a monster in the house! A vicious strange beast! I had discovered the truth. Father had been taken in by the creature and had welcomed her into our home.

"What has happened to the child! Is she quite well?"

"She has tripped, Margaret. She has lost her footing. She is very frail, you see. Not as strong as us."

"Poor thing."

"Up you get, Edith. Are you quite all right?"

And up I got, my face so aflame it could not even be put out by the whiteness of the dress. I was very like a candle that first morning of Margaret. "I am so sorry. So very sorry," I said, and I meant it, though mostly I was sorry for those teeth.

"She talks, then!" said Margaret. "The papers called her mute, and you never said otherwise."

"Yes, she talks."

"Why then is she called silent?"

"It is to lend a great effect. She plays her part very well and we all love her. She is very shy, indeed, especially in public. Nor is she always physically able as you have seen."

That was my first tumble into Margaret. And I considered it a great success, for within it I had learned a great deal. Yet I considered it, too, a disaster, for this was no ordinary new mother. Here was something other altogether and I saw I must keep my cleverness about me.

She spoke, gentling her voice: "There now, Edith, let me study you."

And what study there was. Up and down she looked, and in, and all over; it was as though her staring were pricking me and turning me around and around in her thoughts. So this is Edith; what am I to make of her?

"What a lovely girl she is!" Margaret finally exclaimed. "Sweet Edith, do you need to sit?"

"No, madam."

"She is very dear, I do see that. Edith, your skin is like bisque. How perfectly delicious you are, I swear I could quite eat you up. Come now, my dear child, we are to be famous friends, you and I. Come sit now, sit close to me. There, then, what a good girl."

She sat with me and cooed and smiled and said how well we got on, though I scarcely spoke a word. What an odd girl I was, she insisted. And look at those feet, though. Despite all that, most charming.

Tea was brought in and some biscuits: Norfolk Fair buttons, a local biscuit made with flour and lard, ginger and lemon, with two holes in them like buttons have. They have been sold at Tombland Fair these hundreds of years, never changing their recipe—and why would they, pieces of perfection that they are.

"No Spread?" asked Margaret.

"Edith doesn't like it," said Father.

"Does she not?"

"I could send out for some."

"It is of no matter."

I caught sight of a dead beetle under the upright chair where Father had sat down. I wondered how long

it had been there. It was unlike Aunt Bleachy and her girls to miss such a thing.

So this new Margaret talked on, and she had a most natural manner, as if we'd known each other for years, and soon I felt quite at ease. This was, in its way, more traveling out into new territory than I had ever done before, for she was like no one else I knew. Father even smiled at seeing us close together. Is this, I wondered, a family, one of those that Shakespeare was too frightened to write about?

As Margaret was talking, about horse riding and beaches and the sea—the North Sea is closest to Norwich—Father was summoned down to rehearsal. At Margaret's insistence, he consented to leave us together, as long as Miss Tebby sat nearby in the next room.

"Is that strictly necessary, Edgar? To have a chaperone?"

"Just in case, Margaret. Edith can, on occasion, prove unpredictable. If she becomes upset you can call on Tebby, who has a way with her."

"Father!"

"Do be calm, Edith. All has gone so well, after all! Is she not wonderful? I am so happy!"

As Father left, he touched her hand very briefly, as if to claim her by the gesture.

With Father gone, I would have the woman to myself; the prospect made me surprisingly happy. I must have been mistaken, I thought, about this woman's teeth.

Miss Tebby was sat in the hallway by then, she was holding a playscript, as if Margaret Unthank and I were onstage and Miss Tebby would be ready to prompt if our conversation should falter.

"Have another biscuit, Edith." Margaret offered the plate.

"You have one," I said.

"We shall have a half each," she said and broke a biscuit in two and gave me half. She leaned in then, moved closer to me, and we ate together, *crunch*, *crunch*, the pair of us.

I looked at her slyly. "Your teeth are very sharp, lady. I've seen them."

A silence then. The woman went on chewing for a little while, raised her hand to cover her mouth. I think I heard Miss Tebby tutting. We finished our shared biscuit, crunching in silence. I had offended, I think.

"Awful sharp," I said.

"Oh, Edith," and she kept her hand over her mouth even though she had finished eating. "You've found me out. It is because I always liked to eat as a child. I was always eating, until I wore my teeth down. Sometimes I put my hair in my mouth and chewed on it and that did make them scarred and sharper still. I may have Beetle Spread whenever I wanted it as a child, and it has colored my teeth, and the sugar has stunted them, and the grit has made them sharper."

"Oh, I see," I said.

"Nothing to be done about it now. I just have sharp teeth."

"Oh, I see," I said.

"Are they so terrible to look at? I don't think your father has noticed them. Or if he has he is too polite to mention it."

"Not terrible," I lied. "Just notable."

"What an observant child you are!"

I saw then that there was a loose thread on her dress, a small patch of grey cloth in fact, that had somehow found its way onto her and lodged there. She saw that I was looking at her person, and her own gaze did follow mine. She flinched at the piece of cloth, pulling it quickly from her dress and tossing it into the fire, where it sizzled a moment and then was gone.

"Edith," she turned back to me, "you have written a play, I hear."

"Yes, madam, it will be staged in this very theatre."

"Will it indeed!"

"It is a certainty."

"What is it about, may I ask?"

"It is," and I felt an ache in me then, a shadow of something, a little doubt creeping, a crumb of guilt, "the tale of Mawther Meg."

"Is it though! If I read it, what then shall I learn about my family?"

"Something that no one else has noticed."

"Indeed? And what is that?"

"That over the years . . ."

"Yes?"

". . . in all quarters of Norwich, but mostly from the poorer districts . . ."

"Go on."

"That . . . that children . . ."

"Children, yes. What about them?"

"Yes, children, children have gone missing. In alarming terrible numbers. Oh madam, you must believe me, it is an awful business."

"And where have they gone, these poor children?"

"I don't know."

"You don't know."

"No," I whispered. "But I suspect."

"Yes? Do tell."

"In the Spread," I murmured. "They're in the Spread."

A strange noise emerged from Margaret. I thought at first it was a scream, but then certainly it was a laugh, rather unladylike, the type of laugh they call a guffaw. "In the Spread, indeed! Good heavens!"

"I suspect."

"But you don't know?"

"No. Not actually."

"The suppositions of a twelve-year-old."

"Not *all* of them in the Spread. Probably."

"What a relief!"

"Probably."

"And that is what you've discovered?"

"Yes."

"Well, Edith, *I* know what happened to those children."

"Do you? Where are they all then?"

"Why, Edith, it's perfectly obvious. They grew up. Rendering them no longer children. And after many years they have died their death, which is only natural."

"No. That's not it. I don't think it is."

"I've always thought Mawther Meg is rather a horrid story, really. I'd like to have heard her side of it."

"I think she must have been very hungry."

"I think so too. And she saved the city, we must not forget that. Edith, what an interesting person you are. I am glad of it. It would be awful if you were dull. I think we shall have great conversations together."

"Thank you," I said. I was very pleased by this last comment of hers.

"And, Edith, is it true you have never left the theatre?"

"Quite true, madam," I replied, turning fully toward the fine lady.

"Not once, in all your life?"

"No, never, madam, it is forbidden. I am like the cow of Norwich, which, having lost its way, found itself upon the steps of the artillery tower on the banks of the Wensum, and it wandered up and up until it had reached the top but afterward could not get down, and so that edifice is called the Cow Tower, even unto this day."

"And yet that cow, I've heard tell, was carried down the steps at last."

"Yes, well, I have sat on the steps here often."

"But you've never stepped off, onto the pavement?"

"I came close once, when I was five, I waved my hand away from the theatre and onto Theatre Street, and as I did so I lost my balance and fell back on the steps and broke my arm. No I mustn't step out, it is not safe for me. If I step from the theatre then I shall die."

"Is that so?"

"And not only that, the theatre shall collapse."

"Oh! The theatre collapse? What an imagination!"

"It is true!"

"It is nonsense, Edith. It is too cruel. No wonder you have grown up so strange."

"Have I?" How this woman undid me, yet how fascinating she was.

"Well, my child, how could it be otherwise? No, I can't abide it. That's the truth. As much as I adore your father, I see it as my particular duty to right this wrong. It quite breaks my heart. Now, are we to be friends, my dear?"

"I think so but I can't say yet."

"That is an honest answer and I admire it," she said. "If I am to be happy here, I shall have to have some room to make my own proclamations. I am nobody's dormouse."

She smoothed down her dress, ground her teeth a very little.

"I think, Edith, we must teach you a little of the normal life."

"You make it sound dull."

"Come with me now, Edith," she said, her voice a whisper. "Let us go to the steps together. Child, it is only words that are keeping you here. Nothing more. I can prove it to you, this very morning if you like."

But I was shaking. "I don't think we should. I don't think I'm quite ready. Tomorrow, perhaps."

"Today."

"Today?"

"Now. Give me your hand."

I gave it. She took it.

"Good-bye," said Margaret to Miss Tebby. Clearly alarmed, Miss Tebby leafed through her manuscript, as if she had lost her place.

As we left the sitting room, I noticed again how tall Margaret was—quite the height of the doorframe. If she'd been any taller, she'd have been obliged to duck. "No, don't get up, Miss Tebby. Edith here is going to walk me out."

"Edith?" Miss Tebby asked, looking at me. I must have nodded.

Margaret, still holding my hand, took me down.

"It does creak, doesn't it?" she said as we descended. Her lovely shoes making their particular noise, like an outdoor sound, like a horse on the street.

"It talks, the theatre does. That's how I think of it."

"Is that mold?" she asked.

"It may be."

"How you people live."

She was a cunning woman, this Margaret. Rather than taking Mr. Peat's exit at the stage door, where he was certain to arraign me, she instead asked one of Aunt Bleachy's girls to point the way front of house, and quickly enough we were through, onto the carpet side. Some people cleaning, as was regular, and Uncle Jerome marching up and down, wearing his tragic mask. He stood upright and gave Margaret his bow and put on a smile of comedy for a little moment. There were some ladders and wooden scaffolding up in the foyer, new since yesterday. Repair work being done, been cracks there for ages.

One of the main doors, I saw, was open. The steps were being scrubbed, the building aired. Before I knew it, we were out on the steps.

"Here we are," she said.

Outside again. And all the world.

"We'll do it," she said. "We shall explore, you and I. We need not go so very far, not this time. Say, over to that coffee shop across the road. Yes, that is it. Should you like that?"

I have often wondered over that coffee shop. I have spent many hours watching it. It is close by the Bethel Hospital, but it prefers to look not rightward, to the hospital, but instead straight ahead to the theatre. It calls itself THE THEATRE STOP, and inside it is decorated with tintypes of the theatre people: Father is in there, on the wall, and many others of my family, many expired ones as well. I could just see the pictures from my usual perch in the theatre window, especially with my opera glasses. I liked very much to sit and watch people have their morning coffees or afternoon teas there, just ordinary people about their pies and Spread. Sometimes, when it was warm enough for people to sit at tables outside, they would look at me oddly and wonder why I was staring so. Sometimes I would wave at them wildly, and sometimes they would wave back timidly, but mostly they'd pull up their *Norwich Mercury*s like a screen between us, or shuffle their chairs around so that I was not their view. Some even retreated back inside, or simply paid their bills and hurried out onto the street and around the corner out of sight.

Now here I was, on the theatre steps, with Margaret Utting holding firm to me. The usual morning traffic, carts going back and forth to market, a couple of hackney cabs, the horse-drawn omnibus, once in a while a new motorcar, but mostly the clop of hooves and the rumble of wheels. Nothing untoward. Theatre Street, Norwich, Norfolk, March the twenty-first, 1901.

There are twenty steps, as I say, from the theatre down to the city.

Margaret had me at eleven, twelve, thirteen.

"Just to the coffee shop, Edith, that is all. Do come along. What should you like? A hot cocoa?"

"A pie." I whispered it, because I am not to talk on the public side of the theatre.

"What sort would you like?"

Fourteen.

"Erm, a meat pie?" I whispered.

"You shall have it, my dear. Steak and ale."

Fifteen.

I think there was a cracking somewhere behind me. I daren't look back.

"Whyever do you tremble so, child?" asked Margaret pulling me on. "Do come along."

Sixteen.

One of the windows of the entrance doors shattered then. Glass everywhere. I looked back. Some of Uncle Jerome's staff were on the steps, waving at me to come home.

"Now, girl! Now, Edith! DO COME ON!" And then her mouth was

open wide enough and I saw the pointy teeth once more. They were certain sharp. And the woman herself was tugging hard at me, wrenching me down the steps. People on the top step, then, I saw come running. Uncle Jerome was there, calling out:

"Stop! Stop, child. You must stop. Edith! Help!"

People of Norwich coming out now to watch. As if this were a performance. Out they came, out from the Theatre Stop. Traffic had ceased moving, people were watching. What queer people are theatre folk, never can tell what they'll do, no sense of propriety. So thought Norwich, come for a gawk. Some were heading home from the market, everyday people of Norwich looking for entertainment. There were two young girls in drab dresses holding each other, sobbing. What were they sobbing for? Oh, why won't they all go away?

Another window shattered somewhere—at least I heard a great crashing.

"A very few more steps, my girl. That is all! Come along."

There was a crack in the step. I saw it. The step dislodging. A new crack, I was certain. And I thought, *Oh, the theatre itself is giving way.*

More people come to watch, fifty by now I think. And I may not speak in front of them.

"It is a loose step, child. Only that. Come on, Edith, one at a time!"

"Stay!" Someone calling from the top step, Aunt Jenny it was and in a shriek.

"She must not!"

"Bring her back!"

Other voices calling out—people streaming from the theatre at one end, and people thick on the street at the other, and in the middle Edith and a woman and a drama and a horror.

"Is her," said someone in the crowd. "The one who mustn't go out."

"Going out now."

"Let's watch."

I'm not a play, I thought.

"Let see now."

"Ent that a caution."

"And that's Clarence Utting's daughter, her from the factory, unless I'm mistook."

"By gawd you're right—hello, madam."

"What's it all about then, madam?"

As I pulled my hand free, I looked back at the theatre—and then, in that moment, I saw him again. The ghost of a boy in worsted at one of the windows. The boy from the cloakroom. His mouth wide open in a silent scream.

"Come on, Edith!" Margaret was encouraging.

Seventeen.

And she stepped herself off the twentieth step and onto the pavement. People backed away to give her room.

"See?" she said. "Do you see how easy it is, Edith child? Come along." The soft sweet voice again. "You will stand as surety for me, won't you?" she said, appealing to the Norwich ones. "There's nothing so fearful about Norwich, is there?"

Laughter then. There shouldn't be laughter, then.

"Come along, Edith. Do come along, dear girl. Not girl, not really, nearly a woman, aren't you, Edith? Come along then. Come to me. It is so easy and all will be well."

"Come along," someone echoed.

Words of encouragement: "There's a clever gearte."

"Easy does it."

"Thas the job."

Eighteen.

"That's it. Well done, Edith," said Margaret. "We'll break this curse today. And all will be well. Come now, please to come along. Just a very, very little."

Nineteen.

Behind me, a sound—a smash of something inside the building, I could not say what.

"Look at me, Edith. Look only at me. Come on."

Twenty, right in front.

"Good girl. There's my brave girl."

I hovered there on the twentieth step, farther than I had ever been before. I felt sure my heart would soon burst, Great-Aunt Lorena style. I'd be a cloud of blood myself any moment. Maybe a hundred people on the street now, and behind me a terrible rattling in the theatre, as if it were thinking of its own personal earthquake. I was weeping, I knew that, and shaking so.

And then I heard the great cry and all the city I am sure heard it likewise.

"HOWL!"

Father was on the balcony of the dress circle bar, thundering his noise. And all stopped, all of Norwich I think.

"*Edith!* Step back . . . NOW!" His voice a cannon's noise.

"Come, Edith, come to me." Her voice a whisper.

"NOW. HEAR ME, MY CHILD! RETREAT!"

"But one step more."

"I COMMAND YOU, UPON YOUR LIFE. STEP BACK!"

I stepped back, nineteen. Eighteen. Seventeen. And then Jerome and his people were at me and grabbed hold and hauled me back up the stairs and into the theatre, and they would not leave me in the foyer but pulled me farther back, even onto the stage. And as I was hurried on, I saw how much chaos there was—for the scaffolding in the foyer had collapsed, and one man had a hurt on his head, and a window was busted.

7.

The world gets smaller, then larger.

Oh, what a tale I have to tell. What a story I am. There once was a girl who lived in a theatre and must never leave the theatre, not ever, not once. And this was talked of again and again, so much so that people said Don't you ever dare, Edith Holler. So she didn't. She kept inside. But then, one unlikely day, it came to pass that she got out, or very nearly so, and on that day, on the very hour it happened, though she had ventured only to the bottom step—at the very moment that she stepped so very nearly off it, at that very instant I tell you, the theatre itself began to tremble and cry, it cracked and groaned and it started to break!

So then. It is true. It is proven.

Margaret Unthank did not understand, some said. She was not to blame. How could she have known? That was how some people saw it. Others thought she should be banned. Never permitted back in the theatre, forbidden it for life.

Ah, but she knows now.

In the moments after, I saw them all over the theatre, our working people, all stunned and shaken. A traumatized populace. Every hand, I do believe, shook. Uncle Wilfred was directing his people, propping the building up with wooden crutches and weights. In a terrible hurry he started making a great new load of plaster, bent on hunting for cracks, and when he found them he suffocated them. But he knew, we all knew, that underneath those cracks were buried creeping lines of destruction. Were they stilled now, or were they living yet?

"Will it fail? Will the theatre fail?" The theatre people spoke as if a chorus.

Twelve people resigned their jobs at the theatre that day. They ran off into the city to be at a safe distance. This adventure came to be called the New Blowe, named after an incident from 1648, during the Civil War, when the mayor of Norwich tried to celebrate Christmas and the Protestants complained and the Royalists went about looting for gunpowder. Gunpowder was stored then mostly in the Committee House, a building that no longer exists, in fact the Bethel Hospital is built upon its site. A mob stormed the Committee House, mad for gunpowder, and the store was smashed open. Gunpowder was everywhere, on faces (like me with my ash), in pockets, upon the stairs. People carried it in their hats. And so you can fear what happened next: a great explosion, the Blowe. Forty people died and many more windows all over the city. The rioters were overcome by Roundhead soldiers; eight men were hanged in the ditch of Norwich Castle, along with two old women, Anne Dant and Margaret Tirrel, who were tried at the same sessions as witches. That was the first Blowe, which blew just across Theatre Street two hundred and fifty years ago. And now they do use the word again, though no one has died, not yet.

The main thing I understood after the New Blowe was that I truly must never leave, for there was no doubting now that if I did, the whole edifice would crumble.

"For the safety of us all, Edith," said Uncle Jerome, forced to believe now along with everyone else, "you are not to go out on the steps again. . . . Say you should slip and tumble down them. What then? Stay indoors, at all times. This is not a polite request. It is a command. You need not ask me why."

I nodded. I need not indeed. I am the theatre.

Oh, there is true magic in East Anglia.

There was one carpenter, though, who felt otherwise. A venerable fellow, name of Sutton—should have been retired ages ago, some said. With wild hair under his carpenter's square hat and thick fingers, Mr. Sutton said we were talking rot, or rather we *should* be talking rot. Whether a twelve-year-old girl steps out of the theatre or not, he said, is hardly the point.

What then is the point? he was asked.

"Dray rat," he said. Dry rot.

He showed them a piece of crumbling wood. "It crumbled just like this last Candlemas, and no one said anything other than rat then. 'Tis all it is. 'Tis old wood and bad foundations. And that scaffolding wouldn't suffer a bishy barnabee," using the Norfolk for ladybird. "Been dangerous for years. The wood is soft, is soft everywhere."

Yet Sutton's was not a dramatic enough explanation. There was too little adventure to it. And so it was pushed aside.

Father screamed and howled as I was pulled from the steps, screaming and howling as I was brought upon the stage. "She's all right, she's all right, Edgar Holler," people kept saying, but still he bellowed. It took him an hour to calm, or at least a good half hour, for the screaming to quieten, he had been given such a scare. And I was frightened by Father's animal noise and his wide eyes. But at length his sound did dull, and I tried to comfort him.

"I am all right, Father. I am not dead."

"You did not suggest it, Edith?"

"What, Father?"

"To Margaret—did you tell her to take you out?"

"No, Father, no."

"In no way encouraged her?"

"It was all her idea. I rather fought it, in truth, or tried to."

"Calm, Edith. Please do calm. Yes, yes. I believe you."

"Help me, Father."

But he would not hold me and kept me at arm's length, I was too delicate. Indeed, everyone began to distance themselves from me after the New Blowe, as the New Blowe seemed to confirm that I was somehow a magical one, and a doomed one at that, and they preferred the ordinary. They yearned for life to make sense again.

And that was why Aunt Jenny thought of calling the doctor, because the doctor would tell us no, it is not magic, it is something easily explained.

The doctor she called for was Dr. Cottes. We always had Dr. Cottes available for the family; he came to help us with our twisted ankles when we had been careless onstage, or with our sore throats when we had lost our voices, or from burns from dry ice, or from headaches, or pregnancy, or exhaustion or malnutrition or from ingrowing toenails or swollen livers or pneumonia or pleurisy or dreadful unhappiness. Especially from bladder stones, since Norwich is famous for its bladder stones; the Norfolk and Norwich Hospital contains a collection of some fifteen hundred stones, about the size of marbles. (Some say this is because we

are a poor people and have a poor diet; others, quietly, blame it on the Spread.) Dr. Cottes also comes if we have died here in our sleep, or suddenly while awake, and when he arrives for such a call he closes our eyes and so draws our last curtains shut.

Dr. Cottes was a large huffing man who seemed to need a doctor himself. There was something very solid about him, as though he were the human equivalent of the Octagonal Unitarian Chapel in Norwich's Colegate. But he had a look of pain about him, as if, having so long attended other people's hurt, he had become a receptacle of it himself. He had a tummy which he rubbed as he talked, as if his tummy were an anxious cat that needed stroking. Dr. Cottes had a very sympathetic face; he seemed to feel for absolutely everyone.

Aunt Jenny stayed in the room with me but everyone else was to mind their own. I never talked to the doctor myself, Father said not to. It was better to keep quiet.

"Tell me, Miss Edith, what has happened now."

"An accident, Doctor," volunteered Jenny. "There was a fall, very nearly a bad . . . falling."

"Where does it hurt, Edith? Can you show me?"

"I think it best to examine her all over, Doctor. To make sure."

Off went the dress and the corset and then the underdress. The proof that I was only a little grey human after all. But then the cry from my aunt, and soon the tears down her face.

Deep bruising across my chest, my back, my whole torso.

"Who did this to you, child?"

"A bad fall, as I say. On the steps," said Jenny.

It could of course have been Jerome and his people, when they rushed me back inside, or even the impact earlier that day, when I tumbled into Margaret. No way to be certain. What was certain was that I'd broken a rib. Not too bad, the doctor said gently. Some strange breathing for a while. I was to be careful, I was to sit on cushions, I was to be wrapped up.

"Keep her quiet," he told Aunt Jenny.

"Is that all?"

"The bruising will go at last. She'll feel sore awhile. But she'll mend. It does surprise me how damaged she is all over, but she is young and the young do have a habit of rising again. She has, let us not forget, shrugged off her old illnesses. Fresh air would be a help. Her lungs, too, have a crackle to them. And, this is well noted, since she is so pale: *Sun*."

"Yes, Doctor, we thank you."

"Edith," he says, "you are to have a play on, I think."

I nodded.

"I read of it in the *Mercury*. Well done, Edith, I thought. You do this city proud. Now then, young lady, we can't have you missing your own play, can we?"

I shook my head.

"Then you must take things very easy for a while. No dashing about on the stage. Only rest for you. Until I say so."

The doctor left. Father waited until he had gone, then came in. So white himself, poor fellow.

"Oh, Father! Better now."

"I blame myself."

He feared to touch. "My glass child," he often called me.

"Here I am."

"You must sleep."

"I'm not tired."

"Sleep, sleep." He tiptoed out. Later, when I looked, his top hat was gone.

Quiet days then, We hurt we two did, Edith and the theatre. They patched us up. We'll do, won't we? I did wonder then why I, most particularly, had been so cursed, for it was—it must be—a dreadful bad curse.

We were one, the theatre and I. I was ever struck by the magic of it. We were locked inside each other.

Aunt Jenny, a good Norfolk woman, tried a local cure for me. She brought in a little red pot, and filled it with clippings from my toenails and fingernails, and added to this a little piece of raw beef. This pot, placed under my bed, would help me soonest she said to recover. For a little sun, I was permitted a small fenced-in section of the theatre roof. I could see some of the slate tiles missing—rats will get in, rain too. Whenever I was up there, someone was to be with me; not only that, when I was on the roof I was to wear a harness—like those actors who pretend to fly—which made me ache all the more. The harness was strapped to me and the rope secured to something stable with one of Uncle Wilfred's famous knots, so even if I tumbled over the metal fence I would be living yet—and, most essentially, still at theatre.

For weeks after the New Blowe, I was to be observed by some person or other all the time. I may not be on my own. They could not trust that I would not eagerly escape down the steps and onto Theatre Street. I saw Father very rarely, he was so busy with *Titus*, and often he left the theatre and stepped out into Norwich. And in his absence I grew spies.

Mr. Peat's deputy, Master Cree, who generally came in the early mornings when Mr. Peat was off duty, was kept employed all the day now. A desk was set up front of house when there was no public. Master Cree checked everyone at the door just to make sure it wasn't me, for I have been known to disguise myself. Every now and then I had a hankering to start it all over again. To try out someone else's life for a change and to see how it felt, to get an understanding. I could be male, you see. I could be foreign and different. I could take on age and illness and be someone else trying at living in their own way. Sometimes just having a small clay pipe in my pocket could make me think I was someone else altogether. But since the New Blowe I was mostly Edith, and did keep the costume department and prop room undiminished. Nor had I spent even an afternoon in the great scenery dock, where we kept

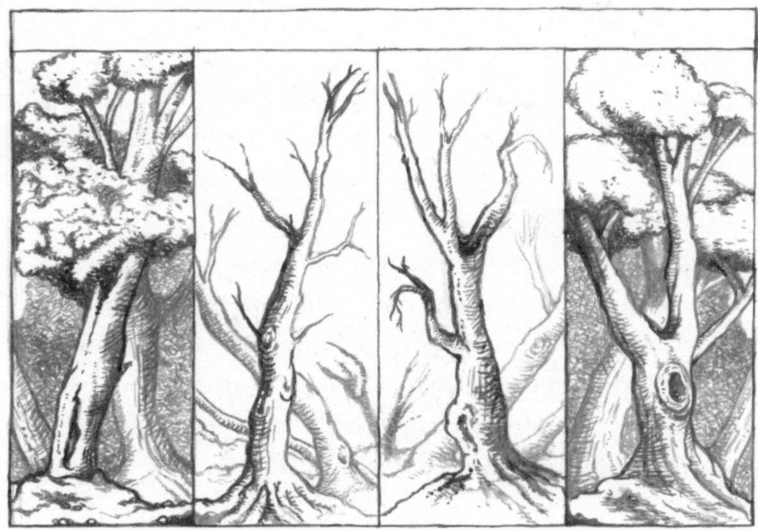

Wing flats for a card theatre.

all our different places hanging, waiting to be called to the stage. In the past I would use them to go for a picnic in Egypt, or to the islands of Prospero or Crusoe or the jail of *The Beggar's Opera*, but these days I did not even visit there to see the backdrop of Norwich, which must have been finished by now. I was kept instead on the Isle of Edith. I needed to keep Edith Edith, to get well for my play.

As I kept still, in my quietness, one afternoon as I sat in the small light upon a staircase that was still perfectly useable, I found a name scratched into the wainscot. ELSIE MARDLE. Oh Elsie, my old friend! She must have written this when she was cleaning one afternoon. I have had no letter from her, but this was something.

"Elsie Mardle," I said.

After a week the theatre was open again, and in came Norwich. The *Norwich Mercury* declared: HOLLER THEATRE SAFE AGAIN AFTER SHOCKING INCIDENT—"NO DANGER AT ALL," SAYS EDGAR HOLLER. My play having been copied at Jarrold's, the original was returned to me, and I kept it in my room, poor battered pages, my sacred relic. Rehearsals would start soon, but first my family must perform *Titus Andronicus*, a great favorite with the Norwich people. Father plays Titus, of course, and finishes the play dressed as a baker, having cooked the treacherous Queen Tamora's two sons in a pie, and oh! the last scene, when he breaks his own daughter Lavinia's neck and stabs the queen—what blood there is, I say! *Titus* has ever been our messiest play, and sometimes the front rows of the stalls may even be a little rained upon during the performance—indeed it is very well that our carpets are so red. Normally I would play Titus's grandson, Lucius—Father cut the five lines given to the part, but had me upon the stage for all to see—but not now. Another child took my place.

Even so, one afternoon Father called me front of house. I was to be seen in public again, for the Norwich public are not always to be contented with a wood-and-cloth doll in a window; sometimes the original must be spied. That day the theatre was very busy and Norwich was eager to see me again. As I came into the foyer I saw a small boy in rough clothing, looking forlorn and rubbing his eyes, he'd lost his mama I think. I was going to go and help him, but then there was Father, calling.

"Look, look there! My daughter. She who may never leave the theatre."

And so the public were reminded of me and did gasp all over again. They looked upon me as something strange and somewhat dreadful. A walking curse. Some of them—only the women really—did come and touch me and stroke my hair. Then, after a moment, they put their hands away and found a distance. When I looked back for the unhappy boy he was no longer there, his mother had surely retrieved him and all was well. I must play my part.

This occasion, coming as it did after the New Blowe, had a different feel to it altogether. When Father summoned me, he brought with him, which was most unusual, a small parcel.

"Here is my daughter who may not travel, but is for her own—and our—safety kept inside these walls, for fear of her death, for fear of the building. And yet, I hereby make known, this small one has written us a play! And we shall begin rehearsals on Monday next."

(Monday next!)

"Of course, as we have been lately reminded, my child's circumstances abide: Should she step out, should she dare herself beyond the property, she will die—and this theatre, the last in Norwich, this very building where you and I stand, shall come tumbling down, and all be lost! So, no, she may not travel. But she may write, she may journey with her typewriter. And where has she traveled in her head? Why, to Norwich! To our fine city. That is where her play is set."

"Norwich!"

"Heavens!"

"Recall that, to her, Norwich is just beyond the window, and yet she has never been there, never once. It is as mysterious to her as the moon is to us. She is, I may say, pure theatre. And so it is understandable that her first play is of our beloved city. She imagines it. And you shall all come and see *her* Norwich. And we may hope that this is the first play of many from my daughter, that in her mind she will travel ever farther than Norwich. And for this reason, and in thanks for her playscript, I have for her here a small present."

With this, he handed me the parcel.

"Do open it, Edith. And show us what it is."

And so I did. It was a guidebook to Great Britain.

People clapped. I cried.

I was crying from delight—to have this book with all its knowledge, to know that Father had gone to Jarrold & Sons the publisher and bookshop, 1–11 London Street, on my account. As I opened its covers and turned its pages, I could see all the book contained: many maps in two or three colors, train schedules, lists of hotels, all provided so that I too may now travel out of the theatre and get about any place my wishes would take me.

As I held the book to my chest, I couldn't help laughing. Laughing and crying all in one confused mess, as if I couldn't quite make up my mind.

"You did well, Edith," Father said to me afterward. "People were moved."

"Thank you, Father. But may I ask, what real reason do you have to give me this lovely guide?"

"I must get on, Edith."

"And, Father, if you please, how is Margaret Unthank? Have you seen her?"

"Edith, I am most pressed."

"Shall I see her again?"

But he would explain nothing, answering only that he must get dressed for *Titus*. I supposed that he was embarrassed to talk of Margaret Unthank anymore, after the New Blowe. He wished never to mention her again. But why had he given me the book? I puzzled over it. It was Father who had always discouraged my learning of places beyond Norwich, for fear such knowledge would worry my mind. He had been known to send back the atlases, the eddas and *Arabian Nights*, not for me the *Mabinogion* or *Mahabharata* nor *Decameron* nor the *Epic of Gilgamesh*, for he was certain such study would be painful to me, restricted as I was. And yet here he was, this same father, giving me a guide to the whole of Great Britain! No, I could not fathom it at all. Did Father have doubts himself, did Father want me to leave?

His gift was written about in the *Norwich Mercury*.

EDITH HOLLER AND HER BAEDEKER.

And in the *Norwich Gazette*:

EDITH HOLLER, BEYOND NORWICH.

That afternoon, I sat me down in the quiet with the book. I smelled it and stroked it and carefully opened its red cover. At the very beginning, before even the title page, was a railway map of England and Wales! Then this: GREAT BRITAIN, HANDBOOK FOR TRAVELLERS by K. Baedeker, with 16 Maps, 30 Plans, and a Panorama! How I gasped and cried at it. THIRD EDITION, Revised and Augmented. LONDON, 37 SOHO SQUARE, W. 1901. This was a special day, a day to be remembered always—the day when Edith was given Great Britain by her father.

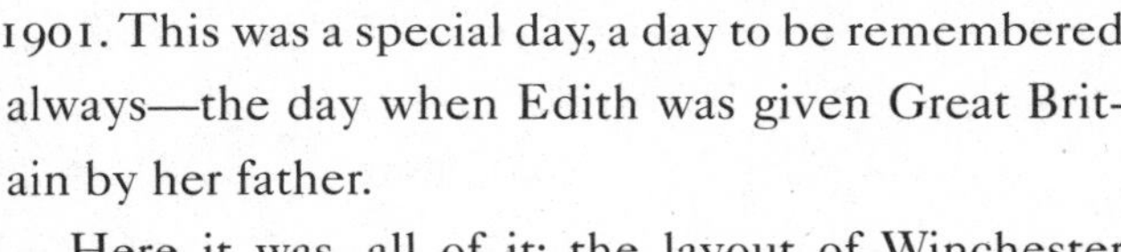

Here it was, all of it: the layout of Winchester Cathedral. The shapes of the isles of Alderney and Guernsey and Jersey. I could whisper words I never said before: Bideford Bay; the pleasure gardens at Kenilworth Castle; Grand Theatre, Birmingham (I wondered how grand it might be, not surely as grand as ours); Great Ormes Head (is in Wales, you know). Then, with a squeal of delight, I opened out the Panorama. In brown and black ink. What a sight: PANORAMA FROM THE TOP OF SNOWDON. Have you ever known such a thing, Edith? Oh no, no, never. What a view I had! The docks of Liverpool! The Derbyshire Peak! Then I folded out the map of Scotland and laid it on my lap: Orkney, the Hebrides, Skye, Mull, Islay. Oh the words, the new language, all quite strange and exciting. I took my time—as you must, when you first encounter new words such as Dog Hillock and Ullapool and Firth of Clyde and Colwyn Bay. Oh, here was great learning.

One name I did not find, at first, was Norwich. But I stayed my hand, did not search, until later, after I had seen it all. But I knew that we of

Norwich were here, too, inside this red bible book. But at last I was ready, and so to Norwich. I turned and kept turning and not finding it until, at last, I had it: NORWICH, page 445. I wondered what it would say about Father; I wondered if I would be mentioned. Would it say, HOME OF THE CHILD WHO MAY NEVER LEAVE?

This is what it said:

> Norwich, the capital of Norfolk and the see of a bishop, is a city with 101,000 inhab., situated on the Wensum. Most of the streets are narrow and tortuous, but in addition to the cathedral and castle they contain many interesting buildings. The town possesses large manufactories of condiments and starch (Utting's; 2,000 hands), bootmakers, iron works, and breweries.

And that was it. There was a description of the cathedral and where to get the best view of the city. (I knew the right answer to that—from the roof of the Holler Theatre!—yet they cited other places.) But of Norwich there was no more. Nothing, not a thing. Surely pages were missing? Surely there were other stories? But no, I turned the page and I was in Cromer, I turned back again and was in Harwich and Ipswich. In my shock I shed a tear, and it did rain a bit on Lowestoft and Yarmouth. To be thought so little of! Here was all of Great Britain, and naught devoted to us but 445 and some of 446. Was that all we were? I turned carefully through the pages one last time, waiting to find something I had missed, and all was Wales and the Lake District, and I fell into Scotland again and wept. I had not been so disappointed since the day—sometime in my seventh year—when ancient Mrs. Stead, who has been in the theatre longer than any of us, who took upon the business of my education, solemnly persuaded me that Jesus was not from Norfolk, as I had always supposed him to be.

"Are we scarcely anything then? It is a dreadful book, a book of lies!"

Yet then as I scrambled through the pages, a little more roughly than before—they were Bible thin and troubled my fingers—I found something else: A map. NORWICH 1:13550. And then the world was better again. We had a map. I traced my finger along the map of Norwich, getting ever closer to my current and permanent location. There the castle. My finger walked down Castle Meadow. Onto Orford Street, getting closer now, onto Red Lion Street, closer, closer yet, and here was Rampant Horse Street (where the horse market used to meet, and where once dwelled the Rampant Horse Inn, where operated the terrible Norwich body snatchers Joseph Collins and Thomas Crower). This feeds onto none other than Theatre Street, my own!

I walked my finger up Theatre Street. There was St. Stephen's Church! But where was the theatre . . . surely we were there. And yet, Karl—for that was Mr. Baedeker's horrible and spiky name printed on the opening page—you have made a mistake. You have run too fast around Great Britain and not paid enough attention. No doubt, Karl, you had many places to travel, but if you had time enough to note that the two best hotels are the Royal in the Market Place and the Maid's Head near the cathedral, you might have bothered a little more about us.

But we were there, I saw finally. After a fashion. Karl had written us down not as HOLLER THEATRE but as THEATRE ROYAL. He had got us wrong.

Very loudly, from my quiet place, I declared: "Karl is an idiot!"

How can Karl be trusted with the rest of Britain if he has so messed up Norwich 1:13550?

I took it upon myself to correct his error instantly. There was a little gap above the word THEATRE, and here I landed HOLLER in ink, in my steady hand. I was going to cross out the ROYAL beneath THEATRE, but I stopped myself, for that would ruin the map, and already the addition of my family's name had the look of vandalism.

Then, in an abundance of caution, I took Karl with me up to the roof. Standing beside the statue, I opened the map of Norwich to see what other mistakes he might have made. But everything else—from St. Giles's Church to the Gas Works, from St. Andrew's Hall to the Corn Hall, even Crooks Place Board school—was where it should be, and so too the Bethel Hospital, and these I know so well as truthful locations and here they were agreeing with the map. There is Norwich, I said, there, there are its torturous streets. Karl speaks the truth. Mostly.

Afterward, I kept Karl with me almost always. Often I opened him at random and wondered over his words: *Leeds the great center of the cloth industry* or *The Episcopal Palace, adjoining Chichester Cathedral on the S. W., contains a fine old medieval kitchen, now used as a washhouse* or *Another popular short walk is to the Two Pots (730 ft.), 2½ M. to the S.* In this way I did learn the world, you see, bit by bit. When I fell to a little sadness over my nutshell, Karl—I saw his name as stern and truthful now—was there to take me away. After a quick sojourn with him to Nuneaton or Edinburgh, Pembroke Dock and Llandudno, I felt more at ease inside my theatre land.

Then did I, armed with my guidebook, tread very careful. We were both ill, the building and I. People went about the place with careful, timid steps. This floorboard, this wall, how safe?

Since the New Blowed I had heard nothing more of the proposed fifth wife Margaret. I presumed that my father's folly was all over with, that the Utting woman had disappeared back into Norwich after the dreadful event, and that I had nothing more to fear from her. No one particularly spoke to me those days, and Father was especially shy. But then, on the day the rehearsals for my play were set to begin, I heard something new: there was to be a general meeting. I caught Aunt Bleachy whispering it to Aunt Nora. I heard Uncle Wilfred telling his stagehands. I did listen about after all—I am not deaf, only rib-broken—and had long since learned that if you keep still enough and grey enough, you may not be noticed, and secrets may come to your ears.

8.

Words upon the stage and in my bedroom.

I was not invited to the general meeting, yet I went there even so. For such an event I knew that Miss Tebby would be upon the stage with all the others, and this gave me the idea: borrowing the veil from the bust of old Victoria—knowing the black would conceal me, I undeaded her temporarily—I slipped under the stage and into the trap room and from there up the little stairs to the prompter's box, where I crouched under the dark cloth. I stayed there, shivering in the cold, until they came: all the uncles and all the aunts, every cousin, the head carpenter, the wardrobe mistress, all the people. Everyone was there except Mrs. Stead; she was not present and the puppet of Death still hung from her door.

From beneath, I heard my father's voice: "Is all our company here?"

But Uncle Wilfred cut in, "You cannot do it!"

"You must not," cautioned Jerome.

"Look at what damage she has done," proclaimed Thomas.

"Please," said Father, "please, please be silent." A long pause, to secure his audience. "I must do it. Ours is the most successful theatre in Norwich, it is true, we take pride in that. But let us remember that ours is the only theatre in Norwich, the others having each burned to the ground."

No one knew how most of these fires had started, but one of them had caused the complete destruction of the Grand Theatre on St. Giles Street. On that night, the audience in the gods, that highest seating area, had not managed to escape; some had lost their lives jumping from the balcony into the stalls. It was not just the theatres that had burned down, the cockpits had burned, the rat pens, even one of the puppet booths—I saw the report that a Punch-and-Judy man went up in flames in Waterloo Park and was burned to ash and all his puppets with him.

That left but one place of entertainment remaining, and that was ours.

"Marrying Margaret Unthank," announced my father, "will ensure the future of this theatre. For her father, as you must be aware, is Clarence Utting, and with the Utting money we will be able to keep this theatre and grow it again. We all have seen the cracks in these walls, the peeling wallpaper, the slouch of our columns, the abandoned stairways. Now we have a chance to find our right angles again."

"But Margaret Utting is the *cause* of the fresh cracking," said Uncle Jerome.

"Perhaps, but she did not know," assured Father. "She knows now. It was my fault, I must bear the weight of blame. I told her, and yet I did not, it seems, *tell* her. She did not yet believe. Now though, now clearly, she has been told. It takes a time, the stepping from the land of business into the land of theatre. The distance cannot be spanned in a single morning."

"And if we do take that Utting money, what shall they want in return for it?"

"To keep the theatre going."

"And nothing more? Will they not demand certain things?"

"They may," confessed my father, "have some small say in our doings. A very small say. For the money."

A lot of headshaking.

"It is the only way I know of keeping Edith alive."

A silence then. Am I to die, is it to come soon: the ending? I panicked so in my hiding.

Then came another voice, one in disagreement with Father.

"Come, come now, enough is enough." It was Aunt Nora. "It is all a tale, Edgar, and everyone knows it. Edith may walk out whenever she wishes. It is a plot of yours to keep Norwich excited in our theatre. You told me so once yourself. They come to see Edith silent in the auditorium or mute upon the stage—alive or not? they wonder. Ghost or living thing? But it is all nonsense."

"Is it? Nonsense?" asked my father, most alarmed.

"Let the child out at last. It was a good idea in the beginning, we were so desperate then, yes a wonderful story. But it has gone on too long. *Enough*, I say."

"It is you that lies, Nora!" cried Father. "If Edith steps on Norwich streets, both she and this theatre will die."

"They never will. Let her go now, Edgar. It's enough. Speak the truth."

"In that balcony there," said Father in a wild sweeping gesture, "Lorena Bignell cursed my daughter."

"Yes, and that is true enough," admitted Nora.

"And after she died."

"That, too, is true."

"There was much blood, you admit that?"

"Some blood, yes."

"Well then!"

"But that curse is just words, and you know it."

"I do not indeed!"

Much arguing against Aunt Nora followed, much citing of truth, of the recent shuddering. All evidence. And my bruising, too, what about that? But what was Nora crying for? Did she want me dead and the theatre rubble? I had never seen her so upset—she was always awkward around Father, and I think she may have had feelings for him—but she had never wailed like this before.

"The theatre cannot last as it is, it shall fall. And so then shall my daughter."

"But only because the theatre, so long neglected, needs repairing!"

"You do not love the theatre! You do not love Edith!"

"Edith has nothing to do with it!" screamed Nora, and then she ran out.

"She is excited," said Father to the others, shaking in his passion. I could see him very clearly now from my spyhole. "What am I to do?" For a moment he buried his head in his hands, a wild thrilling gesture I have often seen him use as Hamlet. I longed to run to him. "Is it indeed true? I cannot tell!" Father groaned. "At times I have doubts myself!" Then, at last, he came out of it. He pushed his hands away as if dismissing a spirit, waving them madly in the air, and spoke once more. "Let us be sensible. May I ask, who believes in Edith's curse?"

All hands go up, mine too inside the prompt box.

"I thank you for your good sense," said Father, wiping his eyes with his handkerchief. "Yes, yes, you have spoken aright."

"And should she wander once more out on the steps . . ." began Uncle Gregory.

"She is to be kept inside at all times," said Father. "Locked in if needs be. She is as casual with the theatre property as she is with her own life. We shall have bars put on every window, and the locks are to be checked upon every outside door, and if faulty, new ones provided. She has no understanding of the seriousness."

I did though, I did.

"Have you not noticed that since the New Blowe she has begun to cough? That new damp patches have appeared on the wallpaper of the royal circle bar?" asked Uncle Jerome.

"Not only that," said Bleachy, "when her temperature is high, the lavatory by the greenroom floods."

"And only yisdy," said Mr. Peat, "when I wer doing the locking up, the exit door on Chantry Road had buckled badly and had to be taken off its hinges and shaved down before it would close again. After the carpenters had finished, I saw Edith Holler near the prop room—and she had a nosebleed."

"I saw her, I regret to say," said Mr. Penk, "I caught her inside my cloakroom. She was banging upon one of the pipes, as if she wished to do the place damage. Are we certain that she does not go about the theatre when she is unwatched and do the mischief herself?"

Oh, I never liked Mr. Penk.

"I too," said Mr. Atkins the fight master, "have seen her kick a wall before now, and deliberately stomp upon a floorboard that is known to be loose."

"She rode one of my dickeys once," said blind Mr. Leadham, "uppards, all along the dressing rooms on the second floor, and the beast was that scared that she did run herself in secret places, and afterward, where she had gone, there was a certain weakening of wood."

"Destruction is in her nature."

"She has always drawn attention to herself."

"We must . . . *observe* her. We must keep her safe," said Father. "Wilfred, do you now put bars on windows and locks on the doors."

"This very day, brother. You may depend on it."

"Make them secure, that we may sleep at last."

"It shall be done."

"Is it safe," wondered Flora Bignell, "to allow her up on the roof? If she tripped?" Murmurs of assent.

"I daresay you are right," said Father. "Yes, Wilfred, lock the doors up to the attic, chain them, triple lock them."

"Yes, brother, I shall."

And so in a trice I was forbidden the roof and its light. When they walled up Julian of Norwich inside her cell, they said the same prayers they used at funerals.

"Now, in summary then, in order that we carry on, we must—I *must*—marry Margaret Unthank. There is no choice. I do it for you."

"Do you not love her, Edgar?" from Uncle Gregory.

"I have played the lover in my time."

"But do you love her?"

"Yes, if it would suit." A silence.

"Everything will be repaired," Father said. "All will be new again. And I am fond of the woman, certainly. She is attractive, and I am attractive. It was a fast courtship. I wrote to her family about Edith's play, it seemed only right, and Margaret invited me to visit her and I did . . . and, almost before I knew it, we were engaged. I was flattered, I admit; it has been some time since there was romance in my life. It did surprise me, but I admit I do undervalue myself. She is my junior by some years. I may borrow, perhaps, some of her youth. I did feel, my dear people," said Father, allowing one of his smiles to shine out, "a little younger this morning."

At this there was nodding from some members of my family.

"She will live here, with us, and with her money we shall have a future."

Some ruffling from the family, but no words. No one asked me how I felt about this woman, who had half dragged me down the steps, coming to be my mama.

Two hours after the general meeting, rehearsals for the new play began.

. . .

"Is all our company here?" asked Father for the second time that day.

"All present," said Wilfred.

"The part of Mawther Meg has not yet been cast," he said. "I find it difficult to imagine a person taking on this role. It is entirely possible that a large puppet may be needed. How can we imagine her portrayed by a human, for she is something other, is she not? I am not decided on this. Perhaps we may try different voices—not an audition, merely an experiment, yes? Good, then . . . Miss Garner, would you do the honors with Mawther? Just the first scene, and then we'll have . . . Mrs. Papworth, yes. Then . . . oh all right, Miss Wilson, let's not get excited. Miss Tebby will read the stage directions. Very good.

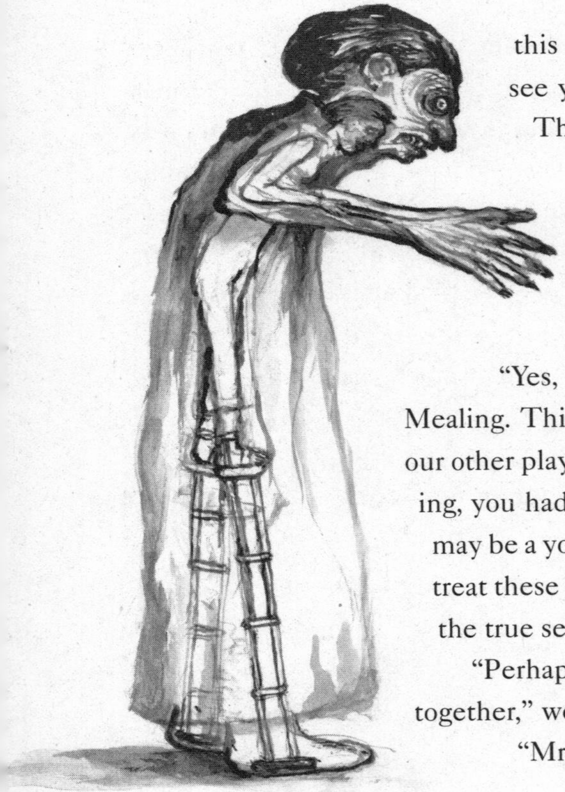

"One final word before we begin this read through," he continued. "You see yonder girl there, dressed in grey? That is the author. I am not used to having my playwrights present. Indeed, I am altogether used to having my playwrights—ah, oh dear—dead."

"Excuse me!" said Mealing.

"Yes, indeed, I do beg your pardon, Mr. Mealing. This is to acknowledge Mr. Mealing, our other playwright. You have a rival, Mr. Mealing, you had better watch out. Our playwright may be a young person of twelve, but we must treat these words with respect and show them the true seriousness of our profession."

"Perhaps one day we shall work on a drama together," wondered Mealing loudly.

"Mr. Mealing," said Father, "this is not

your play, I need no words from you. There is no character here called Mealing. I prefer my playwrights silent, as I also prefer them—oh dear, yes, again—dead. The dead playwrights do not come to mutter at me and to complain. They know their place. I cannot rehearse if the playwright is endlessly chattering at me and having opinions. This goes, too, for you, Edith Holler. You've had your say, here it is on the paper, and now I must have mine. There may be times when we ask you questions, my child, but speak not until spoken to. I am in charge here."

"Yes, Father, but . . ."

"Indeed in general we may not require you in rehearsals."

"Father?"

"Mr. Shakespeare has missed so many rehearsals that I've lost count. Indeed, were he to appear, I daresay it would be a distraction. Don't be a distraction, Edith Holler."

"But it is my play, Father. I wrote it."

"And, daughter, I shall direct it. You give it to our hands; you must trust us. Now then, on we go. We have our chorus of the children of Norwich. Yes, it is quite all right, Miss Thacker, that you play a child, you are small and children are small. Each of you shall speak in chorus, and many of you shall have individual scenes when the Mawther comes to steal you in the night. Now then, Wilfred, is there a quantity of blood ready?"

"Indeed, Edgar. Both barrels are near full."

"We may need more yet—make a note, will you?"

"I shall. And, Edgar, I have a question."

"So inquisitive aren't we all today? Proceed, Wilfred."

"I have read the play and one thing is troubling me: How are we to do the beetles?"

"Yes, that is an interesting question. The playwright gives no suggestion, only commands *the swarming insects* in the stage directions."

"Well, I . . ."

"Not called for, my clever Edith Holler, no indeed."

"I have bent my head to this problem," said Wilfred, "and tried to come at it in a number of ways. But none seemed right—that is, until this morning, when I was using a hammer, and the *noise*! And so a thought: We might make the beetles by sound alone. The people onstage may react to the sound of them. They will hear them, you see? The deathwatch, in the night, in the quiet—you don't see them, no, you *hear* them!"

"Ah, Wilfred," said Father. "How interesting, to make a character of noise alone. In its ambiguity, it may terrify all the more."

A silence then, all looking confused. But to me this seemed exactly perfect, and so I nodded extravagantly and even clapped. And once the clapping started others joined in, for one clap does, oftentimes, lead to another.

"Very good then," said Father, "the playwright has shown her approval by making a noise. So we begin. Miss Tebby, if you please."

"*The True History of Mawther Meg* by Edith M. Holler. Act One. Scene One. The stage in darkness. A backdrop of the city of Norwich in ancient times. The drop rises to reveal, with slowly increasing light . . . the actual city of Norwich in ancient times, the same prospect but now in three dimensions. Many small dilapidated places and, among them, two sizable locations: Norwich Castle and Norwich Cathedral. The two buildings converse with one another."

Silence.

"Go on," said Father, "come, Mr. Emerson, come, Mr. Wighton."

"I am to be a cathedral?" said Mr. Emerson. "How?"

"Are you tall?"

"Yes."

"Do you possess a clear bell of a voice?"

"Well, yes."

"So then, go to it. And you, dear Wighton, are thick and squat. We'll raise you on a plinth and call it a mound. Now then, get on with it."

The two men cleared their throats.

"'We are going backward in time, pull up the ghosts.'"

"'Let the past leak out at last.'"

"'And see that you are now upon ancient Norwich land.'"

"'I am God's house.'"

"'And I am man's.'"

"'I touch the sky.'"

"'I command the land.'"

"'We are the greatest buildings in this our city.'"

"'All others bow to us.'"

"'Other churches, none so fine. God lives within my walls.'"

"'I am power and might, I shall be prison hereafter. Dead men hang from my gates. Kett dangled here, and in my dry moat are hanged the witches. Fear me, O Norwich.'"

"'See me as God, my spire points to Him. We are Catholics now, later shall we Protestants be. What I say is the law. Pray to me or be sent to . . .'"

"'Me.'"

"'Little people strut and strain, they are barely upright but come down again, and are dug in the dark soil of Norwich. Many are underground, silent now that once made noise. We have great plague pits, Norwich loss on Norwich loss, such a crowded dead, a whole city in deep quarries, covered over to keep in their poison breath. O Norwich, new loss is coming! Watch the children in rags running through the streets, watch them whilst yet you may, watch them run unaware of what is coming. See them dart into their homes so dark and dreary—that shall not keep them safe ere long.'"

"'O Norwich look at you, worn-out and cringing.'"

"'The houses do lean and bow, the thatch is threadbare, the tiles fall like teeth. The houses themselves are dying. Homes are being eaten. The city shall come down.'"

"'But not us.'"

"'No. For we are of stone made. From Caen in France do my strong walls come.'"

"'I too, no damp Anglian wood. We stand proud, time cannot touch us.'"

"'Yet we watch. Yet we see.'"

"'Norwich being eaten.'"

"'Norwich falling to dust. And her children soon! Her *children*!'"

"'Hear now a house falling, and the cries from the people within.'"

Said Miss Tebby, "'A house falls to the ground, all others shake in terror.'"

"'Shall we not listen to the complaints of a hovel?"

"'Let us then.'"

"'You there, small place.'"

"'Speak.'"

"'My lords, I am wattle and daub, I am plaster and wood, I am coming undone.'"

"'Stand straight.'"

"'I cannot. I am a hunchback home, my wooden bones are weak. I am thin timbers and leaking roof, holes there are in and out of my limbs, by beetles have I been gnawed and gnawn'. . . . I . . . I can't do this!"

"Gregory, get back in your role."

"No, no I shan't. I refuse. It's nonsense. I cannot be such a puny, moaning thing. I'll not do it. Find someone else to be your daughter's clown. This should not be put on. It is a disgrace. You may feel sorry for your daughter, I'm sure we all do, but this is too much altogether."

"Gregory, there are no such thing as small parts, only small actors."

"That's what you always say, Edgar. Yet there *are* small parts, as you know, and this is one of them. No, I'll not do it! I have suffered enough, why must I be persecuted still?"

"Recall you have two parts—this and the good knight Sir Thomas Erpingham."

“I’ll keep the knight then, but not this ruin!”

“Gregory Holler, what sort of man are you?”

“One that has pride. One of flesh and blood, not wattle and daub. I am a man, not a shed.”

“Listen, Gregory, you represent here the city in peril. You alone must show us the danger of this beetle plague, you must convince us of the pain, of how it hurts. Norwich, here, is in deep danger. You call to us in your agony. We are so moved. Moved to tears!”

Gregory was silent awhile, then. “All right, I’ll try it.”

And on he went, the wind whistling through his small rooms, and showing us his pain and sorrow. It was well done, I say. So it started and so it went on. My story, my play. Oh, to see Mawther Meg eating the beetles and the beetles swarming to her. Oh, to hear the children’s chorus in their terror and the little girl no one would believe. To hear it now, this afternoon, was to set it breathing. My own words, out in the open and thriving in other mouths.

The play was read right through, to the horror ending, and at last all put down their scripts and looked to me. And for a while there was silence. And then, oh my cathedral, oh my castle and marketplace, they clapped and cheered and said it was cruel and dark and sad and so beautiful and who would have thought such a grey girl could write such a terror story of Norwich? It was all actually happening—my play was being born. And I was cathedral, yes, I was castle then.

And did I grin, even though I was forbidden the roof? I did, I did.

Rehearsals then every day, Sometimes I was allowed to attend, but mostly Uncle Wilfred said, “Not yet, Edith, not yet. But soon! Patience, we make your play.” And where is Father? I asked. “Busy, very busy indeed.” And so I must be patient, and so impatiently I listened to the noise of my play coming up through the theatre’s pipes. The very sound of it, the Mawther gabbing and the children wailing.

Afterward, I visited the actors in their dressing rooms.

"How does it go?" I would ask.

"Your father is doing a wonderful job!" said Aunt Agatha Wilson, "and I still harbor hopes for the Mawther."

"How does it go?" to Aunt Jenny.

"He has made changes, Miss Edith," said Jenny.

"What changes? Why?"

"You'll see. Nothing major, Edith, you're certain to approve. There's no avoiding them anyway, they are required."

"Aunt Jenny, please."

"We must keep the theatre, Edith."

"What changes? I demand to know!"

But no one ever said.

It was two weeks into rehearsal, and I was in my room with Karl, when Father came in at last. It was the Friday evening before that particular Saturday. A brief but solid knock. I checked the nose straight off. No line that I could see.

"My own daughter," he said. "Edith, how are you?"

"Well indeed, Father! How are you?"

"I am right well, thank you, Edith."

"What changes, Father, have you made?"

He sighed. "It is muddled in places, Edith. The balance is off, you see. A few minor modifications. You shall barely notice the difference. Well, you may notice them, but you'll see that I am right. It is still your name on the posters and it is still your play. I am still yet to cast *her* and we must hold off a little while now, as you know." And here he paused, a pain came over him. "But, Edith, there is something I need to say. Edith, my own Edith, I think . . . I am not always the best father to you."

The subject of my play had vanished in a fog of other worries.

"Don't say that, Papa."

"We are not like other families, are we?"

"I should hope not indeed! Who would want that?"

"Thank you, that is well said. I mean to do right, Edith. I want you happy."

"And who says I'm not?"

"Are you happy?"

"Yes. Always."

"I think you will like Margaret. She did not mean to be cruel. She did not understand. It was hardly deliberate."

"I do see that."

"And she does regret it."

"I have not seen her since."

"No, I thought it best, we both did. And you shall see her soon."

"We shall be one of those dull families that Shakespeare hates."

"Do you think so? Well, perhaps we shall. All will be well. I think of the theatre and of you and so it must be done. For us all."

"Do you love me, Father?"

"Nearly a woman, Edith. You're quite grown up. You shall forget your old father."

"I never will. Father, why are you so sad?"

"I feel my role running out. Well. Well."

"Father?"

"Well, well, the event."

He had come to the end then, I could feel it. He put his hands into his pockets, but he dragged them out again a moment later.

"Strange," he said, "several mornings now, I find this red grit in my pockets. It was not you put it there, was it, Edith?"

"No, Father. I have been here in my room all along."

"And sometimes, when I awake, I find it about my bedsheets. You know nothing about it, Edith?"

"No indeed, Father."

"Well . . . I suppose not, yet it is most strange."

Another pause then; he nearly returned his hands to his pockets, but he thought better of it. He was a little distracted, Father was. He wanted to leave, but could not find his exit and so I should help.

"We should do this more often," I said.

"Yes, we must. Oh, we must." He got up then and kissed me on the top of my head. As he stood, I saw a small black speck fall from the bottom of his trousers. A beetle. It landed on its back, panicked there a little while, wiggling its legs, but having worked its way toward one of Father's shoes was able by knocking against it to right itself and was soon out of the door that Father had left open. Father seemed not to notice, indeed he had a most distracted and pained look.

"I may come and see you, after you are married?"

"Yes! Now and then, Edith. Now and then."

"Good night, Papa."

"Almost a grown woman."

"Good night, Father."

"Don't let the bedbugs."

The next day was his wedding, though he had not mentioned it. The door closed and he was gone.

9.

In which there is another falling.

They were married in Norwich Cathedral. (*Norwich Cathedral was begun in 1096*, says Karl, *and has preserved its original Norman plan more closely than any other cathedral in England. It is 407 ft. long, 72 ft. wide and 69½ (nave) to 83½ ft. (choir) high*. Which is to say, it is a very, very huge God barn, one of our great wonders, along with our castle and the Beetle Spread factory.) All Norwich must have known about the wedding, which involved the marrying of two great buildings: the theatre and the Spread factory. I was not present, of course, but the wooden and cloth doll of me was wheeled there in a cart in my stead. The whole population of our theatre marched off to witness the contract between one mighty building and another; even blind Mr. Leadham took his donkeys to graze on Cathedral Close whilst the service was conducted. The theatre was abandoned by all save Old Alice the donkey, who was deemed too ancient for the journey, but she was deep down and no company, besides she almost always slept these days.

Master Cree was supposed to stay, to make sure I didn't hurl myself off the building. But he begged me to let him go.

"I don't want to miss it, Miss Edith. To be the only one not to notice an Utting and a Holler coming as one."

"Run along then, I don't mind."

"You won't do anything, will you?"

"There's nothing to do."

"All the doors are locked, you cannot get out."

"I do know that, Cree."

"You do promise not to tell anyone?"

"I do swear it."

There was no one to tell. Not a soul. Silence in the wardrobe, silence in the greenroom, silence in the circle; silence from the fly tower, from the scenery dock, from the gods, from the pit. I was alone in my playhouse, more alone than I had ever been perhaps, for even on the quietest days there were always tens of people working away, I could always take comfort from the noises and voices. But not on this day. No one was here but me.

For a moment, I wondered if the silence might swallow me; if it would persist even after everyone came back; if even when I stamped my foot still it would make no sound. Now and then, that day, the noise from outside would come in for a small while—people walking along Theatre Street, a cart coming by—and the noises would drift and gallop, stretch and grow strange, in the great empty space. But even those street noises that made it inside the great empty cavern of the auditorium lived only a short while before the silence smothered them, and then it was just the two of us again, me and the theatre. And inside it I may wander wherever I liked.

I went upon the stage.

I should not have done that.

There was to be a party on the stage that night—the wedding reception—and all had been made ready. So much food was laid out:

sausages, hams, cheeses, dumplings, and a mountainous wedding cake, in the shape of both the theatre and the factory. And there were huge tureens, all filled with Beetle Spread. It was to be an historic feast.

But I should not have gone there.

The stage, do recall, is a windowless room. There is no outside at all to be seen from it, only a journeying inward. It is a very deep thing, the windowless place.

On that day I heard the sound of that space, you see, as if it were calling to me. It was a subtle creaking, a small breathing, a hushed groaning. The stage was never quiet, not if you listened properly. It was always muttering. The stage was a place where millions of words had fallen, tumbling through the floorboard cracks, but after a while some of them worked their way back up again, floating about like mites of dust and remembering themselves a very little.

As I sat down on the stage, I thought I heard all those bits of words, little spilled syllables lost from their wholes . . . all the dead sounds coming back. It had such a memory, the stage did. And in the quiet that day it was remembering. Gurgling creaking shushing stealing hushing howling moaning, all the ghosts of ages past. But underneath there was a more persistent sound.

Slowly, slowly, out of the near silence, I heard the noise. A constant noise that had perhaps been with us all along, inside our heads and dreams, but that took some great unusual silence to be heard. Yes, there it was: So slight a sound you wouldn't know it unless everyone was gone away. A sort of scratching, is that the way to explain it? No, not exactly, rather a . . . *knocking*. As if someone far away were knocking on a door, waiting to be let in, small pauses between knocks as if waiting for an answer, and then on it would go: *tap tap tap*, *toc toc toc*, *knock knock knock*. Where was it coming from? Now that I had definitely heard it, it seemed to grow in my mind, to get louder. I put my ear to the stage.

The knocking seemed deafening to me. How could I have not noticed it before? I forced myself to breathe slower, and between each steady breath came the knocking, the knocking, the knocking. Something was very wrong. I must get off the stage, I told myself, I must go somewhere else. But I did not. Instead I sat there on the stage, with the knocking in my head, and looked out at all the empty seats, row upon row of them, all the way up. An actor cannot really see the audience when the performance is under way, because the actors are under bright lights and the audience is in deep darkness. But on that wedding day the houselights were up, and I could see all, and there was not a single person in a seat, none in the stalls, none in the royal circle, none in the gods.

Yet wait—wait there! There *was* someone in the gods. You would think it just a coat at first, but it wasn't; no, it was a single person seated in the gods! Look, look!

The little ghost worsted boy. Rubbing his eyes, weeping in the balcony.

No, not truly, Edith. It is all lies and imagination. Close eyes, and when you open them, you will not see him, be honest. And so?

There! There he is.

Truly?

Yes.

"Hallo!" I called. "Hallo up there! I see you. Don't move there, I'll come to you."

And as I called the knocking seemed quieter again.

Something beneath the stage toppled, a sudden smashing sound. Old Alice brayed in distress. I took no notice of her, for there was the worsted boy, right up in the balcony.

"Wait!" I cried, "I'm coming to you!"

I ran through the pass door. Down below I could hear a great rumbling—the furnace, perhaps? I hoped my cardboard people were safe. It was screeching like it had great metal teeth, was grinding them hard together, with a chugging sound and a banging, a whoosh followed by a fearful clang. And above it all, no doubting it now, the fearful knocking.

But the worsted boy! There he was!

"Wait!" I shouted. "Do but wait. I am coming!"

I ran along the side of the stalls, burst into the foyer, and shot up the grand stairs beneath the rotunda, round and round, then through the side door, up and up again, the terrain steeper and steeper, higher and higher, to the very gods. Then I burst through the door marked Balcony and hurried down the stairs, careful careful, holding on to the brass banister, for even I may make a mistake at this slant. There, there, a few more steps and you'll be with him. Careful now.

And there I was, surely I was, and yet he was not. The worsted boy was nowhere to be seen. I looked across the balcony, down into the stalls, searched for him in every seat, but every seat was empty. Yet I had seen him. A boy with a worsted face. Oh, let me not be mad.

Such a strange rushing from the stage side now. The knocking had become a great hammering. A hammering that was surely coming from the stage.

I stared over at the stage itself. Oh, the stage!

At the center, just where I had been standing, I saw a black spot, like a puddle. Yet now came the sound of wood splitting. And then I saw it: The spot was a *hole*. The hole was growing larger. The stage was opening up.

Then, with a great groaning, a terrible cracking—

The stage came tumbling down.

A great sinkhole opened in the floor, and everything on the stage tumbled in: the wedding feast, the Beetle Spread, the Holler Theatre cake and the Beetle Spread factory cake, it all plunged down, falling into the deep, timbering down into the blackness. Deep beneath the stage, the sound of the old donkey braying, until it fell in altogether, our own stage, collapsing.

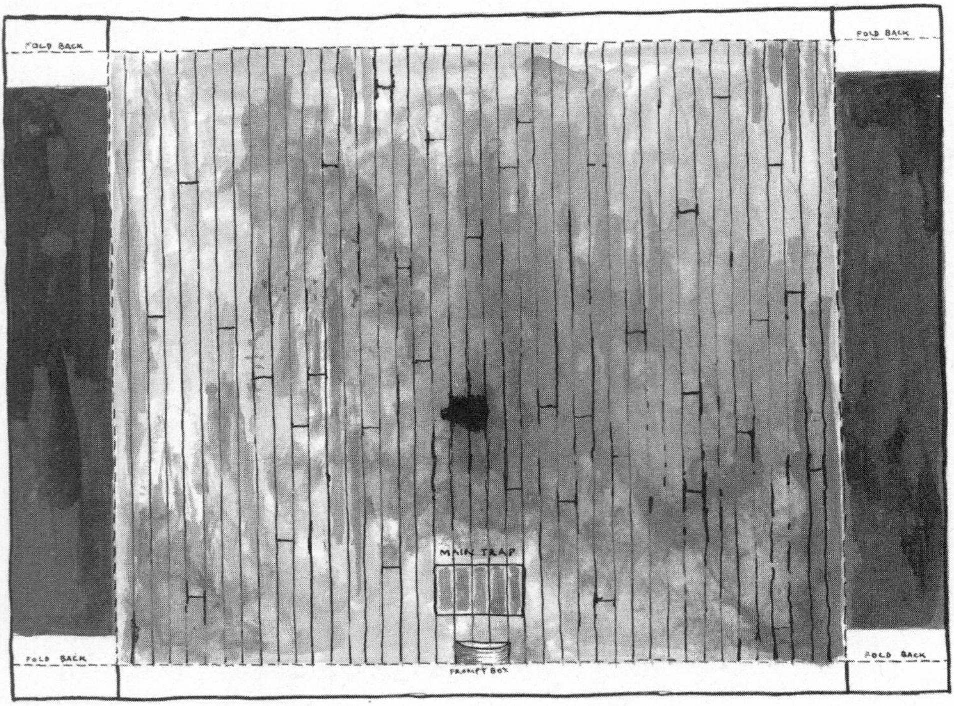

FOLD BACK

FOLD BACK

MAIN TRAP

FOLD BACK

FOLD BACK

PROMPT BOX

FOLD BACK

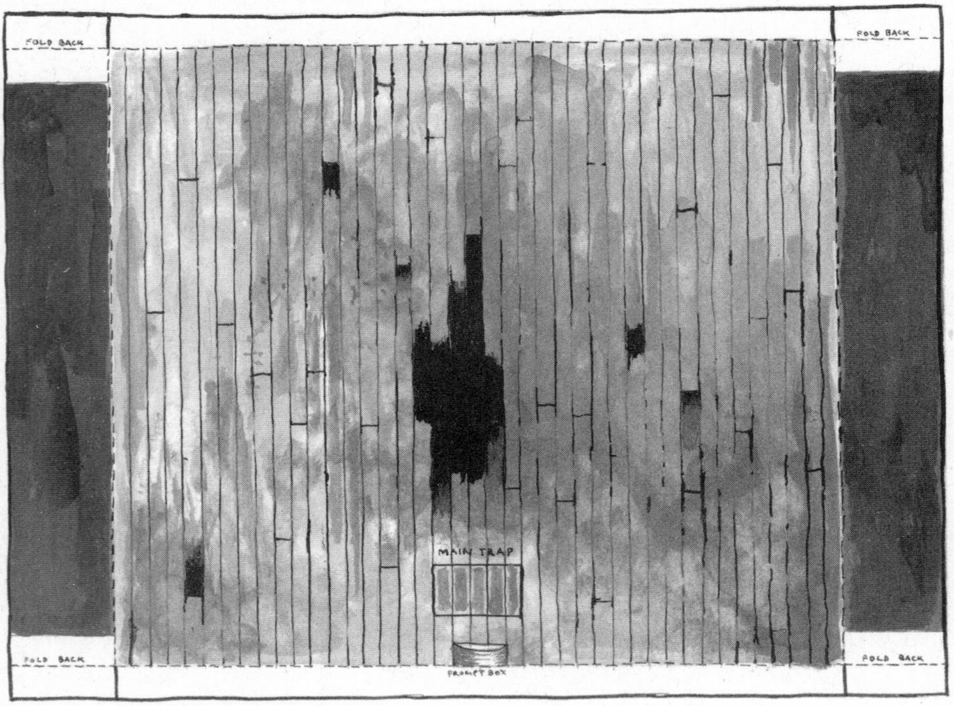

FOLD BACK

MAIN TRAP

FOLD BACK

FOLD BACK

PROMPT BOX

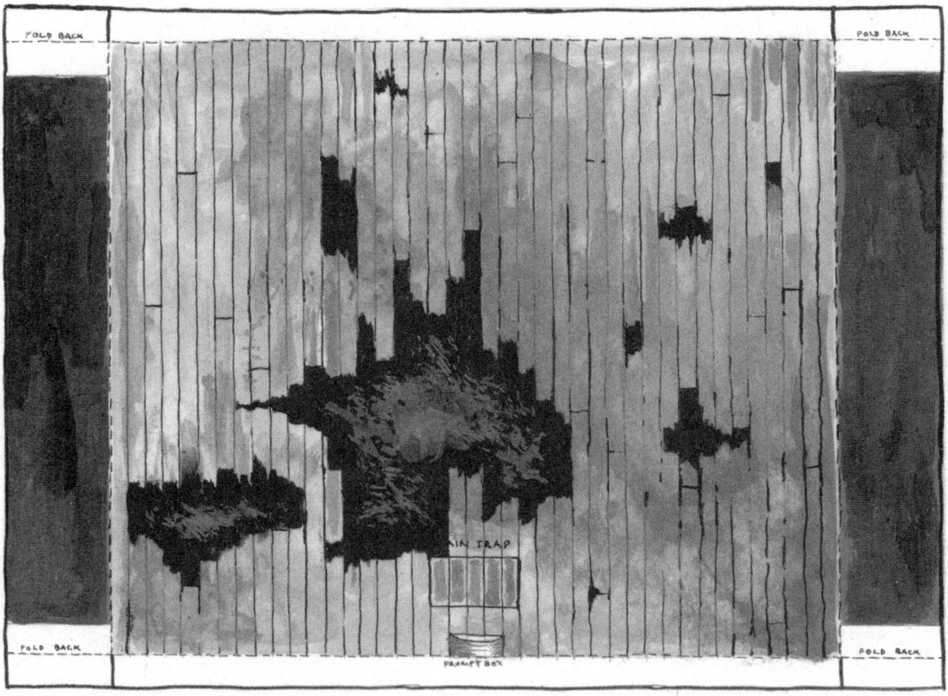

FOLD BACK
FOLD BACK
AIN TRAP
FOLD BACK
FOLD BACK
PROMPT BOX

FOLD BACK
FOLD BACK
FOLD BACK
FOLD BACK
PROMPT BOX

Oh! Oh!

Finally, save for a few torn planks around the edges, it was gone. Nothing but a great vast hole. A huge cloud of dirty dust spread out, laying its filth on the velvet seats of the stalls, the cloud rising up to fill the theatre.

"Help!" I called. "The stage! There's nothing left!"

Deep down, the noise of the donkey bellowing, hee-hawing in terrible agony—until at last she went silent, which was a much more terrible sound.

I held on to the brass rail and screamed into the emptiness. "Misery! Help! Help, ho!"

It was only then, as I held on to the brass rail, that I noticed there was blood on my hands. I'd cut myself. Blood on my legs too. Some dripped down my face.

My body crashed down, right on the seat where I had seen the worsted ghost sitting. It was not a huge bleeding—no need to panic, Edith, just some scratching here and there. How I had come by it I could not say, but two of my fingernails had dark blood blisters in them. I held on to the seat and tried to calm myself. One of the teeth in my mouth felt strange, and when I touched it with my tongue it came away. I spat it out. What was happening?

As I gripped the seat, afraid I might otherwise fall completely to pieces, I felt something tacked to the bottom of the bench. I pulled it free.

It was a piece from my cardboard theatre. It was the children in the wood.

10.

Help! Oh help!

When I stood up at last, I found I could walk only with a limp. My leg felt crushed, though I could not tell why. Perhaps it had happened when I collapsed into the theatre seat. I was very frightened. Frightened for myself, frightened for the theatre. But a limp and a few scrapes are nothing compared with the collapse of a whole stage. I must get help.

I hauled myself down from the balcony, it took such an age despite my panic. So very, very far to descend, and each step a hurt.

I had been forbidden to go near the entrance doors, and it was such a strict instruction—but the stage, the stage had gone!—and surely normal rules should not hold under such circumstances. I hammered on one of the doors that led out to the steps, but it was bolted shut. I kicked at it, slammed my hand against its window, but I could not get out. A knock, I thought I heard, just behind me. Yes, a knock. A knock. It set me screaming, and when I lurched around to look for its source, I spotted one of Uncle Jerome's brass fire extinguishers. I hauled the thing up and swung it against the door; it left a great dent there, which was something, which gave me hope. Led on by my galloping panic, I heaved the thing once more, twice, four times, and at last the door groaned open. I stood on the steps then, on the top step, and I called out:

"Help! Please help me! The stage! The stage!"

But no one was there, no one on Theatre Street at all. The businesses were all shut up, everyone had gone off to the wedding. No one at the Theatre Stop, no one at the Assembly House—the Norwich School for Girls dead inside, no one in sight even at the Bethel Hospital.

"Help! Help me!" I cried till my voice was hoarse. But no one came.

At last I sat down on the steps, wailing. I feared to go back inside, I was terrified of the theatre now, it was all ruined, oh everything is ruined.

No one in sight for so very long.

At last came a sound, growing louder. I thought at first the terrible knocking had followed me out, but slowly I understood it to be the noise of someone running. At last I saw a small figure coming down Theatre Street: Master Cree, sprinting in advance of the crowd returning from the cathedral, so that his attendance there would not be noticed. If only he had stayed! The service must be over, for the cathedral's bells were shouting out again, only what should have been peals of joy seemed to me to be howls of calamity. And when Master Cree saw me as he bounded up the steps, he saw my face, and—perhaps reading the horror writ so clearly upon it—he did scream himself.

"Miss Edith! What is the matter? Why are you here? The door! What have you done?"

"Ah, Cree," I managed. I was shivering then, though it was quite warm, and such a throbbing in my head. "I have been waiting. Waiting for a very long time. You should not have left, it was very wrong of you."

"What has happened?"

"Will you go inside, Cree, and tell me if the stage has gone?"

"The stage, gone? What can you mean?"

"I may have dreamed it. At least, I hope I might have. Will you go and see?"

Master Cree dashed in to find out what had occurred during his unlawful absence. I stayed on the steps and heard music coming toward the theatre. The Norwich Philharmonic—at least those of its members who could carry their instruments and play at the same time—was loudly marching my father and his bride toward their home.

In a moment Master Cree returned. What a face of horror. He looked at me and sprinted away again, running toward the oncoming music. Oh dear, then, it had come down.

Soon enough, actors came panicking up Theatre Street. Such was their distress that they rushed past me without a glance, hurling themselves through the door. A moment later, I could hear their screams and wailing. More and more they came, more and more they made their sorrowful noise. Then at last Father arrived, and Margaret Holler, née Utting, formerly Unthank, at his side. Father was sweating, his hands were shaking. He looked, I thought, as if he had aged since last I saw him. The people on the steps all stood aside to let Father and his bride through. And then one by one, and then severally, all the others followed. I stayed on the step, shivering though it was not cold.

What silence then. I could hear nothing from inside the theatre; perhaps my heart was pounding too loudly, or perhaps that terrible knocking had finally deafened me. At last Aunt Jenny came out. Her cheeks were nervously shaking. I thought she might hug me, but instead she pulled me rather roughly by the arm. "Your Father wishes to see you," she said. "Come along."

She noticed my limping.

"Whatever is the matter with you?"

"It hurts to walk."

"Edith, now is no time for your theatrics."

"But it does!"

"This is not about you, this is about the theatre. Edith, what's all that brown on your arms and legs, on your face?"

"It is dried blood, I suppose."

"It is the wrong color. It is paint."

Our blood in our barrels always stayed very red; it is possible that Aunt Jenny had confused true blood with fake blood in her mind.

"Nothing, Edith, nothing at all, can hide you from what's coming."

"But I didn't . . ."

"I'll not hear it! I do love you, Edith, but sometimes you make it very hard to like you."

She said nothing more as she took me back inside, through the foyer and into the stalls. Everybody was gathered there, all along the wider side aisles, holding on to one another. They stood around the seats, huddled against the walls, but none of them were sitting, as if there were actually an audience filling the seats and this was all part of a play. All faces turned to me, staring and pointing, as Jenny marched me down the center aisle. Father was at the front of the stalls, by the railing above the orchestra pit, as close as he could be to where the stage once was and now was not. The new Mrs. Holler sat in the front row of the stalls, nearest to him. She alone was seated. Father had his back to me, his hands to his face. I saw him straighten up now, put down his hands and turn my way.

How terrible his face. I never saw such a look. I thought I had known all his faces, but this was wholly new. Nobody made a sound. All waited for *his* noise.

At last it came. "Oh, Edith," he said, not so loud and yet loud enough that you may hear it, I was certain, in the balcony. A pause, and then: "What have you done?"

"Nothing, Father."

"You cannot blame *this* on Margaret."

"I do not indeed."

"Edith, I ask you again. What have you done?"

"There was a terrible knocking, Father. A loud sort of tapping. And the tapping, it grew and grew, and then there was a little darkness on the stage, and it grew and it grew, and all fell down."

"You tried to leave."

"No, Father, no!"

"Tried to leave us, knowing the consequences."

"I did not."

"Why would you do such a thing? If not for yourself, for the others? For your family here?"

"Father, please, I did not. I did not!"

"To hate us so."

"I do not, Father. I love you all!"

"How far did you go? As far as the castle, to the river even?"

"Father, I never left. I daren't, you know."

"Do you, my only child, my love I thought, expect me to believe that this stage, which stood for hundreds of years, died unprompted on the one day you were alone inside the theatre? With Master Cree safely distant at the stage door? When at any moment you could have broken down a door, walked out upon Theatre Street, gone for a stroll in Chapelfield Gardens without fear of witnesses? That the stage chose as the moment of its death the single occasion when no one else was present? Look at this, Edith, do but look at it. This *ruin*." He stopped for breath; I thought his heart might stop altogether.

"To my own grandfather I swore to protect this theatre, to keep it going," he went on. "This theatre which killed my father, but not me. I thought, *I am strong, I shall keep it alive* . . . but look. Do but look!"

"O Father, don't do this!"

"Tell me straight, daughter, what caused the death of my stage?"

"I do not know."

"A wandering daughter."

"No, Father, no!"

"I have done everything for this theatre, thrown all in: my sweat, my bones, my blood. And by my strength, only just, did we keep it alive. Years of anguish, years of fear. Always wondering, Do we make it another week? Can we mount another production? And, at last, at long last, when all seemed safe, when it seemed we had arrived at a new era, when our futures after so long a worry seemed secure—only then do you, my own child, choose to play with our light, indeed to blow it out! I see Victor Holler on his deathbed, pleading, pleading. And all for this.

"Go now, Edith. Run away if you must, I open all doors. Get you to Great Yarmouth, find yourself Cromer and Brancaster, seek Lowestoft even. Trip-trap to London if you must and so bury us all in rubble. There is no more theatre, Edith. I did everything for you, my own, but you cared nothing for it. I can no longer protect you. Go, Edith, go. Run!"

"I cannot leave, Father. You know I may not!"

"Edith," something else coming to him, "are *you* hurt?"

"No, Father. Not particularly."

"You are certain?"

"I lost a tooth."

"*I* am hurt."

"Are you, Father? I'm sorry to hear it. And Father, dear Father," for something alarming had just occurred to me, "my play . . ."

"I cannot look upon you today, my only Edith. Seek the small, dark places, keep yourself there out of my way. For I swear, for now, I have no such daughter."

"Father, you are being too dramatic. Do stop it now."

"My Edith Holler says so?" he whispered.

"Yes, Father, your Edith. Here I am," I replied quietly, going to him.

He seemed to soften a moment, but then let out a loud wail.

"Do not approach! Your tears mean nothing to the wound you have caused me and all our people. Do look upon them, Edith, my sometime child, study their faces and comprehend your deed. Norwich has no theatre now, and thus shall never understand itself, not ever again!"

"But, Father!"

"No more words." He put his hand out so that it entirely blocked my face from his view. "The rest is silence." And then he turned away, my own father.

"I did not leave! I did not leave!"

I stamped my feet, but then everyone in the theatre was shushing me and hissing so loudly that my words were all drowned out.

"Selfish child."

"Abominable girl."

"To be so jealous."

"To destroy your father's happiness."

"And ours!"

"Just because he fell in love."

"Just because he married."

"He *is* married you know, no matter what you've done."

"Poor Edgar, poor abused man."

"And on his wedding day!"

What sobbing there was, what great woeing among the theatre community. What calling of *Edith! Edith! How could you, Edith?*

"I did nothing!" I cried. "I went nowhere!"

Old Alice the donkey had died when the stage fell, they were eager to tell me of that. Mr. Leadham was down below with the corpse. All the ramshackle populace seemed broken by the news, clinging to one another in the aisles. And then, in all the growling and moaning and shushing, a new, clear voice.

"We shall rebuild it." It was Margaret, speaking from the orchestra pit, standing on the conductor's dais. "We shall make a new stage and all can begin again. We shall make it fresh and we shall make it strong: we shall make it *stronger*. Come now, come, my new family, this is not an end, not on this day of wedding. This is a beginning. The stage has fallen, let us have it back again. We were Victorian, now let us grow Edwardian. A new beginning. No expense shall be spared. This I swear, no expense."

What a thing to hear. A beautiful woman in a wedding dress, her voice so clear, her message so strong—it quite shut them all up. To be addressed so, and by someone who was not one of us. Quite a shock, such commanding words coming not from Father, who before now had alone steered us, but from his new and immaculate bride.

Margaret's last words—*no expenses spared*—lasted in that hall longer perhaps than any words ever delivered in the theatre. They stayed up and sang, and when at last they had shrunk and withered, there followed a silence. And then, from somewhere unknown—perhaps it was from Mr. Mealing, indeed I think it came from there—a single clap, hand upon hand, and then more and more and yet more, all my people clapping now and cheering and Father standing there useless and in love. It was so easily done, the crowning of Queen Margaret.

She was loved, then, by everyone—everyone but Edith.

"And," she said, turning to me, "I shall watch over this child. Do not blame her. I, for one, give no credence to this curse. This is an old building, a dear but dangerous palace. The ground on which we tread is so often perilous. An accident surely, a collapse. We must be grateful that no one was upon the stage when it fell. My dear new family, please be kind. Just a child. An innocent. And an implosion."

Noises of disagreement, but Margaret would not let them win. She spoke over them. "I shall care for her now. Give her to my keeping . . . to me and my own child here."

Behind her, coming up from the orchestra pit, like some cheap theatrical entrance, was someone else. Someone who must have crept up behind her when the orchestra gate was opened. A person I had never seen before. A girl. About my age. And this new upstart child was smiling, and curtsying, and all my theatre people were bowing back at her.

"This is Agnesia," said Margaret. "The theatre's new daughter."

11.

Some sistering.

She was the child from Margaret's first marriage, with dead Mr. Unthank. I was presented to her that afternoon. "Edith dear, you are not to blame yourself," said Margaret to me quietly. "These people are a little primitive, but do not fret. I am here now. And, lord knows, you are filthy and must get yourself cleaned up. It is not good to go about so disheveled. But soap and scrub shall sort that out. Other matters may take longer and harder work. I know your father will not talk to you, but allow me to intercede. I am your friend, Edith, I alone. Oh, I mean to mother you so. I will make all well again, though it may take a little time. And how to fill that time? I have the very thing for you. Edith, there is someone you need to meet."

She stepped back, and there she was again, this other girl.

"Here is your new sister. This is Agnesia, my darling. My love, my daughter. Now, Edith, you shall never be lonely again. Isn't that a wonderful thing?"

But I *liked* to be lonely. There was only me. *I* was the daughter of the theatre. No others. To look at this one now, in her smart dress, a little taller than me, with pink in her cheeks! She had rather a snout, I thought, not the mother's nose at all, but larger and rounded, as if the dollmaker had applied a dollop but then was called away and never got back to finish. Bright blond was her hair, of an unnatural hue. She curtsied, her horrible little curtsy again, and so I must bow in return.

"How lovely," said Margaret. "I'm sure you'll soon be the best of friends and love each other very much. You must have so much to talk about. Agnesia darling, do you have any matches?"

"No, Mama."

"That's my good girl. Play then, my children. Go now!"

And we were propelled, me and the daughter, by these last words. Each of us shuffled along a bit, to be out of the way. And then there we were, just the two of us.

"How old are you?" asked Agnesia.

"I'm twelve," I said.

"I'm thirteen. I shall always be older than you."

"Not if you die first." (Do understand, I was most upset.)

"What did you say?"

"You heard, I think."

"Is it true that you never go out?"

"I may not. It is forbidden."

"That's nonsense, isn't it? I wouldn't stand for it."

"I have a terrible curse upon me."

"Do you though?"

"A deep dark curse it is. I wouldn't come too close."

"I don't fright."

"Besides which, why would I ever want to leave?"

"If you can't go out, I'll stay in and keep you company. I'll call you sister."

"I have company enough already," I said to the pleading thing. "I was born here. It is my place."

"Well, it's my place now too. Show me around, will you, Edith?"

"I will not."

"We must play, Mother says so."

"I shan't."

"I only want to be friends."

"I have everything I need right here in this theatre. I don't want anything else. Leave me alone!"

I ran from her then, though the pain stabbed at me, along and out the passageway. My foot dragged as though I were the last Plantagenet, though like Father in the role I could still move fast if I wanted. And as I went, I howled, "My play! My play! My play! My play!" Yet despite all my noise, I heard a voice behind me. There was no mistaking that voice.

"Edith! Edith, come back now. Edith!"

Her mother calling to me. Not mine, not at all, though I had sometimes hoped for it.

The way she said my name was like so many hooks, but I didn't stop. Into the foyer, round the back of the ticket office, up to the circle, and then back to the side door and round the rubble on the stage, and I did not stop until I was in the furnace room and crawled into the second furnace, and there I wept and angered, and ached and hurt.

After a time, a pang of hunger overcame me and I slunk back into our apartment. I went to the kitchen and that was where she found me at last. With a sausage from the cold box in my mitt.

"No, Edith, I don't think so. No food just now. Perhaps later," she said, taking the sausage away. She marched me back to our rooms, which were filled with uncles, Jerome and Wilfred and Gregory and Thomas.

"We must learn our lesson, my darling," she said. "I think earlier you were not so nice to Agnesia. We do want you to get on, and so you must know that when I call you, you will always come. I am going to make this place a home to you, a normal home where people follow rules. If rules are not followed, there will be consequences. We need to know where you are, for your safety. It is important. I have made a promise to look after you. Now, Edith, don't look so angry."

"I am angry."

"I see that, indeed I do. But consider that everyone is upset."

"They hate me!"

"I'm sure they don't. And consider this, you have me."

"Only this morning there was hope in the world."

"I am your friend."

"I want my play to be put on."

"That is difficult without a stage."

"But it must."

"Edith, you are thinking only of yourself."

I needed to speak plainly. "I hate you and I hate your ugly daughter."

"Edith. Edith dear. Do please try to be reasonable. . . ."

"Get out of my father's sheets."

"Edith, don't be crude."

"The rank sweat of an enseamed bed."

"Edith, this is not the way."

"Who are you to tell me what is the way?"

"Your new mother, Edith."

"You have horrible sharp teeth. I've seen them."

"Edith, I must warn you."

"You're not a mother, you're a monster."

"Edith!" That was Uncle Jerome.

"Do not worry, my new brother," said Margaret. "I shall look after her. Edith dear, now listen to me. I am going to help you. You have gone astray. I do not blame you. It is hardly surprising that you have got a little lost, growing up in this dangerous place."

"I want my father. I don't want you. I don't know you."

"I am all you have, and I am here to put you right."

"You are a devil monster!"

"No, Edith. No. I see I shall have to introduce the first lesson."

I was put in the coal room, which is directly above the furnace room, the two connected by a soot-blackened chute. I was handed a small shielded lanthorn giving weak light. I was to sit in there that I might learn my lesson. And so, with the furnace of my stomach groaning and protesting, I sat with my brothers and sisters of coal and contemplated my lot. Only after two hours would I be allowed to come out again. When I looked down, I saw that one of my toes had gone completely black. At first I thought it must be the coal dirt, but then why would it hurt so to the touch? Am I dying then, dying away in the coal shed? Will Norwich come out for the funeral? I had such rich imaginings of the event that time passed swiftly and soon Margaret was with me again.

"What do you say now, Edith?"

"I say hell and damnation!"

I was left inside a half hour longer, and then—as I thought I lay in my last moments—the door once more.

"What do you say now, Edith?"

"I am sorry, madam."

"How lovely! How well you do it. I am so proud of you. Now you may come upstairs and have a little bread and milk. Edith dear, be civil or we must have you put somewhere else until you have found your manners. Come along, quickly now, stop that shuffling. Walk properly."

I was thinking of the dining room, but Margaret said no, Father was there having his meal with the uncles, and I must not see Father for now. So I ate it in the kitchen, feeling very downtrodden indeed. But that was not all of it.

When at last I returned to my room, I found Agnesia within it. She had been about my objects, I could tell; she had fiddled with all my stuff; some of the letters on Leadenhall Street were bunched up on the roller.

"These are my things! Mine!" I cried.

"We must share," said Agnesia. "Mother says so."

"You are a monster!"

"Now then," said Agnesia, "what have I done, that I grow the title *monster*? You mustn't go round calling simply everyone a monster, you know. I consider the label downright unfair. I consider that a slur, I do indeed. And I require compensation."

"You are about my things!"

"Now then," said Agnesia, "this magic lantern will do it well enough. I thank you and we'll say no more about it."

"But it is mine! It is all mine!"

"Come now, you sound like Bonaparte. It is mine now and so I'll be Wellington, shall I?"

"It is not right! It is not fair!"

"Come and be civil and we'll talk no more about it. I want to know all about you."

"Look what you have done!"

In my absence, Agnesia had taken hold of my childhood. All my old nursery days had been brutishly manhandled. She had trespassed upon my Book of Outdoors, that volume of pressed leaves that had blown into the theatre and that I had collected up over years, and so many of those leaves had been set free again and crumbled into dirt.

"I'm sorry, I did not mean to, it just fell apart."

Worse yet was the little fireplace in my room. It was burning bright. A stack of papers was its fuel—and then I understood what was burning.

"My play! The original! All up in ashes."

"Oh, Edith, I am so sorry, I thought it rubbish. It was so ripped and stained, and I like a little fire."

"But my play!"

"I have said I'm sorry."

"Hagseed!" And so I hit her. I had to. A strike across the face, hard. The fear in her, and then the anger. She ran to her mother.

Margaret was not so nice after that. There was the sign of my hand upon Agnesia's face, in red did the ghost of my hand show upon that accursed cheek. She had little sympathy for my torched manuscript; copies had been made, after all, so why such alarm? Margaret had made a decision, she said, to ensure that Father and I were kept apart—in order, so she said, that Father might recover himself the sooner, I was no longer to sleep in my own room. Instead, until I was forgiven, Margaret told me in her deliberate, sweet voice so that it hurt all the more, I was to go down to Aunt Bleachy (she said Belinda) and that until further notice I was to call Bleachy's address my own. Uncle Gregory and Uncle Thomas stood by as this happened, doing nothing at all.

"But this is *my* bedroom!"

"Now, dear Edith, it is all for your own good. Your aunt Belinda will see you are washed and dressed every day, and you shall be a clean and presentable Edith then. Do go down and be washed by your aunt—for you must learn to love yourself, Edith. And you must be cleaned up, for indeed you look as if you've been to an earthquake and not a wedding reception. Let us not be wild, Edith. I shall civilize you. So, the first step, a bath. To your aunt Belinda."

"This is where I live, in these rooms, in this apartment. It is my home!"

"Now, Edith, you are getting upset."

"Yes, yes I am!"

"Edith, listen, you are just another girl. Nothing more than that. Don't exaggerate your worth. Why indeed must you be so singular?"

"I am Edith Holler, who must never leave the theatre."

"You are a child grown up with strange notions."

"All of which are true."

"Well no, actually, that's the point isn't it?"

"Is it?"

Storm Scenes to fit Most Plays

1.

2.

3.

4.

"Oh, Edith, it's been a bit rotten hasn't it?"

"Has it?"

"Yes, I do think so. Let us put an end to all that. No more stories now."

"But I like the stories, terrors though they may be."

"Downstairs you go."

"This is my home! I want to stay!"

"Quite feral, my dear girl."

"My home!"

"It may seem unfair, even perhaps unkind to you now. But when you take some time, and when you are older, you will see that I am doing all this for your own good. And then you will thank me for it. And, Edith, think of me for a moment, I have been in this imperiled building the smallest of hours, and it is up to me to rescue it. Do you see now? There is so much to do. Do not add to it, Edith. You must grow up. You must become a lady."

"You're taking me away from my own father!"

"No dear, I am not. I am going to calm him and make him well, and then you shall be together again. I've never seen a man so miserable, and upon his wedding day!"

"Oh, when will he be well again?"

"There is much to be repaired."

"But it wasn't my fault."

"I believe you but let us not travel back three spaces. Let us, rather, go onward."

"Father!"

"To Belinda's with you. Hurry now. Hurry along. Don't make a fuss, do stop that ridiculous limping. I'll come and find you later, and keep close watch on your progress. Go down, Edith, go down now."

And she shut the door upon me.

Exit Edith.

III

She stays.

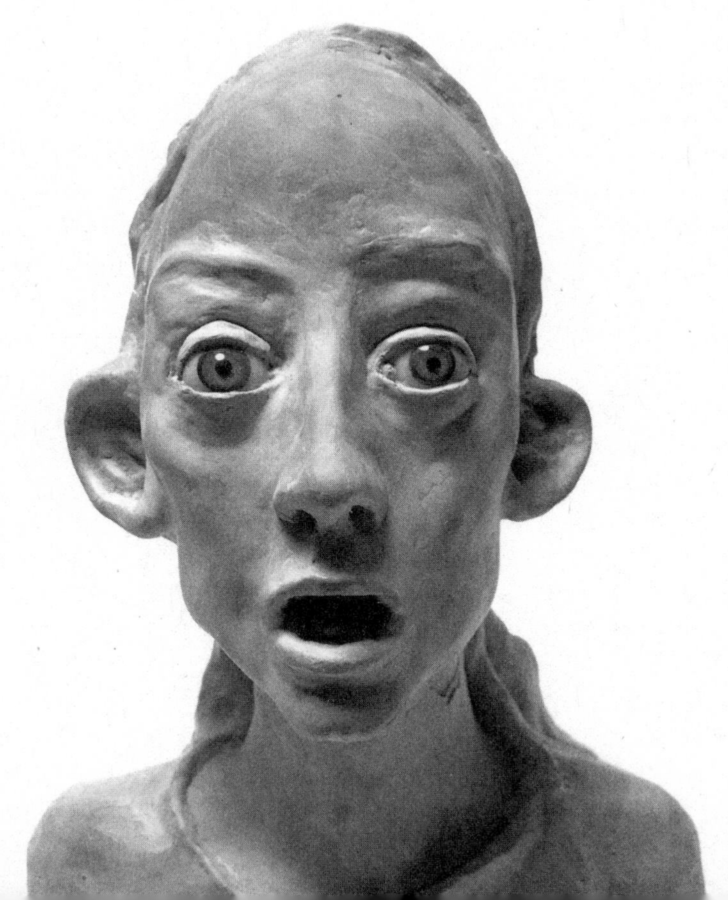

12.

My aunty Bleachy.

As I descended the steps toward my aunt, down into darkness, I saw that Uncle Wilfred had put up a new sign: NO MORE THAN THREE AT A TIME UPON THESE STAIRS. Along the dressing room corridor there was a group of children. I didn't know them, and when I came by they moved along a bit, but they stopped at the far end, watching me. Norwich children, I supposed, hoping to get some food from the wedding feast.

I knocked at Bleachy's door, and when I knocked the children scarpered. From the land of Bleachy came a noise, and the noise said, "No."

Aunt Bleachy lived, if it could be called living, in her former dressing room, dressing room 11. And even if she weren't Aunt Bleachy, still her quarters would be avoided, for the room next door was dressing room 12, and that was where Father's unhappy wife Ada had hanged herself. (There is no dressing room 13, by the by; we pretend the number doesn't exist.) We always ran by 12, and so mostly we always ran by Aunt Bleachy's too. Yet here I was.

The door of dressing room 11 did not say MISS BELINDA HOLLER. Instead, in the spot where the actor's name would normally appear, was the label from a packet:

for Spring Cleaning use
CALVERT'S No. 5 Carbolic Soap
F. C. Calvert & Co. Manchester, England

It may once have been a dressing room, but long ago all the costumes, all the greasepaint, all the actors' makeup sticks—the flesh pink, the grey green, the bastard amber, the violet and carmine—had been taken away. In their places were Aunt Bleachy's children: bottles and buckets and mops and brushes and so many packages of supplies for cleaning. Bleachy hoarded these and kept them fast about her, so much so that her dwelling appeared more broom cupboard than dressing room. She felt safe in her room with all her favorites, all her soldiers, and she their proud general. Twice a day, Bleachy would open her door and admit her cleaning staff, her miserable brood of Norwich women and girls who would come in to pick up mops and pans, polish and bleach, and at the end of the working day the well-used tools would be returned to their homes. Bleachy would count them every one, and bless them.

This is where I was to live now, if only temporarily. I knocked upon the door again.

"No."

"It is Edith, Aunt Bleachy."

"Oh no."

"I have been sent to you."

"Scrub harder."

I opened the door.

"Hullo, Aunt Bleachy."

"Hullo, dirt. Hullo, dust."

"I have been told to come here."

"I don't like it."

"No more do I, Aunty."

"But, stain, I must admit that you have done me a big favor."

"I have?"

"Despite all the mess, all the dust and rubble everywhere: you took away their precious stage. I would never have thought of that."

"I didn't do it, Aunty."

"You need not be modest with me. Don't stand there by the door, not a duster such as you."

And so in I went. The room itself was a dank little space. There was a bed, a metal-framed single cot, its thin mattress speaking always of the shape of Bleachy, whether she was in it or not, as if Bleachy's ghost lived there when the flesh Bleachy had vacated.

"Come in, come in, my little cobweb."

I had never known my aunt so loquacious, so happy. She even stroked my hair a little before wiping her hand and washing it. Then she lay down a cloth upon her bed and bade me sit on it, seating herself there beside me.

"You'll tell me by and by, I'm sure. But for now here you are, my own blot. I think we understand each other at last, as we never did before. I thought you one of them, but you're not, you come along to my side. And you've done such a thing. Oh, their faces!" And now she laughed. It was an odd laugh, something like a scraping or screeching. Aunty Bleachy's laugh had, I believe, been so long underexercised that now, finding itself out in the open once more, it failed to fly right—just limped and stammered, then puttered out altogether. But she rallied enough to

offer a word of encouragement: "Watson's matchless cleaner is the best soap for all purposes." And she nodded to me and I nodded back.

"I have made up a little bed for you," she said, pointing to a corner where some old and very battered mattresses had been stacked. I recognized them immediately—they were a few of the many used under the stage to catch an actor when he fell through a trapdoor into the trap room. The room that had now, in part, descended upon a donkey.

"I shouldn't be here. It is not right."

"Satin polish," she nodded, "satin brown cream."

"I want to go home."

She looked worried a moment, then cheered herself. "Peerless dyes are the best." Aunty Bleachy, like my father, like everyone else in that big house of ours on Theatre Street, liked to speak other people's words. To their minds, words set down by another had great authority, had a wisdom and a determination that their own words lacked. Speaking the words inscribed on cleaning products, reciting advertisements on soaps and polishes, made Bleachy feel bigger. Like my father spouting Shakespeare, it gave her the feeling that, if even for a moment, any of us can hold something immortal. After all, the thinking goes, how much of us is ourselves after all, and how much is just borrowed bits and pieces? We are only whispers in the moment, and afterward nothing at all.

"Pears' soap, recommended by Mrs. Langtry for improving the complexion," decided my aunt Bleachy that day. "So then, my little lint girl, some rules: You may play with the brushes and mops—a child must play—but do put them back where you found them. You do still play, don't you? Still some child left in you? So then you may borrow my brushes. What else? This room is locked between half past seven a.m. and three p.m., twelve noon if we have a matinee. During that time: no admittance. Then am I to be found about the stage side, doing my business.

"On Sunday I do not go to church. I lie in, you may likewise."

I said nothing.

"And first of all we must have you clean."

"Aunty, can I not have a sleep first? It has been such a long and horrible day."

"First a bath, then a sleep. I'll not have you in my sheets so dirty. Let us scrub you up and have you readied for your new home."

There was a large zinc tub, and water was brought up for it. Steam all over Aunt Bleachy's room, great white clouds that smelled so different to the dry ice.

"I'll not do it!"

"You will, you must. Off with your clothes."

"No, no, it's private! My body! I'll do it alone, I promise I will."

"No, I shall see it's done properly."

"I won't have it!"

"Nonsense. Why such preciousness?"

"Leave me be!"

"It's only a body, everything common in that."

"But it's mine!"

She was stronger than me and not to be put off. She was performing her own play, a one-act drama of cleanliness. Since theatre does deal with the metamorphosis of a character, so that the character at the end is very different from the one at the beginning, I was to go into the water a filthy thing and come out shimmering. And yet not so.

When my clothes were peeled off me, it was discovered that something was wrong. My body had a change about it. Since the morning a huge and angry growth had appeared upon my chest, a great map of woe it was. An invasion. Dark and black in the center and spreading out very livid. Something clinging there.

"As if you were rotting," whispered Aunty.

"What is it, Aunty?"

Front of house wallpaper, Holler Theatre.

"I've never seen the like, not on a person before. Old wood surely. But on a twelve-year-old girl, never. However did it happen?"

"I don't know, I've not seen it before. Will you take it away, Aunty? Oh, I don't like it."

Aunt Bleachy called for reinforcements, and Aunt Nora descended from her cloth to look upon the strange discoloration. She lightly stroked it as if it were velvet, but pulled her hand away.

"It is true then, after all."

The new stain upon me resembled the red wallpaper from our front of house, only with a large darkness of mold in its center. We did have wallpaper in just such a condition, on Uncle Jerome's side, but only on our walls, never yet on our skins. Dr. Cottes was summoned again.

I cannot remember his visit because I passed out.

I had fallen backward into darkness.

With no stage, the Holler Theatre had gone dark. And a theatre dark is a terrible and woeful thing. It meant failure, it meant no public, and we needed the applause of our Norwich public; we lived on it. All stories had been put away; there were no tales to come out; the life of adventure, of tragedy and comedy, the stories of brave men and women, of love and betrayal—all these were silenced. With no stage our lives had gone dark, stripped of all color; like dull Edith, they went about grey and ashen, quiet and distraught.

As I lay in my sickness in Aunt Bleachy's room, and as my family waited for Margaret's builders—she had insisted on her people doing the work, it had been so poorly repaired in the past—the theatre people were all lost souls without purpose. Before they had always fought and screamed and sang and hated and loved one another, but now they were all sealed up. They all kept their distance, one from the other. If one of them opened a door and saw someone else in the corridor, that person would shut it up and go back inside. You could hardly hear a word. Everyone's life had been reduced to a party of one. Each kept away from all the others, all were selfish. As if to come in contact with another was to court danger, that to speak to another may even be inviting death in. What dull and lonely days!

I came to think of this time as the End of Stories.

The only things that could grow in all those storyless times were sadness and anger and quiet seething. My people all looked at one another, but they could divine no plots. They were only human bodies keeping their distance, living only mechanically—for to stop living, to pull themselves out of their suspended state, would create a plot of some kind, an arc, a journey. For now, within a stageless theatre, they all were mannequins, just dummies with blank faces. My people, with no expressions. My people forgetting that to be human is to speak, to touch. Instead all they had was *Ssssh* and *Ssssh* and *Sssssh*.

They had forgot themselves.

I'd thought them very tough and dependable, my theatre folk. But now it seemed they were such delicate things and we should surely have treated them gentler. We should have shored them up while we had a chance.

How I missed the noise of striking swords.

How I missed the cranking of the wind machine.

How I missed the interval gong, hurrying the audience back to their seats.

How I missed the whispering of the pipes, for in those blank days the pipes were mute.

How I missed the sound of voices.

From the orchestra pit there was naught but silence, for that is all that was available: a symphony of silence, a quartet of silence, a solo.

In my delirium, in my sickbed, I had horrible dreams in which I was drowning, or running and looking for people but finding no one at all, only Margaret's tall form hovering over me. They wondered if I might die. The theatre, after all, is well acquainted with death. The theatre believes in ghosts—we have them all about us in our plays—and I think the ghosts must know this and so come here in happiness or unhappiness to be remembered. And the people coming to the theatre are much more likely to believe in ghosts when they are with us, even if they doubt once more after leaving. In the theatre, you are in direct contact with the dead. Sometimes, in my illness, I thought I saw my own lost mother come to fuss over me. But it was only Margaret. Sometimes I felt the mother was gnawing at me. Again, just Margaret attending. In illness you are vulnerable to all the monsters; in my fever I could see them all about me, and I was scared. Even the cleaning rags in the corner of Bleachy's room seemed to be breathing.

Margaret fussed over me a great deal; she mopped my forehead; she chivied Dr. Cottes. In the worst of it, Bleachy told me later, I kept calling out in the night the stage manager's line, those words of great hope: "Act One beginners please, Act One beginners please." But what I remember most was another dream, in which there was only me and a brass fire extinguisher and I talked to it like it was my own child. "Ssssh, it's a terribly sad thing, you know, but someone ought to tell you after all. Listen up: I think that everybody's died."

Two weeks passed before my fever broke and I became sensible again. When Margaret was not beside me, Aunts Nora and Jenny and Bleachy took their turns, encouraging me back into Edith. I never once saw Father, though surely he must have come.

To aid in my progress back to my natural greyness, my caretakers saw to it that my rash was covered at the start of each day in a bread-and-milk poultice, which was removed in the evening. Aunt Jenny tied a skein of scarlet silk loose around my neck with nine knots in it that was said to help most particularly with ague. But what seemed to soothe me most of all was Aunt Bleachy rubbing linseed oil into me—this was her own particular way of doing things, she was speaking her own language, and it worked very well. Sometimes she polished my nails with a drop of Brasso, or put a little floor wax in my hair, which gave me a wonderful good smell.

Slowly the black on my skin retreated, at last the wallpaper red faded and became grey again, grey like the walls backstage, no longer the livid crimson of front of house. My cough grew much less frequent, and soon I hardly sweated at all, and soon I was strong enough to sit up and look out through the bars of Bleachy's small window. This was something of a comfort when Bleachy was away at work. The bad dreams, though less frequent, could still sometimes be quite vivid. I thought I saw a hermaphroditic person eating a child like it was a chicken leg, I was quite certain of it. And one foggy morning, I spied a man in a topper strolling up and down Chantry Road. He didn't seem to be going anywhere, just walking back and forth. I wondered what he was about. He was a very tall and thin gentleman, taller, I thought, and thinner than almost anyone I had ever seen. And then, in my panic, I understood that I *had* seen him before and even knew his name.

"Mr. Jet," I whispered.

There he was, walking up and down. Trying to see where he might get in. I screamed for Aunt Bleachy, but by the time she came running Mr. Jet was no longer there.

"There is no Mr. Jet," Bleachy said, "not really."

But I knew different.

"It's your illness making you worry. It is but a fever dream, Edith. Do calm yourself. What a fuss you do make, you've upset everyone with your noise. The whole theatre heard you crying. Your new sister from upstairs is just outside asking after you. Shall I let her in?"

I shook my head.

"Too tired?"

I nodded.

"I'll send her off, then."

I was certain I had seen Mr. Jet, and I was proven right. The next day, worried because of my calling out, Miss Tebby, the prompt, had come in early, and there was indeed a trace of smoke along her corridor. She followed the trace to her own room, and when she opened the door, the room was all ablaze! Up went *Henry IV*, both parts, up went *Richard III*, *The Tempest*, *Lear*, and *Othello*, up went *As You Like It* and *The Taming of the Shrew*, up went all words of not just Shakespeare but Marlowe, Middleton, Rowley, Boucicault, Molière, Mealy—all their worlds turning to the same black ash—and among them, in the thick fog and flame, up went *The True History of Mawther Meg*.

Miss Tebby ran from door to door.

"Fire," she whispered, "fire, fire."

"What, Tebby, speak loudly, girl."

"Mr. Jet. It's Mr. Jet."

"What say she?"

"Can't make it out."

"Mr.," she moaned.

"Yes, 'Mr.,' got that. And what breed of Mr., then?"

"Jet."

"Mr. Jet! Is he in the house?"

"Yes," came her small reply.

And then it was heard: "Mr. Jet is in the house!" And afterward that sentence was the only sentence in everyone's mouth. What rushing followed! Soon everyone in the theatre was busy with buckets and the fire was put out and the corridor sealed off. And yet, even so, every play in the history of theatre was burned to death.

"My play? My play!" I wept at the parting.

"All gone now."

"But not all," I said, "surely not all. The actors, they each had a copy."

"No, Edith, I'm afraid not," said Tebby, her voice quieter now after her unusual exertion. "Word came from your father that all be gathered up and kept in my office."

"When was that?"

"Only yesterday."

"Oh, my play! Mr. Jet stole my play."

"Yes, yes he did."

"I wrote a play," I wept, "and it was beautiful, prompt."

"I am a girl of twelve," said Miss Tebby. "I have written a very good play full of folklore and history but it is all gone now, it is only dust and ash. I am not doing well and have an ill look about me, I have fallen from the lighter rooms to those where the air is less pleasant. There are firestarters about us, and I myself look half-burned. Even so, I do bless this theatre. Oh, Edith, the plays!"

"We might all have died," said Bleachy. "We have been lucky."

"I'd rather be dead," I said.

Black those days were, black as the hole in the theatre, black as my burned play. There were no colors then, all was come monochrome, like the card-toy theatre characters, which arrived plain and stayed that way until the juvenile owner colored them in. (It cost tuppence to have colored ones, twice as much money.) In those one-penny days, Grey Edith, under the influence of Aunt Bleachy, became a little whiter.

I closed myself off after the fire and lay in bed in silence. I won't speak at all, I told myself, I think my voice has gone quiet now for always. I am a doll, I am a prop. Margaret visited and tried to get me to talk, but nothing would make me.

It was Aunt Bleachy who worked most faithfully to encourage me into conversation. One day, she returned to the room carrying a bucket.

"Look what I found today."

She tilted the bucket. At the bottom were fifteen or twenty dead deathwatch beetles. "I keep finding them, in little corners. I stamped on a good few and they leave a terrible mark. I don't know where they are coming from, but we are getting them more and ever more. It must be the warm weather brought them in. I'm going to try a new carbolic, see if that'll do the trick. Stubborn they are, but the carbolic will see to them."

But the carbolic did not see to them, for at the end of each day there were always more beetles in her bucket for me to see. I never said a word in response.

"Mostly they are found along this corridor, or upstairs in the apartment. Indeed, look how the bucket fills up! But I always find them, for nothing can hide from Bleachy. I know the theatre better than anyone, all its little secrets. You can't hide from Bleachy!"

She kept the corpses, proof of her labors. The dead mounted up.

One night I came awake with a start. There was something at my leg, something under the sheets. I was only very vaguely aware of it at first, I thought it was part of a dream, but then I could feel it certain on my calf, crawling there—and then biting, swift sudden hard little bites, piercing the skin and then burrowing in. I pulled back the covers. A beetle there! Chewing into me! And out came words again:

"Help me! Aunty Bleachy!"

I'd barely screamed before Bleachy was there, slapping at it.

She scraped the beetle free of me. It fell onto the floor, and then, quick as anything, Bleachy squashed it with her bare foot. What a bloody mark it left.

"I thought them dead," Bleachy said, "but were only sleeping. I'm going to put them all in the furnace now to be certain."

"Why was it biting me?"

"It was confused, I daresay. That must have been it."

"It mistook me for wood!"

"A lone crazy beetle, pay it no heed. Is dead now."

Next morning she said, "What you need is employment. You'll help me rid this place of beetles for good. Face your enemies."

"I won't clean."

"You will, it's been decided."

"By who?"

"By your new mother up the stairs. To make you learn yourself."

"Father won't stand for it. You wait and see."

"Where is he, then? I've caught no trace of him."

"Yet he will come."

"While we're waiting, I have nice cleaning overalls for you, an apron, a little cap if you like."

"But I'm . . ."

"No."

"Holler."

"That name's losing its mettle. It's my name, too, and I shouldn't like to wave it about. Got a bit of a smell to it, if you ask me. You won't mind cleaning, not after a bit."

"But I will, Aunty."

"A good scrub does the world of good."

"But I'm meant for playwriting, not lather."

"Best to forget all that. Time to muck in."

"But I can't."

"You can and you shall. If not for yourself, then for me. I'll get you a mop, you'll be safer along with me, I reckon. Some people are not saying such nice things, after all."

"What things?"

"I give them no heed. Better to muck in, better for you to clean now."

"I shan't do it!"

I confess I screamed then. And Bleachy sent for Margaret.

. . .

"It is a great cruelty!" I spat at Margaret.

"But why, Edith?"

"I am playwright."

"And so you are. But why insist on keeping yourself so singular? A playwright tells stories, and a storyteller must always want to see the world anew. I am not going to march you out to the steps—I think it all a nonsense, of course, but I've made my promise never to force you, and so I shan't. Instead I will help you to step out on your own terms. I want you to be an ordinary, happy girl."

"I am Edith Holler."

"And I would like Edith Holler to do a little cleaning."

"No."

"Edith, sometimes we must do things we don't necessarily wish to."

"I'm too ill."

"Cleaning will make you stronger. You want to be well, don't you?"

"Leave me alone, I need to sleep."

"I think it is good medicine, Edith. Agnesia works sometimes in the factory, and it made her a much more reasonable person."

"I am not Agnesia."

"No, you are not, my darling. But I need you to be strong and brave."

"Why don't you mind your own business?"

"You are my business and I want to help you. Edith, listen to me, my darling, you have a strand of unhappiness in your family. Your own grandfather went across the road, as you people call it. Let us not have that strand grow new roots. I fear all this make-believe can encourage it. I would not have said this, indeed I had decided not to, but I cannot tell how else I may convince. Your father, Edith—"

"My father!"

"—he is unwell."

"I must see him."

"The doctors have said no, for his sake. He is beset by a great melancholy, and he cannot find his way out of it. It has made him cry like a babe."

"I will help him!"

"Yes, I know you will. And this is how: by not seeing him, just for now. He believes that you are the cause of the stage's collapse and the doctors fear that seeing you will make him worse."

"My own poor papa."

"Give me time and I shall convince him, and when he is quite himself again, when he can see plainly what is before him and not howl over what is gone—for indeed he does bray like a donkey, and no man should bray like a donkey—it will be my dearest pleasure to show you to your papa."

"When will that be?"

"Give me some time, Edith. Until then, let us make sure that you are well and do not fall into your familial malady. Let us have you upright and fit and full of health."

"Yes."

"Will you clean for me?"

"I will clean for you."

"There's my good girl." Margaret turned to Bleachy. "Now, Belinda, whyever are you crying?"

"I'm not, really I'm not. The lye."

She left and Bleachy came forward and gave me a hug, which was very unlike her.

"Here now, Edith," she said, "I have something for you." In her hand was a Meg Peg. I must keep it with me at all times, she told me. By using it, she said, I could help her by extinguishing the beetles myself. "Call them to you, summon them with that clacker and then stamp them all to death. Do your part to protect the theatre."

I did not like the thought of it. But Bleachy insisted I was to have it about me always. She used the knotted ribbon Aunt Jenny gave me to make it as a necklace, and then she tucked it away beneath my smock.

My time with Aunt Bleachy was like a tiny world of its own, a box cordoned off from the rest of the theatre, still in its time of no-stories, that blank, dull time where all my family resented me. In Bleachy space the stench of soap insisted upon itself, and so behind the door marked CALVERT'S NO. 5 CARBOLIC SOAP I was safe—until at last Dr. Cottes declared that I was better, and I was ready to make my first steps out again.

13.

I clean the theatre.

When I'd gone into Bleachy's, I was still Edith Holler. When I came out, I was someone else altogether. And I could not yet tell who that was. This new person was obliged to stand beside the cleaners of the backstage. I thought they'd never allow it, they'd know me instantly as a fraud, but they permitted me noiselessly into their ranks, barely giving me a second look. I stood beside ruddy-faced women and their disheveled offspring. One girl smiled at me, and I clung to that smile like arms around me. These are my people now, I thought, and I am one of them.

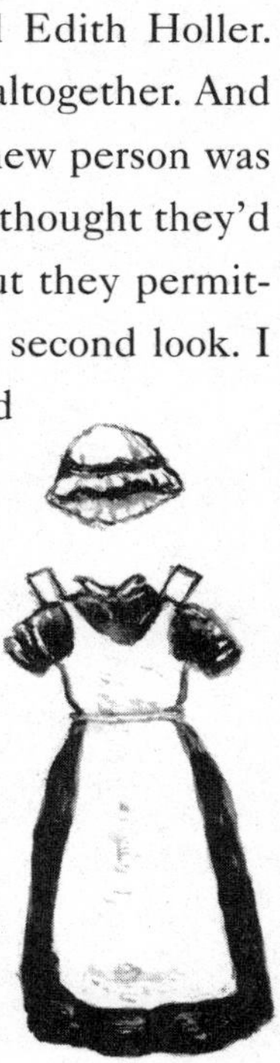

"Edith, here's your bucket."

Hello, bucket.

"Your mop and soap. Go with Polly Borthwick, she'll show you."

I went with Polly Borthwick to one of the small theatre lanes. She showed me the way, though I knew it well enough. "New parts are closed up," she said.

"Watch yer step." The back of the theatre is a place as narrow and torturous as the tiniest street on a Norwich map; indeed I have often pretended that our theatre is just a copy of the city of Norwich, reduced to a single property. You that are not of the theatre, expect no great secrets in a theatre's back rooms, for they are very plain and dull. The scenery dock and the prop room, of course, are exceptions; those are small factories of wonder. But mostly it is doors and corridors and steps, for there is no way to do life, I suppose, but doors and corridors and steps.

"You do this one," Polly said. "I'll take the passage the other side."

"What do I do?"

"You mop, you scrub, what do you think?"

I started.

"What are you doing?"

"Mopping."

"The mop is not even touching the floor. Dint do it like thart, must make contact! And the mop it is dry. Fill the bucket with water from the tap, hot mind. And add the soap from the tin. You do know to add the soap, yis?"

She showed me and could not but laugh at my ignorance.

"Come along, slummockun!"

The bucket filled with water was very heavy.

"Yar slopping everywhere!"

I slopped everywhere. I did not put enough muscle into it, that I was told often enough, and I was too slow, that too. But I got quicker, and in time I grew new muscles. It was like bathing a body, washing the theatre, an old ailing body, giving it comfort in its pain. I thought I'd get to hear all the stories of my fellow cleaners, that I might write a play from their histories, but there was never time, so much work to be done, and at the end of it we were all exhausted.

I feared, at the start, being seen in my new position by one of my old theatre family, but I need not have worried on that score, for all the doors were shut. If someone did come out of a room, I made sure to keep my head down, but no one ever looked at me, not once. This must have been how they treated Elsie. Sometimes I heard the footsteps of Margaret up above me, the particular clop of her boots, like some wonderful goat set loose upstairs, but she did not come down to my level. I longed to go upstairs, to find Father again. He was my father, after all, mine alone, and it is not right to keep a daughter from her father. I knew I would mend him better than any other; he does love me so and my love itself would heal him. It was this great muscle of love that made me suddenly set down the mop one afternoon and climb the stair. Back home I went, to a place where I'd been forbidden to trespass. But you cannot trespass on your own home, can you?

"It's all wrong," I whispered. And I opened the door to our apartment.

I heard the voices first of all. Then I saw them, in the drawing room quite crowded about: Mr. Collin and Uncle Wilfred and Dr. Cottes and other people I did not know. Most of all, I saw Father lying on the sofa, blankets pulled up to his neck, withered and gnawn. Poor dear Papa. He looked to me, saw me come in. We stood watching one another for a small moment. His jaw dropped open, and then he muttered:

"Get her out."

What a thing to say. It must be the cleaning clothes, I thought, the bonnet: he does not recognize me. I tore the bonnet off so that he may see me clearly.

And then again, louder this time and more distressed: "Get her out."

My own father. Margaret was there, and she took hold of my arm and steered me away, led me back to the front door of the apartment, and closed that, too, so that we were fully two doors from Father.

"He didn't mean it," I said. "It was the bonnet. The clothes. But he didn't mean it."

"Edith, it is what I feared most."

We sat down on the steps outside the apartment door. Just me and Margaret. She stroked my hair and held me close. To look at her, I thought, is to be away in some new address, for she seemed a kind of handsome architecture.

"You're beautiful," I whispered.

"Thank you, dear Edith. We are friends, you and I."

How she looked after me in my upset. Tight her grip. I held on back like she was an island. But Margaret is no landscape I can understand. I cannot read this person, she does not move like other people. How can I peel her open and look inside?

"Thank you, madam."

"You may say, 'Thank you, Mother.'"

"I want to know you."

"And so you shall, my child"

"You're not made like us, are you?"

"Am I not?"

"We're rather small and wooden structures, but you're made of stone from Caen."

"Are you quoting your own play?"

"You've read it?"

"I have."

"When?"

"Recently. Before the fire. Your father's copy, before it was gathered up."

"What did you think of it?"

"I'm no expert."

"Tell me."

"I've no understanding of theatre."

"Tell me."

"Do you want me to be nice or to be honest?"

"Nice."

"It was very interesting."

"Honest."

"I hated it."

"Oh."

"I think, Edith, that in your eagerness to make something new, you have made instead something rather upsetting. What will they think of you? Not a child for Norwich to delight in, I daresay, to create such a horrid little piece. Almost criminal. So much blood and slaughter. You will make the good people sick."

"Oh."

"Why not write something nice? Something people will want to see? You make Mawther Meg a murderous hag, but what if she wasn't? What if she was loving, what if she was loved? That story, or something else altogether. Edith, I ask you, think of the Beetle Spread business. You may cause it harm, with such stories, and then people would not have the Spread on their morning toast, never on a crumpet at tea, not in their mugs in winter beside the fire. No more Spread in the house, for fear of who it was that first made it. And if no one should buy the Spread anymore, the business is lost and the jobs are lost and the people without work are poor and the city stumbles and all is poverty and starvation. Consider that, Edith."

"Oh."

"Edith, it is no great disaster if, after all, you are not a writer."

"I am a writer. I think I am. I have to be."

"Of course, I know nothing of these things."

"It took me months to write."

"What of that?"

"I put everything into it."

"And yet."

"What about the children, though? The ones of Norwich, all the dead children?"

"What about them?"

"They died."

"Children will always be dying about the place."

"It is not safe for the children."

"No, it is not. It never has been. Not since Herod, I suppose, or before. Why so much fuss about children, anyway? More can always be made. Lord knows, we are not running out."

"Where did all those children go?"

"To adulthoods, thence to their deaths."

No more talking then, just sitting upon the steps. The stuffing all taken out of me.

"I shouldn't have come," I said. "I see that now."

"No, Edith, my darling, it was wrong. As I'd warned you."

"I'll go back down now."

"It would be best, I think. There's my good child."

I put on the bonnet and descended. And as I stepped down and down it was not Dame Julian's words in my head, but only Father's: *Get her out* and *Get her out.*

It was an awful play, I told myself now, all of it stolen from fairy tales, thieved and poorly restitched. The Norwich Snow White, with the dwarves all poor children. It would never work. I could see the audience booing, walking out of the theatre. Good, then, to let it go. What an arrogant, spoiled Edith. What an abomination. Oh, you are a rotten Edith, grey and reprehensible.

I vowed to keep quiet, to go unnoticed, to cause no more trouble. I was all bonnet then. Bonnet and mop.

I bathed the theatre in my penance.

I found other words scratched onto the walls, COAT WILL I AM or 10 POTTERGATE, and then just scratches that were unintelligible, and around a corner DEEP CAT or STILL DRIP or MARGERY MARGERY. How long they had been there I could not say, but the more I looked for them, the more I found. And it wasn't only that, it was the theatre, too. When I coughed, it always seemed to me that the echo of my coughing was not an echo at all, that it was the theatre coughing back at me. Sometimes I thought I could hear a donkey crying out, but in this I was right: it was not the ghost of poor Old Alice, but Mr. Leadham's other donkeys, which had been moved from the understage to the safety of a dressing room. One of the donkeys was lying on the bed, as if it were a person. Mr. Leadham's lanthorn was on a hook outside the door, the only door that was open.

"Who's thar agin?"

But I hurried on.

Once, when I had snuck off to rest in a water closet—one of the newer ones, with a chain and big metal tank above the porcelain bowl with the wooden seat—a beetle came under the door. I crushed it with my boot, but almost as soon as I did, I became aware of a dripping above me, a dripping that grew until it was actually raining inside that little room, much as it was outside. I fled the place and went back to the passageway I was supposed to be cleaning, yet soon enough it came again, a drop, a drop. And soon the rain. So I screamed out, and as I staggered down the corridor, God's truth, the rain, the damp patch above me, followed like my own personal weather. I was wet when I came home at last—but the rain did never follow me into Aunt Bleachy's. Bleachy dried me and I was washed and changed. I was getting stronger, Bleachy said, and then an order: I *must* get stronger.

A question: If the theatre's so rickety, why then do we live in it?

The answer: because it is our home.

To be frightened by the only place you can be—there must be many people, I supposed, like that.

In the days that followed, everywhere I went, I found sawdust on the floor. Always grains of it, never shavings. In the corners of rooms, in drifts on the stairs, on shelves and under chairs.

"Devil stuff," Bleachy said. "Used to use sawdust to soak up all the blood that spilled during a show. I was friends with sawdust then, but

I was also in command of it. And now, Edith, my own dear brush, did you know that the blood barrels have both grown quite solid? No more blood now. Hard as a rock, it is."

Now the sawdust, unchecked by blood, grew wild all around.

One morning, when I was supposed to be cleaning an empty dressing room, I found a message scrawled into the plaster, presumably by some bored actor: CATHY LONGLEGS. An insult of a colleague, perhaps. Going about my day, I happened to look out the window at the streets of Norwich. People hurrying by, busy with their lives. Come from the market, come from St. Stephen's, girls running to the Norwich School. Who are you all? How real you do seem! I stared deep into them: *Notice me, notice me.* Soon I became aware of people coming out of the theatre, people upon the very steps where I had had my accident. A huge, hunched figure going out and behind him a couple of tiny men, like a giant and two dwarves. Who were they? I'd never known them before. The giant turned around: it *was* a giant, the giant from "Jack and the Beanstalk," wearing an old mac and a flat cap. He turned around briefly and looked up at me, tipped his hat, and off he went, followed by the dwarves, disappearing into the gloom.

"Wait!" I called. "Come back!"

Others on the steps, then, too: a thin young man, a dark look about him, in patched working clothes, his face pinched and ill. I'd seen him before. *Hamlet!* Hamlet is leaving. Then three old men, huddled together, shivering and gabbing; one was blind, I saw, and another wore an old flower in his hair; it was the Fool and Gloucester and Kent, but done up as pensioners of the city of Norwich. And there were Falstaff and Justice Shallow sharing a hip flask between them; they looked like they might sell root vegetables in Norwich Market. A man with a red nose, burst with drink—that was Bardolph, surely. Then, finally, came Lady Macbeth herself, wearing a Norwich shawl. Oh, where are they all going?

Out of the theatre, all of them, and into Norwich.

I ran from the window then, to try and stop them, and soon I found people walking along the backstage corridors on their way out. I bumped into a fellow, looked up at the strange face. Oh, it was a troll!

"Mornin'," said the troll and shuffled on.

"Don't go!" I said.

And the figures kept coming. There were thin, awfully thin, young women, more like dolls really, but with hunches beneath their shawls; surely there were wings there, fairies being evicted. A great stream of them. Oh, all the parts are leaving, keep them in, keep them!

I ran back through the theatre, to the stage door. There I stood appalled as role after role went out into the drizzle: Oedipus in a sou'wester; Argan the hypochondriac, sneezing convincingly into his dirty handkerchief; the Pied Piper in patches, with a rat in his hands, feeding it a piece of cheese; Medea, smacking her lips as if she'd forgotten to put her teeth in. Last was Britannia. Her stockings had holes in them, and her dress was very greasy, I could see it beneath her long woolen cape. She was smoking a roll-up.

"Don't go!" I begged.

"Not wanted, Miss Edith," she gurgled. And then I knew it was Aunt Agatha Wilson I was seeing, after all. They were all our old actors, shuffling out onto the streets.

"You mustn't go," I called.

"Can't stay."

"No! Please!"

"We'll be back, when the theatre's open."

"Don't leave me."

And they did.

It cannot be a theatre with all the actors cleared out.

"Is Mrs. Margaret, hinttut?" murmured Mr. Peat. "She's having a clean-out, the pootrud mawther. When will there be an end on it?"

Out they went, all the actors, evicted from their dressing rooms. It was Margaret that had done it. No need to keep them on, she reasoned, not when we have no stage. Besides, she had said, it was not safe to keep so many in the theatre, it was adding danger to the building. Let them go, then, until all is repaired. In this way the actors were removed, until just the technical workers remained—a few carpenters, some lighting people, a handful from wardrobe. Mr. Mealing was kept, only because he had made himself agreeable. Beyond that were left only my true blood relatives.

Mr. Peat was nervous about it all.

"Who else?" he moaned. "She'll have the building empty, she's that stingy. Botty mawther."

Most of my fellow cleaners were let go. Margaret's bidding, Bleachy told me. "Something is surely wrong," Margaret had announced, "if a building's sole purpose is to be cleaned. Clean for what, for whom?"

Bleachy and I were left to our mops, left to our floors.

"We'll keep cleaning, shan't we, Edith?"

"Yes, Aunty," I said, for she looked so unhappy.

"Do you still have your clacker, Edith?"

I showed it to her on its red ribbon.

"Good, my bucket. Keep it to yourself, mind. They've been forbidden. You won't find one all over Norwich."

"But why, Aunty?"

"On account of them being insulting, it seems. A cruelty to the Utting legacy. A mocking toy. Utting's been to the courts over it for years, and they have ruled at last: No more Meg Pegs. They're dangerous, it's said, and boys are hurting one another with them. News to me, that was. So they're gone: in the toy shops one day, nowhere the next."

Empty corridors and rooms then, Edith lonely amid the desolation.

14.

Discoveries upon the grid.

The best plays have a change of scenery. They might go from a castle to a wood, for instance, or from a place on the low ground to a place high in the mountains, or a kingdom on the clouds, or else might go lower down, in a dark cave deep beneath the earth. Let us climb up and down, the theatre tells us, so that we may be taller and we may be deeper, that we may view the world from different angles. I needed a new perspective in those stale days, to get me out of myself, to feel a little different, to dust off Edith. I hid my mop and bucket at the bottom of a stairwell and set out.

The highest part of the theatre—excepting the roof, which I could no longer visit—is the grid. The grid is far above our heads, in what we call the fly tower—the home of all the windlasses and the drum and shafts and counterweights that are used to haul our worlds up and down. It is a dangerous, lofty place, the lid of the stage. If I could climb that mountain, what would Ben Nevis be to me?

It was an early summer's day when I left. As I stepped out, I felt it was far from certain that I would return, and yet, a little tight of breath, off I went.

I climbed up and up the first ladder, and came to a little galleyway where I could rest awhile. There were wooden passageways like balconies up there—bridges, they are called—where the stage people move their canvases like sailors. Indeed some of our stagehands were sailors in their time, from Lynn and Yarmouth and Lowestoft, and knew how to work the ropes. This land is called the loft, or the stagehouse, and it was stacked with scenes that lay still and neglected now, like my own card theatre in the second furnace. But even above this there is a higher where to climb. And so I ascended the mast of the theatre, higher and higher and ever higher, beyond the last bridge—the blackness a river of death beneath—until I was at the loading rail, which is the highest a scene may ascend within the theatre's throat. Here was the scenery stacked up.

And here I found among the backdrops something I had never even hoped for:

Scenes from my own play.

Here all along, proof of it.

"Edith Holler," I said, though my voice was dry.

Here upon canvas, pieces of me. I took off my cleaning bonnet and let it fall down and down into the darkness. Bleachy would scald me for it later, no doubt, but in that moment I didn't care. Here was Norwich, ancient Norwich, completed now. Behind it the interior of Maw Meg's hovel, and behind that a portion of King Gurgunt's deep chamber. All was here, wrapped in darkness. As if my own play had been calling me. And in that moment I loved it again. Look, Edith, at what you've done! Oh, what beauty.

If the play is still hanging here, I thought, perhaps there is still a chance for it.

I asked myself: You remember the play, don't you? Much of it, at least? Well then, why not write it down a second time? If I'd done it

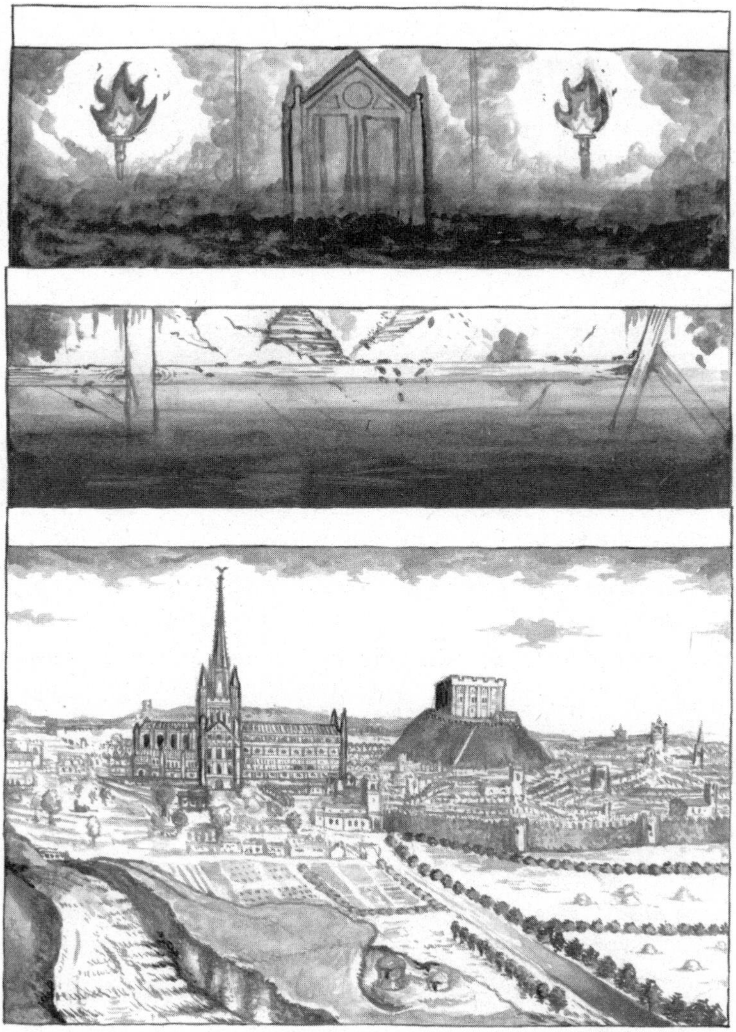

ABOVE: A stack of backdrops for a card theatre.

BELOW: A pair of wing supports for a theatre, right and left, to be glued to the proscenium arch at one end and the back wall at the other.

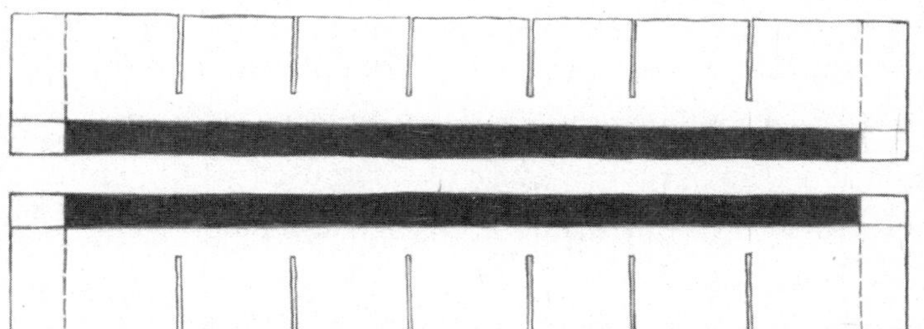

once, I could do it again. What a fool I was—of course I could. The play had been there all along, in grey Edith's grey brain. All I needed was to tip it out from the bony basin.

I reached out to stroke a little Norwich scene, and then it was time to finish my ascent. A little climb and at last I had reached heaven. I was up there with the stars, the grid itself, that most high of all places—the very limit of travel.

I crawled out across the thick slatted wood. It did bend in places where the wood was weak, and in parts it appeared rather worn, yet still I ventured out onto this great crow's nest, to look at all the wooden machinery that made the worlds seem different down below—the great drums and wheels that pull the rope and allow the world onstage to change. This was the very brains of the theatre. Here come and go all the different lands that give our plays their settings: the heavy backdrops, the side tabs, the castle, the mountains; all the cities of man. Here may you play puppet master with landscapes.

It is very busy at this level. I must step over the shafts and around the drums; I must be so very careful not to trip upon the ropes that stretch across the great space, as if a god had been playing cat's cradle here. There are holes everywhere in the grid, square holes between the ropes, where you may brave yourself to contemplate what gravity is. From that dizzy height I could look down and down to the stage—but no! To where the stage *used* to be, but was no longer, and now even deeper, all the way down into the secrets of the underground. The hole in the Holler Theatre seemed to lead to the very core of the earth, Hollow Theatre should be its name. And, just for a moment, I felt it calling for me to tumble, spinning and screaming, into its depth of death. But Edith did not.

I was not alone in that highness. Hidden by one of the windlasses, I came upon a little mound: a pile of scraps and cuts of material—worsted, it was. How I leaped to find it there! Another proof of a different sort. There was no ghost boy inside it, though I wondered if this was one of his sleeping places. Perhaps for years he had lain himself upon a worsted bed and looked down onto the stage, seeing from that seagull position all our entrances and exits. To think: if only I had looked up, I might have seen his tiny eyes looking down.

Yet this worsted was nailed into place here. Was this to punish it? To keep it safe? Or was it left here as scarecrow to keep trespassers away? To ward off ghosts? To keep Edith out? I did not like the nails, was the ghost pinioned underneath them? No, this was his private home, I felt sure. The nails were just to keep all in place. But why so many of them? That question I could not answer.

I took a piece for myself—certain confirmation of him.

As I lay there on the high wood, watching eternity, I sensed something down in the darkness. Something moving. I peered through the grid and there it was, deep in the black: creeping legs, hairy body, and all around it, thin films of thread. A monster! A huge, many-legged thing with a girl's head. Close your eyes and look again, poor disturbed Edith.

Ah, but no! It was no great monster in the broken hole of the stage depth, but only a spider, spidering away close at hand, just beneath the grid, no more than an inch in length. I laughed to recognize it, a spider, such little life. It threaded its way out of sight—but with its absence there came a knock.

The knock again.

You grow so bold.

Then, on the other side of the grid, quite at my eyeline, a beetle came trip-trapping, then two, then four and five of them. Again the sound: *knock, knock.* Not waiting for the dark, but in the daytime now. *Oh, the theatre,* I whispered, *I think the theatre will fall.* The grid itself seemed to me to shake a little. I scrambled for the edge; I tripped on some ropes and fell—not far, just a bit—and split my lip; but I knew I must go on, I must get off the grid before it falls.

Rung and rung, descending. Wrung and wrung, with a galloping horror. As if something were trying to pull me from the ladders. I looked up: a beetle crawling on the ropes just above. Come on now, Edith, move! On, on, slipping now and then, down I went, the scream for now kept inside. Then, at last, I was again on the rim of the stage, on the very edge of the fall.

And then: a *bang*!

And I nearly fell in.

A bang again!

I followed it straight, off the stage area and into the first of the dressing room corridors.

BANG!

There! There was the noise and there, in the same place, was Uncle Wilfred, with his hammer, sending a nail home. He had his back to me.

"Uncle Wilfred! Uncle Wilfred!"

Bang! went another nail. He was hammering a sign up. It said:

KEEP OUT

CONSTRUCTION SITE

NO ENTRY TO THE STAGE

"Oh it's you, Edith," said Wilfred. "Shouldn't you be cleaning?" He banged in another nail. "The building starts any day now. And they shan't use our carpenters. Utting's people only. Get it done proper."

"Uncle Wilfred, the beetles are eating the theatre. It'll all be dust!"

"Edith, we know. The builders will put it right."

"Then I am not to blame."

"It seems not."

"And yet I've had no apologies, Uncle. Not a word."

"Who's left to apologize?"

"Father must know then that I didn't do it."

"Edith, these are hard times for everyone. But it shall be made right again."

"The builders must come quickly, Uncle. At once! Or it shall be too late."

"Any day now, it's certain. And so you must tread no more front of house, Edith."

"Just once more, Uncle, whilst I still may."

"One last time then, my dear niece, until the stage is done."

15.

I am come to play; Mealing writes a play.

The beetles' knocks that I heard upon the grid, so loud in the daytime, had little echoes that lived on after the initial sounding. Those echoes, the children of that dreadful noise, danced all about the backstage, bounced along the corridors, whispered in the empty dressing rooms and the empty greenroom, in the wardrobe, in the puppet mistress's room. In they went, those trespassing echoes, darting before they died—mayfly noise that they were—inside the heads of all the remaining people of the theatre. To most of us, the knock and its echo offspring caused little more than a sudden intake of breath, or a pang in the heart, or a twitch in the bowels, or a flare of acid in the gut, before all was forgot and dullness came back upon them. And yet, in some heads and bodies, the echoes nudged and bothered and caused them to stand up and to speak out.

Knock it went upon Margaret.

Knock it went upon Agnesia.

Knock it went upon Mealy.

• • •

When all imagination was shut up, and all fanciful things were covered by sheets and tarpaulins, when all players had been dismissed and there was no story to be found inside the entire building, then truly were we in the thick, treacly days of Beetle Spread. Then truly did the deathwatch beetles command the theatre.

And in that dark age Mr. Mealing, who spread dullness everywhere, felt quite at home with the world. In the instant of those specters of beetle knocks, something seized that undramatic man, something dark and misshapen, a strange little ugly thought, and he began to knock a little himself. That knocking was the knocking of Mr. Mealing's unimaginative heart, as it set up shop in his left ventricle, and there it grew. It echoed within him until at last he found himself at the door of Father's apartment. He saw the daughter Agnesia step out, and he stepped in, knocking as he did upon the open door. Margaret, seated and studying the designs for the rebuilt theatre, gave him permission to enter. "Ah, Mr. Mealing, ah, *Oliver*, how good to see you."

"Dear Mrs.," and here I break off a moment to say that Mealing pronounces Mrs. as *Meeesiss*—a little direction for anyone who happens to find themselves playing the role of Mealing—"Dear Mrs. Holler, dear, dear Mrs. Holler. Fine lady." The Mealing pump was pumping harder, something new stirring inside the oily little man. "I found myself, of a sudden, compelled to approach your person."

"And you are most welcome."

"Is there anything I can do for you, anything at all? To ease your entrance into this theatre life?"

"Well now, that is kind, I must say. And actually I have been thinking, Oliver. You are: Oliver, a playwright. Is it not so?"

"I do count myself a bit of a scribbler indeed. I have penned, oh, a few dozen monologues and three whole plays, all of them set in the drawing rooms of fine London houses. Perhaps you may care to read . . ."

"No, Oliver, no indeed. I don't. You, Oliver, may care to write—"

"Yes?"

"—a *new* play, Oliver."

"A new play?"

"For me. For the theatre. To save it. I have this wonderful notion, for our future. It will be a great work, Oliver. It will be the play you were born to write."

"Oh!"

"*O* for Oliver, indeed! And let me tell you of the play's subject."

Then followed some words which were so quietly laid out that they were impossible to hear, and indeed they were further obscured by the short gentleman's ejaculations of the first letter of his first name, sent out like smoke rings—no doubt in part thanks to the unaccustomed proximity of a large and breathing woman. In the end, it seemed that sufficient information had fallen out of Margaret and into Mealing, for Mealing to grin, nod vigorously, and retreat from the apartment.

This is conjecture, for I was not there. But I pieced it together later.

Fighting that beetle noise, I went all about the back stage gathering wonders, and then to my little room with the plate glass window to perform, for Norwich, one last time while I may: the dumb show before the great performance. (This is a practice done in older times, a show of the upcoming play performed solely through silent gestures.) So now did Edith, while yet she might, reveal to Norwich: THE TRUE HISTORY OF MAWTHER MEG.

That afternoon, before all was forbidden me—with no time for rehearsing but with gathered props and clever business here and there—all was quickly ready. I pulled the cord to open the curtain. Now may Norwich see me well. See what? A strange old woman in dirty garments (me, thanks to Nora) and before her a great cauldron (a large pot for a plant, dragged over from the foyer). I stirred the pot with a great spoon (a broom handle), and as I banged my head against the pot, I looked up through the window and saw a child standing there watching, eating a pork pie. Then another young fellow came to join him, and next their mother probably, and then an older couple out for a stroll, and an office worker shirking off and some wanderers from the market. And so it went on, Norwich people come across the road to look. As they pointed at me and nodded, on and on I mimed, stirring and stirring my cauldron, making large dramatic poses, my eyes as big as saucers. Then I looked, as if in great alarm, and pointed here and there, and from my pocket I showered dead beetles (from a bucket of Bleachy's). So now they knew it was the Mawther Meg story—a story often told, one that they all were familiar with—but then the twist: From behind the pot I pulled up a doll of a child (a prop we used for Young Macduff's body) and I dropped it in the pot and stirred with glee, putting my hand to my stomach and letting out a silent cackle. Now the Norwich people stared! Most confused, they were, but hooked. Then another doll of a child (one we used for a prince in the Tower from *Richard III*), and another (the other prince), all of them in the pot. Then, one final child (this was the Boy from *Henry V*, murdered by the French at Agincourt). With a nod to the boy with the pork pie, to ensure that he paid particular attention, I put the child doll to my mouth, and employing an old bit of sleight of hand, I seemed to bite its head off.

The boy in the window dropped his pork pie.

Then I ripped open the doll's canvas chest, and out poured a flow of blood—red rags and red ribbons—and these I mimed eating all withal.

And I saw, then, Norwich silently screaming.

Oh, I did have them, the people of Norwich, Norfolk! Yet then,

"What are you doing?" someone in my room. Agnesia stood there.

"You cannot come in," I whispered, my mouth covered. "I'm doing my play."

"It's disgusting."

"Go away."

"I've been sent to get you. Mother wants you, you're to come back to the apartment."

I wrapped the doll in my own Maw Meg clothing, and followed Agnesia up the old familiar staircase.

"Careful!" said Agnesia. "No running on the stairs, Mama said so."

Along the way I saw a new sign: NO MORE THAN TWO AT A TIME UPON THESE STAIRS.

On the way up we passed Mealing on his way down. He looked most content, I noted. Turning toward me with a frown, he spoke with a strange significance:

"Edith indeed! A tragedy!"

And hurried along.

"You're breaking the rules, Edith," said Agnesia. "We are three on the stairs!"

He went down and I went up. The door was open. So then must the heart be too.

"Father! Father, I have come home!"

No. Nothing. Only Margaret. And Uncle Jerome, I should add, and two official-looking people I did not recognize. And a policeman, for some reason, standing at the door. Whatever for? It is not like us to have policemen in the theatre. The murders we have upon the stage, you know, are all pretend.

"Father?"

"Hullo, dear Edith," said Margaret. "How lovely. How are you? What have you been doing?"

"Father?" I called. "Father, I am here!"

"Your father is elsewhere, child. But, Edith, why were people peering through your window?"

"Hello, Uncle Jerome."

"Hello, Edith," said Jerome, nervously, "it is good to see you."

"You have not forgotten me, then?"

"No, certainly, indeed not." Very red was Jerome.

"If not for Father, why then have I been sent for?"

"Can we not be friendly? Are you unhappy to see us, your own family? Indeed, we have not spoken since we had our talk upon the steps, and how I have missed you."

"I have found the backdrops, Uncle Jerome. I have not forgotten my play."

"I know of no backdrops," said Margaret.

"I have great hopes for it still."

"Give them up, Edith dear. You know you must."

"No, of course not! I shall write it out again."

"Write what, child?"

"My play, of course! I shall put it on paper once more."

"Edith, I thought the matter settled. Edith, we have no stage."

"We will again."

"Thanks to my involvement."

"Indeed! We are so grateful! A new stage, and soon. We all, I'm sure, thank you!"

"It is noted, my dear, that your manners are improving. And also you have been cleaning for us and this progress must be rewarded, and so, of an afternoon or morning when you are called for, you may come again unto these rooms and then you shall, in keeping with a child your age, play with your sister."

"To play?"

"With your sister."

"Yes, madam."

"You may say, Edith: yes, Mother."

But I could not.

"Yes, madam."

"Not ready yet? I do appreciate your honesty, Edith. One day, let us hope, you shall think of me as your mother."

"Thank you, madam. Thank you for repairing the theatre."

"That is lovingly said, Edith, and I bless you for it. We are friends again."

I was sent to my sister and down below the iron descended and the theatre was cut in two.

The room where I'd lived was no longer Edith's. No evidence of her there. All I knew had been removed. Gone, too, were my belongings, my wallpaper, my carpet. You would not know it was a place formerly called Edith's room at all; only the shape of the room was the same. It was like the stage, I thought; it could change its personality utterly, it could become a different scene from a wholly different play. Did it remember the girl who used to live here?

"This was my room," I said. "Though you would not know it."

"Does it not look well?

"Even Leadenhall Street. It's very wrong, I'm sure of it."

"What's the mutter?"

"My typewriter."

"It broke."

"I shall write my play out longhand, I don't mind. I have neat writing."

"Did you have any other toys, Edith?"

"No," I said, "there is nothing else."

"I heard about toy theatres."

"No," I said.

"Well, then, we are to play together. Mother says so. I offered you this once before, however, and you turned me down. So now we shall have to be more discerning. I shall audition you."

"You audition me?"

"That's it. What shall you do then? Will you dance for me?"

"No," I said.

"Will you sing for me then?"

"No," I said.

"Will you clown for me?"

"No," I said.

"What will you do? How will you show yourself, how entertain the heir of the Utting fortune? Come now, I am looking for quality."

"Nothing," I stammered.

"Ah!" cried Agnesia, clapping her plump hands together. "I have it! If you do nothing, then *I* shall do something. You're my doll, aren't you? Yes, that's it. I have seen a poor boy once, one of the factory workers, and he kept his best toy in his pocket. And do you know what his toy was? I'll tell thee, 'twas a rat! He had a *living* toy. What a notion! And how he loved it. It was truly an impressive thing to see: that boy and that rat. I told on him, of course—you cannot have a rat upon a factory floor—and he was sent up to Mother's office. Whatever happened to him afterward, I cannot say, for I never saw him more."

She continued. "So now I have a doll of my own, but a very drab one to be sure. I must color her up. In dress, in makeup. I'll change her now!"

"What are you doing?" I cried.

"A doll, you know, cannot talk. Not a word from you, doll. Not until five of the clock. Then you may go down again, and I shall have my dinner."

And she let out the loud and exaggerated laugh of a stage villain.

Agnesia was in fact mostly gentle with me. She never stripped me of my own shabby gown, only added bright garments over it. My hair was brushed, tenderly even. Makeup was added to my face. It was even, at times, pleasant. She showed me great affection and sometimes held me close and rocked me back and forth. She was, in her particular way, sisterly.

In those strange days, it seemed, only Agnesia was allowed to fashion stories. The knock had made her a little storyteller, and she found little doll histories and tragedies where all the rest of my family, drooping about the knocking theatre, found only sleep. At first I was only her silent doll, but soon I was a crowd of others:

If she glued a beard upon my chin and put a crown upon my head, I may be king.

If she gave me an eye patch and a cutlass, I was pirate.

If she gave me epaulets and a rifle, I soldiered.

If she gave me whiskers and a tail, I catted for her.

If she gave me a doll much smaller than myself, I gianted.

I took on so many roles, stood in such different fashions, and let the costumes guide me. Agnesia let me speak then, and so intense was our play that I felt, truly felt, I had left myself behind. I was everyone then—everyone but Edith. I would wake in the morning with Aunty Bleachy and wonder: Who shall I be today? I traveled so far without ever leaving the theatre. I had so many fresh dramas that I quite forgot about writing down my play.

"Oh, you are wonderful!" cried Agnesia.

She was often very close to me and would demand that we held each other tight.

"What does it feel like, to be Edith, Edith?"

What could I say to that? "It comes to me naturally."

"May I wear your old smock? I'd like that very much. Please, oh please!"

I let her, and soon was down to my underclothes.

"What is the red ribbon around your neck?"

"Nothing—a gift from my Aunt Bleachy."

"Oh, I don't like her, let's not think of her, not now that I'm Edith Holler!" she cried. And she clung to the role for the rest of the afternoon. She tried very hard to be me, and I aided her to better her performance. In a way, there were two Ediths then.

"Well done," I said. "That's very like!"

"I am learning what it is to be a girl, to be an Edith. Do I convince?"

"I would swear," I lied, "that you are the legitimate and I the mere doll."

"I feel it so. I do! I am Edith herself! I've quite taken over!"

She did go on, rather.

As the playing continued, elsewhere Oliver Mealing dabbed a little rouge onto his cheeks and said, "I am come into my own." Up in his little room he sat, knocking away at his typewriter—and under his hand a play began to form. At first a germ, a little smudge in the darkness, but Mr. Mealing fed it with ink and little by little the dreadful thing grew. Bit by bit the smudge increased to the size of a flea and then a fly, then of a bat and then a rat, next of cat proportions was it, and shortly after swine-sized, and then it was a great black bitch dog, like old Shuck itself. By then the knocking had grown so loud that Mealing could control it no longer.

Now the play controlled Mealing and not he it. Not only did the play drink up all the ink and demand ever more, it even began to eat away at Mealing himself. In his days of inspiration, out of daylight, the playwright grew thinner and paler and weaker, and soon there was less of Mealing than there had been before. The more play there was, the less Mealing. He smalled himself, gave himself over to the great black play, which grew finally to the size of an elephant, a dark and oily elephant.

And then at last, marking a new stage to that time of playing and playwriting, came the builders. With them came much disturbance and you could no longer hear the knocking anymore, instead all was:

Boom!

Boom!

Boom!

16.

Quarter House, Theatre Street.

They never spoke to anyone from the theatre, the builders didn't. Not even Mr. Peat, who let them in and out every day. We had long been yearning for them, yet when they came, there was no communication between us few remaining and the builders. I stood by the stage door to watch their arrival.

"They are here to get their work done," Margaret said, "not to talk to you."

They were Utting's people, the builders, not theatre people. It was like we were two different species and had no understanding each of the other. They barged right through and would not shake hands when Uncle Wilfred offered his. It felt as if we had been invaded, as if some foreign army had come to take the theatre by force.

They had arrived at last to fix our stage, but we could not cheer them.

We never saw them in their work. We were strictly forbidden to enter the building site. We only observed a great supply of steel—girders and winches and great metal sheets and so many metal pipes. We had always been a wooden and stone people before; how it hurt, this growing into metal, this becoming modern.

Once the iron was down, I was stuck on the stage side. I could no longer get to front of house, that luxury place full of light and red, nor to my little room in the front, with my doll dressed as Maw Meg. Instead I must stay stageside, in that darkest of places.

Our address was Half House, Theatre Street, Norwich. Yet now, it seemed, we had only half of half the house because the stage was forbidden us. Quarter House, Theatre Street.

All about the theatre in those terrible months was the sound of drilling and hammering. Clanking and tolling of metal upon metal, a clamorous shrieking that would go on for so long—minutes on end, sometimes an hour—before letting off. Great new holes were being made in the roof to make way for new chimneys so that finally the theatre, which according to Margaret was desperately drafty, might be comfortable for the people of Norwich. But how this transformation hurt the poor building.

Those noises were with us so persistently, from the moment the builders arrived until they left in the evening, that we unhappy few remaining residents felt that we ourselves were being drilled into, hammered upon, cruelly smacked about; as if our own bodies were undergoing a terrible metamorphosis. How my bones ached! Aunt Bleachy told me, in our white pocket of communication, that my pain was surely growing pains, that I was becoming a more adult Edith; they were the feelings of my young ivory frame morphing into a different creature. I wondered what sort of creature I was shifting into, with such new hair about me. And what also were these red welts about my arms and legs and forehead? As if nails were being driven into me? Mosquito bites surely, said Bleachy, or the spots that young people get on the road to adulthood. Yet why, I wondered, were there small teeth marks upon my skin? They would be far less red if you never scratched them, Bleachy told me as she bathed my wounds. My chest and head and bones hurt. I lost weight. Aunt Jenny was no longer around to offer her strange medicine, I missed it now, I believed in it.

At length, Dr. Cottes came back. He put the stethoscope to my chest. Around us, the builders boomed on.

"I hear nothing," said the doctor. "There's too much racket." He seemed very nervous and unhappy. He tried again; again the theatre roared. "No nothing, no sound. No sound at all."

A great hammering.

"Is this Edith herself?" the doctor wondered. "Or the doll?"

"Do make sense, Doctor," said Bleachy.

"Indeed, I've never heard her talk, never once."

He looked me over.

"Edith, you are even now growing into a woman."

But it hurts, I thought.

"How can I help her?

"It is impossible to think in this clamor."

"What can be done?"

"Rest and fresh air. And silence. Indeed, I must leave you. Call me again when this building is not at war with itself."

I lay still and imagined myself upon my deathbed, the theatre all evacuated, no body left but me. And in this vision, at the very moment my chest sunk for the last time, at the end of my final breath, so died the theatre, all fallen in on itself. We were gone together in an instant. What a cloud we'd make all over Norwich.

After the builders came, the playing with Agnesia would not come right. I was still shut in with her, but in my unhappy state, no costume she pillaged from the wardrobe ever sat correctly on my person. I could no longer feel the part, not with all the noises shaking the furniture and our souls. Our game playing turned unhappy and tense. Agnesia would shove me, or leave me standing in a corner, and there I would remain until she was called away for tea. Sometimes, in my fear, when she was just outside the periphery of my vision, I fancied that her face had turned strange and ugly, that it had shifted into a different state, or that her whole head had turned three hundred and sixty degrees. Yet when I turned back to her it was only Agnesia there, a girl very nearly my own age.

My ill humor did not escape her. "You used to be fun!" she cried.

And sometimes this sister turned spiteful. One day she put me in her toy trunk, with all her dolls, and sat upon it, and she would not let me out.

It was best then to think myself somewhere else, to picture myself not inside with this new sister but anywhere else that Karl knew about. But holding on to the idea was almost impossible, for no matter how hard I tried, some great hammering would come along and ruin everything and I would be back to myself and my aching head, with Agnesia nearby prodding and goading me. Sometimes she even told me her secrets, as children are wont to do with their dolls. Up until last spring, she confessed to me, she had been a pupil at the Norwich School for Girls, but she had been expelled on account of starting a little fire by accident in a lumber room.

I remembered this well because I had been on our roof during that incident and saw the smoke. "But, Agnesia," I asked, "did you set light to Miss Tebby's room?"

"Shush, Edith, I'm telling you my secrets."

She told me that she was in love with a handsome man of Norwich, so graceful and well dressed, such a warm gentleman. So she said. I did not believe a word of it. Then she leaned forward and kissed me on the lips, her eyes closed, her face so close to mine that I could see all the little hairs upon it.

"There then, kiss back."

I did.

"We kiss like this, like this."

And so we kissed.

"Let us pretend we are me and him," she said. And then we lay together and stroked our bodies, and were very somber about it, and our breathing was uneven, and she smelled so like an animal. And this was a brand-new falling—or was it a flying after all?—but she stopped suddenly and her back went rigid and she pushed me from the bed.

"That's enough. It's so you'll know how it is, at least once in your life. The kissing business, poor doomed thing."

And she laughed at me, at my sadness.

One time, Agnesia held me by the window while she tried to train a focused beam of light onto me with her magnifying glass.

"Now tell me, you must tell me, how it feels to be on fire. Keep still."

The sun, briefly, came out. A bright circle of light on my arm.

"Is it wonderful to be so burned? To actually feel something!"

"It hurts, let us stop now."

"How does it feel, dull Edith, do tell?"

"It is wrong to do it, Agnesia. I know it is."

"But I like it."

"But it hurts!"

"Yes!"

Our time together was running out. One afternoon—it would prove the last day of my playing upstairs—I was dressed as Joan of Arc—here I am, Mother, playing your part—when a beetle happened to crawl out from under the bed. Without thinking, I crushed it with my boot. What silence and shock upon my sister's face! Pushing me aside, she knelt down and, with considerable care, prized the corpse from the carpet.

"Why did you do that? The baby!"

She lingered over the tiny wreck as if were the remains of a beloved pet.

"Very dead," she whispered. "Most over with."

Then she looked back up at me and there was some slapping and many how-could-yous and I was turfed early from the room. I was not to come back again. It was summer then, and that is ever our quiet season. No one goes to the theatre then. The days are long and stale. It is the worst season of the year.

My sister was taken out of the city, traveling vast distances so that her toes and legs, knees and thighs, ribs and tummy, arms and elbows and shoulders and neck and hair might drape upon the sea. To faraway Cromer she went, to dine on dressed crab and jellied eels and whelks bought in paper cones and her noises were all of barrel organs and the hush-hushing of the salty wet, but most of all to her pleasure were the fireworks on the pier.

It was some Utting secretary who took her away, however. Margaret stayed behind, Margareting everywhere. She did ask if I would accompany Agnesia; the trip would do me such good, she claimed. But how could I? I belonged to the theatre.

And so, staying there, I witnessed them together: Margaret and the building. And whenever I was alone, I escaped to the second furnace, where on the backs of old bill posters I began at last to write—that is, write again—my *True History of Mawther Meg.*

17.

Margaret certain.

Margaret was everywhere backstage then, in and out of rooms, wondering aloud whether there were still too many of us altogether. The building could not take it, she insisted. Blind Mr. Leadham was dismissed. On the morning of his eviction, he'd awakened to find his donkeys gone and no one could tell him where. We never did discover who took them. I watched him tap his way down Theatre Street. How strange to see him without his donkeys; he didn't look complete. After Mr. Leadham left, the only evidence of him or his creatures was the lanthorn that remained outside their old room.

In the cramped stage door office, I saw Mr. Peat, he who was always gruff and full of Norfolk confidence, looking petrified.

"Tell me," asked Margaret, "did you not, at one time, work for Utting's?"

"I sought new employment and won it here."

"Mr. Peat, you are old, you are frail."

"Missus?"

"You need rest, you need to take things easily."

"I shall not go! Mr. Jerome, Mr. Wilfred! She means to dismiss me!" He ran to my uncles. "I am suffun savidge, Mr. Hollers. I am east angrier!"

My uncles were horrified on his behalf. They went in search of Margaret.

"On what authority?" they asked.

"Why, dear brothers, am I not here to rescue the theatre? It is, I recall, close to bankruptcy. There are no new monies coming in, only a considerable amount going out. The theatre is closed—it is dark, as you fellows call it—so then how can we keep employing so vast a number? To save the theatre, we must make sacrifices. If we do not look about us and find savings, if we do not seal up the gaps in our leaking pockets, why then I am very much afraid the theatre shall cease altogether."

"Truly, it is as bad as all that?"

"Worse, brothers, worse."

And so poor Mr. Peat was let go. He stood just beyond the stage door, out on the street, and let out as many curses as he could find inside him; they were several indeed, and he went on a good while, but he could not be heard because the door was shut and bolted upon him. Even so, he ranted until Margaret called the police and they took him roughly away down Theatre Street.

And so Master Cree became *Mr.* Cree, and sat in his office as if he were the manager of Norwich Union Fire and Life Insurance, and whenever he saw Margaret he purred like a kittycat.

After Mr. Peat had been shuffled off, and Margaret had won the backing of my uncles, then came the last stage of her great purging: the remaining wardrobe staff was let go. Flora Bignell screamed at Margaret until she was carried out by force. She claimed she was loath to do it, but that she was willing to be unpopular if it saved the theatre. By then, Margaret had enlisted the local constabulary to stand guard at the theatre and to come inside whenever they pleased. She showed them around as if the place were hers. And when she was ready to let people go, she had a policeman nearby to lend a little weight to her argument.

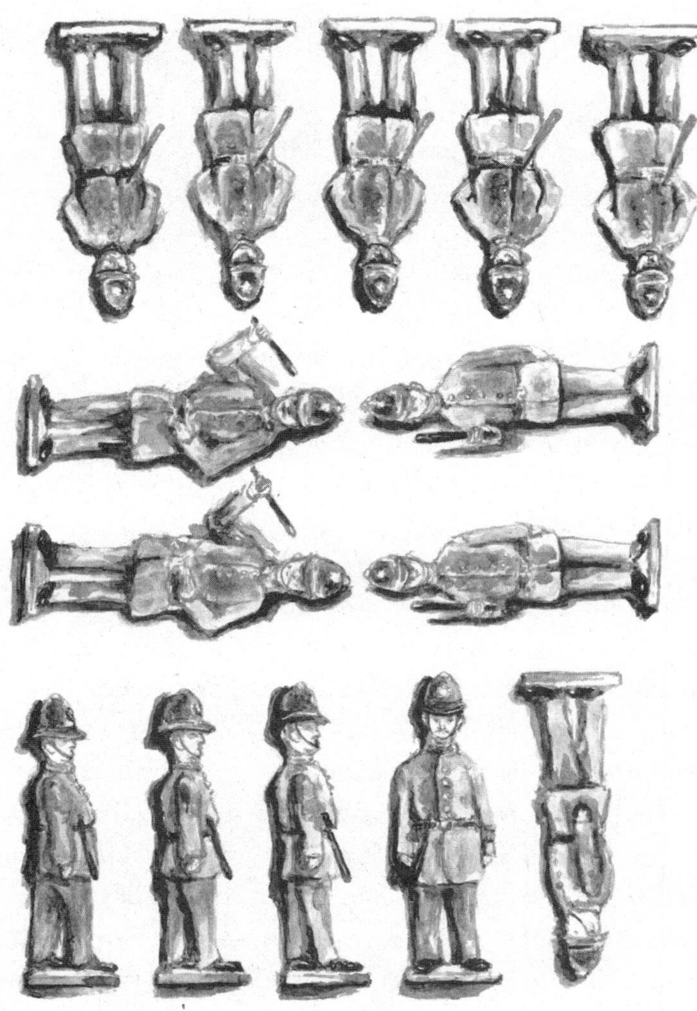

One night, as I lay in bed staring out of Bleachy's window, I saw a familiar figure, tall and thin, rushing along Chantry Road.

"It's Mr. Jet! It's Mr. Jet!"

Bleachy, out of bed, came and opened the window wide.

"Who's there? Show yourself!"

There was a rustle in the trees, the noise of some rubbish blowing about the street.

"It is nonsense, Edith," she said. "Don't give in to it."

"I saw him!"

"Is only the wind."

And was it the wind? How can it have been the wind if the very next day terrible news came into the theatre in the form of the *Eastern Daily Press*, which Bleachy gave to me. NORFOLK AND NORWICH SUBSCRIPTION LIBRARY BURNED TO THE GROUND. All the history lost, all the beautiful books, all the words, all the stories of Norwich.

It was from the library that I first came upon the names of the missing children.

Who would believe me now?

"They've burned Norwich," I said.

"Only the library, my dirt."

In those dark days, it was impossible to see properly. All was foggy and strange. The light in the theatre was all wrong, it played tricks on you, and there were odd meteorological happenings within our walls, as the builders raised their clouds of dust and dirt. Walking down a corridor, you suddenly found yourself beaten by a tempest. One time, as I was about my mop and bucket, I found more scratches on the wall—AN COAL GATE and further on CLOTH and BLOOD PERCY. As I was bathing the poor building, I saw down the corridor—at least I thought I saw—one of Uncle Wilfred's stagehands who should have gone by now, the young man called Hawthorne. Suddenly there came a darkness about him, and I lost sight, and then a strange red cloud surrounded him—a sort of eruption, like you may catch sometimes at sun's rise or set, a brief red sun—and then it was gone again. When I reached the place where Hawthorne was, it was all Hawthorneless. There was nothing but the red again upon the floor, a quantity of it, flowing down the corridor as if it were in a hurry.

The light in those days. It played such tricks with you.

Miss Tebby, too, was among the losses.

"Good-bye," Margaret said. "You kept so quiet, I nearly missed you."

"I am the prompt," she insisted.

"But the theatre is dark," said Margaret. "To whom are you giving service?"

"I know all the plays."

"Then you must be able to entertain yourself wonderfully well."

"Where is Edgar Holler?" cried Miss Tebby, for the single occasion in her life raising her voice. "Can he let this happen? Dare he show his face? Where do you hide, Edgar Holler? Are you too ashamed to bid farewell to the woman who fed you your Shakespeare?"

"Put her out, Mr. Cree."

And Mr. Cree did, he forced the little woman down the steps and into the street. That walking library of dramas and dreams, who could in a split moment direct you to any scene of any act of any play, went forth onto the limited stage of the streets of Norwich.

I knew then that, if Father did not come when Miss Tebby called, he must be chased out at last. I had the sudden revelation that he must be in the Mourning Room all this time and cursed myself for not having thought of it sooner. Fully determined to break the door and haul him out, I ran up the stairs. *Here he is! Here he is! All will be well now!*

But the Mourning Room door was wide open and all was empty inside, save a painter in overalls with a wide brush.

"What's happening?"

"Is painting."

"I see that, but why? Where has everything gone?"

"Is only painting, slow you down."

She meant to blot Father out, to remove all Father from the theatre. Footsteps on the stairs, the weary ascent of my uncle Jerome.

"Where is Father?"

"Ah, Edith, hello to you."

"Where is my father? He is your own brother, you know!"

"I do not think he is very well. He is being looked after by Margaret."

"Is Father dying?"

"No, no, I'm sure nothing like that. I am told he is very tired and must rest. When the stage is finished, and when the theatre opens up again, no doubt his recovery shall be swift."

I sought out my remaining family.

"Have you seen Father, Uncle Wilfred?"

"Not personally."

I came upon Uncle Thomas, listless in the greenroom.

"Have you seen Father?"

"Not for a while. It is Margaret who sees to him. A wonderful woman. Where would we be without her? And where has Gregory gone to, that's what I'd like to know."

"Aunt Bleachy," I asked, "have you seen Father?"

"No, Edith, my bucket, we never speak, your father and I."

"I think he must be in trouble."

"He could generally take care of himself. It was, as I recall, his principal concern."

"I would so like to see him."

"Well, don't worry me about it. I've found an enormous puddle, bigger than all the others, and no one knows where it came from. Blessing is, there's so much sawdust to soak it up with. Go along Edith, my own basin, I'll see you later. Something is quite wrong with the building. I've half a mind to quit it myself. I surely would, if it wasn't for you."

"But Aunty, I must find Father!"

She slowed then and turned to me, and a misery blossomed on her face.

"Do you know what I think, my only bucket?"

"What, Aunty, do say?"

"I think he must have gone across the road."

"No, Aunty. Don't say that."

"Where is he, then?"

"I'll find him."

So then I must do the thing myself. I went up to the private region of my former home to the new mother that lived there. A timid knock.

"Enter," said Margaret.

18.

Some beetles.

Enter," said Margaret.

I did. There were shoes lined up against one wall, a tidy row. Her shoes all of them, ladies' boots. All in the same style, but some larger than others.

"Who?" her noise.

"Edith," I said.

"No, not welcome, Edith," she called from the dining room. "I am even now about my luncheon. Run along, my darling."

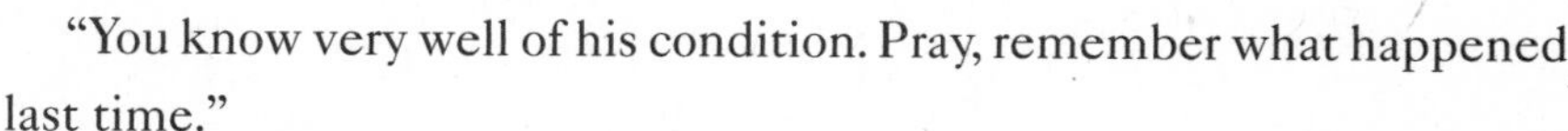

"I wish to see Father."

"You know very well of his condition. Pray, remember what happened last time."

"Even so, I must see him."

"Go down, child, do learn your place."

But I would not leave, not when I was so close.

"Good-bye then, madam."

"Good-bye, Edith Holler."

I closed the door but remained inside. I heard Margaret in the dining room, quietly slurping, her spoon against the bowl. I proceeded carefully toward Father's bedroom, even turned the handle. The handle silently obeyed, but the door as I opened it purred a little, and a few yards away, in the dining room, the slurping stopped. All was silent. I stayed still. At last the noise of spoon on bowl returned, and I crept into the bedroom, closing the door behind me.

It was very dark inside, but there was no doubting the great oblong of Father's bed.

"Father," I whispered, stepping toward the bed. "Father, are you there? It's Edith. Father, it was the beetles that ate the stage, it was never me. Father, here I am opening the curtains—so!"

Father was there, sitting up, resting on many pillows. I could just see the shape of him.

"Hello, Father!" I called in wonder. "I am right glad to see you at last. How are you faring? Why have you not come down to see me? I have been very ill, did they tell you? Perhaps you came when I was sleeping. And you have been ill, dear Father. No one's seen you these many weeks. It's not like you to be so shy, indeed it is not!" I paused; heard silence; continued. "I have found the backdrops in the fly tower, Father—oh, they are so beautiful! We will put my play on, won't we, Father, when the stage is back again? But what have you been doing all this time sat up in bed? It must be very trying. Have you been learning a new part? I'm not supposed to be here, that's why I'm whispering. We should whisper, I think—don't let out your great booming voice. Well, here I am again and there are you at last. A family reunion. My darling papa! I forgive you everything now that I see you again. But how are you, Father? Will you not speak?"

Silence again.

"No words for me, none at all after all this time?"

No. None.

"It is very cruel of you, Father, it is indeed."

It was.

"I love you, Father. Please speak to me."

He did not.

"Father, I won't have it," I said. "It's not right. I'm going to light this candle here so that you may see me plainly, your only Edith child, and I may see you, my father."

There were matches beside the candle. The little flame grew as it caught the wick, and the room, like the stage, was illuminated and there was a daughter and her papa.

How pale he was. His skin so shiny.

"Father!"

So cold to the touch.

"Father, you are not dead, are you?"

Not only not dead—I knew it then—but never alive. The eyes, I suppose, were glass. The hair was surely horse. The mouth, I think, had stitches in it. The father was false. It was the dummy of him we used when we played *Coriolanus*. Father is switched for that dummy at the last moment, so that the audience may gasp to see the knives truly going in, and in the cavity of the dummy was so much stage blood that did spurt out. It was magnificent; it always made me scream. Come now, this was that dummy, wasn't it?

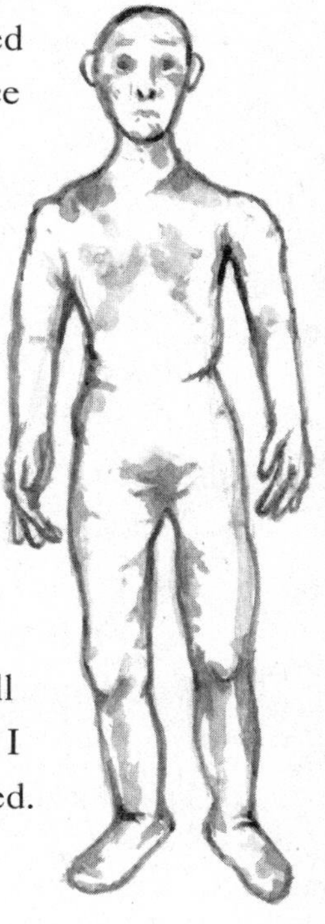

It looked like Father, but then so did the dummy.

"You're not Father," I said. "You can't fool me."

And then the doll's jaw dropped open. And from out of the mouth something shifted. Something small and black. It dropped out of the mouth and fell onto the counterpane. I stood up, stepped back. But the beetle, for such it was, came on. I withdrew further. Still the beetle followed. I reached Father's dressing table, I got up on the chair that stood before it. The beetle stopped.

It put its head to the ground, it banged its head upon the floorboard, making a small tapping, and as it tapped, there came another beetle, and shortly after a third. They went straight to the original and likewise began to rap their heads, the noise amplified now.

I looked back at the dummy, whose mouth was even wider open now. More beetles were spilling from it, rushing to join the others beneath the chair.

It was not a quiet tap, then.

Between the taps, I heard a spoon dropped into a bowl, a chair pushed back—and footsteps, her footsteps, coming my way. She had been summoned, Margaret had, by the beetles. But then another sound, a different tap, a hurried knock in fact—on the apartment door. Margaret changed her course. The apartment door was opened.

"Yes, what is it? Am I to have no peace?"

"It is I, Nora, from the wardrobe."

"Yes, I see that. And no, again, I have not seen your husband. You must take responsibility for your own spouse."

"It is not Gregory I am here about."

"Then what is the matter?"

Nora's voice was thin but steely, very like a needle. "Overalls is the matter. Working suits is the matter. It's bad enough that I must struggle alone, but these hands here are accustomed to making clothes for kings, for heroes and for villains. I may sew fairy wings if I am asked, I do patchwork peasants, that I own, I do clowns, too, gaberdines and gauntlets, I trouble myself with doublets, with corsets and crinoline. But never once with overalls. And such a number at that."

"Nora, if you'll but listen . . ."

As I stood upon a chair in Father's bedroom, hearing Nora plead her case, I watched beetles pouring from the dummy—so many, indeed, that the dummy seemed to lurch forward, even to move in spasms, as if it were alive. Its arms began to lift, too, as if they were reaching out to me, until I realized that those white arms had begun to bulge at the seams. The arms pulsed horribly, until finally the seams split and out fell beetle after beetle, and the empty arm collapsed lifeless onto the bed. The new beetles, hundreds of them, dropped to the ground and joined the others tapping their heads upon the floor, so that now their sound became a very definite knocking, as if of a small child or a feeble adult, trying to catch attention by rapping upon a door. She is sure to hear it, I thought, and any moment.

". . . these working clothes are not what you think of them."

"I can tell you what I think of them."

And with that the dummy's belly tore open and a great black cloud of beetles burst out, covering the bed and deflating the dummy entirely, until it was just an agonized head. Beetles everywhere, beneath me, amassing under the chair, all knocking their heads until the knock was no longer that of a feeble individual, of a weak hand, but of a full and healthy adult.

"The working clothes are for the stage, Nora. They *are* costumes."

"Costumes? How can that be?"

"For a new play, written by our own Oliver Mealing. A very great work that shall be the glory of the reopened theatre."

Mealy's play? What about mine? But some other time for that. The beetles were all around me now.

"What's that? Someone's knocking."

"Indeed, I hear it too."

"It's coming from my brother-in-law's bedroom."

"Ah! Strange!"

"Are you not going to answer it? What a noise he does make!"

"He can be dramatic, as you know."

"He sounds in a terrible fit!"

And indeed by then the whole floor of the bedroom was swarming in beetles.

"Please, dear Nora, go back to your wardrobe and let me attend upon Edgar."

"I would rather see him myself."

"Is it not for a wife to look to her husband, to be his nurse?"

"Poor Edgar! I had no idea he was so bad!"

"Go then!"

The door slammed shut.

I was quite desperate. The floor was a lake of beetles. There was nowhere for me to step. I heard the door slam. I was done for. What shall she do, when she catches you here, an island of Edith on a beetle sea?

Yet even as Margaret sped toward me—and my doom—I became aware of a new sound, a creak of wood. One of the panels in Father's room, about two feet off the ground, had begun to screech and shiver. Oh, I thought, here they come. Here lies Edith May Holler, cause of death: beetle.

The panel swung open, yet no beetles came out.

Instead, behind the panel: A pale face in the gloom. The ghost of the boy in worsted. Like a coat with a face grown out of it, hoodlike. A fold in the face opened. A mouth.

"Quick now, to me!" he whispered, his voice so faint and muffled I could barely hear it. "Do not step on the beetles. Go to the table and come to me that way, do but hurry."

I climbed upon the dressing table and scrambled over to the open panel. The boy pulled me toward him, with his cloth-covered hands; I felt a prickling shock, like static; and out of the room I went. And, as if it were all rehearsed, the moment the bedroom door was opened, the panel was quietly shut. All that was left, to show it had ever been open, was a single bisected beetle that had tried to follow me and only half succeeded. The front half joined us within the walls. The other half, the rear of the beetle, fell back inside the bedroom.

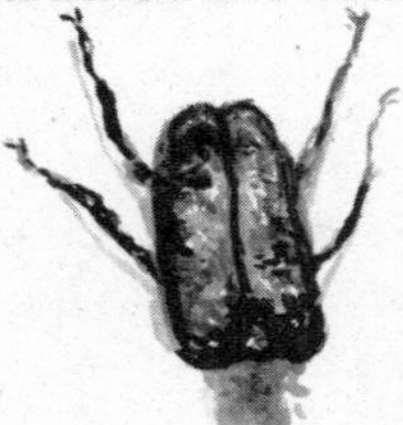

19.

Some more beetles.

Keep still," the cloth boy whispered, "not a sound."

We could hear Margaret inside the bedroom.

"What is this?" Margaret called. "Why have you all come out?"

Who was she talking to?

There followed a knocking and clicking, somewhat different from before, as if the beetles were speaking back to her. A strange, shifting noise, like bones being rubbed together.

"Come now," whispered the cloth boy to me, "we do not have long."

He took my hand and pulled me along, within the very walls of the theatre. Such a thin way to go, wooden slats and plaster either side. I didn't know there were such passageways—I, who felt sure I knew the structure's every corner. But here I was, wedged inside, dust and dirt in my eyes and mouth, as if I were being buried alive. He pulled me along, and like that beetle who went in two directions at once, I must have left something of myself behind, some tears of my dress and hair, some of my own grey skin. But he was exhausted now, and I think had ripped himself until he could pull no more.

"We'll have to climb out," he said. "You must be very quiet."

He felt about in the dark, unlatched something, and the light flooded in.

"Follow," he whispered.

He had opened another panel. This one to the dining room of my old apartment. A single chair had been pulled back. The table was laid for one, with a napkin on the tablecloth and beside it a bowl and spoon. Here was Margaret's lunch. A deep dark red soup.

"Whatever is she eating?"

"Sssh!" He pointed in the direction of the bedroom.

We could hear her talking to the beetles and the beetles knocking.

"Quick then," he said, "and not a word." He carefully turned the handle to the apartment with his gloved hands and we passed through. He closed the door quiet behind him and we were out.

"Run!" said the boy. And we did, as far as we could from that apartment and those beetles and that woman.

"Follow *me*!" I said, for this was my theatre and he should be aware of it. I raced past him, and he followed swift behind, like a rag blown by a wind. We did not stop until we reached the furnace room.

"I thought that was the end," I panted.

"Close to it, I suppose."

"I'm very much obliged to you," I said.

"Not to mention."

I saw him then a little better, the dusky boy. His own face was of worsted, as if there were a veil of material over it, and yet at the same time he seemed most boy-like, the likeness of a boy. The cloth, you see, it was so person-shaped.

"I don't believe in you," I said. "You're not here."

He did slump a little at that.

I reached out to touch. And did touch. Moving cloth.

"There you are at last," I said. "I'm not frightened."

"Do you see me?"

"Yes, I do."

"Then I must be here."

"I've been looking for you, all this long while," I said. "Have you been avoiding me?"

"I've been watching you."

"Well, it's not polite. Is it?" I said, and then because I must: "Excuse me, cloth, excuse me, worsted, excuse me, boy, may I ask you a question?"

"You may *ask*. I may not answer."

"Excuse me, but are you the remains of a person that once was living?"

The faded human shape beside me said, "Yes."

I gasped.

"You *are* a ghost. Oh, that is wonderful! And dreadful! All at once."

"Is it?"

"I've always wanted to know a ghost. Yes indeed: a ghost of a boy. You're my first dead person. Well, the first one that talked to me. What a special day this is! Oh, there *are* such things!"

It *was* a special day. For I was suddenly aware that someone had lit a fire inside me, some angel had touched me unawares. Someone new had come and sat beside me, a living thing I had heard of before but could never yet call my own. Something unusual, unsettling, and awkward. Something shifting in my blood. I thought it wasn't for me, so grey and flat-footed as I had always been. But I was wrong, and I discovered it that day, that afternoon, in the furnace room.

And the leaping sadness! My sudden love—the pain of this—he was dead.

"How did you die, poor boy? Will you tell me?"

"I'd much rather not."

"Please."

Nothing from my stitched fellow.

"Dramatis personae: a young woman of Norwich. And beside her, a ghost."

"Well, don't hark on it."

"I've never known a ghost before."

"I'm not surprised, the way you go on."

"What is your name, ghost?"

"Is Aubrey."

"Aubrey? Aubrey, the ghost of a boy. I'm Edith Holler, the playwright."

"I do know that."

"Aubrey. I am sorry you died."

"You may come to it yourself, one day. It may be sooner, the rate you're going."

"It is a little bumpy, just at present."

"That woman upstairs, she does not like you."

"I don't say that she does."

"You should come hide with us. We do hide wonderful well."

"And who are *us*?"

"The others that live in the secret places of Norwich. Will you come and hide?"

I looked at him then, at his beautiful head, and I nodded. Of course I did. I'd go anywhere with him.

"Yes, yes I think I will, Aubrey the ghost. I would like that very much. Such kindness! And I do like to hide."

"I must warn them, for if you come without warning they may be unkind to you. I shall tell them first. For your own safety. They might bite you. Ghosts do eat, you see, or they fall into dust, like Earth's proud empires. It will be all right, after I've told them."

"I don't entirely like the sound of it."

"It is there, I suppose, or your death. For she'll kill you certain. The woman upstairs."

"I don't know about that, but did you hear her with the beetles? What a thing!"

"And you'll be dead."

Barely a moment's thought. "I'll come then."

"Five o'clock. We'll meet back here."

The shape went out of the cloth; the cloth fell and then was gone altogether. A true ghost!

"Wait a minute, Aubrey! Do you know what's happened to my father?"

He was back a moment later, and not happy for it. "He was in his bedroom, last I knew."

"No, there's just a dummy there."

"I'll ask about."

"Please, Aubrey, and thank you."

"I'll find you back here then. Don't go to that woman meantime. Leave her be, most particular."

He was gone. But I called him back.

"Aubrey! Aubrey!"

"What now?"

"You are real, aren't you?"

"Yes," he said. "I was."

Just then the door burst open. It was Mealy.

"Whatever are you doing in here, Edith? I heard voices. Who were you talking to?"

I sat still. Beside me, an old pile of worsted.

"I was practicing voices," I said. "Please go away."

He looked a moment at me, glanced at the ragged pile.

"I've been thinking of you, Edith. Most particularly."

"I'll call out."

"You need a wash," he said.

"Please go."

He shrugged. "I come and I go as I please, but I'll go now because that is what I wish. There's nothing for me here." He came very close, leaned forward, and gave me a pinch on my inner thigh.

"I am writing a play."

"Go away, Mealing!"

"It is an excellent new play, it shall be performed in this theatre."

"My play shall be next."

"It has been destroyed, poor Edith."

"There is one copy left."

"I do not think so."

"Who cares for your thoughts?"

"Say *Oliver*. I should like to hear you say *Oliver*."

"Please go."

"Say *Oliver*, then I shall."

"If you promise to leave."

"Say it, then I go."

"*Oliver*," I whispered.

"Not so difficult, was it?" He gave me another pinch but then shook his head and was gone again. I spat. I turned to the worsted, and it too had gone.

"Aubrey?" I whispered.

But he didn't come back that time.

It was certain that the best course for me was to spend the next few hours inside the second furnace, thinking Aubrey thoughts and trying not to dwell on that swollen mannequin upstairs pretending to be my father, or for a moment think of the awful playwright who had pinched me. The second furnace had always been my safest place, I would look at my card theatres, have Karl to guide me, and feel calmed, safe among the pages of my remembered play. I would think of love, love for a dead creature, and how might I wrap myself in that. Perhaps it was perfectly right for a person like me to love a ghost; I was almost part ghost anyway, grey as I was. Perhaps I'd just lie down and die in the furnace and then we could be dead together. Yet when I opened the door a terrible smell rushed out, like a guilty person, and inside it was all very black.

There was nothing in my own second furnace: someone had taken my theatres, my belongings, most especially the new pages of my play.

In my misery, I reached inside to make absolute sure, and found something was there after all:

A thick floor of ash.

What a wailing then, the childish sobbing of an unhappy girl. Unable to stop myself, I ran back out into the theatre, but my misery was stopped almost immediately by someone else's—the sound of a man moaning.

"Father!" I called.

The noise was coming from the prop room. I rushed there to find not Father but instead Uncle Wilfred, standing before a pile of rubble, in clamorous upset.

"The throne," he said. "It just . . . gave up on me. Crumbled upon me, soft as dust."

"Uncle Wilfred," I said, pulling at his sleeve. "Someone has burned my new playscript and my card theatres, and there is a dummy in my father's bed filled with beetles."

"No more tales now! The throne!"

Uncle Thomas came in. "Wilfred, have you seen Gregory? We've sent out search parties, but still no luck. No one's seen him for ages. I daresay the old sot has wandered out into Norwich, most likely he'll show up again before long. But if you happen to see him . . ."

"And where's Father?" I asked.

"Look at this throne, will you?" cried Wilfred. "Just look at it!"

"Seen Gregory . . . have you? No? Well, give a shout if you do. Many thanks."

"He never did love the theatre, not really," whispered Uncle Wilfred after Thomas had gone. "Oh, the throne!" A silence from Wilfred, he was stilled a moment by his thinking. "You must stop it, Edith, whatever you are doing, stop it now, child. All the wildness in your mind."

"Do you think the theatre will fall?"

"I can't say."

"Do you believe in ghosts, Uncle?"

"What, Edith? No!"

"I think I've seen one."

"Edith, not now."

"Am I ill, Uncle?"

"Damn these beetles."

"Beetles!" A cry from Aunty Bleachy. "Beetles everywhere. But no matter how many buckets I fill and how many I pour into the furnace, there's always more."

"It was Margaret brought them in," I said. "Like Queen Elizabeth. In 1578, when she came to visit Norwich, she and her retinue brought the plague with them and afterward thousands died."

"I never liked them beetles," said Bleachy.

"What beetles?" That was Margaret herself, suddenly in the prop room with us, towering above Uncle Wilfred. "What beetles?" she repeated.

"The beetles ate my throne," stammered Wilfred.

"What nonsense!"

"Is true," cried Bleachy. "Is certain true. I've burned bucketloads of them. So many beetles. Can't walk in certain parts without stepping under them."

"Do you walk on them, Belinda?" asked Margaret.

"Oh yes, whenever I can. I stamp and thud."

"And you burn them, do you?"

"To a crisp. But there's never an end to it."

"Then it's obvious what to do."

"It is?"

"Summon the pest man. He shall have to come and exterminate. And right away. I do not know why you have not done it already. I shall see to it. I know many pest men, and they know me."

"Thank you, Margaret. What would we do without you?" said Wilfred.

"Edith dear, I have been looking for you. Where have you been?"

"In the prop room here, with Uncle."

"You have not been upstairs in your old apartment?"

"No, madam, I asked but you would not let me in. So I came down here to my uncle Wilfred in his sadness."

"Well, don't go hiding in any prop room. I require you. Your sister has returned and she has missed you terribly. And there is someone new come to tea, whom I wish you to meet."

"May I not stay with Uncle? May I not help Aunt Bleachy?"

"Come along. You should be with people your own age, and you must meet our new guest."

Putting her hand on my shoulder, she marched me upstairs, to the rooms I so recently had fled.

With my shaking hand, I closed the apartment door, but only most of the way.

"Come into the dining room."

I did.

"Close the door, Edith."

I did, but also left this door a little ajar.

"Agnesia shall be back in a moment, and in a few minutes our guest shall call. As you see the table is laid. Will you sit?"

"I'm to join you?"

"Yes, indeed, do sit."

"Where is Agnesia?"

"She has gone across Theatre Street to the coffee shop. Look out the window. You may spy her there getting some treats for us. Isn't that nice?"

I went to the window. Indeed, inside the Theatre Stop I could see Agnesia, just as Margaret had said. But this sister wasn't collecting food to bring over; rather, she was sat at a table eating—and not alone. At first I couldn't quite see the other person. A gentleman, I could tell that much, from the top hat alone. Agnesia was with her gentleman! And I thought for a moment of Aubrey and was glad of it. Oh, everyone who wants one should have a gentleman!

I could just make out the collar of Agnesia's fellow's dark coat, which was pulled up high despite the summer weather, when the man shifted forward to whisper something to Agnesia and then I saw him properly.

"Mr. Jet!" I said. "Agnesia is talking to Mr. Jet!"

"Now, let us be ready to receive her properly," Margaret said, ignoring my cries. She tucked a napkin into the top of her dress. A butcher's knife was placed before her. "Come here, child. Are you hungry?"

"But it is Mr. Jet!"

"I think not, Edith. That is a story."

I looked back and he wasn't there any longer and Agnesia was having pastries wrapped in paper.

"I can't see him now."

"There, then, what did I tell you?"

Had I dreamed it? "Oh, what is happening to me?"

"Do sit down. Aren't you hungry?"

"No, I'm not."

"Never mind, I am hungry."

"You've just eaten." I pointed to the bowl which yet remained upon the table.

"Yet I hunger still. Let us have some quiet words together, just the two of us. Edith, I want you to understand how lonely a business it is carrying the weight of this theatre. I must make hard decisions for everyone's sake, and few do credit me for it. And, Edith, I must seize my moment, even before our guest arrives. I have called upon our guest most urgently, I was going to wait for him, but I'm not sure I shall any more. You see, Edith, I think . . . I think you want to do me harm."

"I beg pardon, madam?"

"I have read about you in the papers these twelve years, and I wondered if it was you. After all this time, Edith, I think it is. It was easy to get at all the other children. They'd come out onto the street, or else I would employ them in my factory. But I could never get to you. And then you'd be there in the newspaper again, mocking me. And so, in the end, I came here myself."

"I don't understand."

"It hardly matters. But you won't hurt me. I'm too clever for you, and I'm too hungry."

"I don't want to hurt you, madam."

"I had other plans, I thought I might have someone look after you for me. I did warn you about the play, though you would not listen. I think now I shall see to the matter myself."

"What matter, madam?"

"Do you know, Edith, I think some people have wishbones. Do you have a wishbone?"

I knew those words. "I wrote that. It's in my play."

"Hello, Edith."

"May I go now, please."

"Come to Mother."

"I hear someone calling."

"There's nobody there, just us two. And I have such a hunger up. Please, at last, come to Mother."

"What will you do?"

"Oh, child," she said. "Can you not tell? I thought you knew. I mean to eat you."

She opened her mouth. The jaw, it dropped open—huge, it was, and it took up more space than was possible. Like the open mouth of the furnace. Then she snapped it shut, such a clack.

No one has a mouth that wide. It wasn't natural.

I stepped back toward the door.

"But that's enough now, madam. Too much of theatre."

"Come, come. Mama's hungry. It shall all be over in a minute, and then you'll have nothing to worry over, ever again."

"Please stop, you're frightening me."

"Come close now, come on."

"I must go down. I hear someone calling."

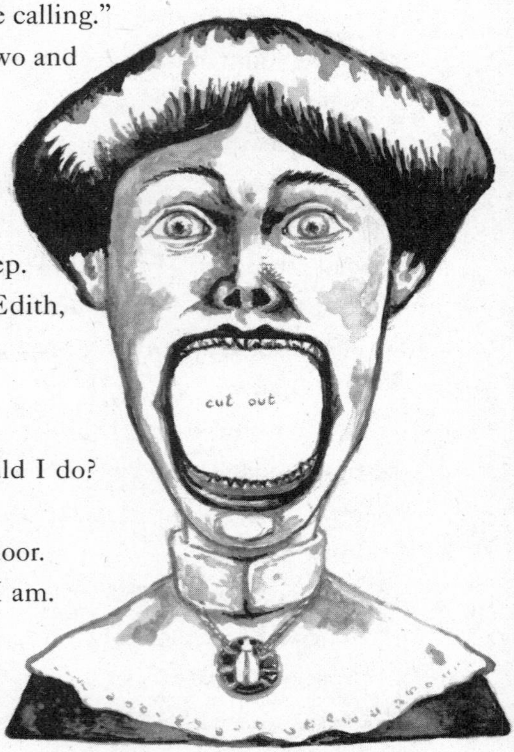

"There's nobody there: just us two and the dinner service."

"Please. Please don't."

"You should say: 'please don't, Mama'."

"Help. Oh, help." I began to weep.

"*Mama*. Say *Mama*. Come now, Edith, step into my mouth."

"I shan't."

"But you shall, Edith. Come in."

She was so very close. What could I do? Nothing to do but . . .

"Mr. Jet!" I said, turning to the door.

"Not again. Hello, Edith. Here I am. What's the matter?"

I looked back at her. The teeth were gone away. The mouth a normal size.

"Why do you look so shocked?" she asked, her face full of concern.

"You tried to eat me."

"Edith darling, come now."

"Just now, your teeth."

"Are you unwell?"

"I know that you did. I know what you are."

"Oh, my dear child," she said, tears in her eyes.

"Why are you crying? It is for me to cry!"

"You're frightening me, Edith."

"No. You frighten me."

"To see your face. Poor child."

"Don't come close. Stay back."

"Edith, dear Edith."

"Mr. Jet. Mr. Jet!" I said and louder. "MR. JET!" I cried. "MR. JET IS IN THE HOUSE! MR. JET IS IN THE HOUSE!" Recall, I had been trained in the theatrical arts. I knew how to throw my voice.

I shoved open the dining room door and bellowed for my life.

I screamed so loud that Aunt Bleachy came pounding in, and Uncle Wilfred, and even Mealing. Then a policeman, too, and Aunt Nora soon enough. Uncle Jerome at the end.

"Whatever is the matter?"

"Mr. Jet? Where is he?"

"It is just more tales from Edith," pronounced Margaret. "Tales upon tales. How will we ever teach her? When will she ever learn?"

"She tried to eat me!" I protested.

"What new trick is this, my darling?" said Margaret, laughing.

"She is in such a panic!" observed Bleachy.

"Good afternoon. Am I intruding?" A man at the door, a new man I had never seen before. Tall and upright and well dressed, with long black sideburns and thick black eyebrows.

"Dr. Chapman!" cried Margaret. "You have come just in time!"

"I have?"

"Look at the child," said Margaret, pointing in my direction.

"She tried to eat me!" I screamed.

"You hear her now. Such stories!"

"It is truth!" I yelled. "I know the truth better than anyone."

"Nonsense, darling. I've tried to teach you but you won't learn."

"I will tell the whole truth of Margaret. Help me, Aunty Bleachy!"

"Miss Holler, please to calm," said Dr. Chapman. "You may tell us in your own time."

"She tried to eat me!"

"Come now, Edith, no one can believe that," said Bleachy.

"Thank you, Belinda, some sense at last."

"She brought all the beetles here."

"Quite unhappy, you see, Doctor."

"She's hidden Father!"

"No, child. He merely does not wish to see you."

"Open the bedroom door, then."

"I shall do nothing on your say-so."

"There's a horrible thing in there, do look! A dummy-man filled with beetles!"

"What nonsense! The poor girl."

"Where's Father then? Why isn't he here when everyone else is? What have you done? Oh! Oh!" I screamed, suddenly understanding. "He would surely have come if he could. Oh, you *have* killed Father. It was no dummy I saw then! You have eaten him, and what's left is being picked at by beetles. Oh, God! The truth at last! Father is dead!"

"Edith, enough at last. The child is a devil!"

"Did you eat him? Oh, why did you eat my father?"

"Horrible girl!"

"I know what you drink in your soup bowl. That horrible red."

"What? Do you mean my borscht?"

"No borscht. It was blood. I saw it!"

"Blood, was it? Oh, Edith, child." But her voice was not as certain as it had been before.

"Oh, police, arrest her," I pressed. "She has murdered my own papa!"

"Listen to her! Must I bide all this?"

"And I know what you have in your mouth! Open your mouth that all may see those horrible, murderous teeth!" It was all making sense at last. "She's not natural! She talks to beetles! And she eats people. *Eats* them."

"Edith, my own bucket, please do calm."

"Even her feet have been growing! Not natural, not at all."

At this Margaret looked away, and when her face returned there were new tears in her eyes. "Oh, Edith. How you hurt us. We try our hardest for you and yet you come back at us with such cruelty. Do you not see, Doctor?"

"Edith," said the man, "I am a doctor. I understand that you are upset. I can help with that. I can make you calm again. If you'll come with me, I'll see that all is well."

"Come where?" I asked.

"Not far at all. Such a little way."

"I may not leave. The theatre will fall down."

"More tales," said Margaret. "And note what opinions she has of herself."

"Please, madam, it is for me to speak," said the doctor. "Not far, Edith, just across the street."

"Where exactly?"

"To the Bethel Hospital, for some rest."

"No! No! I will not! I must not! Aunty!"

"Calm yourself, dear bucket, do calm."

"I won't! They put grandfather and Thomas Jeckyll in there and they never returned."

"How she wails."

"A wild animal," said Margaret. "And, to be honest, a little pathetic."

"I'd never have written a play if I'd known it would come alive."

"Oh, my bucket!"

"I am Edith Holler!"

"All right, Edith. Nothing bad will happen. Sit, do sit. It's all right. Tears are fine, tears are good even. There now, breathe slow. Good, my child."

"But she *did* try to eat me!" I wailed. "And she *has* murdered Father!"

"Yes, yes. It doesn't matter now."

"But it does. And I can never leave. The theatre will fall. Truly it will."

"We'll make sure it stands. We'll keep a good eye on it."

"Bleachy will look after it," said Bleachy.

Men in butcher's aprons appeared then, three of them. That wasn't right, was it? Do people in the Bethel Hospital dress like butchers?

"Who are those men there, why have they come?"

"They are with me, Edith," said the doctor. "They're here to help."

"I can't leave! All will come down!"

"Edith, be reasonable."

"I will not! The theatre! Oh, help!"

"Bind her, gentlemen."

"No! No! You must not! You're hurting me! Help me! *Help!*"

They flung a blanket with buckles over me. Suddenly there was no movement but by their doing. I screamed.

The doctor came close, with a handkerchief and a bottle. He poured a little onto the handkerchief and put it over my face. As if to wipe my face away. And in that instant my iron safety curtain came down, as if someone had sliced the ropes, and I went quite blank.

Exit Edith.

IV

I leave.

20.

The Bethel Hospital.

It was white all around me when I woke again. The stage setting: Just me and a simple bed with a metal frame, not unlike Bleachy's really. And an enamel chamber pot. A window, barred, and the glass painted white so that I could not look out. The floorboards were white, too, but much scuffed and scratched, like our old stage floor. The room lit by gaslight. In the corner, too, a chair, like the simple wooden chairs in all the dressing rooms. How many chairs are this same shape, yet live at so many different addresses, with so many different stories to tell, always taking the human bodies, carrying their weight awhile? (Here is a thought, an idea for a small production: an empty stage, perhaps a table or a bed; knock on the door; the door opens, enter a chair, tottering onstage on its four legs; now follows the chair, and the table or the bed, in great conversation with one another—such deep and meaningful and helpful words, only we can't hear them. What we might learn!)

Sitting up, I saw the door that led out of the room. It had a little window in it. I crossed the room to try the door, but it was locked. I was in the Bethel Hospital. I could not tell which way the theatre was, though

I knew it wasn't far. I had traveled farther than ever before in my life. Yet I was still in my old smock, and underneath it, hanging from Jenny's ribbon, was the Meg Peg that Aunt Bleachy had given me. That was something. Proof, you see.

"I am Edith May Holler," I whispered. "The theatre's daughter, the playwright. Here I am, and here is my setting; this is my world, and I am in charge of it."

I know who I am. I do not forget.

"I am Edith, the theatre's . . ." But no—I clapped my hands on my mouth. The theatre! The Holler Theatre must have fallen. Oh, the poor people. Did they get out? Was there perhaps yet time?

And another memory: "Oh, my father!"

I hammered on the door. At last the sound of the key in the lock. A voice.

"Stand back please, I'm coming in."

A nurse in her strict uniform.

"Up at last," she said.

"Hello to you."

"You *do* talk, then. It was all pretense and lies."

"I am Edith Holler."

"I know."

"The theatre's daughter."

"I know who you are."

"I need to go home."

"You're here now, let us be comfortable."

"The theatre will fall without me. And the woman must be arrested, my father . . ."

"Let's be quiet, shall we?"

"You're not listening!"

I was slapped on the cheek.

"Be silent, didn't you hear? No words. You do not speak, no sound from you."

The hurt on my face, the tears coming, and the outrage.

"Where am I?"

"No," she said. "Any more noise and I'll put the gag on you. Do you want that?"

I shook my head.

"Can you be sensible?"

I shook my head.

"Orderlies!"

"Don't you dare!" I screamed. "I must go to the theatre. You must let me. Great danger. I am Edith Holler. Help! Help me!"

The orderlies came in and put something over my mouth and I went away again.

It was dark when I woke. The gaslight was off. It was the same room, but everything black now: black walls and black floor, black at the window, black my sheets.

I went to the door with the window. Small light there in the corridor, and beyond it just a dull grey landing, nothing save a candle burning low in a wall sconce.

When next I woke, all was brown. The same setting, but browned like a roast. "Hello," I said. "Hello, anyone?" I went to the window in the door. "Hello? Hello."

No one came.

Next time, all was white again. The nurse brought some porridge. I was hungry and I ate it all up.

"Norwich rhymes with porridge," I said.

She didn't say anything.

"I'm much better now," I said. "I've had dreams," I said. "But much better now."

"Are you going to talk?"

"I shall be the pattern of all patience: I shall say nothing."

"Good then."

"Except?"

"Well?"

"My father died."

"Poor lamb."

I could bear the waiting no longer. "Does the theatre still stand?" I asked.

"Too much altogether!" she replied.

I raised my hands and put them to my mouth. I decided to be good.

A little later, the doctor at last.

"You took your time," I said. There's cheek for you.

"How are you, Edith?"

"I am very well, thank'ee."

"I am glad to hear it. Edith, what is that about your neck? Under your dress there."

"A present, it was given me."

"No personal objects here. You should not have it."

"I like to have it."

"Not allowed, Edith. It is very wrong of them not to have taken it. Shall you give it to me or must I remove it myself?"

I untied the knot and gave it to him. He placed it on the chair before turning back to me, sitting on the side of the bed. "That was very good of you, Edith. I'm very pleased."

"I'd like to go home now."

"Not just yet I think, Edith."

"And what about how *I* think?"

"That indeed is the question."

"Does the theatre stand?"

"Last time I looked."

"And when was that?"

"I have been very busy."

"Please, please I do solemnly, humbly beg you, tell me!"

"Edith. Edith. We are here to be calm."

"I am not calm."

"No, you are not. You have got very muddled. Edith, we must help you make all a little clearer. You have been told many lies."

"No."

"Edith, a building doesn't fall down if a person leaves it. Unless there is dynamite. The stories that you've heard, that you've seen upon the stage, they are not good for you. To most people it is clear that they are not true, but you, Edith, have become confused. Let us put all these monsters away."

"There are witches."

"No, there are not."

"Then who was hanged in the castle moat?"

"Unhappy women."

"Witches."

"No."

"And my father is murdered."

"It is not true."

"Oh! Have you seen him then?"

"I have not, but I am sure he is quite well."

"Perhaps he will haunt you then for your ignorance."

"Edith, I am sure he is well. But we must understand that when people die, the dreadful truth is that they are dead, and that is that."

"They don't come back?"

"No, they don't. I am sorry but that is how it is."

"My father might. Just like Hamlet's father."

"But that is just a story, Edith. And Hamlet in *Hamlet* never changes, he is only words, he is not a real person. Whenever you see *Hamlet* it is always the same."

"He always dies."

"Yes, he does."

"It is such a sad story."

"And that is it, Edith, it is only a story. Hamlet can only be the words he was given. He will always die in the end, by poison. Every night the play is performed he will die; his death is already decided before the curtain opens. There is no other outcome for him. The ghost shall always appear upon the battlements and it shall set in motion the play's unhappy outcome."

"I've seen a ghost."

"No, Edith, no you haven't."

"I bloody have. He was right there before me!"

"Now, Edith, no more tales. We're done with that. You are a real person. Unlike Hamlet, you may write your own life. You can go where you please."

"No, I can't!"

"Not now perhaps, but later."

"You'll keep me here, won't you? And never let me out."

"Edith, with rest you may be your own self again, and not let anyone else be the hero of your life."

"What did you say?"

"It can happen, you see, that a person may become too obedient, too much in servitude of another's thoughts—a father, say, or a mother. Or a person can be too much influenced by their surroundings. It may so hap—"

"Stop there. What is your name again, Doctor?"

"It is Chapman, Dr. Chapman."

"No, no it isn't."

"Christopher Chapman."

"No, I don't think so. I know you."

"We have met."

"Mr. Collin is your name."

"Dr. Chapman, Edith, no more tales please."

"You're Mr. Collin, the understudy. And you nearly had me!"

"Edith, I am Dr. Chapman. You must believe me."

"You're Mr. Collin in a wig and glasses, with eyebrows and sideburns. You've put cotton in your mouth to change your cheeks, you're wearing makeup, No. 2 flesh I would say, but even so you're Mr. Collin true enough, no matter what you wear."

"I shall call the orderlies."

"And you'll still be Mr. Collin."

"I'll have you gagged."

"And you were born in Broadstairs, Kent."

"No!"

"Yes, yes you were."

"Still so far gone, Edith. I should have been called earlier."

"I can prove that you are Mr. Collin. Then all the world must believe it."

"And how may that be done?"

"By a tugging of the nose!"

I grabbed for his nose then, to pull the false one off. Gave it a yank, pulled and pulled, but it would not come. "Such strong glue!" I cried. And he shoved me back, hard and rude it was, my head against the frame. He stepped away and he held his nose, Mr. Collin did, and it was indeed most red after my tugging, though it was still most certainly affixed.

"I will not have my patients violent."

"Stubborn nose. Off with it."

"I shall have you strapped down now."

"Oh, did I hurt you?" I said, of a sudden in genuine distress because of the man's fury. "I never meant to."

"You may not be violent."

"I did not mean to."

The orderlies came and I was strapped to the bed. I didn't struggle too much then. (In truth I could not, as an orderly had his knee and weight upon my neck, so I let him at his business, even watched as if it were merely interesting.)

"We shall have those stories out of you, Edith. And then you shall be well again."

Very busy they were, about me. Afterward I could not move, stiff as board. A gag clasped me around my mouth until it was sore and I thought I was certain to be marked by it. They did not bind my eyes, so—unlike Gloucester—I could still see. *I'll think nothing,* I thought—*nothing at all. That will save me. Here is my body, but my thinking can still slip away from it; you may catch a body but not the mind,* I say. *That will learn them.* Calm and calm and white and still and no one indoors, just the quiet tides of my even breathing, so small, little little living.

Sssh, Edith has gone away.

It is summer and the theatre is closed up.

Be white now, in a white room. Nothing more.

But my mind wandered, and it worried.

Oh, Edith, you are forgot, and you shall never come out again.

Such a small play, three acts at most and then the curtain, even though it is still only morning. Well then, that is the story. They say this place is for curables, but that's only to get you inside without making too much fuss. Once you are properly inside, they grow such fondness for you that they hold you hard, with straps mostly it seems, until the life has gone out of you. Do not scream at it, for they are stronger than you and they have straps, and they say, *Here is Edith at this address*, and they are most persuasive.

Just a plain room it was, with small furnishings. On the chair, I saw my beetle clacker on its red ribbon. He'd forgotten to take it, wrong of the doctor not to take it. I'll pretend it isn't there.

Still, still.

Then, in the corner, a little movement. Some small skipping and dancing, such wild running, such exploration. A beetle came under the door. It scurried forward, the little thing, toward the bed. I lost sight of it then, somewhere under the bed. Should I call out? I wanted to call out. *I can't call out, I'm all shut up.* No sign of the beetle still, but I knew it was there, somewhere under me. And then there it was at last. At the foot of the bed where I lay. Then—yes—on my feet. And not stopping there. *It's coming on. All along the terrain of Edith. My body's a country.*

Here it comes, the tin mines of my Cornwall, thence upon my Fenland, over my Yorkshire moors, north it tramples, to the Scotland of me. On my face now, upon my cheek.

I closed my eyes. *Firm shut, Edith.*

Now it was at my eye, hoping to open the curtain and out the vile jelly.

I cannot stop it, it bites there and wants in. I keep my eyes firm shut.

The door opened and someone stepped inside, approached my bed. I kept my eyes firm shut. A hand on my face, knocking the beetle away. Then the slam of a foot, moving from side to side. The beetle then, I presume, was deceased.

I hear a voice: "Watson's matchless cleaner is the best soap for all purposes."

I open my eyes. Aunty Bleachy there before me. I say nothing, I cannot.

"I oughtn't to do it. But I can't just stand there and let it happen," she went on. "This here, Edith Holler, what is happening now, is called a crime, though others may term it an escape. And I find I can't let it happen. They took my own father this way, Edith, and no one protested. Across the street he went, and only I wailed at it; the others just stood tall and sensible, and after there was no talk of my father. When I screamed and cried, they said I was unhappy in love. But I wasn't, it was for Father I bellowed. They wouldn't have that, my fuss about Father. They warned me that I would follow him if I wasn't quieter, and then they gave me the mop. It was never unhappy love, not of their sort at least, it was because my father had gone across the road. I'll not have that again. No, I won't. I'm taking you out. It may be very wrong of me, yet in the inmost part of me I feel it's right, and that's the part that's won me over, and so I'm doing it. I'm fetching you, my bucket, though I shall no doubt be in such trouble for it."

This speech is called a monologue. And in addition I shall confirm that I am this woman's bucket.

She took off the gag.

"Aunt Bleachy. You didn't forget me."

"None of that."

"You came for me."

"Now listen, Edith, and concentrate hard. There is something you must understand: You're not in the hospital, bucket. You never left the theatre."

I could not believe what I was hearing.

"Your uncles, my brothers, foolish thin men," said Bleachy, "but they would not allow to have you taken out. So they hired on staff from over there, at Margaret's expense, and they had this done over, like a stage set, see. Though the doctors and nurses are not actors, no, they come in and out, rushing across Theatre Street. But, even so, you're not in hospital. No indeed, you're in dressing room 12." I made wide eyes at that. "It is a terrible deceit. But not for much longer, my brave Brasso girl. I'm going to hide you. I'm going to keep you a very deep secret. I hope it's right, to do this. I cannot tell, I don't want to harm you. But they are harming you already. Look at your face! They say the harming is right. But how can it be? So then, an escape." She'd unbuckled me by then and I could move.

"I shall leave the theatre this day!" I cried. "You'll take me and I'll see the world?"

"Not quite, Edith. For I, too, fear the curse so badly—the theatre may fall without you in it—so we'll keep you here. But hidden. Here's the plot of it: I'm going to take you down, down beneath, in deep rooms that are forgotten. But Bleachy knows of them, because I know this building better than all. I know how deep it goes. The cleaners, you see, always know more than anyone else. Will you come with me, and not call out? I shall visit you and feed you, and after a while we'll work out what is right to do next. Will you come with naughty, wicked Aunty Bleachy?"

I nodded.

"So then, we should do it quick and silent."

She moved, and behind her, slumped against the wall, was the doll of me from front of house. I looked at it, most alarmed.

"I'm putting the doll in your place. It shall give us, perhaps, a little more time. Oh, why do all this, Belinda? Why take these chances? And yet I feel I must. More than anything I've done in my life. Oh, Edith, this is living. How you make old Belinda live again! Come now, let's put dolly to bed."

"Aunt Bleachy?"

"You must be silent, my little limp lint girl. Do only what Bleachy says, though she oughtn't to do it. And quick now, basin mine, quick as we may."

And so the dummy was put in my place, strapped down, and even gagged, its face turned away from the window, so all might assume there is a person there, though there never was. It was all very theatrical.

"Look, here's your clacker," said Bleachy, quickly knotting its ribbon around my neck. "Come along then, though I oughtn't to do it."

"Aunt Bleachy?"

"Only silence now, and I lock the door and we come along."

She took my hand and led me on.

"Not a word, bucket."

Steps into the dark. With each step trusting myself to the blackness and to Bleachy. Can't see, can only feel. The wall broken in places, the air damp and thick, her hand strong and living. The stairs creaked so, and down we went, first to where the donkey died; then to a hatch, pulled open and more steps there, only they are stone now; in we went and closed the hatch behind. The air grew damper, I could smell the deep earth, down and down, into the darkness. Step after step. Feeling each one. Going round and down, ever darker, ever damper. A foul wind came past us and I reached for the wall. I slid sometimes, for the steps were damp and uneven, Bleachy, too, though not as much. Round and around, never an end to it, until there was. We'd built up such a rhythm then, cascading down in the dark, that when at last there were no more steps, I didn't expect it and came plunging down, struck ground hard. This effect may be done upon a stage, I could not help but think it. You have a spiral staircase that is slowly pulled up from the stage floor into the fly tower, and the actor on the stairs runs down and down as the stairs are pulled up and up, until at last the actor gets to the final steps and drops down upon the stage floor. It is ever wonderful to see and gives an exact impression of going down and down, and the audience fully believes that what they are now watching is deep under the ground. And so the actor hits the stage—and so I, in actual truth, fell upon ungiving ground.

Bleachy helped me up.

"There then, they'll not find you here."

"Aunt Bleachy?"

"In the undercroft."

"Aunt Bleachy?"

"Old cellars of the Swann Inn, what once stood in this place. We are in one of the deep rooms, a whole great series of chambers that have been forgotten. They covered it over when they made the theatre, but it's still here. And here's food and water. Here's candle and match. But use sparingly, Edith, as I do not know when I can get back to you. I ought not to have done it, truly I am such a bad one. But I couldn't leave you there, could I? So stay, bucket, and I'll come back with more just as soon it's safe. But I must leave you now before I'm missed."

"Aunt Bleachy?"

"Needham's polishing paste. Dazzling, mirror finish."

And she was gone away. And that is how I came under.

21.

I come under, the company.

I sat with candlelight for a long while after she left. A spotlight upon me, and beyond it the undiscovered country. Something more than dirt floor and cold flagstones, some old rags in the distance, lost for centuries perhaps; someone's used this place as a dumping ground. How the theatre keeps revealing itself, you think you know it all but then more and more is shown. It shall never be fully known, I think. I held on to the candle, clung to it. I must be brave, though. I can't have light all the time, or I'll have no light to turn to and be lost in dark perpetual. I've come away from the stage, I thought, so far away. It is quite usual for the hero of the play to take some rest in the fourth act, I reminded myself. Hamlet does it and so does King Lear. It is to give the actors something of a break before the grand ending, they leave the stage for a little while. At last I took a deep breath and blew the candle out, and the darkness leaped and drowned me, until all that could be heard on the stage was my breathing, unsteady now but at last a little quieter.

"Hello," I whispered. "Is it moles and worms that burrow at this depth? I've never been so under in all my life."

Nothing.

"Is only me, Edith in darkness, lone and lightless."

I kept very still, slowed my breathing that I may hear all the better. And in the silence, I found it out, there was the very slightest breath from close by. Some wind, no doubt, falling through this lonely chamber from the place I came.

"I'm not frightened of the dark," I said to no one. "Not even the dark of death. I've thought about it often, like Sir Thomas Browne does in his famous writing. He lived in Norwich, Browne did, and Norwich people may wonder over death same as any other. We may be eastward, but we are not backward. I practiced my death often enough as I lay in my sickbed. May I tell you, dark darkness, I was alive once!, and it was a very pretty magic. I had my own sun inside me and I shone. Yet I *did* hear something! For there it is again!"

Something brushed against me, something at my arm and then a nip.

"I am bitten! Is it rats? Leave me be! I'll snap your necks!"

It did not come again, yet now I sensed a certain movement in the distance around me—not just in one place, but before and behind, on all sides.

"I shall defend myself! I'll kill all rats!"

And then I heard a sob.

"Not a rat, then."

And another sob.

"It sounds very human."

Small noises of a person weeping.

"Are you hurt? What makes you so unhappy?"

More sobbing.

"Can you not speak?' I asked.

"Simon Pottergate," came a small voice.

"Oh, I've heard of you!" I said.

"Cathy Mancroft."

"Anne Colegate."

"You too," I said. "You're in my play."

"Lolly Bowes."

"William Gostlin."

"They are just words, words from my play, Edith," I told myself. "Mutterings of noise. They're not real. Though they sound so like it. It is just a fancy. This noise you hear, it does not happen."

Out came all the names, from all around me. And at the end, after a pause, one more:

"Aubrey Unthank."

Aubrey was there. The worsted fellow among the voices.

"Aubrey again! Come here, Aubrey! I might manage that," I called to him.

"I am here."

"I can't feel you. Come close."

"Yet here I am."

A touch of damp cloth, just behind me.

"Oh!" I screamed at it. Real cloth, true cloth. Damp and old.

"Please to calm, Edith!" he said. "You are safe. And we are here. There is plenty of land at this depth. We may move from undercroft to undercroft, we may cover miles if we like. There's another city under Norwich, one unnoticed by the guidebooks, and the undercrofts are a large part of it. They are joined by old passageways—what is left of the old chalk mines. We are under Theatre Street and we call it Untheatre Street; you may stretch out from here to Unassembly House, Unmarket Place, Unmaddermarket, Unbridewell, Unlondon Street. Hear me, everyone," he called out to whatever else was down in the dark, "here is Edith Holler beside us."

"Edith Holler the playwright?"

"Edith Holler who'll tell the world of us."

"So famous with us on account of the play."

"Aubrey, how can they know of it?"

"We stole a copy of your play upstairs. We did joy to see our names therein."

"All my characters! From my play!"

"Yes!"

"Are you true? Are you really there?"

"Yes!"

"Yes!"

"But no, no," I said to the darkness. "That is enough now, please to go away. I cannot trust in you."

Silence then.

"Have you gone away?" I asked.

Silence then.

"Were never really here, were you?"

Silence then.

"I am most relieved by it."

But after a bit, very quiet.

"Yes, we were."

I was surely in tears by then and shaking wildly. I had spilled myself.

"You must prove it," I whispered. "For I have doubts."

"How may we?"

"Give me the copy of my play that you took."

Silence then.

"I thought so," I said.

"Ah well, is not as one anymore."

"We all took our names out, the bit about us."

"Tore them and kept them for a while."

"But not the rest so much."

"Been bedding and such."

"Dropped here and there abouts."

"Blown by wind or fall in the dirt."

"And gone everywhere mostly."

"And well, it's not what it was. No."

"Lost," I said, "quite gone then, my play."

Long quiet after. When will Bleachy come? I wondered. I would like Bleachy to come.

"How many fingers do I hold up?" asked Aubrey at last.

"Are you still there, Aubrey?"

"Never left. How many fingers?"

"I cannot tell, truly, I am blind, blind and quite confused in truth."

"Would you like to see? I could light your candle again and then you could see everyone," said Aubrey.

"I should dearly love a little light. Though I fear it now likewise."

"You light it then, Edith."

I struck the match and there was the little flame, and then the candle caught and the light grew a little bigger.

"You may do this upon the stage," I said in my nervousness. "It is cheaply done indeed. You have all in darkness, then light a match or candle, and the small light catching faces gives a most dramatic effect. The faces appear distorted and strange!"

But when I shone the light and looked about, the candle revealed no children. Only old spent clothes, empty of people and thick with dirt and grease: shirts, dresses, blankets, all manner of garments, shoes too and old trousers, shorts, and nightcaps, nothing there but secondhand clothing scattered on the floor, dismal and neglected. And silence.

I must get back to the light, I thought. *Anything must be better than this uncertainty in the dark*. I shone the light about. Leaping candle shadows, but nothing more.

"I am all alone," I said.

But then: "Here."

Another: "Here all along."

"Where?" I cried.

"It's us."

"I hear the voices," I said, "but see no people to match them, only old clothing."

"She can't see us."

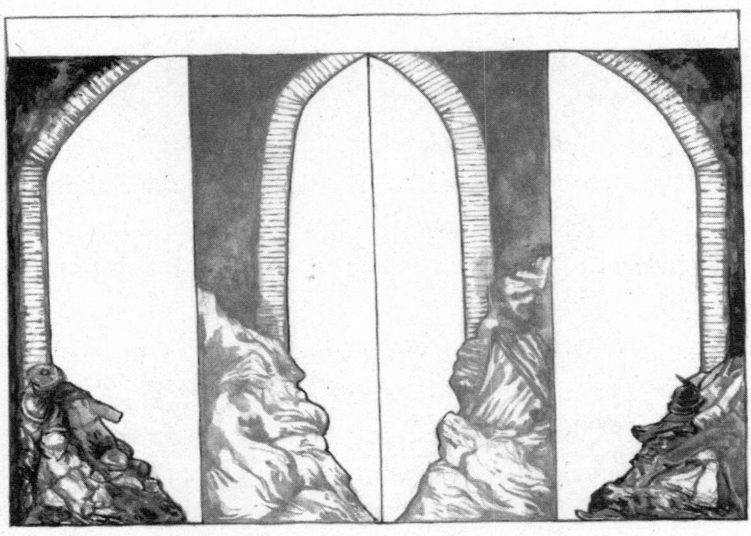

"Let her see you," said Aubrey, "stop your hiding." I could hear him, just behind me, but not see him, I feared to turn around lest he shouldn't be there.

"We shy."

"Oh, all reet."

"That there, right before you," said Aubrey, "is William Gostlin."

By the weak light I struggled to see what at first seemed a dirty overcoat but soon I spied a grey face peeking out. It was a strange, lopsided face, and as the candle danced, the face rather than getting clearer seemed to blur, and then stutter, until it was only coat again.

"Keep still, William. Shuffle up."

William Gostlin shook himself, and when the ruffling faded, the coat opened a little as if the wind or some unseen hand had unbuttoned it, showing something else within it.

"Oh, a little grey boy!"

"She's seen him!"

"She can see us!"

"Edith Holler can do it."

It was a little boy, an ordinary, grubby, lovely looking boy. Oh, break heart, I must weep now over an old coat.

"Why are you crying, Edith Holler?"

"Forgive me," I said. "It is because you are all true. True all along."

"You found us in paper."

"Yes!"

"And now in clothing."

"Yes!" I cried. "But I cannot tell how it may be so."

"And yet it is, you see us."

"But you should not be!"

"And yet we are!"

"It is all too much indeed!" I wept.

"Here we are, all about you."

"Be not afeared."

"Yet I am so very frightened."

"Come about us," said Aubrey. "Get acquainted."

"I am so glad to meet you, poor children all," I said as I reached my shaking hands out toward the old coat. "You are such truth, every shirt and skirt of you. William, darling coat."

"Will you tell her what happened to you?" asked Aubrey.

"I did burn, I do own. I fell out of life when I fell into a furnace. At Utting's it happened."

"And something else, William Gostlin, now?" coached Aubrey.

"I was pushed. She dint oughtera done it."

"Dear William, I'm right sorry for thee," I said. "Are you a little murdered boy?"

"Yes, Edith Holler."

"And us! And us!"

"My play," I whispered, "is come alive. I am living inside my play."

"You may call it your play, but it is our lives to us."

"Look at you all!"

At first they all seemed just old cloth, but when you stopped and stared and let your mind free, they shifted and revealed something else altogether: a faded curtain became a girl with long hair, a patched woolen dress would grow feet and hands and a mouth. I met George Hungate and Martha Tombland, Simon Pottergate and Alice Lemon. A dark bundle of knotted yarn called Ethelbert, and a mobcap beside him had Elizabeth Fooley under it. Some had grown large in their deaths: Margery, who was of great size and quite damp, who I thought at first a horsehair mattress. Cathy Mancroft, who was unlike the others on account of having many legs and was not far from a spider, though a very large one and did alarm me most particularly. And there, too, was also Jack Thaxter, who had distilled to about the size of a handkerchief.

Oh, what strange and what newness. It was like seeing a creature entirely unfamiliar—as when a cousin of mine brought me a frog from the Wensum in a glass jar, when I was only five years old and had never seen one. I screamed, certain that the very devil had been brought to me. Its every movement shocked and horrified—the great eyes, the warty skin, the mouth of it. But within half an hour, less, I came to accept that there were frogs in Norwich, that they were part of all Norfolk, and that frogs and humans are in East Anglia simultaneously. So then, here was another thing new to learn: odd-shaped people, all of them dead.

One ripped creature, who I thought at first a piece of sackcloth, went by the name of Anne Colegate. "I have been here three hundred years," she told me. "Three hundred is a long death, three hundred since Utting's took me out into the salt marshes at Titchwell and weighed me down for a witch. But I come up at last and no one knew me. Over time, I found that by taking hold of a sack, I could hang on awhile longer. So, you see, it was I who found that out, and now we all are able to do it. The holding of the clothing keeps us more solid, the rags are our skellingtons. By friendship with material which outlasts us, we do come a little more substantial. And so still, though cloth-seeming, am I Anne Colegate."

"I know your name, Anne! I saw it in the books and wrote it down. I found you."

"You remember us, when all else allust forget."

"Sometimes you did forget us an'orl."

"So then we done bit you in the night."

I marveled. "It was you, then!"

"To make you larn us."

"And we wrote our names. On the walls."

"Yes! I saw them. In the theatre!"

"And all over Norwich, but no one noticed."

"No one said my name for hundreds of years, until you did."

"Hello, hello," I cried.

"Hello, Edith! Dear Edith!" A filthy towel was standing over me. Underneath it was a puddle, a dripping where it stood. I could not see the face, just a blur as in one of the old daguerreotypes, made when a person moved too much in front of the camera.

"Hello," I said.

"Hello, Edith, it's me!"

"Hello to you," I said again.

"She drowned me, Edith," the towel said.

"I am so sorry."

"I did not work well. I was so tired and she drowned me in one of the water tanks, and then I was put in the Spread."

"I am so sorry, poor child."

"Edith! Won't you call me by my name, don't you know me?"

"I'm sorry, I don't seem to. I'm sure I shall in a moment."

"I did write the letter for you, Edith. But it was an unhappy letter."

Oh! I knew her then.

"My breaking heart. Are you Elsie?"

A gush of liquid from her, like she's poured out a whole tub of water. And then I saw her.

"I found you, Elsie! I did not expect you here. Indeed, I wish you were still above. Nobody told me. Oh, my Elsie Mardle."

"That's my name. There, you said it. Am I so very different?"

"Elsie, my love, you are changed. There's no color to you."

"Yis, I am dead."

"When all is at its worst and I feel I am in danger, or when I want to cause a nuisance," said Elsie, "I do—though it does hurt a bit—become a leak. I drip and fall on the floor, and when they rush upstairs to see where I'm coming from, I drip all myself off and go into hiding. You may

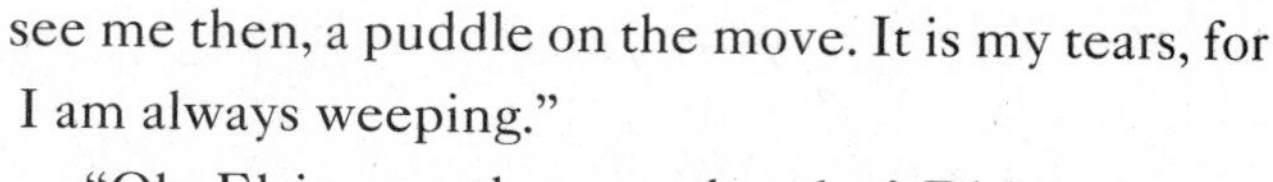

see me then, a puddle on the move. It is my tears, for I am always weeping."

"Oh, Elsie, was that you that day? Did you weep on me?"

"I did, yes! It was I!"

All these children had suffered some such fate: had been charred or crushed, drowned or scalded, slashed or poisoned, starved or bloated, locked up or let out, buried or exposed, fractioned or gorged, frozen or exploded. They had received, among them, centuries' worth of crimes. And in death they had found one another, had come to share tales of their various exits and to murmur in the dark their sadness, and to diminish, to grow strange in their long nights. All the poor murdered. All pointing the same finger: at Utting's. Utting's dead, every one of them.

"What keeps you all here, my poor clothing?" I asked.

And together they said it: "Revenge."

22.

Like Peer among the trolls.

There are surely gnomes and dragons, djinni and golems, that live in other locations in East Anglia, and in Thetford Forest the body of King Edmund searches for his head, and there are kelpies grouping upon Blakeney Point. But here, under the ground, are gathered the missing children of the city of Norwich, Norfolk. Are the true fairies then actually in fact the dead, and we have mistaken them?

They that are dead under Norwich do touch life, they sniff at it.

"Oh, you are so hot!"

"How do you keep so warm?"

You were once warm like me, I remind them. Life and death, we pet each other. Be careful, tread lightly, lest the ghosts run out. They who are remembered less and less urge us: *Remember me, listen, listen.* Wave upon wave of their little sentences, tide upon tides of them:

I had these fine friends, I was most sought after, to see me run—cor to heck!

I shouldn't oughta have hurt Percy that day.

It was such a pike I caught an'orl.

I sawd the old woman died and she smelled and I shouldn't ha seen it.

I stole two happenies from Mrs. Barton.

Their bare bottoms and the noise they made.

She yawled like a cat and was allus yawlin, and then she died and didn't yawl then.

I seen it at Mundesley and it did sparkle so, was cold though I only went up to me ankles, dissent go no farther, but I shoulda, wish to God I did now.

So fast it went, and all the way to Diss, and all the land running alongside, keeping up.

Every night I felt her lips on my forehead, I pretend to be sleeping but no I wasn't.

Them sherberts were wholly good, and lickrish, too, I do miss the wittles.

The final voice, more urgent, asked: What's that? Who's there?

I listened out. Couldn't hear it at first, but then I did.

"I think it is my aunt Bleachy returning," I said. "I think it must be."

"I am sorry I didn't come sooner," she said, catching her breath. "I never had the chance. I mustn't stop long—it isn't safe. What a fuss they are making upstairs, bucket. The whole theatre turned inside out, all on account of Edith Holler. You're that famous."

"How long have I been down here, Aunt Bleachy?"

"It has been a full day, I'm sorry to say, and a night. I oughtn't to have done it. It was very wrong of me. I do have food for you, and some milk."

"I'm running out of candles."

"I'll bring more next time, and you can take my lamp. But I must be careful, they all are looking at me. Cree came into my room without knocking. But, my dear, how do you fare? Are you quite well?"

"Yes, Aunty, I am."

"You look warm."

"Aunty, will you shine the light around and tell me what you see?"

She stepped about, swinging her lamp, and then: "Oh!" says Bleachy.

"What is it?" I asked.

"Only rags and old rubbish. But for a moment . . ."

"Yes?"

"I thought I saw a person sitting there."

"So did I, Aunty."

"But is only rags. Nothing more."

There they all were, all the children and Bleachy staring at them, and they staring at Bleachy, but they never recognized one another. Too, too far apart.

"I must go upstairs. It'll die down again in time, won't it? I'm sure it shall, Edith. What'll we do then? We'll think of something. Be brave meantime. I'll come again."

"There are streets and streets under the ground, Aunty."

"But you must stay here strict, in the theatre undercroft, and not stray to any other."

"For fear of the theatre?"

"Of course. If you leave, you know, its whole weight shall come tumbling down."

"It is safe here in these underlanes," said Aubrey. He came to me once Bleachy was gone—first the words, quiet and calm, then the shape of him as he slowly comes solid. "Now Maw Meg's in residence above, we seek the deeper ground."

"Old Maw Meg?" I asked. "Above?"

"Though you are so clever, yet sometimes also slow, Edith. You may call her old, but she looks fresh enough. And is just called Margaret these days."

"But it cannot be the same! She is Maw Meg from centuries ago? That's nonsense!"

"Is truth."

"No person could live that long."

"And yet she does."

"Look at me," said Lolly, "I am four hundred years dead."

"Oh, Lolly, you do indeed look old, yet at the same time you seem not above seven."

"I am, but I am kitten next to her old mog."

"She is a morrigan."

"She is an old witch."

"She is ancient spirit."

"She is death."

"A devil is what she is, and a poor one at that. Satan wouldn't take her, such a hapless creature. So she was left here on the ground—a joke in hell, maybe, but not to us."

"All do prop her up and make much of her."

"But she's dirt really."

"She's a clown."

"A murderous one."

"Never was human, some say, but an old spirit from ancient times, when such things were common. She and her sister, they lived in Thorpe Marshes. But then the marshes were dredged to make for Norwich land, and the sisters came to live among us and nearly starved to death. That is, until Margaret came to beetles."

"And since then, there's been one Margaret Utting in every generation. They say they're all different, the new Margarets that come, but thas squit. It's allus the same Margaret as afore, but changing her clothes to fit the age."

"She has a great command over them beetles. Though she kills and cooks them, still they do love her."

"And she has another hunger. How many children has she eaten this long time?"

"And still at it, Edith," said Elsie.

"Oh, my Elsie friend."

Then a voice from another corner. "Hello, I am Archibald Pointer."

"Hello to you, Archie."

"You didn't catch my name in the play."

"I shall now, I make a note of it. Will you tell me who you are, then?"

"I was a boy up there in Conesford. Now in death I cling to this bowler hat." (The bowler is a Norfolk hat, designed by Coke of Holkham to protect his gamekeepers from harmful branches.)

Other shapes announced themselves.

"I am Francis Moore. I found a corset."

"I am Kitty Cardle, I like mostly twine and wicker."

"I am Ernest Ridings and am all about working boots."

"I am Cecily Pardew, and I have three shirt collars."

"Over there is John, he comes to us freshest."

A young man came forward; you'd think him almost living except every little while he silently exploded. His poor body burst and was no more, and then those bits collected themselves together and he was himself again, until the next time.

"I keep losing bits of me. It's very awkward. I lost two fingers by now. I can't help it, I can't stop myself from coming apart. It will keep happening. Like being sick, but an acute case of it. I'm better since I took this tweed jacket from Norwich Market, yet even so I can't seem to keep me all together."

"I think you were once Hawthorne, a stagehand. A lovely fellow you were."

"Excuse me, I feel it coming. Beg pardon."

Hawthorne silently exploded again.

"Adults come join us sometimes," another said. "She kills them, too, when she has the urging, but they never stay."

"My father," I said. "Did my father come down?"

"Some shadows do fall here whose name we can't quite tell. Mostly they come like a burst of wind or fog and then are gone."

"I felt a sudden wind coming down the stairs."

"That was probably one then."

"Could it have been my father?"

"Who can say? Was someone spent, most are like that. Some do sit with us a little, but they never stay long. Gregory Holler's quite new, too, but we can't get him to be sensible. He has not accepted his death and is in a most confused state. The frightened ones keep to their own company and they don't last. Sometimes they are with us a mere few minutes. There's Mr. Gregory now, poor fellow, over yonder." I was shown to a dirty and ripped bedsheet that sometimes took on a vague human shape.

"Excuse me, sir," I said. "I don't mean to intrude, but were you once my uncle Gregory?"

The exhausted material seemed to sit up then, and as it stretched itself toward me, I heard something very much like a rustle of cloth, a whisper: "Have you seen her teeth?"

"Yes, yes I have."

"How are they, then?"

"They are terrible sharp!"

"Oh yes they are. And is there a smell?"

"Yes, yes!" I cried, "it is foul and rotting!"

Then poor Uncle Gregory shrunk to the floor and began to tie himself in knots.

"That smell you speak of," said Elizabeth Fooley, "is the smell of dead meat. Little pieces of old human get stuck between her teeth and they stay there for centuries."

"She tried to eat me," I said.

"She takes the youth and she drinks it and she grows younger and what she doesn't eat goes in the Spread."

"Boys and girls that come out to play."

"Never more see the light of day."

"She ate me."

"I was her lunch one day."

"And I her dinner."

"I was breakfast."

"I was tea."

"I was stewed."

"I was baked."

"Roasted."

"Boiled."

"I was raw. She took me in a hurry. Had me called upstairs in her office at the factory. The door had scarcely closed before she sliced my belly open and took out great scoops of me. I watched her do it for a while in my horror until my lights went dim."

"All the missing of Norwich . . ."

"Yes, she ate them."

"And you are then . . ."

"The leftovers."

Here they were chicken carcasses, pheasant bones, here they were bacon grease and pasty crusts, here they were pork rinds and gristle, scrag ends and offcuts, pigs' tails, ducks' beaks, quails' feet.

"But you are most beloved!" I said. I had my beetle clacker from Aunt Bleachy in my lap, and in my love for them I let it sound out a single noise.

"What was that?"

"It was me," I said.

"A Meg Peg!"

"Yes."

"You mustn't. You mustn't ever."

"Give it over!"

"Destroy it quick!"

"No, never," I said, hiding it. "It was a gift from my aunt, and it means much to me."

"Hide it then, and swift, put it away. Or we'll break."

Such a fuss.

• • •

They were like demolished houses and old shrunken lanes, they were shadows of time spent, they were forgotten objects thrown out on the dung heap, they were old bits of the undigested past—and, one and all, they mourned for life. How cunning they were to keep in Norwich still. They had to disguise themselves when out in public as old garments, and if someone worried at them, they hurried along strangely fast, pulled up a collar or down a hat, or else they made themselves shadows where there shouldn't be shadows, little patches of coldness.

But here, in the deep dark, they could be themselves. And they talked of how they would gut Margaret and drown her, pierce her and punish her in ever so many ways.

"I'll tug her."

"I'll trip her."

"I'll rip her eyes out."

"I'll pull on her tongue till it gives."

"I'll know the inside of her soon enough, I'll put the bits on display. Drape them on the ramparts of Norwich Castle."

"I'll eat her, I will. Is only fair enough."

But their reverie was interrupted by a noise above.

"What's that there?"

"It's only my aunt Bleachy again."

"No. Not. There's two coming down."

"Get in that far corner, Edith, we'll lie on top of you. Move yourself!"

I lay down and they draped themselves over me. The noise on the steps grew louder, and voices with them. A man and a woman.

"Edith? Edith, are you down here in the darkness?" Margaret's voice.

"If you're down here, you must answer." Uncle Wilfred in response.

"It's your sister who's hidden her, I feel certain of it," said Margaret.

"I don't think Belinda would do that, Margaret, she'd know the danger."

"Edith! Edith, if you hear me now, it's very important that you come out."

"Don't hide anymore, Edith. She was ever a good hider."

"She'll die down here. Slip and hurt herself. Or starve."

"Come out, Edith. Give it up at last. It's not safe."

"What's this? Is it food? Is it proof of her?"

"It's wrappings. I cannot tell if it is new or old."

"I'll murder that Belinda. To play such games with a child's life."

"But no, looks old to me."

"Shine the light over there," Margaret said. "What's that?"

"Old blankets and rags. So much of them. And all filthy and rotten."

"Edith! It is your mother! I command you to come out! This is not a game!"

"Edith! That's enough now. Be sensible, girl!"

"How came the rags here?"

"Who can say? They look old and worn out. All rotted away. Been here a long time."

"Edith! It is your mother! I command you to come out!"

"She may not be here, Margaret."

"And yet also she might!"

I felt a foot moving in the children around me, a solid, human foot.

"Is it not safe down here, Margaret."

"Certainly not safe for a twelve-year-old child, already so frail. Oh, Edith, I beg you. Come along now." The foot gone then.

"It feels wrong to come to a place so long abandoned."

"Not more superstitions."

"This a dead place. No one comes here."

"*She* might. Where else can she be? Edith! Edith, I say!"

"Who would hide in such a place? Cold as death."

"A desperate person. A child who doesn't know better."

"We should go back."

"But what if she's here?"

"She cannot be. She does not know of this place. Only I know of it, and I never told anyone."

"You told me. *Edith!*"

"Only because we'd looked everywhere else. I had no choice."

"It is indeed a doleful place. *Edith!*"

"I am sure she is not here. Remember how easily she is frightened. *Edith!* She could not stand it here. *Edith!* No more can I."

"Yes, very well then. *Edith! Edith, this is your last chance.*"

"*Edith!* We're going up, we'll leave you here!"

"Nothing. Very well then, Wilfred. Lead on."

Steps away, quieter and quieter. The slam of the hatch. And silence.

"They're gone," I said.

And silence.

"It's safe now," I said.

And silence.

I crawled out of my hiding place. I lit Bleachy's lamp. They all kept so still. All but the dirty sheet that was once my uncle Gregory, which let out a small groan, then laid himself down and ceased to move.

"Uncle Gregory!"

"He's gone, Edith," said the worsted, taking shape.

Just a thread of uncle left, then nothing at all. Poor Gregory.

"Oh! Uncle Gregory is dead!"

"He was dead already. It's just now his ghost has died along with him."

"I just saw him stop. Just there, just now."

"It's the panic probably, that she'd come so close. But his worry is all finished."

"He's at peace now. Or that's what they say, anyway, but who knows?"

"You may be Edith Holler, but you've a lot to learn," said another bundle, sitting up.

"She brought Margaret here, and so close." A new cloth, shaking.

"Things to be done down hare, things not."

"She should never have brought that killing thing among us."

"Her herself."

"She sounded so reasonable," I said. I did not tell them how close I was to calling out.

"Haven't been so near to her since . . ."

"Nor I."

"Nor I."

"Smell her still, she's in the air here."

"If she's come down once, what's to stop her coming again?"

"We should hurry further off. Find another undercroft. Move house."

"Yes! Yes! On we march."

And they began to shift away from me, all that clothing gathering up. As in a storm, newspaper and rags blown along the street.

"Don't go!" I cried. "Please don't go."

"Must. Onward."

"Don't leave me."

"Come with us, then."

"But I'll be away from the theatre, and the theatre will fall!"

"Dull Edith."

"Hollowhead Holler."

"Knock on the hollerhead—is holler indeed."

"I must not. The curse."

"The curse said '*on* the streets,' didn't it?"

"Yes, yes it did."

"Are we on the street?"

"No, we're not."

"Under, aren't we? *Under.*"

"Yes."

"So then."

"Get you gone!"

That was the first time—the first time truly—I ever left the theatre.

23.

Unnorwich.

Can you hear me, O people of Norwich? In the lonely early mornings when the streets are empty, do you hear someone running underground? Can you hear footsteps, the scuffing of a skipping child? Does it stop you in your tracks? You stand still and listen: Oh! Someone is below.

It is me all along! Here I am, Edith, underneath! I may run under the Cornhill, beneath the cathedral, in the tunnels that spread like veins along the Norfolk and Norwich Hospital. I have been to every place there is. Under St. Andrew's Hall. Beneath the Wensum—oh, the fishes! I am such a traveler. I have been all Unnorwich. Hear me: Just as Will Kemp, who first played Dogberry and Bottom and Falstaff, did famously dance from London to Norwich in 1599, now do I skip down all the Norwich underlanes in like fashion. No one can stop me! I have never run so very far and near. I am the city, I touch it—oh, I touch it, my fingers all over the deep body of Norwich. Here and here and here again. I am everywhere! I am in all the roots, all the cellars and basements, all the tunnels and wells, so much underneath. Undercrofts from the time of the plague, hidden cellars that survived the great fire, older than Kett, Saxon even! In this way I race through time. I am Tudor. I am Georgian. Only the area of the Beetle Spread factory do I avoid, where the chalk has all been stained red—that I leave well alone. Sometimes, in our running, we find a beetle in a tunnel, and then we are on the hunt; we chase the thing, and when we find it, we stamp upon it severally. Here is Edith indeed. I tread all over the past. And the past comes up from the dirty ground and talks to me. Here I know everyone! Everyone dead, that is.

Oh, wonder! How many good creatures are there here! How beauteous is mankind!

I have been beneath Cathedral Close, with the plague dead. I meet everyone. So many bones come to me, lost whispers from the great plague pit. Fine at breakfast, dead by supper. Whole families, whole streets of Norwich lost, but kept here in tight places—great crowds of them. They are just voices in the dark, but I hear them.

"People die sore in Norwich."

"Is the sickness ceased?"

"It is gone," I tell them.

"You are lucky then to live when you do."

"However is my girl Charlotte? Is she well?"

"I have not seen her, dear lady, I am sorry."

"I never wanted to be buried by Giles Upson, he stinks in death as much as in life."

"Lord have mercy on us."

"The spots, the blistering."

"I am Sarah Betts, hallo, hallo. Can you hear me?"

"Hello, Sarah, who is there beside you?"

"I am Thomas Betts, husband."

"I am Alex, son of Thomas Betts."

"I am Alice, daughter of Thomas Betts."

"I am Robert, son of Thomas Betts."

Such lives. All lost.

"Remember me? Take our names. Take our lives when upstairs you go."

"I do remember you," I say. "I note your name. All the dead Bettses, I bless you with my breath."

I keep a tally of all these lives. They call out their names and will not stop until I repeat them. I have you, poor city of dead under the streets. I hear you all and you are many.

We visit the plague people, Aubrey and I, though we do not go often. They are very crowded down there, and I think it upsets them when I call. But I have met so many. I have seen the Grey Lady herself. She is younger than me. Her feet don't touch the ground. She is very nice. Sometimes she laughs, remembering her childhood. We even sing old songs together:

Maw Meg, Maw Meg,
Big-bellied powder keg
She ate more meat
Than fourscore men;
She ate a cow,
She ate a calf,
She ate a butcher
And a half,
She ate a church,
She ate a steeple,
She ate a priest
And all the people!
A cow and a calf,
An ox and a half,
A church and a steeple,

And all the young people,
And yet she complained
That her stomach wasn't full.

Aubrey took me to Dame Julian. She is still there, under the church of St. Julian. She is all white, and when you sit by her, there is a great calmness. She gave me an old round nut, an ancient object, pressed it into my hand.

"Tak this little thing."

"What is it?" I asked.

"It is all that is made. It lasts and ever shall, for God loves it: and so hath all thynge and being through the love of God."

She held my hand.

"The devell above seeks thee. Keep ye downe."

"What should I do?"

"Patience is necessarie for you, for in that shall you keep youre soule."

"Thank you."

"The Holy Ghost is in your soule."

"Thank you."

I have talked with Sir Thomas Erpingham and he has drawn for me the Battle of Agincourt in the Norwich dirt. Again and again, we do relive it. And I pretend to fire the bows that defeated France. Glorious knight of old, pride of Norwich.

"I pray for thine victory, Buried Edith. May you be returned to light."

I have found Robert Kett under Mousehold Heath, among all the roots. His body long and

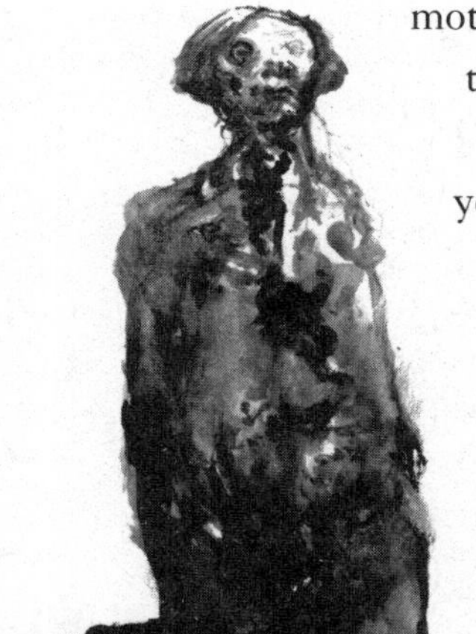

mottled since it hung from the walls of Norwich Castle, full of stretched holes, but he holds his ground.

"I would that all bond men may be free. Are you free, Edith Under?"

"If I stay hidden, I think I am."

"That is not freedom. Break Norwich! Pull it down."

"I am just a girl."

"So was Boudicca, and look at all she did."

"She lost. You lost."

He spat in the dirt. "But I am not forgot?"

"Never."

"Make an army, tell Norwich that Robert sent you."

I have met Sir Thomas Browne. He has a huge urn and rests in it beneath the church of St. Peter Mancroft. His head is fainter than the rest of him.

"I have seen your skull, sir, up above, and will have it returned to you if I can."

"'Tis no matter, is all one to lye in St. Innocents Church yard, as in the sands of Aegypt."

"How is death with you, sir?"

"Bones, hairs, nails, and teeth of the dead. We must all come this way. Why dwell you down with us? It is not your time. Why make you bones your company, when flesh you have still?"

"I hide from her above."

"You should not be here, you trespass."

"What can I do, grey child that I am?"

"Rough diamonds may sometimes be mistaken for worthless pebbles."

"How was Charles II, dear doctor, when you knew him? I know it was he who knighted you."

"He is as much bone now as I am. Go find your purpose before your own skull peeks through."

Such are the people down below. But mostly I am with Margaret's dead children, for they do follow me about and I am dear to them. And most of all is Aubrey. We stick close; he shows me every shade. And I was so happy! I wanted, I thought, to live here ever.

"Is there a King Gurgunt as well?" I asked him.

"Of course there's not. This is death, Edith, not folklore."

"I knew it wasn't true."

"You did believe it afore now!"

"I wanted to. It was a lovely idea. If there was a King Gurgunt, he would save us. He and his army would pull down Uttings and put a brute end to Margaret."

"But he isn't true."

"King Gurgunt!" I called.

"Hush, Edith. There is only us. Come along."

"Still, I'd like to go under the castle."

"It is but cells and rats, and the ground is not safe for such as you. People fall and are never found again. Stick by me, don't get lost, or you may stay lost."

24.

Notes upon rewriting a play.

Summer was soon finished up above, and autumn stole it, and next autumn mourned into wintertime, and I stayed there in the underland of Norwich. Sometimes the police came down with powerful lanthorns, searching the underlanes. They called my name as if they knew me. We always hid from them, and after a while they went up again. Margaret's children journeyed aboveground when they may, and found light, but I stayed under always. I had a lanthorn of my own after all and so illuminated Edith a little, and where she walked it was always a little lighter.

The children who ventured up would return and tell me the news from above. Sometimes I longed for it and sometimes I hated it. There were bill posters of me, which they brought down for my perusal: URGENT MISSING FRAIL CHILD EDITH HOLLER. My own missing poster! I am famous again up above, famous for my absence. But soon enough other posters lost my absence from sight, and I was missing all over again. Am I forgot then? Do they know me yet up above? I am deep down, after all. I sup with the dead.

I returned often to the theatre undercroft, for Bleachy left me food there, and I took it back with me farther off. The food was taken, so Bleachy must know I am still living, and I left her small messages, written on pages torn from my notebook: *I am quite well. I have made friends. I am with the children. I am still here.* Other times the children stole food for me, from the market mostly: small nuts and fruit, and once a baked potato, though it scalded poor William Gostlin, who had been burned to death. But most of all I stole the food myself. Through the undercroft passages I could get into many of the cellars of Norwich houses, using ancient forgotten doors. They were bolted on my side, many of them, but I forced the rusty bolts and found my food that way. What are you missing, good people of Norwich? Cox's pippins? Salted cod? Fermented plums in jars? Potatoes? A cold pie or two? A whole cured ham? (Never the Spread, I wanted no Spread.) Don't blame the mice, it is Edith who did it. Don't set the rat traps; I leave them all alone. Set, rather, a large Edith trap. For I stole and stole. I must, how else could I live like a mole?

Sat in chalk tunnels, my lanthorn before me, my ghosts about me, I wrote—and so much better than before—*The True History of Mawther Meg.* The ghosts came to help me, to put it right. Indeed, I saw now how wrong it was before. It was just as well the old play was burned.

"I am starting afresh."

"We are the drama!"

"A great drama," I said. "God grant me the gift to do you justice."

"Put us down there upon the page."

"Yes, do make us substantial."

Down in the dark, time passed strangely. And I stroked worsted to keep me from fear. I wore it down. Held him like he was my life's comfort. When I was not writing, we went running and leaping together, and held each other in the dark, and sometimes our mouths so locked together I did feel flesh at last and not worsted. I am alive and this is my body.

I turned thirteen in the underdark. I should have been having my play on up above, so that all Norwich might learn the truth of Beetle Spread. Instead I lived in the foul earth and wrote. Aunt Bleachy left me a hot pie that day from the Theatre Stop, and put a candle in the pastry. It was still a little warm when I found it.

Aubrey came close.

"Oh, Aubrey," I wondered, "why are you dead!"

"Because she killed me."

"Oh, Aubrey, would that it were not so."

"Promise you'll stay down always? Promise you'll never go back up."

"I won't go yet, not yet. Not until the play is done."

Here did I grow into myself, with the whispers and whines of the ghostfolk. I was someone mighty down there, the only living thing amid the shifting rubble, the wardrobe of the apocalypse. Me and my play pages mounting up. Those indeed were better days, my best days. I had never felt quite so myself before, even among all those old roots. I climbed out of myself and made me over a goddess. And also, most of all, was Aubrey by me, lit by lamplight. Where's my ecstasy? Oh, here's my ecstasy: I could touch him, put my hands inside him if he let me, and it did feel different then, my filthy fingers trying to learn the shape of him. Better to shut your eyes. Wild Aubrey, dead and gone. (I am like a widow, I thought. And I shall never stop mourning.)

"Whatever are you doing?"

"Learning you. I do like you, Aubrey, can you not tell?"

"We are bound together, you and I."

"With such knots no one can undo."

"Not even her."

"Do not talk of her."

We played the lovers. And we meant it, so that's not even playing, is it? Not truly. And yet we *were* playing parts, weren't we? We were frantic with love. We showed it off to everyone about, we were so proud of our story. Norfolk people do provoke a wild passion: our own Anne Boleyn was born just thirty miles from Norwich, at Blickling, and King Henry could not keep his fingers off her until at last he found that he could. Edith and Aubrey, we sounded so ordinary, but there may be an average Charlotte and her Fredrick who live up above, and can be seen walking down Rupert Street or Cambridge Street as conspicuous as any lamppost, or perhaps a Matthew and his Mary in the Rosary Cemetery all covered up, yet planted there together, and when they were upright they were of passion agitated and could be found on a summer's evening walking and whispering along the banks of the Wensum. I was so glad of it, to have known such loving, to add it to my life's worth.

But sometimes, even so and increasingly, there were such doubts.

"It's not good for me down here, Aubrey. I don't belong."

"Lie still, Edith."

"I want to get up!"

"Don't leave me, Edith Holler."

"No, Aubrey, not yet. Not until it's finished."

My Aubrey sometimes faded so much that I feared, like Uncle Gregory, he'd flicker out, the worsted would grow so tattered and exhausted. So I fed him. I would prick my finger, and he would suck upon a little blood. After we'd lie down and we would listen to my heart and wonder at its working.

In the early mornings, when Norwich was asleep, sitting upon the ancient tombs, the children would assist me with the play. They would tell me how many she ate, and how many went into the Spread, because the Spread is dull without some child in it. It is child that makes the flavor. What tyranny, Norwich! Do you not see the agony that runs through your streets? It does not stop in the deaths of these children—

that is only the start of it. All those devasted families, all the pain passed from generation to generation. The word *Norwich* itself comes from the Anglo-Saxon, and means "north farm," but I think "gnaw witch" is a better meaning. Always the ghosts would worry at me. Am I in there? Show me. Let me see it.

"There, see?"

"It is not right. Tear it up and start again."

Some days it was the very best of plays and they proclaimed me genius, yet other times it was a dismal work and I the failure. Then, with sloping shoulders, I would put it aside awhile and go walking Unnorwich, but always thinking of my play.

Sometimes the ghostly children would grow unsociable and drift off in the darkness when they were unhappy with my work, lose themselves down tunnels or dig up the earth and bury themselves in it. Or, in disagreement with my progress, they would fight one another until they were just knotted bundles all about and it took me hours to untie them. They told me of fallen fellow spirits, who had ventured up above to seek Margaret out alone, only to grow so frightened in her presence that they appeared only as some dirty rag, a patch, a mere thread. And Margaret, finding them, would simply burn the scrap and the ghost would come no more.

Beyond the play, the only true advancement they made in their revenge was in collecting spiders to eat the beetles. The children gathered them from the city and countryside and brought them back, where they kept them in an old lead coffin inscribed with the name FLORITUS TAYLOR.

They fed the spiders and grew them, a great living multitude, their swarm of living toys, to protect them from the beetles when they came spying. That was all the action they dared. But sometimes Margery or some other ghost, feeling hungry, would creak open the coffin lid and steal a spider or two for themselves, as a snack, and general recriminations and wailing would follow.

"I must eat to keep going!" cried Margery.

And in all the howling that followed Margery's theft I felt my own despair grow.

"I must get out!" I cried. "I am buried alive!"

When I panicked in the dark, they brought me new sheets of paper, stole it from Jarrold's, pressed it to me with greater urgency. They would have me put new tragedies into the drama. But it grows too great, I would protest. I must cut back.

"No!" they said. "Listen! Listen!"

"Listen, Edith Living, I tell thee," said Cathy Mancroft, sitting beside me as if I were the stunted Miss Muffet from the nursery, and all the ghosts gathered around. She folded her many arms about her, and one around me, and she spun her tale. "Are you ready? Do write it down now."

"Yes, I am ready. Speak to me."

In her childhood, Cathy had worked at Utting's, and once she had seen a spider come out of the sinkhole in the workers' washing room. A great big spider it was, and it felt its many-legged way down the wash trough and out of the room. Cathy opened the door to let the spider through. It was a great harvest spider, like a plum on twigs, and off it scuttered into the factory like a stroll down London Street. Then the spider saw a beetle—for there were of course always beetles about—and then, oh, it ran. It was such a thing to see, the spider and the beetles. It trapped ten in a minute, ate some there, and wrapped the rest in its knitting for later.

"What a spider was that!" cried Cathy Mancroft.

"And then what happened, Cathy?"

"Well, then," she recalled, "and I do remember this because, you see, it was the last day of my life. The foreman, he comes calling out, *What's this? What's this?* And he sees us crowding around—though many of us did scatter—and then he spies the spider, and in an instant he blows his whistle and what a business followed. You should have seen them, the men dancing around trying to stamp on the thing, and the children laughing. What a dance it led them on. But all dances come to an end, and at last one of the men did stamp upon the spider and it was done for good. The laughter stopped all at once. Then Margaret Utting came up. 'Who let the spider in?' she says. 'Who done it? Who done it?' And another girl, who I had thought was my friend, she said, 'Please, miss,' she did, and pointed at me. And I was to go up to Margaret Utting's office then, and so I went."

In Margaret's factory office, Cathy was interviewed. I wrote down the dialogue.

"You like spiders, do you?" Margaret asked, and with such a smile.

"Not p'tickly, missus."

"And yet you let a spider in here."

"I didn't think it would matter much."

"You didn't think at all, did you?"

"I am that sorry, missus."

"Of course you are. You should be. But it shall do you no good, your sorrow. I don't care for it." As she said this, she was busy preparing something, sloshing liquids about. "What is it you like about spiders, girl? There must be something. Is it perhaps their appetite? Is it their many legs, their particular way of perambulation?"

"They do wander wonderful strange."

"Do they not, child! How would it be, do you think, to have so many legs?"

"You'd be a deal quicker, I suppose!"

"Yes indeed! Would you like to try it?"

"Oh, I don't think so, missus!"

"Though it would make you so fast, to have so many legs?"

"I do get by, with just the two," said the voice, a little quieter that time.

"Nonsense. Let us have several about you. Let us see you creep and crawl. Drink this."

"Thank you, no, missus. I would rather not. May I go now, please?"

"You may go, but drink this first."

"Must I, missus?"

"You must, miss."

Cathy drank it. It was like the Spread, but there was something else in it. Margaret made sure she drank it all down. Once Cathy had put the cup back on the table, she began to feel funny. She needed to get down onto the floor, she felt that, onto her belly. Her legs and arms began to stretch out from her, to grow longer and to bend the wrong way. But it wasn't just that: they soon had black hairs upon them, such as may come in due time but now were here upon her of a sudden. And then more legs grew out of her, and even more, and it hurt her, this growing of legs. Until she had eight thin legs all to herself, and her body had shriveled and darkened.

"Oh, my mama!"

"Mama shan't know you anymore, my dear."

"Oh, help!"

"I shall help you."

"What are you doing?"

"This will help."

"I do bleed. I do bleed! I am running out."

We were all transfixed now. "And I did run out," Cathy said. "Right there on the floor. My blood fell into a pail, and she was lapping at it like she was a dog. And afterward they threw my odd body into one of the great vats in the factory and I was dead. Dead, save I was still here! I went home to Pockthorpe, but no one knew me. I banged on the door in the dark. Father came out—he was drunk—and he thought I was a rat or some such, he couldn't place me, and he kicked out at me before cursing and going inside. He closed the door on me, my own pa did. When at last a couple of the ancient children found me, I was in St. Giles's churchyard, lying in the shadow of a grave. I was surprised at being noticed. 'What are you there?' the grey children asked. 'Come out, be not lonely. Come along with us.'

"And so I spidered along and they showed me down into an undercroft, under the Bridewell it was. And since then, I have noticed these long years, the spiders they often do come to me, as if I am a sort of mother to them."

Oh, what a story that was. It would be its own scene, and how magnificent and terrible would her transformation be.

I do quite well, I told Aunt Bleachy in a message I left her. *I'm not frightened. I am with the children. They tell me such stories. I need more fuel for my lamp and writing paper please. I am warm enough. I hope you are well.*

In that deep land, however, I was molding. The dirt was finding its way into me. My hair was growing longer; I could feel it stretching as I sat there, my nails too. I was turning monster, or perhaps I always had that monster about me, and that now my fellows are dead and strange, I have simply let her out. Monster Edith, a thing of hair and scratching. I was finding stuff about myself that I'd never known before, the darkness brought it out of me. What a stench I was then: how I could breathe me in, the strong odor of Edith May Holler. I had grown all fungal. As I changed into my own oddness, in the deep places beneath Norwich, I truly became the playwright. I set down the ghost children's stories, found the best way to have them upon the stage. Many were histories very like one another, and so the storytelling must be compressed, that one history should represent many—but all must be acknowledged. I wrote the collected child murders of Utting: an accusation.

I wrote and I wrote and grew wild with it all.

And yet there was one story I had not yet been given.

"She never ate me," said Aubrey one night as we lay together, "never once."

"How then did you die, dear Aubrey? Will you not tell me at last?"

"I caught my death by her. Your Margaret mother."

"Not mother, Aubrey, stepmother."

"And so was she to me, stepmother I mean. But I am the very last story, Edith. I think you've written down all the others."

"Yes. Tell me."

"But then the play will be finished."

"There will be work after. And I have yet to understand how it might best end. Tell me, Aubrey, for I must have you in the play."

Such stories, Aunty. Such histories here in the dark, I have found them out. Do bring more fuel for the lamp, most urgently. And paper please.

25.

The scene with Aubrey in it.

I could picture him standing alone upon the stage. Aubrey, ghost of a fourteen-year-old boy, to the small audience before him, a girl of thirteen: "I was born here in Norwich, Norfolk, in 1877. My mother, she died in childbirth, like many another Norwich mother, and I never knew her. Sometimes I do think I feel her and she is just out of sight, but other times I sense she is just gone and dead and there is nothing left anymore, as if the world never had her in it, as if there's not a trace, not a hair of her left. My father, he was a magistrate at the local courts. He was very busy always and I was often told I may not disturb him. He was not a bad father, not at all, though he could be stern for days and days and liked the house kept very quiet. He did come to me in the nursery and would read me Bible stories in

the night. When I was in my fourteenth year, Father told me he was to marry again, that I was to have a new mother. I was happy for him and shared in his joy. For a time at least. I even liked her very much when I first saw her, and she was very kind to me. She brought me a present—a suit it was, made of worsted. It fitted me very well, and to begin with was a great comfort. They said it made me look different, like I'd aged, like I was no longer a boy of fourteen but a young man of twenty. How grown up you've become, everyone would say. And how handsome.

"But it was a strange suit. It had a life of its own. To begin with it improved me—I felt the best version of myself when I wore it—and I came to fear being without it. It was my security. I felt I could not go to school, not even to sleep, without it. Children do have such objects, I have seen it before, the clinging to a blanket or some stitched toy in the shape of an animal; I had never been like that before, but I was now. I felt I could not brave the day without my worsted. But it did not stay that way.

"It was infecting, that suit, I do say. It was an evil thing. In time, the suit hunched me over, made me look like an old man. It was eating at me, that suit was, pinching and starving and aging me. I took it off only at night, and once in my nightclothes I saw how shriveled I'd become. The trouble was, when I was in the worsted suit, I never felt I could eat anything. It stitched me in close and robbed me of all my appetite, but though I grew so thin and aged, Father could never see it. And why was that? Because, as I discovered, the lady was about him too.

"One night, creeping out of my room, I found this new mother unstitching Father, and letting his blood out. When she'd gathered a few bowlfuls, she sewed him up again. Night after night, I watched her do this. I whispered to Father, I told him what was happening, but he only laughed—how unlike Father that laughing was—and said that if she should try such a thing, it would be sure to wake him and he would catch her at it. But he never was awake, I discovered, for each night she drugged him with a tainted mug of hot Beetle Spread. So as the days went on, there was less and ever less of Father, and his voice grew faint and dreamy.

"He was happy, this foggy Father of mine, and did never once complain. So then she felt at ease to gnaw the more at him; she would take some kidney one night, a portion of lung the next. Father began to look lopsided, but he was still very happy. When she had emptied Father out too much and he began to look a little baggy in public, despite his broad smile, she began then—in the night, when Father was sleeping—to fill him with sawdust. Soon there was hardly any real Father left at all, only the pelt of him.

"As my father was failing, my new mother began to grow something. She put a pillow up her dress and said she was pregnant, but she was not, or at least not in the way it is usually understood. But she was growing something. In a room at the top of the house was a little maggoty thing in an empty jam jar. I discovered it there one day, and at first I thought very little of it. But then, next time I was up there, the creature was twice its size—and the bottom of the jar was pocked with drops of red. Blood, I am certain, my father's blood. It was a maggot, or larva, of about a foot's length, and it wriggled alarmingly, as if it were very hungry. Its mouth had a redness about it. Its skin was creamy and covered in yellow hairs. For a while I was unable to go upstairs to see it—I was unwell, you see—and next I climbed up, the larva was more pink than cream and had grown to the size of a pigeon. It was in a large glass box

now, thick glass it was, and at the bottom was about an inch of blood. It still had the yellow hairs, though, which had grown longer, but what was most alarming about it was that the face, which before was certainly a beetle face, was now rather closer to a human's. It looked, to my horror, like a small girl's face—though with rather large eyes. I ran from the place and vowed never to return.

"All this while, thanks to that suit, I was diminishing. And, like Father in his fog, I never could seem to call out for help at the right time. She had both of us under a spell. Though sometimes I was certain what she was about, I never did manage to proclaim it in public. When I was out in Norwich, all my suspicions and dreads would vanish until I was alone again. And all the while that suit, which held on so to my skin, drew closer and closer to my bones. It was eating into me. My own skin was growing worsted patches. When I begged her to let me take the suit off, she only added a new stitch, which did me up tighter. It never came off anymore, I wore that suit day and night. Its thread was entering into me, mixing up with my veins, tying itself around my organs. And when I complained to Father, or the scarecrow that was once Father, he just smiled me away, saying what a fine woman Margaret was. When I screwed up my courage and told him of the beetle creature upstairs, he warned me of the dangers of telling lies.

"Those days, as I lay in bed, I heard a knocking sound coming from the top of the house every night. I knew it was the calling of the deathwatch beetle and I knew that such a sound meant that there was a death coming, and soon. Shortly after, it was announced that Margaret had given birth to a daughter. Her name was Agnesia.

"She was born with very blond hair, a quantity of it. I knew she was grown up in the attic, and from my father's blood. I wrote letters to the *Norwich Mercury*, to the *Eastern Daily Press*. I said that my mother was a cruel and evil woman, that she had filled my father with sawdust, that she'd sewn me into a worsted suit that was both starving me and making me older, and that she had grown a creature in our attic. The next day, when the postman arrived, I intended to toss the letters to him from my window. But Margaret found the letters before I could do it. She always seemed to know what was happening in that house. Only later did I realize how she did it: it was the little beetles that were living by then all over the house—in the walls, under the boards, in our beds—that found me out. She screamed at me, called *me* cruel, to so threaten her and her daughter. Said she'd grown many daughters before, but they had none of them lasted. But this one was different, she said. This one was perfect.

"'I have tried so often,' she told me, tears in her eyes, and she was so sad that I found myself moved by her telling, despite everything. 'All the others grew for a few months, no more than a year, before dying out. I had three that lived past their fifth birthday, but then something went wrong in them and they died on me. One had a love of water and drowned in a bathtub; one was obsessed with flying and fell from a roof; one would eat only wood and a great splinter caught in her throat. They were never quite right, those darlings. But now it is different, now I have made a true and beautiful daughter. And none shall threaten her! Those who do shall pay dear. Now, boy, stepchild, I shall be your busy seamstress.'

"She stitched more and more stitches into the suit, did me up ever tighter so that I could not hope to take it off. Then she locked me in my room and sealed up the door. She took away the doorknob and she wallpapered over the door, so that no one would suppose that there was a room there at all. Last of all, she heaved a huge chest in front of the opening, so there could be no hope of help. By then, the suit had tied me to my bed and had sewn up my mouth.

"And in that bed I did starve quite to death.

"Once I realized that I had died—it took me a little time to understand—I shifted open my bedroom window and dropped lightly to the ground. And then, for days, I wandered the city until at last I was found near the Guildhall, by a grey child. 'Do you mind if I make an observation?' he asked. I said I minded not. He said, 'I think you are dead.' And I said, 'I am in agreement with you.' And so I came under."

"And yet still you wear your suit?" I asked.

"It's all I am now, this suit. Even in death, I cannot get it from me. It clings to me as much as it did in life. It is strong, her spell, I cannot undo it. We have become so bound up in each other that I fear sometimes that if we were to be finally parted, it would be the death of both of us. I do poke holes into it, now and then, and snag it deliberate upon nails, though the tearing does hurt like it were my own skin. Sometimes I rip bits off me, but it always grows back."

"I saw a piece of it, up on the grid."

"Yes, I nailed a bit up there and fled from it. But it's no use."

"My poor Aubrey. You shall be my favorite part in the play. I shall have you die upon the stage—all the best parts die, you know—it shall be a very special death. I want you to know that."

26.

Which has fresh murder in it.

I did adore having Aubrey with me, but just not all the time. I must be by myself, too, to work on my play, but he was often there muttering at me. More and more I returned to the theatre undercroft, to get some peace from the noise of the ghosts. And so it was that one afternoon, as I sat there, I heard the hatch opening at last. I nearly called out to Bleachy, then an instinct told me to stay myself, and hide with my papers under a dirty blanket in a corner.

"I left her, that first time, just here."

It was Bleachy, but she was not alone.

"Yet I see no trace of her now." Margaret there.

"She does wander further off. I do tell her not to."

"What a terrible thing you have done, Belinda."

"You would have her across the road!"

"Certainly. She is a danger to herself. If I'd had my way she'd be safe there now."

"They'd never let her out again."

"There must be consequences, Belinda, for what you have done."

"I do regret it now, surely. I do fear for her life."

"When did you last feed her?"

"It's been a day or two. She must get food from somewhere else."

"Belinda Holler, how you will answer for this. Like an animal. The poor child."

"But I've told you now, haven't I? I've come clean. I was trying to do the best by her. She will be looked after, won't she?"

"And who else have you told?"

"Only you, I come only to you in the end. The notes she leaves me—something wrong in them. I fear she may be very ill indeed. And so I told you at last in my agony. To save her. I could see no other path."

"And you told no one else?"

"None at all, so help me."

"And what has she written that caused you such honesty?"

"Such an unhappy child, to think those thoughts."

"Come, Belinda, out with it."

"She says she's not alone down here. That she's with other children in the dark. It's her fancy, of course it is. But she writes of them all the time. She says she's with those that have gone missing for hundreds of years. The ones she writes about being in the Spread. And not only that, she says you . . . she says you eat the children."

"Poor girl. Quite, quite disturbed. And what else?"

"She says you're Meg herself, she does. Mawther Meg. That you're hundreds of years old."

A pause. "She says that, does she?"

"She says you, ah, grew your own daughter from your late husband's blood."

"Well now, I think that's enough."

"I don't say I believe it myself."

"I suppose I must thank you for that."

"I say, how tall you've gotten."

"I am tall, Belinda."

"But you're taller now than you were before."

"Dear Belinda, how worried you look."

"You make me so uncertain. You won't eat me, will you?"

"No, I won't. Do behave, Belinda Holler."

"That's a blessing then, isn't it."

"For you don't look very appetizing."

"Ha! You're funny, aren't you. I didn't think you were funny. Here's not the place for it though, not down here. Try me again up above. And how tall you've grown!"

"I told you, I am tall."

"Very! What are you doing? What do you hold there?"

"I'm sorry, Belinda."

"Calvert's No. 5 carbolic!"

"Awful sharp. All done now."

My aunt Belinda fell slowly to the floor.

"I shall seal this place up, Belinda. With you inside it and the troublesome child, no one may come down here ever again. I am so sorry, but it is for the best. I am in charge, and for everyone's sake I must remain so. You do see that, don't you? I may kill all I like, and they never stop me. Rather, they say have another and another, and so I do, I do. And they love me for it, they always do. And I love me for it, too. I always have.

"Do you not find me handsome, Belinda? Come now, you'd kiss me if you could. You're still looking at me, Belinda, I think you see and hear me yet. Let me tell you something else, then: They know I put dead children in the Spread. They've known all along. Even though they don't quite say it to my face, they know there are children in the Spread. And they simply don't care."

She stroked Aunt Bleachy's hair.

"And I shall tell you one last thing." Such a soft and gentle voice. "No one loves children more than I. For they taste so well."

Steps going away, then the hatch.

• • •

A mound on the floor, not moving. Quiet, quiet. The lamp is lit, the children come running, complain of the smell. *Mawther, Mawther,* they say. She was here again, among. She left something when she came. The puddling thing here. Oh, wicked! Here lies Aunty Bleachy, mound of a woman. She loved her father, that I know. She stroked the mop-heads because something was missing. There now, there now. Approach at last, and do penance.

Above the mound, a patch of white fog began to grow. A thin cloud it was, like worn-out muslin. A small voice to it.

"Oh, is it Edith at last? I never had such loving before you came."

"Here I am, Aunty."

"Where ever have you been?"

"Here and there abouts."

"Have you kept your clacker, then?"

"Yes, yes I have."

"You're a good girl."

"How are you feeling, dear Aunty?"

"I shan't lie to you—not quite myself today."

"My aunty, my aunty."

"She came on your Belinda. There was a knife, a very quick knife."

"My aunty, mine."

"Oh, Edith, I see the children now."

"Yes, here they all are."

"I thought you'd made them up."

"Steady her, Edith. She's all of a flutter."

And Belinda Holler the bright cloud, fretting so, turned into a thin white fog, like a burst of dry ice, and drifted upward, onto the ceiling. We could see her a little while, and then not at all.

"That was my aunt Belinda," I said, "and I loved her very much."

27.

Of dolls and kings.

It happened on one of those afternoons when Aubrey had been up above because I had grown so unhappy after Bleachy's death and he was escaping my grief, letting himself be blown around the people on the streets, hiding in shadows, galloping along Tombland, singing in the cathedral. He even spat in the Communion wine—that was a great habit with all the ghosts—but he was never seen once. I was about my thieving in a cellar, helping myself to some fresh apples, laid out on newspaper for the winter, and idly reading the *Norwich Mercury*, when I came upon writing whose subject was mine own self.

> At long last this reporter can reveal to the people of Norwich the troubling story of Edith Holler, who has lived all her life inside the Theatre Royal Norwich (soon to be renamed the Utting Theatre, due to the benevolence of that august family). As many people of Norwich will remember, the child was often witnessed through a large window at the theatre's front. There, from time to time, she would mount strange one-person plays of her own, dumb shows every one, performed for the curious

passersby. These were invariably unsettling dramas of an unfortunate child; indeed, it was thought by many to be a great cruelty that she had been shut up so long inside the building. When the child was not at the window, a replica constructed of stuffed calico, with a head of more substantial material, took her place. The doll was considered very similar to the child, but there was something a little corpse-like about it.

Last April, you may recall, we began to make reports in this newspaper regarding the child's absence. She had not been seen at the window for many a week. At around the same time, the theatre itself had suffered some unexplained internal collapse, and no plays had been performed for some time. Nor had the theatre's then director, Edgar Holler, been seen, alongside his daughter, causing much speculation among our readers.

Those who have asked after the missing child have received no satisfying answer. The police were informed and a missing person case was commenced. Bill posters were seen in our streets, reading URGENT MISSING FRAIL CHILD EDITH HOLLER.

Yet still, for many weeks, there has been no sighting of Edith Holler.

This newspaper has now ascertained that the missing person case of Edith Holler is no longer ongoing. The police have dropped the matter. And yet Edith Holler has not been found. What can be the reason for this?

This reporter has unearthed the answer, and can now finally reveal to you the true story of Edith Holler. It is simple, and perhaps a little shocking: Edith Holler is a puppet. That is, no real Edith Holler ever lived. She was an idea made by her father to draw attention to his theatre.

Think only of her full name—Edith May Holler—and you will see how we good people of Norwich have been gulled.

No doubt the people of Norwich will be shocked by this discovery. They may even feel betrayed. The theatre is under new management now, and this new management has apologized for the behavior of the previous owners.

This appears to be the end of the strange matter of Edith Holler.

"It is lies, terrible lies, foul lies."

"Poor Edith."

"I am alive yet! I am here!"

"Edith, do calm."

"I've been forgotten!"

"No indeed, Edith," said Aubrey back down in the underneath. "I think now you are likely to be remembered for a very long time."

I let out a long loud groan, of the kind I have often heard coming from the Bethel Hospital. A creature in torment. An animal keening. And the grey children came rushing.

"Hush now," called Margaret's children.

"I am dead! I must be."

"Why's that, then?"

"It was printed in the newspaper. And now all Norwich thinks it. Oh, I am dead."

I lay down. Kept still on the cold earth. Not dead even, not according to this. Never living. They don't believe in me. No such person. Never was. A doll with high opinions of itself.

"Edith. *Edith.*"

I do not move.

"She's pretending."

"She keeps so still. Is she breathing?"

"All too much for her. Been miserable since the old woman died."

"You're living, Edith Holler!"

"Go away," I muttered. "No, take me to Bleachy first. Let me lie down beside her."

"How may we convince you?"

"You may not."

"The words from your mouth."

"Just a dream."

"Remember your play."

"I have doubts!"

I closed my eyes, kept very still. Let me drift away from my body.

"She's breathing less and less."

"What color there was is draining from her."

"And how cold she is."

"Did we kill her?"

"What do we do? Oh, what?"

"We've played her to death."

"Take her to the king."

"What was that?"

"Let the king tell her."

"The king! The king!"

"But he hates to be disturbed."

"E'en so. We must do it at last."

"Under the castle with her," Cathy Mancroft said.

"You must not, Cathy Mancroft!" begged Aubrey.

"I shall indeed. I'll take you, Edith, tie her on my back."

"No, no, she must not go!"

"Why not?"

"Please don't," was all he said in reply.

"She needs to see living."

"Let her be dead with me."

"There are hundreds of them there, beside the king, Edith," said Elsie as they helped lay me on Cathy's back. "I was taken when I first came, and it gave me huge comfort. But Aubrey said we mustn't, for fear you'd provoke the king's army and leave us."

"Come along, all of you. To the king! The king!" said Cathy.

Only Aubrey, who wanted me dead, stayed behind. So mad was his love for me.

Down burrows and shafts till there was just earth and damp, and then, in the deepdown, at last a vaulted chamber.

"Here then, Edith Holler, here they've been all along."

"Sit her up."

"She's so cold, so cold."

"Let her see at last."

"Open her eyes."

My eyes were opened. How to tell it?

Say now Greenman, say now Jenny Greenteeth, speak of Peg Powler, Pyewacket, Yallery Brown, Tom Hickathrift. Remember Barghest and Black Annis, Habetrot and Fat Lips, William of Lindhome and Robin Goodfellow. Who goes there if not Nanny Rutt, there Dunnie, there Freybug. Bogeyman, bogeyman. Long line of lost things that we forgot to give credit to and so made them shy. Kings too: Bladud, Lear, Leil, Rud Hud Hudibras, Morbidus, and Gurgunt. Which sounds like *grunt*, or the noise of gristle stuck in the throat. Gurgunt, king of the roots, cavern king, his body wrinkled like old potato gone long to seed; strange weeds grow out of him here and there, moss his eyebrows. Whittled man, not what he was, time has bit almost to his skeleton, such thin clothing around it. Think it dead, yet it blinks. Old seat the hoary thing sits upon, stone seat, druid work surely. Crown of gnarled root. They call him king, but seeing him you'd think more like leather bogman, face so squished. Every hinge in him calcified, hear him move, how he does crack.

About him, his army. All laid out upon stone tombs, like they have in old churches, I've seen the drawings. Like the brass rubbings shown me from the church of St. Peter Hungate. Not dead but gently sleeping, beauty of men—but something wrong with them, their skin all leathery

and shining. Mudmen. Their armor all leather and the roots grown about it all, and mushrooms and toadstools stretching out of them, that move in the wind as if they were at the bottom of the ocean. Old men down in the mud, each lying in sleep, each holding a sword that has grown brittle with rust. Some have fallen to the floor, others are blue with age. Oxidized after so long a stillness. Shouldn't be allowed to live that long. The skin hanging loose on the man on his throne carved out of old fossil bones. And him a fossil too.

"Your majesty! King Gurgunt!" said Cathy.

The king spits, blood on his chin. Black it is.

"This is Edith Holler," she said.

"Is dead?" His voice without moisture, burned chicken bones cracking.

"Very nearly almost."

A stick snapped in half, twigs crunched, old leaves underfoot. The king in motion. As he rises roots tear behind him, the ivy comes away.

"Let me look at her."

He puts his hand upon me and I feel so heavy, so very heavy, and I think I'm with a tree and the tree is moving.

"Malnourished," he says. "Bony. Unattractive. Stained. Thin life. There's the skeleton now. Soiled itself. Smells of filth. Fish far from water. No wings, is there? But a quality here that I seem to know. Something almost gone, but not quite: something Norwich of it. Dragged out of a ditch? Found in the graveyard? Looks very mortal. A chrysalis. Oh, it's not dead then. Is growing under there sure enough, but something is trapping it. No room for movement, can't get out. There, see. Thick hair, too fast, too tight. I shall cut it." He took a great knife, held a lock of my hair, and then a sawing. "See now, it gives way. There, looser. There it is, that thing underneath, hiding. Let it out, let it breathe, bring it to the surface. Come out, come out."

What a breath I breathed then. Under the earth so long.

"There, then. There she is. A growing thing."

"Look how she grows!"

I grew right before them: an inch, two. God's truth.

"Then she'll do."

"The king has spoken."

"Lady." He nods to me. "Speak."

I forget how.

"Speak, I say."

I cough. I sit up. Me and the leatherman, king of the tuber, monarch of the corm.

"Your Majesty," I manage.

"Yes, yes," he says.

"I thought you to be a story," I whisper.

"And now?"

"I see you to be the king in the hill, the king under. Norwich is a blessed place."

"It is, certain."

"Your Majesty, you must wake your knights."

"Must I?"

"Mawther Meg is up above."

"She is a wicked one."

"Will you come? Can you stir your men? Once more unto Chapelfield, dear fellows! Awake, awake, and all to battle at once. I'd have called long ago, but I never knew you were here."

"They will not wake unless by my bidding."

"Then bid by all means."

"I shall not, lady."

The king, I saw then, had lost most of his teeth. He had a spot on his cheek that looked a cancer. His eyes were bloodshot. And the knights, they smelled. Rank they were, of spoiled milk, and moldy cheese—no, of filth and sewage, of creatures no longer up above.

"Your men breathe, yet still they are dead to life. Wake up, I say, wake up, won't you? Come now, awake!"

I shoved one, tried to haul him off his tablet, but he would not come.

"Oh, you are men of stone!"

"They shan't wake, unless I call them."

"Then call away."

"Indeed I shall not."

"You stink as a king. Like a rancid goat."

"You stink as a lady. Like an unwashed woman."

"I've not come here to be insulted."

"Go further off, then."

"Dribbler! Do-nothing! Lump! What's the point of you?"

"I am here to protect Norwich, which I do love with all my heart."

"Then prove it! Shift yourself! Children are being eaten up above!"

"Indeed, it is lamentable."

"Children murdered and put in jars."

"I weep for them."

"I don't need your tears. No good, are they? Shift, move yourself! I was told there were living yet beside me, but it was a lie. Here are just more corpses piled up."

"We do live. We do breathe."

"Prove it! Help me!"

"I shall not."

"Slugabed! Worm!"

"My subjects have grown rude."

"Do you doubt my cause?"

"Not for a moment."

"So then, step lively!"

"No, I shall not."

"Why? Is a dead child not a dreadful thing?"

"It is *the* most awful thing."

"Come along then, at last. Wipe your eyes and we'll talk no more about it. Which way shall we march? Storm Castle Meadow, then up Theatre Street? Oh, to see her face! Tallyho!"

"No, no, I shall not."

"Shiteabed!"

"Even so."

"Oh, what's the point of you?"

"To protect Norwich, should she need me."

"She needs you now!"

"Yes. Perhaps."

"And so then, come along!"

"But what if she needs me after? I may come only once."

"*I* need you."

"And so may others later. And so I must stay awhile and rise at the end of Norwich."

"We are very near the end, I reckon!"

"But not at the end."

"You're not coming, though there's such evil?"

"No. Or there'd be no hope left for Norwich after."

"When will you come?"

"By and by."

"And what if I am killed?"

"Then you shall be dead."

"And still you'll wait?"

"And still."

"Oh, what sort of a story are you?"

"A Norwich story."

"I think you are a dreadful king," I said in fury and disgust. "A king of what? King of the bedpan. You will be forgotten."

"But I'll still be here."

"Margaret's unhappy children have stories, and all of them are better than yours."

"I am a wonderful story. I give such hope."

"None."

"Children know me. All Norwich knows me!" He was so agitated that he leaned forward and struck his throne with his fist, and as he did so his old body let forth a great crack, as if to enhance his argument.

"I am a playwright! I'll cut you out of my Norwich play!"

"Who sees this play? Is it popular?"

"Not yet, it was, very nearly. But it shall be. I swear it!"

"So do it."

"I will! I see it now! I know how the ending goes. Oh, I have it. It is wonderful! Better than anything a resident Mealy could ever do."

I wiped my damp face, took a deep breath. I felt better. I felt full of life and hope. Here is my ecstasy. "Yes! Thank you, great king! I am Edith again! Cathy Mancroft, we shall begin rehearsals this very night! And you, all of you shall play your own selves."

28.

Preparations, up and down.

A great business afterward, wondering how best to perform the screams, how to show the horrors. The grey children did fright themselves all over again, just thinking of it. Up above us I knew they must be preparing for the pantomime season already; down below I was director, actor, stage manager, and they—why, they must be themselves. It would take some practice, but practice we did: one after another calling out their lines in the damp dark.

All save Aubrey Unthank, who remained in an obscure corner, perpetually unthanked. He had withdrawn his part, forbidden me to include it. Yet did we proceed without him.

"I'll want you upstairs and onstage, when the time comes," I said. "The theatre is certain to be packed once they open again, ready for the Christmas season. And when they do, we'll be ready. It will be such a pantomime that shall never be forgot."

"And what of the actors? The theatre people?" asked Elsie, who knew the theatre well enough. "Are they going to let us just take their stage?"

"We'll lock them in the dressing rooms. I know where the keys are."

"Lock them in? They'll hammer and groan."

"You won't hear them. They'll be far enough away from the stage. And Uncle Wilfred and his sort . . . well, I'll make them understand."

"They'll never believe us."

"They will," I said. "If it's in the theatre they will. But only there. It's the only place it can work."

"We should take it slow." This from William Goslin. "Start with those of us who still find our old shapes. We shall go so slow, until they understand."

"Yes, William!" I cried. "We'll bring them along with us, so that they can know your story."

"But what about you? What'll you do?"

"I shall be chorus. I introduce you all. I set the scene. They know me, the people of Norwich. They'll trust me."

"But they know you as a doll now."

"But they'll see I'm not."

"Then they'll just think it's another of their plays meant to entertain of an evening."

"At first they might, but then they'll begin to understand. When they start to see the clothes moving onstage, they'll look harder. They have never seen anything like it . . . and yet, well, perhaps some of them have. There is always that possibility. Seen it but never spoken up. And do not forget, you more recent ones, some of your relatives will be there in the audience."

"Oh! They might be!"

"Up in the gods."

"And they'll know you, even though you are so changed."

"My own father didn't know me," said Cathy Mancroft.

"That was different. It was dark, then, and he was drunk."

"It'll still be dark, and most like he'll still be drunk."

"And if it's the play we ourselves perform of our lives, or rather of our deaths, then who will play the role of Margaret Utting?"

And, almost without thinking, I said, "Oh, I will."

I had not until that moment conceived of trying the role myself.

"Shall you?"

"Yes. But someone must go up and steal some clothes of hers."

"I'll do that," said Elsie.

"And I'll need a disguise. They mustn't see me until it is time. They mustn't know it's me."

"You may wear us. Go covered in ghosts."

"Ghosts of us that look like clothes."

"We may be jackets or trousers, top hats or flannel shirts."

"Can you imagine what an entrance I'll make?" I bellowed. "It will be the finest piece of theatre in the history of the stage. Oh, I'll do it! How many do you think could hide upon me?"

"Why, very many. Fifty, I should think."

"'Tis wonderful!"

"Many of us are small enough that we can hide in pockets. Others can shy ourselves so much that we're little more than a length of hair. Simon Pottergate can hide himself in those old spectacles, can't you, Simon?"

"I can, I do!"

"Well done. I shall carry as many of you as possible. In the meantime, let us practice our parts."

Aubrey was so unhappy at being left out. He did not approve of our rehearsals. He skulked about the undercroft as our rehearsals advanced, muttering through his worsted: "It isn't right, shouldn't ought to do it, no good will come of it, and even if she does succeed, which she won't, the revenge will mean our deaths, we only linger for revenge, we'll find our rest, she'll put us out, it is not right to do it, why do you listen to her, she's not one of us, the play's a disaster, you look ridiculous, sound ridiculous, who'll come with me under the market, who'll come with me to mix up the letters of the general post office, who'll come keep me company, who'll come, anyone, no one?"

No, no one came. Aubrey was left lonely, and though he picked and tore at himself, all he found was worsted there, and he would not stand for it. He wanted to ruin everything, but how to do it? He went to Floritus Taylor's old lead coffin, where Cathy Mancroft kept all her spiders, and he shoved the lid open. He wanted to destroy things, to hurt our progress, and he acted without thinking of the consequences. The spiders came swarming out. They crawled all over him, biting into worsted, but soon they went elsewhere, for Aubrey was not enough for them, small meal that he was. Up they went, through the cracks.

All about the theatre went the spiders, spidering. Under the doors they hurried, they had such a hungering, and into the rooms. To think of them learning all the land of my playhouse, as they played with the beetles here and there, as they followed their nature, and what great life was taken as they did. Beetles dead on the staircase, dead in the greenroom, dead on the new stage, dead in the wardrobe, dead in the scenery dock, dead in the understage, dead beside the sleeping people, dead in the bathtubs, dead in the sinks, dead under tables, dead under beds, dead on Theatre Street, dead on Chapelfield East, and dead upon Chantry Road. Dead, the unsuccessful fleeing ones, in Chapelfield Gardens. Dead in front of the Bethel Hospital, before they could seek help inside.

As the spiders spidered their great massacring, so did I spider in the dark of my dreams, spinning a horror tale by candlelight: a mighty tragedy, a history of eating and of blood, a great accounting of the dead of Margaret Utting.

Then, in the morning: a scream.

It woke us up, Edith and the ghosts. All save one: Aubrey was nowhere to be found, only tangled sheets of worsted, more than we had ever seen.

And again it came: the scream.

The noise of some twisty dame.

What distress it was! What an alarum. There is a woman way upstairs, I said, stopping everyone from sleep. Is she on fire? Are her bones charcoal already? What distress!

All that morning, after the screams subsided, we could hear people running around and calling out above us. Twice beetles came down in the dark, and twice Cathy ate them.

"There'll be more, I'm sure of it."

She was right. Ten came down. Twenty. Thirty came.

"All thanks to Aubrey."

"Look what you've started."

"Aubrey! Aubrey!" we called, but he never came.

We could not wait for him, nor go hunting. Every one of Margaret's dead children was in a panic. Some flew upward to be out of the deep, promising to wait up in the fly tower, hanging like bats, but mostly we kept in the undercroft and continued our preparations.

In the undercroft, we had always used a spy to keep abreast of the progress above. Cecily often volunteered, and also Ernest; dear Elsie she went up, too, they took turns. When Cecily returned that morning, we thought her a crowd of beetles at first, but she found her human shape.

"It's tonight," she announced, breathless. "The theatre is opening tonight!"

"We're not ready."

"We can't do it."

"We must, I think. We must be ready. Tonight or never."

"And there's something else," said Cecily, most nervous.

"What then? Show us, old friend."

And she did, a playbill:

UTTING THEATRE ROYAL,
THEATRE STREET, NORWICH

FOR ONE NIGHT ONLY
FRIDAY, 22 DECEMBER, 7 P.M.

EDITH, A TRAGEDY
OR, THE TRUE HISTORY
OF EDITH HOLLER

BY O. MEALING

"Whatever can it mean?" Hawthorne asked.

"Mealing always said he would write a part for me."

"Is there a play called *Edith, a Tragedy*?"

"It seems there must be."

"I thought we were putting on *our* play," said William Gostlin.

"We will, but for the theatre to be open they must have a play of their own."

"I don't like the sound of it."

"No more do I," I said. "Well, we shall have to change the script."

"Are you all right, Edith?"

"Do I look like I've seen a ghost?"

None did laugh at that.

"We'll do it," I said. "I do fancy myself a better playwright than Oliver Mealing."

Knock, knock, in the dark, The beetles are coming in, hundreds of them now. If I stood in their midst, they'd be up to my shins. I don't stand in them. All the others have gone. Some have run from the theatre, but others, I am certain, do remain. No sign of Aubrey still. I am atop of Margery, she is pushing me up. I find the stairs and climb up and up, some new route that the ghosts are old friends with. Margery blocks the passage, the beetles can't get past her. She stays there, a perfect cork, though the crawling liquid beneath her does bite and bite.

"Thank you, Margery. Oh, thank you."

But Margery says nothing.

I keep climbing, up and up.

"Do hurry, Edith!" calls John Hawthorne, old stagehand, whom I'd known in life.

"I do come."

We'll play our play, so help me.

And tonight.

Exit Edith.

V

I return.

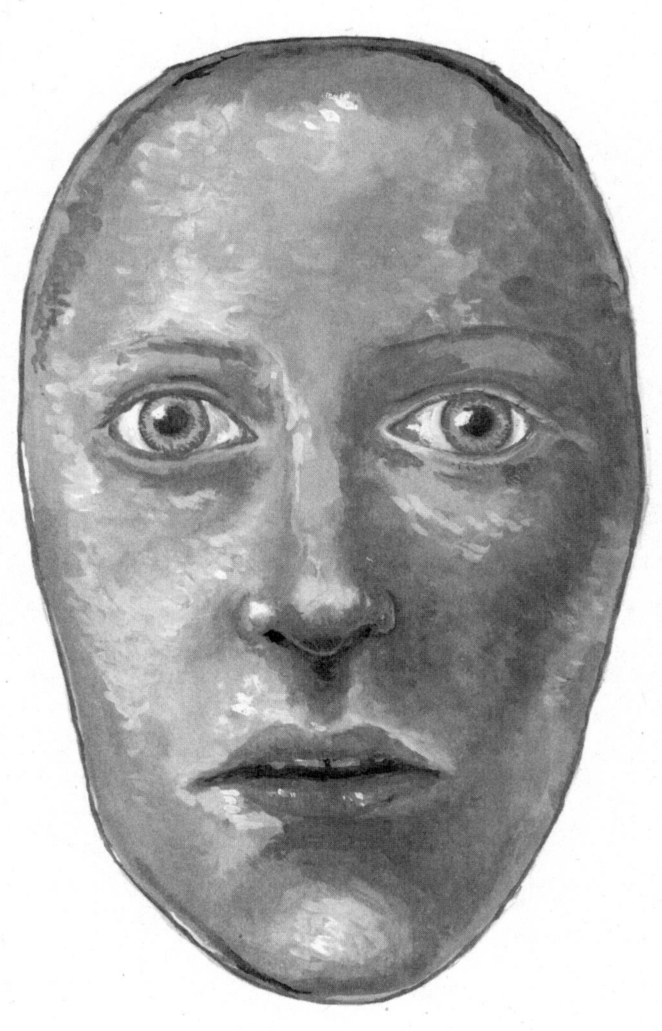

29.

Act One beginners, please.

The orchestra was playing when I came up again and breathed at last the upstairs air. How the Norwich light did sting, I shed tears over it. I came up between the walls inside the theatre's fireman's room, which is filled with buckets of sand and brass fire extinguishers. I had never been allowed in here. But now here I came, out of a panel in the wall, and so many of the grey children waiting there for me.

"The orchestra is playing," I said, "we should have come sooner."

"And the audience is going in, too."

True enough I could hear the people outside, the noise of the Norwich herd, a general hum, a mass of people that I had not been near for so many months. Laughter now and then. A name being called. The general noise of the theatre crowd before a show is ready to begin. Then the announcement from Uncle Jerome.

"Ladies and gentlemen, please take your seats. Tonight's performance of *Edith, a Tragedy* will begin in fifteen minutes. Your seats, if you please."

"Fifteen minutes! We'll never do it."

"We must shift, and fast."

"But what about backstage, locking the actors in?"

"Too late for that, I suppose," I said. "We must think of something other."

"What other? Oh, here is disaster!"

"No, no, all will be well, you must just follow me."

"Follow her? Why would we follow her?"

"Edith Holler found useless."

"Falls at the first hurdle."

"Listen, all of you," I cried. "Listen now, and stand close. I've had enough of your groaning and wittering. I am here to tell you: follow me and all will be well. What have you to lose, you dead things? I alone am living and do go to it. But you, my friends, shall be ever remembered after this night, for this is the night of Edith Holler, and those of your kind who are away and hiding in Norwich shall grieve forever after that they were not here on Edith Holler Night. Stand to, you ghosts! Are you yet shades of human child? Will you come with me?"

"Oh, listen at that."

"Is good saying."

"We'll cling on."

"We'll come."

"Most brave are we."

"Good then, my darlings, dress me, dress me."

So they came, all those ghosts several, and I was armored in layers of dead people. What a dressing up that was, like getting swathed in something forbidden, like wearing filth. They did not weigh much of anything, and yet I had never felt so terribly heavy. I was covered in dead—it was like being buried alive, I say. I must have worn fifty ghosts that evening, and how many people can boast of such a thing? Cecily was on my cheek, looking more like the display of some nasty illness than a birthmark, Archie was my hat, George Hungate my hair, my coat was much of it Anne Colegate, one boot was Elizabeth Fooley and the other Martha Tombland, old boots they were and rather shapeless—it didn't do to look too closely. Simon Pottergate was last and he fell upon my nose and I saw less than previously.

"You must carry us."

"We must lean on you."

"You must bear our weight."

"Or else we'll move separately."

"And then they shall know it's wrong."

"Yes," I said, "I understand."

"I will walk beside you," said John Hawthorne. "I shall force myself to stay together and try to prop you up if needed."

"You won't separate on me, Hawthorne?"

"I am feeling most unified, right now."

"I will puddle in the shadows," said Elsie. "I will drip locally."

"I wish I could see myself properly." The reflection in the polished brass of the fire extinguishers was distorted and not encouraging. "I must be well over six foot."

"You look fine," said Hawthorne. "Like a tall old man, a thin one who has lived a long while. You look a little previous century, if you'll not be offended. But you'll do.

"Well, then," said Hawthorne, "are you ready now? I shall try to steady you. Are you prepared to carry them all?"

"I am ready," I said.

"And so let it be now."

What a load descended upon me! I crashed against the wall, but just about stayed upright. What luggage I had, it robbed me of air. I thought my lungs would never fill again, like I was being terribly smothered.

"Small breaths, small taste of air, Edith. Come now. Breathe."

I did.

"Well done!" the dragging children said in chorus.

From beyond the door there was Uncle Jerome's voice again.

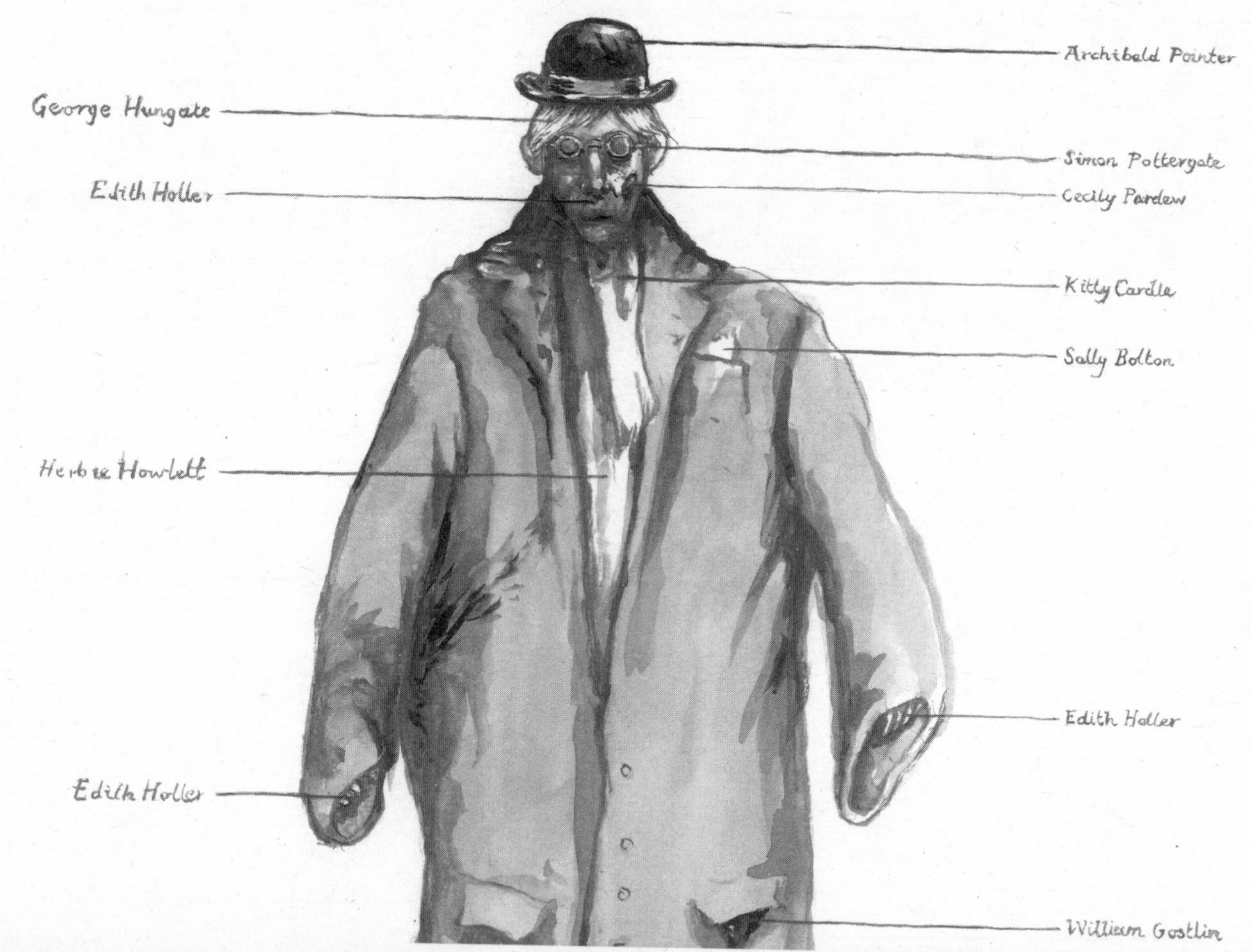
Archibald Pointer
George Hungate
Simon Pottergate
Edith Holler
Cecily Pardew
Kitty Cardle
Sally Bolton
Herbie Howlett
Edith Holler
Edith Holler
William Gostlin

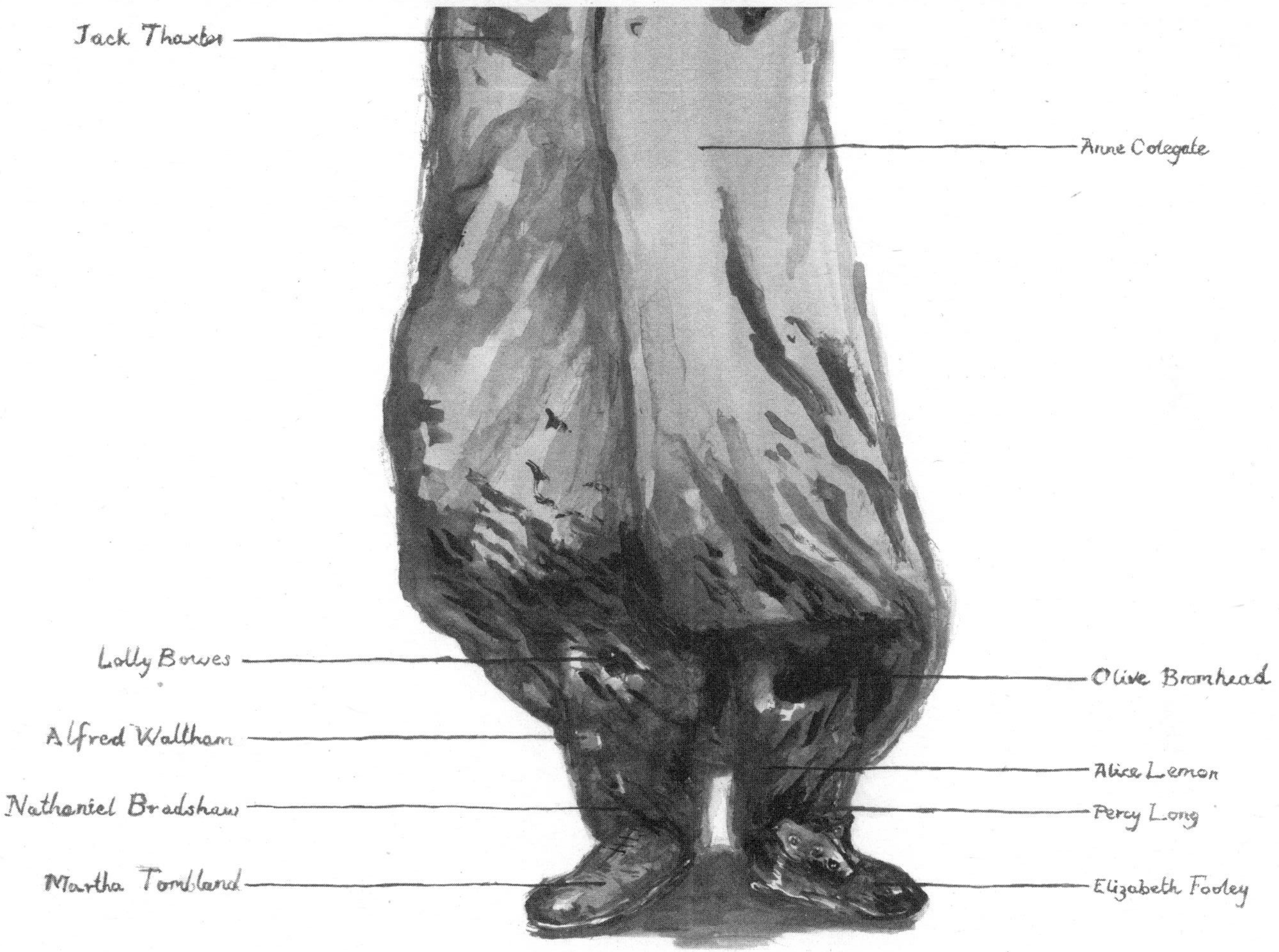

Jack Thaxter
Anne Colegate
Lolly Bowes
Olive Bromhead
Alfred Waltham
Alice Lemon
Nathaniel Bradshaw
Percy Long
Martha Tombland
Elizabeth Fooley

"Ladies and gentlemen, please do take your seats. Tonight's performance of *Edith, a Tragedy* will begin in ten minutes. Your seats, if you please. It is time."

"Let us go then, Edith," said Hawthorne at the door. "I'll open the door, and out we'll go among them."

"Yes."

John Hawthorne opened the door and the noise of Norwich came unto us. I could feel some ghosts about me ruffle in their fear.

"Steady now," said Simon Pottergate upon my nose, "hold on tight."

"Once more into the breeches," I said, but only to myself, and forward we staggered.

At first I made only small progress, each step a journey, but I grew better at it quickly. I learned to use the swaying of my hips and legs to distribute the weight of them. I have no doubt now that many people in life must carry heavy ghosts about them while never knowing of it. I carried my own army. I was that horse of Troy.

The foyer was packed as I stumbled out. Hawthorne stayed close to guide me—he who, after all, had spent his life in this building. All people did look to me, but none did recognize. I think I must have been a strange sight, this tall scarecrow. And there was something else I had not fully considered. We had a bad smell about us. I had not washed since going down in the dank dark, so I had grown a powerful stench of my own, but I had also, surely, a terrific reek of death about me, so much that people stepped wide around me, some holding handkerchiefs to their noses.

I put my hand on Hawthorne's shoulder and he led me on to the great room under the rotunda. I was back in my world, yet felt such a stranger to it. The looks of the people said that I did not belong here. That there was something outlandish about me, something other. Perhaps they knew deep down in their Norfolk souls that I was carting death.

My home, as I say, and yet not so.

The theatre had been rearranged. The mourning ribbons and bombazine and Norwich Black Crape had been replaced with Christmas decorations, but not our usual ones. Instead of candles and stars, pictures of Father Christmas and a large Christmas tree, were hangings of crepe paper in different colors, but every one of them cut into the shape of beetles. And that was not all. The portrait of my father as King Lear had been removed; so too had the Hamlet Holler. In their place were two new bold canvas likenesses in big gilt frames, two usurpers in our theatreland. The first nearly pushed me off my ghostly stilts: it was Margaret—and for a moment I thought the painting not a painting but the actual Margaret herself, she did stare out so.

How she does terrify! I thought. But she was framed, this Margaret was only marks on canvas. And next to her was not Victor Holler indeed but instead a large and old man staring grimly out from his frame. Beneath was a label large enough to be read from a good distance: CLARENCE UTTING. The father by his daughter's side, staking his claim.

What a crime it was to have those interlopers upon our walls. The theatre had been infested and sullied. Our country had been invaded by a foreign power, pillaged and raped, as King Sweyn had done to Norwich in the ancient days. How could they have allowed it? How could Uncle Jerome have so cast off his family, so betrayed his blood? Uncle, lily-livered man, how can you exhibit yourself after allowing such a

thing? Shame, eternal shame, nothing but shame! I'd claw them down myself.

Police stood in front of the portraits, one by each. For fear, I supposed, of an incident. How far had we fallen, that we should have such need of police in this house! The theatre is a place of joy and stories, a place of freedom. It should require no constraining of life. Humans come here to escape their burdens, to be free for a few small hours—we take their weight from them, let them rest and be transported elsewhere, and then, when our tale is all told, they may take up themselves again with new thoughts to help them as they set back out on life's road. But how may that be done if police are standing guard to measure it? Look at the people of Norwich! They come unarmed. Look at the police of Norwich, however: they have truncheons. And truncheons say beware, be meek O Norwich populace, or we'll knock upon you until you bleed, we'll crack open your shells.

By a nudge from Hawthorne and a drip from Elsie, I became aware that I was being stared at, and not with affection. It was Mr. Penk, that cruel governor of coats and hats, who detains outer clothing during each performance like a prison warden. He places the coats and hats and scarves upon hooks as if he were stringing up dead birds in a butcher's window. Mr. Penk, the cloakroom dictator, had seen me, and there was enough wrong in what he saw to make him leave his cloakroom stable and trot out into the bloodred pasture of the foyer. I could feel his eyes upon me, even though I had turned my back on him.

"It is Penk," I said to Hawthorne. "We are being pursued."

"What then?"

Mr. Penk weaved his way toward us, through all the Norwich lives. What escape could there be from such a determined Penk as that one? He was quick upon us.

"Excuse me," he said, in that voice that was no pretty instrument, a cheap ill-tuned fiddle. "Excuse me, now."

And so I stopped, and my army likewise halted. About turn we did. I moved my armada to aim it squarely toward the creature called Penk. And we did look, altogether, mighty sorrowful.

"Excuse me, at once," fired Penk.

"Yes?" I managed. All innocence.

"That is a large and heavy coat you are carrying."

"Yes."

"And a . . . hat? Of some kind?"

I felt Archie breathing heavily, pressing hard upon my skull as if searching for a hiding place.

"Yes," was all I had in me.

"I take the hats and I take the coats. You have a scarf, too, and I take the scarves. Let me then unburden you of the great weight of your overgarments."

"No need," I replied and began to sidle away from Penk. But Penk had his eye upon Martha Tombland.

"It is perhaps the biggest coat I have ever seen. I'll hook it, if you please. Indeed, it shall likely require two hooks, three."

"No. Thank you."

"I'll have it, I tell you! I mean to have it!"

"I wish to keep it on."

"Can you imagine the irritation you will cause to the people sitting around you with such a coat and hat?"

"I keep them."

"I think it's best if I take possession. It is my employment."

"No."

"Such strange garments too. Come now, shall I help unbutton you . . ."

His hand came forward, touched, and shot back again in shock.

"It is very frigid, sir, your coat."

"Yes."

"It has perhaps just come out of cold storage?"

"Yes?"

"Then that explains it. Now do come along, sir, step this way. It is just a very few footfalls to the cloakroom. You will feel so much more comfortable."

"No. No."

"I do insist upon the matter, sir."

Hawthorne came between us. "No thank you, sir. He wants to keep his coat."

"And who are you?"

"I'm with him. Good day, sir."

And we left Penk behind us.

We tried to lose ourselves in the Norwich census. But I was that much taller than the rest of them, and could be spied without difficulty. It is a hard thing to be anonymous when you carry so many along with you.

The general fuss about us was broken by a new arrival: A flurry toward the entrance announced that Clarence Utting, Clarence the great beetle himself, was crawling into the auditorium. His people milled around him, Uncle Jerome fawned and scraped, wearing his largest smile. And the thing about Clarence Utting was that he was as strange a figure as us: Where we were slender he was great, where we were feeble he was lively. Mr. Clarence Deathwatch Utting.

"He's not true," Cecily whispered in my ear.

"Not a real human," said someone else farther down.

"Though he has bits of human about him. He is a patchwork person."

"Though he does have human parts. He is sewn-together skin and he is full of gas."

"My breath is inside him."

"And mine."

"She took our breath, and with it she pumped him up."

"He is a kind of balloon!"

"And there's a very bad beetle inside his head, inside the engine that moves him forward."

"He's a puppet!" I said.

"Yes, and he don't come out much. Mostly she keeps him safe in her office, pumping him up whenever a little air's got out. Taking one of our lives away to keep him working."

"He must have forty human lungs inside him."

"But even so, he ant real."

"He's one of her doings."

"Could we pierce him?" I asked.

"He has been patched and mended so many times. Like the tire of a motor vehicle."

"Ever so thick it is, his pelt."

"She must be up to something big, to bring him out."

Uncle Jerome was ushering Clarence Utting toward the royal box.

"We must go now. To the pass door. Our only chance."

Such a long way there, into the auditorium and all the way down the stalls and just by the stage itself. And only then did I comprehend something terrible.

"We've no tickets!" I cried. "They won't let us into the auditorium without tickets."

"Can we not steal a ticket?"

"We are ghosts after all, and do pilfer regularly."

"But how to get a ticket and where from?" I asked.

"Everyone here has tickets, everyone save us."

"Look, look about, they have them in their hands!"

"Let me do it," said a usually quiet girl called Sally Bolton, who was serving as a stale handkerchief in my top pocket. "Off I go now."

She hopped down, growing darker as she fell. Once on the floor she skittered along the carpet, very much like a mouse; she seemed to take on the carpet's color, rendering her very near invisible until I saw her dart up a moment—you had to know where to look—and take the tickets from a very smart husband and wife in fine garments looking most pleased with themselves. The gentleman who had been holding the tickets quite failed to register that he was now holding the dried and hard wings of a dead bird, a rook that Sally Bolton happened to keep in her pocket.

But before she could make it back, Penk was upon us once again. He had perhaps overhead some of our conversation.

"Gentlemen, your tickets please."

"But you're the cloakroom attendant," I said. "Not the ticket taker."

"E'en so. Tickets."

"We don't have to."

"I'll call the manager."

"Then call the manager."

Uncle Jerome was still busy with the great inflatable Utting, that hot air balloon being lowered into his seat.

But just then a policeman, unawares, had trod upon Sally Bolton. She was trapped under his leather boots (Norwich made), the two tickets peeking out from under his sole. To add to the panic, Uncle Jerome was out now and Penk rushing toward him, pointing at us. Jerome frowned briefly, then reinstated his smile as he came forward for this unwitting family reunion.

"Oh dear, oh no."

"What is it, Hawthorne?"

"I feel myself separating from the whole. I feel it shall happen."

"Keep together, Hawthorne, hold on!"

"Excuse me, sir," Uncle Jerome said to me. "Do you have a ticket?"

"Yes, of course."

"May I see it please?"

"Now?"

"Yes, now if you please."

"Ah yes, of course. I have it here somewhere about me."

As I fumbled, I heard a different commotion at one of the entrances into the stalls. Someone had tried to get into the theatre with a pair of dead bird's wings. The policeman moved to intervene, and a moment later the recently trapped Sally Bolton slipped two tickets into my hands.

"Here you are."

"Oh. Thank you."

"I do not know why I have been thus singled out."

"I do apologize, sir."

"I am most unhappy."

"Please, sir, accept my apology."

"I am a theatre critic from the *Times* of London," I said. "I shall be certain to put this incident in my review."

"Oh no, sir, please I beg you."

"Never have I been treated so. And by such a provincial theatre."

"Please, sir, let me make amends. I shall show you to your seats immediately. Allow me to personally see that you are comfortable. Please, please, do follow me."

"My ear," whispered Hawthorne, "it's coming undone."

"Shush now, Hawthorne, hold it in place. A few moments more."

It was a very busy night, All the seats were taken. Listen there: the noise of Norwich. And look: the scaffolding all gone, and all repaired at last. Down we tottered, down the central aisle of the stalls. Everyone looking at us.

"So honored to have you here," bobbed poor Uncle Jerome. "Such a privilege to serve you. Anything I may do to help, myself personally that is, you must but raise your hands and I shall come running. Now then, sir, sirs I mean, your seats are just here for you."

The front row of the stalls. In the center.

"Thank you."

"Is there anything else I may do for you?"

"I wish no more to be disturbed."

"No, sir. Of course not."

"Good-bye, Uncle Jerome."

"Good-b— I beg your pardon? Excuse me, sir?"

"Good-bye," said I, "I wish to be left alone."

Off went Jerome in a considerable sweat. I stood with Hawthorne beside me, clutching his head. The pass doors from the stalls onto the backstage were both closed, of course—that was to be expected—but what was different was that policemen stood in front of each. They'd go soon enough, I thought, once the curtain was up and the play begun. Then we might find our way through. I turned around to face the audience. With my back to the orchestra pit, I could see the whole of Norwich laid out before me.

"Everyone has come," I whispered.

All the gods was full, all the upper circle, all the royal and all the boxes. There was the bloat of Clarence Utting, filling up much of the royal box.

"Edith!" Hawthorne was tugging at my sleeve, which is to say he was pulling upon Anne Colgate. "Edith, I fear for my nose! My left ear is already absent!"

"Come, Hawthorne, let us sit."

"Oh, oh, I am coming undone."

"Sit, sit down, everyone is watching us."

We sat, but one of Hawthorne's feet didn't follow and stayed on the carpet. As he reached for it, the hand slapped away under the seat; the other, thinking it a wonderful game, set off with it. Then, as he leaned down in agony, his very head rolled off.

"Hawthorne!"

"I'm sorry," his head called from under the seat, "I so hate it when this happens! Good-bye and good luck!" Hawthorne spread out very quickly, and soon there was nothing in the seat beside me.

"Just getting settled," I said loudly, in an attempt to mask Hawthorne's departure, "making myself comfortable."

"What now?" wondered the boot that was Elizabeth Fooley. "How do we get to the stage with the policemen there?"

"We'll do it. When the police have gone. In the dark, when the play's begun."

"That's good, that is."

"They don't know it yet, those in the wings," I said, "but here we all are."

"Yes, here we are."

"Birnham Wood has come to Dunsinane."

"Well done, Edith. We'd not have managed without you."

"Thank you, Archie."

"Even if this is the end, still it's been worth it. Never felt so alive."

"Shut it, Archie," from here and there about me.

The orchestra stopped.

We sat, a hundredweight of ghosts exhaling about me.

The houselights went down.

The iron went up.

The red velvet curtain parted.

30.

Mr. Mealing's masterpiece.

The curtain parted. The stage was dark. Slowly the footlights came up and the stage lights, slowly we saw the scene. It was not like any stage set I have known before. Nor was it what I would suppose Mealing should have chosen for his setting: no drawing room here, no armchairs, no comfortable furniture to speak of. Behind me, the people of Norwich gasped; then, after a brief moment, a tremendous burst of clapping began, waves and waves of clapping at this new scenery. I had never heard clapping for scenery before.

What appeared onstage was an industrial setting: furnaces and great walls of brick—actual bricks, or so they appeared, not painted on canvas. Giant pipes ran up the walls, and huge vats stood confidently upon the stage. The scene, then: a factory. The thing was, it looked as if everything there actually worked, that it was all real. A whistle blew. A jet of steam rose from one of the pipes. The people oohed at it, though it was only—I suppose—a little dry ice, a magic very easily obtained. Still, it was disquieting, to see such a modern setting on our stage. Nothing fancy about it, no pretend. Simply a grim workplace.

Another whistle. Everyone jumped in their seats. Next the loud noise of a handbell. And then the great double doors at the back of the stage opened wide, letting in yet more smoke. They do overuse the dry ice, I thought, we'll all be coughing in a moment.

Could see nothing through that fog. Amateurs, I thought, to overdo it so.

And yet it didn't have the smell of dry ice. There was something sweet in it, sticky.

The audience all looked forward in excitement, taken in by it all.

As the smoke started to clear, figures began to emerge from the gloom—many of them there were, too, twenty, thirty, I should say. All of them stomping forward, behind them the rumbling of a great machine.

Here they are, then: the actors on the stage.

I look out to see who is who—to see my family again—but I recognize not a single soul on that stage. All these figures wear the same work overalls and, most notably of all, man or woman, the same face: a blank dull mask, repeated over and over. It is a pale face, with no warmth in it nor indeed any horror, not laughing or smiling, just blank and open-eyed. Each figure had the same small mouth: an expressionless slit cut into the mask. This face, over and over and over again.

All comes present now and we are here and this is it.

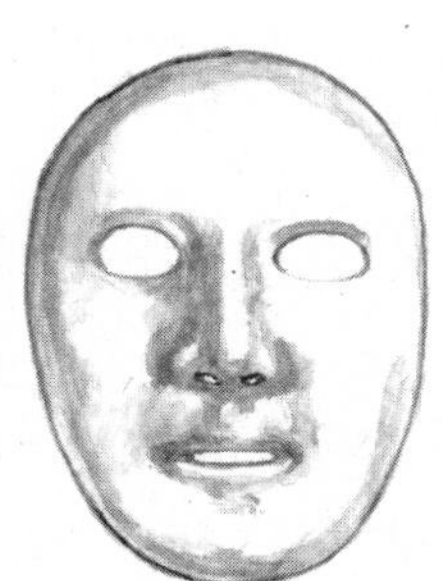

They move forward, in step, an army of blandness. They come downstage, ever closer to us with the dull thudding of their working boots. They stop and then they speak.

"Woe!" says one mask.

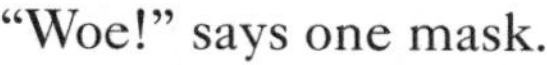

"Woe!" comes another.

"Woe!" a third.

This is not good, I think. This is not promising, is it, Mealing? Yet all around me is Norwich, Norfolk, breathing it all in.

"We work the factory."

"We work the furnace and the pumps."

"We turn the wheels."

"We shovel the coal that makes the fire."

We are a little tedious, I thinks.

"We are of Norfolk."

"We are of Norwich."

But that was my idea! It was my play that was set in Norwich, Norfolk. Mealing stole it from me!

"We grind the beetles."

Oh, that sounds familiar.

"We make the paste."

Some small cheering and clapping from the audience then.

"In each beetle there is a story."

"In each beetle a tale to tell."

Hold on, I think, sitting forward. This is something new yet.

"The beetles move about Norwich in the night."

"To all the sleeping people in their distress."

"The beetles beetle in."

"Crawl into ears, up noses, through open mouths."

Oh, wait! I like this, I think. This is good misery. What a terror! Bumps in the night!

"And inside."

"Yes, inside."

"The beetle bores, the beetle robs."

"It takes the tales. The tragedies, the comedies. The bedtime horrors. The sadness and the loses. We take away the pain."

"We stop the stories."

"We collect the stories."

"We hide the stories."

"We stop the stories."

"And when the beetle is dead, then may the people eat the stories, but only the husks, all life smashed out of them, boiled and boiled until the story is lost. Now all stories taste the same. And there is but one story left. Only ever one story."

"Our single story."

"We tell the tale of Maw Meg. Maw Meg who saved us."

"Maw Meg, the beetle queen. Maw Meg, Norwich savior."

But *I* was writing about Maw Meg! Oh, it isn't fair, it isn't.

I look around me at the audience then. What's this? they murmur a bit, but they listen on. Is new, surely. Is it theatre? Where's harlequin? Where's a giant? What have they done with the murdered king?

"Only one story."

"One story."

"We crush the other stories, we smash and grind them."

"And we pour the broken stories into small jars."

Good lord, Mealing, I never thought you had it in you. More juice than ever I gave you credit for. This is theft, yet there's good in it.

I feel the ghost children shifting about me.

"When do we go?" Simon Pottergate whispers.

The policemen are yet at the pass doors. "We'll watch a little more," I say.

"Edith!"

"Ssssh!" I say, as any theatregoer should when they hear a whispering after the play is begun. Don't break the spell, not now. Later, surely, once the curtain's down again. But right now—the play! The stolen play!

"Look out! Look out!" cry the chorus.

"Here comes the foreman."

"The story crusher."

"The story breaker."

"The story eater."

Then a bell, a siren. The audience look around them uneasily. It is the very same noise, I know, that is used to call workers to the great factory in our city. That must summon so many people in this audience to their labor each morning.

A single man comes forward. He is in a working suit and has a cap unlike the others. He wears no mask, and yet there is something false and contrived about his face; perhaps it is his greasepaint. The audience is clapping again—whatever has got into them?

And then I understand. How has it taken me so long to see it? What has gone wrong with me? Too long in the damp and dark, must be losing my reason. I know that man. I've known him all my life. And the people do cheer, for they know him too.

"Father! It's Father!" I whisper. "He's alive! All this time living!"

"Edith," says the coat.

"Edith," says the hat.

"Edith," say the spectacles.

"Edith," says the mole on my cheek.

"Edith, Edith, we must get on the stage," comes my boots two.

"Papa! Father!"

"Ssssh!" says someone nearby.

"Ssssh!" says I back at them, "I am the theatre, after all! Who are you to shush me?" And yet I quickly grow quiet, for there is my own papa upon the stage, where he ought to be.

"Edith, we should go," says my clothing. But I ignore it.

Up on the stage, my father is delivering a speech, a great long speech about collecting stories. Everyone in that great hall is with him and his words.

"I take them all," says my father, "when they come here, as you see, and police these people hereabouts. Together we keep Norwich safe. Without us all would come apart."

It is rather a bald way of writing, Mealing has. Is interesting, I suppose, but there's altogether too much declaring. My thoughts must have drifted off, for the next thing I hear is:

"Edith."

Oh, leave me alone, you clothes, and let me adore my own found papa.

Yet again it comes, "*Edith!*"

"Ssssh!" I say, but it is not Dripping Elsie who is whispering *Edith*, nor even my noisome attire. No, I understand now that my name is coming *from the stage*. From my own father.

"Edith," he says again. "It is Edith telling tales. Edith the story creature. So many tales she tells that there are tales told about her: That Edith is but a doll. That she is a doll but also a girl. I tell you now, Edith is a breathing thing and she is here among us. She has been summoned to this great room. How good it is that she breathes! For all breathing things must die. The tales of Edith, they spread from the theatre out into the city. What noise does this one Edith make! This Edith that puts a bad mark on all other Ediths. But the world will see no more Ediths named after this one, for who would subject their own child to such a blight? This Edith passes lies from person to person, and she tells her lies in such a way that the people of Norwich start to believe her. Such terrible untruths she whispers out from the theatre on Theatre Street, like a bad gas it is, and it does enter into every head. The most devastating stories. Stories of twisted love and dreadful murder, tales of fathers made of canvas, tales of collapsed stages and crushed donkeys. Tales of mothers with teeth. Ill tales of beetles. Tales of hiding and being hid. Bad tales that have fallen into the River Wensum and mix now with our drink."

That's not right. And that's not fair.

"What's this?" ask my clothes.

"Lies, all lies," I whisper.

"Yet I have caught her finally," says Father upon the stage, says Father about his own daughter. "I have caught her lying on the streets and have brought her here. Yes, it is good that she is living, for now she can die. Die and never lie no more. Come now unto me, Edith, bad Edith, truant Edith, Edith the liar, Edith that doth of murder speak. Step forward I say!"

I rise a little in my seat, though my clothes weigh me down so.

But there is no need for my getting up, I see that very quick.

For now a new character enters. It is a little girl all dressed in grey. With a grey face. Looking like she's seen a ghost. Or is one, perhaps. All one color, this Edith. She is not, I admit, so very pleasant to look at.

"Oh!" comes out of me. No way to keep it in. Here's more thieving.

"I am Edith," says the liar on the stage.

"She does speak then an'orl," someone in the audience mutters.

"Could talk all along," adds someone else, unnecessarily.

"I am Edith," from the thief once more. But she's not, of course, no she's not.

She steps forward, this grey girl, and I lean forward in my seat, despite my heavy companions, to draw closer to this mock Edith. Something familiar in her gait.

I know this Edith that isn't Edith. It is my sham sister, the firestarter.

It is Agnesia there, dressed as me.

"You have been telling lies, Edith," says Father.

"No, sir," says fake Edith.

"You told everyone you could never leave the theatre. And yet here you are."

She is still at the theatre! She never left.

"It was Father that said so. A terrible curse."

"It is a lie, of course. You may go where you please."

"No, no. The theatre will fall down, all will be rubble."

Some nervous muttering then from the audience hereabouts.

"It still stands."

"It cannot."

"It does not need you to keep it upright."

"It does, oh, it does!" wails fake Edith, and in such seeming agony that I feel myself quite moved by it. "Please! Please! I must go back!"

"You shall never see it more."

"My home!"

"You are to be made into Beetle Spread."

"No! No!" she cries. (Overplaying it, in truth.)

"No one will come and save you. You have lied to everyone and they have turned their backs on you. You are alone now."

"Help, help ho!"

"No one will come."

"Father! Father!"

Father says, "He cannot hear you!"

"Will no one help?"

The audience is worried for fake Edith now. I see two handkerchiefs held to faces.

"No one will help you."

"Will no one help me?"

Up until then, Mr. Mealing's play seems to have been going pretty much according to script. I can see him in the stalls, twitching a little with excitement. I am a playwright, he says to himself, I did this. He is quite moved by the general effect, I can tell, and untroubled by thoughts of thievery.

Only then comes the upset.

"I will help!"

The actors on the stage look at each other in confusion.

"There is no help," improvises Father.

"Yes! Yes, there is!"

The audience looks around, trying to see who has spoken the last lines. To their surprise, a tall and old man in the audience stands up and waves his arms.

"I shall help!" says the old man, who is me. "Come," I say to my clothes, and to the puddle at my feet, "the time is ripe."

"It is not in the script!" squeaks Mealing.

The audience looks about, wondering what to do, wondering if this is some new theatrical ploy. I step forward onto Mr. Fenwick's ramp, which connects the auditorium with the stage.

"You cannot come up," says Father.

"Yet here we come," I say.

I cross Fenwick's ramp unsteadily, until I stand at last upon the stage.

"Who are you?" cries Father, and very well, too, for it did set me up excellently.

"I am Edith Holler," says Edith Holler.

31.

The Mawther revealed— Part One.

"I am Edith Holler," I say.

The audience, at first confused, does now laugh—at least a few of them do—at this bewildered old man. For they know Edith, you see, they have seen her through the theatre window.

"I am Edith Holler," I say, for these things are best done in threes.

Again they laugh, but soon the laughing stops. For now, before their eyes, one of the most fabulous costume changes in history begins to occur. Now do I, thirteen-year-old Edith, begin to shed my ghosts. Now off comes Archie who was my hat, and off comes Anne Colegate who was my coat, and out from the pockets spill Jack Thaxter and William Gostlin, my scarf Kitty now falls, more and more am I Edith. The mole on my cheek floats off and stands as Cecily, now I step down from boots and one is Elizabeth Fooley and the other is Martha Tombland. Now I step forward, and last come my spectacles, who were ever Simon Pottergate. And now am I girl again, in the very last hour of girl.

"I am Edith May Holler."

There is some shrieking from the audience, and a host of loud noises of surprise at all the falling clothing, and the strange and wondrous shapes of ghosts of children beside me as I stood now among them. They see me clearly then, the audience does, and all my strange companions. Up in the gods somewhere two hands smack together, and then more and more all over the theatre, until the clapping and cheering goes on and on.

And I do bow.

To those upstairs in the gods. To the circles. To the stalls right and to the stalls left, which is to say to all the wards of Norwich, to Conesford and Wymer and Mancroft and Over the Water. Then I step backward and regain my part, which is myself.

"I am indeed Edith, and these are my friends."

At this point, it is true, some few members of the audience do leave—perhaps five in all, I do not think more than that. The police likewise leave their posts, sensing danger and wary of it. One woman begins to weep uncontrollably and an usher takes her out. One man is a little sick down his front. But, for the most part, the attendance stay in their seats. And out in the audience I am able to see now, among them, some people I know.

Up in the gods a man waving. "Gearte! There's my gearte!" It is Mr. Peat.

And in the upper circle, standing up and likewise waving at me.

"Prompt!" I say.

"I am a girl of thirteen," calls Miss Tebby, "long missing and feared dead, strange in aspect and difficult to fathom but with a heart that still beats. I have found a new group of alarming friends with whom I have thrived. I am the last crumb of a theatrical dynasty. Yet here I am again. Here among us! Back again! I am, indeed, Edith Holler!"

And now, seizing the opportunity, I begin to introduce my fellow actors to Mr. Peat and Miss Tebby and to all the audience. "Here is my friend Elsie and here Martha from Tombland . . ." I announce them all, and with each new introduction my friends do bow. Some of the audience shake their heads, or lean forward trying to understand what they are seeing. Others, comprehending more clearly, applaud for each new member of my traveling troupe.

But I find myself having to speak louder and louder, and soon I realize why: There is a growing commotion backstage. The other actors and Uncle Wilfred's stagehands are standing in the wings, waving at us to come off the stage at once. Most of the actors have fled into the wings during my costume change—even Father among them—and the orchestra pit had likewise been abandoned, but now they are growing braver again.

Then, from the corner of my eye, I catch a glimpse of a certain fabric amid the drab canvas of the offstage people. It is a dress—it is *her* dress!—I know it in an instant. Margaret is backstage and leering in the shadows. Mad is Mad Margaret. I can hear her calling on them to close the curtains: "She's not alone! She has help. End it, end it now!"

"These are my friends," I say. "They are the children. And they are ghosts. Every one of them. *Ghosts!*"

Some gasp. Others, I admit, laughed a little at my proclamation, for stupid people think that the way to present themselves as sensible people is to scoff at ghosts, until one comes up very close and says to them some winter's eve in a damp water closet on Botolph Street: *Hello*.

"Do not let them close the curtains or bring down the iron, my friends! Stop them, do stop them."

And then, in a flurry, my former clothes are suddenly airborne, a sight that might be taken for either rushing material caught in a wind or else children running. The laughter in the audience quite dries up at the sight of it. Now others join them. Cathy Mancroft, who had been curled up in the fly tower, spins her way downward. There are some yelps backstage, and a hush from the audience, though some seats do creak as people brace themselves within them as if for protection.

"Now, now, *I* take the stage."

This last was addressed by me to Agnesia. We stand upon the stage together, one grey girl and another grey girl.

"Get!" I command.

"We should share. Mother says so. . . ."

"Get!" I command Agnesia, and she gets, for Cathy Mancroft and her friends are coming for her and she fears their touch.

Quiet now on the stage, quiet now in the foggy blackness off the stage, quiet now in the up and down of the audience. Me alone upon the downstage.

Deep breath.

"I have a tale of Norwich here to tell," I begin.

Not a sound from the audience. Except one.

"No! No! No!" It is Mealing, tearing out his hair, running from the theatre. His play defeated.

"Step forward, Elsie, come now, do come."

Out of the darkness comes a timid girl.

"This is Elsie. My old friend. Come here, Elsie."

Elsie takes my hand.

"Do you see her?" I ask.

"Yes. Yes," a woman cries in the upper circle.

"No, I din't. I don't. Wait. Now, I do. Thar she is." This from the balcony.

"Elsie is a ghost," I say.

Elsie nods.

To help the audience understand this, Elsie falls into a puddle and pulls herself out of it.

Some applause, of course. I hear someone near the front whisper, "Done with mirrors, that is."

"When Elsie was twelve years old, she was murdered."

I let that sink in.

"She was drowned in a vat of Beetle Spread."

Not a sound from the audience.

"It happened here, in this city of Norwich."

No sound.

"A witch did it."

Oh, I have them, I have them.

"Witches are true. There's one that lives here. Here in Norwich."

No sound.

"She is with us right now in this very theatre, beside us."

Small sound, a little gasping for air, from somewhere offstage.

"I know her name. Shall I tell you?"

Small sound, offstage. Then from the audience, here and there:

"Tell us. Do tell us."

"Her name is Margaret Utting."

A wail from backstage.

"All of these children were murdered by Margaret Utting. Every one of them."

A gasp from the crowd.

"Uttings have been murdering for centuries. Have you lost a loved one while he or she was working at Utting's? Yes? Well, she was responsible. Did your child go off to school one morning and never come home again? Yes? Well, she is to blame."

From somewhere up in the audience, a cry:

"Oh, Elsie! My little Elsie!"

"Do any of you here know Archibald Pointer, from Conesford? She slit his throat one autumn down Rose Yard."

Then another:

"It's Archie! Oh, I think it's Archie, gone these twelve years."

"Who does remember Elizabeth Fooley, last seen Westwick Street, soon to be found in so many jars of Beetle Spread?"

"Is it my Bess, my lost Bess?"

"Do any know this child here, Nathaniel Bradshaw? He was ripped open in Pilling Park."

One by one, as they call out from the seats, the ghosts come forward to stand in the hard stage light. With great care they undertake to re-assemble themselves, try to show the shapes of the people they once were. And from the audience the names continue.

"Natty! Natty Bradshaw!"

"Sally Bolton."

"Reggie Noble."

"William Gostlin."

"Herbie Howlett."

"Lolly Bowes."

Some of the ghosts now are waving to the audience, blowing kisses. At the calling of their names the ghosts remember themselves better and stand much more like themselves, to great cries from the audience.

"Here they are then, the missing children of Norwich!" I proclaim. "Time now to tell the tales of Utting murder. Foul, foul black stories. We will show you, so that you may forever know." I clear my throat to make my aside: "To your places, everyone, please."

But then something I had not quite expected:

Down the stage walks Aubrey Unthank.

"I have a tale to tell," says Aubrey. He is wearing his worsted very loose, I notice. As if something is underneath it.

"Aubrey!"

"Hello, Edith! Something has happened, Edith. I yearn to tell it."

"We could not find you."

"I would tell it now, if I may."

"Yes. You say: I was born here in Norwich, Norfolk, in 1877," I prompt.

"A boy who, through cruelty, became a dirty and ripped worsted suit. And yet one day . . ."

And then Aubrey begins to tug on the worsted. He tugs and tugs, he rips himself, claws at himself, patches coming off. *Oh, he will quite destroy himself,* I think. But he does not. The worsted comes away, and it doesn't grow back. And there is Aubrey Unthank in front of me, made of flesh and not cloth, like Adam before him. Something solid. A new Aubrey, his face not white but pink. Aubrey is a flesh boy again! Can it be real? Aubrey made true again?

"The spiders, Edith! The spiders ate the worsted and broke the spell! I didn't die! I was never dead, only trapped. She trapped me in worsted."

"You are real!"

"I am!"

"Oh!"

"Oh!, indeed," laughs Aubrey.

"Yes: Oh! There was one other living then in the underlanes, beside me all along!"

The audience claps to see the miracle. They cheer and some weep and some cry, *Encore!* Aubrey there in all his newness, in white shirt, blazer, corduroy shorts.

"You're live!" I say and hold his warm hands.

"I am, I am. I wasn't dead. Just worsted."

I turn to the audience. "This is Aubrey. A child of Norwich. See him here in his fine clothing. Note that I do love him so. This Aubrey walked upon the same streets that you all walk upon—before he was so miserably imprisoned."

I walk up to start the story. I am standing a little in front of the prompt box.

"I will tell you how it all happened, I will show you now." I begin to pull at my grey smock. Underneath it is Margaret's dress. I pull the grey away and stand there in red.

The audience whispers and calls out: "There she is! O there she is!"

"I," say I, "I am Margaret Utting!"

I have scarce finished the last syllable of her name when the trapdoor springs open and I fall from the stage into darkness.

32.

The Mawther revealed—
Part Two.

The moment I fall through the trap, I feel a sudden gust of dry ice. Then, as the fog clears, in the very place where I had stood dressed as Margaret, stands now Margaret in another dress of the same hue. The very actual Margaret Utting herself.

Great clapping from the audience, and great hissing and booing, for it must be said that her timing was impeccable; she has taken the audience like a true professional. Margaret stares at the audience, her lip curling, then turns upstage toward Aubrey. Aubrey steps back one pace, two.

"Where's Edith?" He trembles.

"I am Margaret Utting."

"What have you done with Edith?"

"*I* am Margaret Utting."

"Edith?"

"She's Edith Holler *pretending* to be Margaret Utting!" someone calls from the audience.

"Come here, child Unthank. Come here, come to your mother do."

"Edith? Yet you do look so like *her*."

"Come along, Aubrey. We are telling a tale."

"I don't think I like this so much anymore."

"Come to Mother."

"I'd much rather not."

"Come along, don't keep the audience waiting."

"Must I?"

"You know you must."

"You look so like . . ."

And, as if he is operated by a puppet master, Aubrey comes along to Margaret then, without ever wanting to.

"There you are, Aubrey. What a picture of health and life you are."

Aubrey whispers, "Is that you, Edith? Under all that? You look so much like *her*."

"Stand up properly. What clothes are these? I gave you a suit, do you recall? Now we are here to tell your tale. What sort of tale is it?"

"It is a terrible cruel tale, with murders several."

"Is it indeed?" She turns to the audience. "You know me, good people of Norwich. You *know* me. I have always been among you and you have always been fond of me. We are old friends, you and I."

Some nod then, bow their heads at her.

"Now then. Must we believe in this nonsense?" she asks.

Many shake their heads then. A few cries of *No!* from the audience.

"Do we truly believe this talk of murder? Is it likely?"

"No," comes quickly then.

"No."

"No."

"Of course not, for you are people of Norwich and people of Norwich are good and sensible." She calls offstage then, sotto voce, "Agnesia darling, bring the sharp knife, will you?"

"Yes, Mother."

Agnesia enters in a different dress—one of her own now, so that it is clear she is playing the role of Agnesia. In her hand is a large butcher's knife.

"This is a large butcher's knife," says Agnesia instructively to the audience.

Now then, you who are watching this. You had better sit up and pay good attention, for what is about to happen is going to come very fast. So then, take a deep breath, here goes. It is a game of relay, do follow the baton. Whoever holds it is dead. Swift now. *One. Two. Three. Breathe.*

When I fell through the trapdoor, I fell hard and quick; there was no mattress to catch me. I could have broken my back—no doubt she had hoped for that—but I landed hard on my coccyx. (I think I may have snapped it in my landing, so that it is at an angle, so that I have a tail now.) I spend a long moment panting before air returns to my lungs.

I look around me at the new trap room, which feels like the underbelly of some factory machine. Up above me is the stage, and onstage I hear Aubrey's voice . . . and Margaret's too.

"Aubrey!" I cry.

But it is no use—no one can hear me in that below room. I clamber along the floor until I find an opening, a vent of some sort, and I squeeze through. From there I fall out onto one of the dressing room landings. There is old Mr. Leadham's lanthorn still! I strike the flint attached to it by a shoelace and it comes alive. Yelping for my busted coccyx, I rush upstairs to the stage level, pushing past any cousins or uncles or aunts milling along the backstage passageways—all of them wearing that blank mask we'd seen on the stage. *Quick, quick,* I think, *your Aubrey, he needs you.*

"Out of my way, you puppets!" The masks part and I run on and on until I am backstage, then in the wings. Stage left.

"This is indeed a large butcher's knife," says Margaret upon the stage.

"Whatever are you doing with that?" asks Aubrey.

"I am going to murder you with it. This is a murder story. You said so."

"But that is not how it went."

"Now it is."

Margaret slices the knife in the air in a wide arc—such a bold gesture—and steps back so that the audience might better see Aubrey. There he stands upon the stage, my worsted Aubrey. He speaks no lines, though he has two mouths now: The first is the one I knew, with its lovely pink lips. The other opens wide on his throat, with terrible red lips, and sprays red out, far out, into the audience. What a great jet of red it is.

Oh, very well done. So convincing. Hear the audience, how they scream and scream. For the audience is getting dirty.

But no—it is real.

It is true murder!

"Oh, my Aubrey!" I scream.

Poor Aubrey, alone in focus upon the stage, a child dying. Poor Aubrey, spilling out. And soon he spills out so much that his knees give under him and he tumbles to the floor and his clothing grows damp with red.

"Oh, my Aubrey!" I scream.

My scream is heard of course—it is a scream, I say, and not a whisper—and so it is likely heard down Theatre Street, right around Norwich Castle, perhaps even to the cricket grounds on Mousehold Heath.

"Oh, my Aubrey!" I scream the third time.

Standing in front of fallen Aubrey, Margaret smiles at the audience—a great, sickly smile—and the wide hoop of her dress quite covers Aubrey from sight.

"You there, spot me."

She walks downstage, a spotlight upon her. The rest of stage is dark. Aubrey can no longer be seen.

"Listen to me, my dear people. My Norwich ones, listen, listen only to me." It takes a while, for some of the audience are booing and shrieking at her. "Only *I* was born Margaret Utting. You know me. You do not know that boy you think you just saw fall. You never saw him before. And, please, look up in the box. There is Clarence Utting, my father."

Stern Clarence looks down at all Norwich, and Norwich looks up toward him, their employer, and a lonely clap becomes multiple, and then someone invites three cheers and three cheers are given.

"Thank you, thank you," says Margaret. "No harm done. I forgive you. Nothing did happen here. Of course it didn't—what can you think of me? It was to entertain only, a spectacle to launch this new building, the Utting Theatre." She bows, Margaret does, and calls quietly to Agnesia: "Pull the body away."

Agnesia looks uncertain.

"No one died, you see. That is not a dead child." And more quietly, "Pull away, Agnesia."

In the darkness, she begins to.

"When the stage lights come back up, you will see that no harm is done."

As Agnesia moves toward Aubrey, I rush to him, too, thus appearing a second time in view of this audience. I shine the lanthorn upon my dead boy. Oh, but look at him.

"Come, Aubrey. Come again."

The light shows him clearly. Agnesia takes hold of the lanthorn, trying to pull it from me, and in the struggle—oh, to see the light rushing back and forth, it is most dramatic—the lanthorn falls and the glass shatters and the flame is set free. It is a good and hungry flame. See how quickly it catches hold of Agnesia's dress! See how it climbs up her person. Look! Look there!

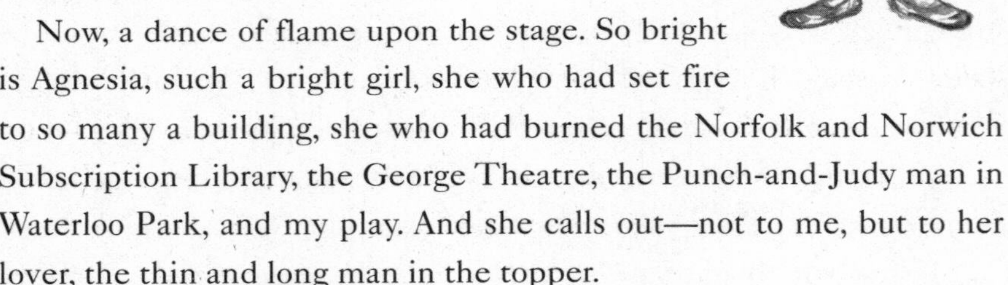

Now, a dance of flame upon the stage. So bright is Agnesia, such a bright girl, she who had set fire to so many a building, she who had burned the Norfolk and Norwich Subscription Library, the George Theatre, the Punch-and-Judy man in Waterloo Park, and my play. And she calls out—not to me, but to her lover, the thin and long man in the topper.

"Mr. Jet! Mr. Jet!"

How she cries out in her personal inferno. Such an Agnesia bonfire!

"Mr. Jet! Mr. Jet!"

Now, nothing gets a theatre staff moving more quickly than the name of Jet. Uncle Wilfred raises the stage lights. Uncle Jerome raises the houselights. See the panic on Uncle Jerome's face; see him rush with bucket and hose; see beside him his people, similarly armed. But are you listening properly? For she says not calmly, "Mr. Jet is in the house," the proper way to alert the proper people and gather them to action. No, indeed, she has merely screamed "Mr. Jet! Mr. Jet!" And though her wails do bring forth my Uncle Jerome and his aquatics, still it is such a loud clamor that it can be heard all the way out there in farthest Norwich.

Agnesia has not summoned the proper people. She has summoned the man himself.

Mr. Jet was just then scorching the kitchens in the boarding school of Crooks Place. He had hoped to see many dressing gowns and pajamas go up in smoke before the night was out. But he hears the call that came out from the theatre, and it stops him. He is quite a small Mr. Jet now, about the size of a rabbit. But he speeds up his work, and is soon quite as big as a pig. He is in his top hat and suit as always and his mouth a wide O. Which would have surely answered the distress call with a great

"Agnesia!"

of his own, but he had no words other than *crackle* and *whoosh*, and so he crackles and whooshes and speeds his way out of the school kitchen and across the playground, diminishing rather as he goes. But as he speeds his way into Chapelfield Gardens, his breath making white clouds, he touches some trees and sets them afire, and he grows taller then, and taller still as he hugs the park gate. There is a cart in the road and he touches that, too, so that as he rushes his way down Theatre Street and reaches the theatre steps, he has grown to about the height of a streetlamp.

As Agnesia dances onstage in her state of inflammation, and Uncle Jerome runs up and down the stalls with his sloshing hose, his boys behind him, Margaret—a mother also, you may recall—wails to see her daughter so energetic. She longs to get at her, to put her out, to end the child's suffering, but she cannot get to her.

Something is in the way.

And that thing in the way nips and bites and scraps at her. That thing, in fact, is many things, of all shapes and sizes—ghosts of children, every one of them, ghosted from childhood by her own self. How they do haunt her now in her moment of distress! Nor do they care very much when she waves a bloody knife in their direction; rather, they yelp and squall and persecute the unhappy woman. (And how many Norwich people present in that moment will later find small bite marks about themselves!) So then Margaret called out in agony—not to her daughter, for she cannot get to her, but to something else altogether,

"Help me, my loves! Come now to me! One and all, come now! Come my beetles, come to Mother!"

And she gets down on all fours, as if she is in the same vein as Cathy Mancroft, and she bangs her head upon the stage, and that is a horrible thing to see.

And elsewhere in Norwich, and in the theatre, and in the houses all about and in the factory, the ground begins to shift. More and more a knocking grows, and the streets of Norwich have a shimmer about them as if they are alive and on the move. Like a tornado, a dust cloud, a great weather event of beetles comes hurtling along the city streets, growing larger and larger until they reach Theatre Street and even the theatre steps there. By then they are about the size of a herd of cattle. Still they hurtle forward.

At that same time, upon the royal box, Clarence Utting—shocked to see his daughter and granddaughter, or at least his maker, in such distress—begins, against his true will, to inflate rather. He grows and bloats until he knocks over the other chairs in the box. As Clarence Utting staggers to his feet, the chairs around him fall over. It is not a beautiful advance, his. Like some large opera singer, he puts his arms out toward the stage with a desperate sympathy. In a horror to watch Agnesia's dance, which is more black than red now, Clarence Utting dances a little in his unsteadiness, a dance with an invisible partner. Stumbling, sometimes dropping, sometimes rising, he finds himself at last even upon the very edge. In his urgency Clarence Utting totters upon the very edge of the red velvet box, standing high upon it, dangerously perched and twirling himself, beyond his control, around and

around. Then, as he struggles for balance, his foot slips, and up he does rise for a little moment, and then down he does plummet—down, down into the left-hand aisle of the stalls, about the size and weight of a full-grown bull.

Finally Mr. Jet himself, just ahead of the herd of beetles, bursts into the stalls—to the absolute horror of Uncle Jerome, who now has fire all round him but only one hose. But as Mr. Jet rushes himself down the stalls, his mouth open and crackling and whooshing, there comes a different whooshing sound, and with it a gagging noise—and, looking up, Mr. Jet sees a rapidly approaching Clarence Utting, who lands with a great incredible burst right on top of Mr. Jet and so doing puts his lights out, until he is naught but a pile of dust, and then no more at all, only a very crushed hat.

How the audience wails at the tumble of this weighty Utting, deflating atop a small smoky gentleman. Even as they struggle to make sense of the bizarre double accident, however, they are distracted to feel something shifting at their feet. At first they wonder if some timid youth named Graham, for example, has grown brave at last and was playing footsie, or if only the children in the row behind would keep still—that is, until they start looking down at their feet for the source of the disturbance, and one by one begin to scream, for now under their seats, touching their feets, runs a great swarm of beetles.

Beetles then everywhere! On comes a great wave of beetle, covering the whole red carpet of the stalls, heading straight for the stage, using up all space possible. In every corner of the theatre people stand upon their seats in horror at the creatures, to escape their touch as they pass, to stay as far away from them as possible. (One child from Hellesdon, seated in the upper circle, complains that it is unfair that he does not have any of the beetles, which are exclusively on the stalls floor. Well, young man, perhaps in future you might encourage your parents to invest in better seats.) The tide of beetles causes Uncle Jerome and his boys to drop their buckets at last, sends them fleeing up the staircase, and so it is all too late for Agnesia, who is by this point quite bacon.

When the sudden sea of beetles comes upon the sagging remains of Clarence and the extinguished Mr. Jet, they decide, rather than go over them, to go under. And so it is that the bodies of these two notables are swept onto the stage by the wave beneath them—the beetles!

On the stage now, a mighty clash of beetles and ghostly children, and from the audience a barrage of cheering and waving—some calling out for the beetles, others yelling on behalf of the ghost children. The beetles swarm around Cathy Mancroft, an astonishing ghost with much of the arachnid about her, until they have altogether covered her, until it seems she's grown an entirely new and moving skin of beetles. Now poor Cathy topples with all these beetles about her into the orchestra pit, and all the ghosts and all the beetles rush to follow, some to protect, some to attack. Beetle after beetle, ghost after ghost, all fall into the orchestra pit until they are quite lost from sight.

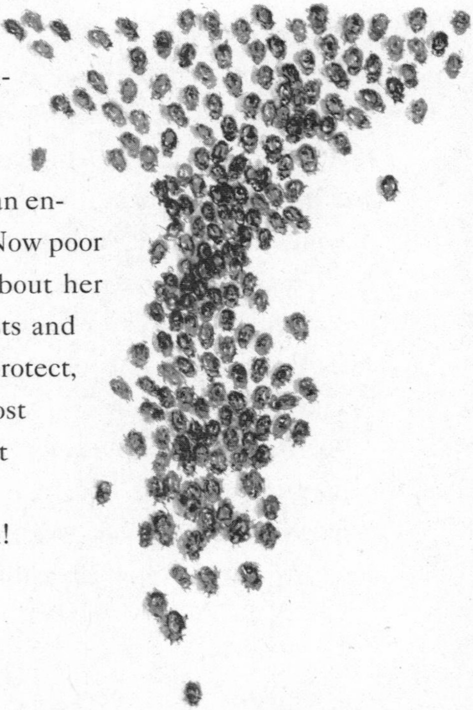

Such clamor from the audience then! Such hurrahs and whistles of approval.

And when everyone else is gone, I am left alone onstage with Margaret.

Are you ready now? We are nearly there. One last big breath and all will be done. Here goes. (But be steady, this theatre is old, do not move too swiftly or your seat may shriek.)

"You!" shrieks Margaret, "Look what you have done! My babies!"

I step back a little, make myself a very little farther from her, though still on the stage and still very well lit.

"It is my life!" she wails. "My life you have killed."

"My love!" I cry. "My love lies dead!"

"And now you must die for it!"

She lifts the knife—the sharp butcher's knife, you remember it. And she runs for me, aiming to plow the blade right through me. I stagger back, but she is too fast.

In it goes, deep.

But it doesn't hurt, not really.

"I want your life!"

She pulls the knife out—it takes some tugging—and strangely there is no blood with it. Down it comes again, in goes the knife, and at last she tugs it free and I tumble to the floor. Yet what a strange doll it is that lies there, poor lifeless Edith—for it is not me after all, but the doll of me, which has been switched and now lies stabbed upon the floor. I am still uncut.

"EDITH! I WANT EDITH!"

Margaret screams, and as she screams she seems to increase, to grow larger with her anger, her fury filling her until she is twice the size—no, much larger than she ever was before. Here is something ancient and eastern and Anglian. Old history still living. A horror Faerie upon the stage.

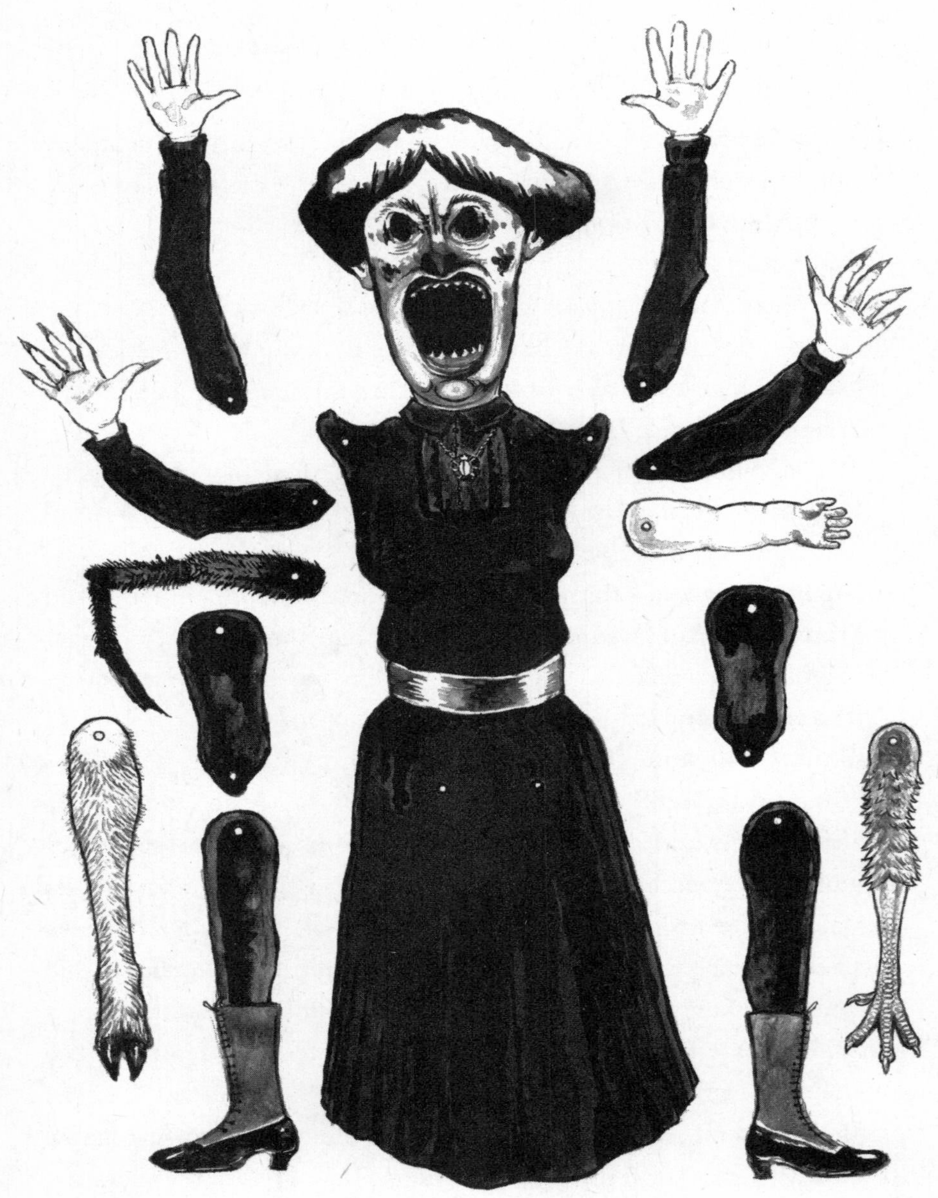

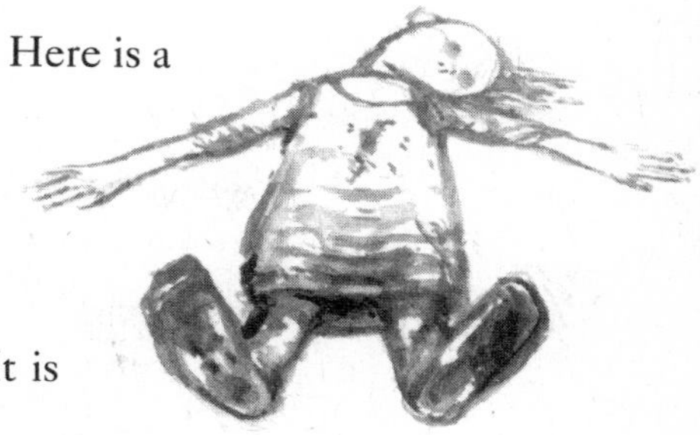

Ah! the audience cries, a giant at last! Here is a marvelous giant!

"Who did this?" cries the monster. "Who switched? Who?"

"I did."

An old woman out of the darkness. It is Mrs. Stead at last. The puppet mistress.

"Who are you?" Margaret demands.

Mrs. Stead steps forward, as if she is made of very old wood, and speaks.

"Come, you must remember. Your own sister, after all."

"My—" She stops. "Agnes?"

"Hello, Margaret."

"I cannot believe it. How old you are!"

"And you yet so young."

"You live! And here?"

"Here I am after all these years."

"Hiding? Here?"

"Among the puppets."

"I'll cut your strings."

"I cursed the child to keep her safe. I had one of the old actors do it. I gave her the idea and she made much of it. She was ill and spitting blood, her death was very close, and this added great weight to her argument. And when she cursed the child—and she, being an actress, did wholly relish the part—she put so much effort into it that she did hurt herself in the process and died shortly thereafter. And so Edith was cursed and safe from you. And then, when I could, I fed her the idea of you. And she made the part her own. Edith was so natural at it, she was born to do it. See, Margaret, I kept the child safe! See what have I done."

"And see, Agnes, what I may do!"

Like a maddened barber in a desperate hurry, Margaret swings her knife swiftly, and the old woman comes smashing down to the floor, cut precisely in half.

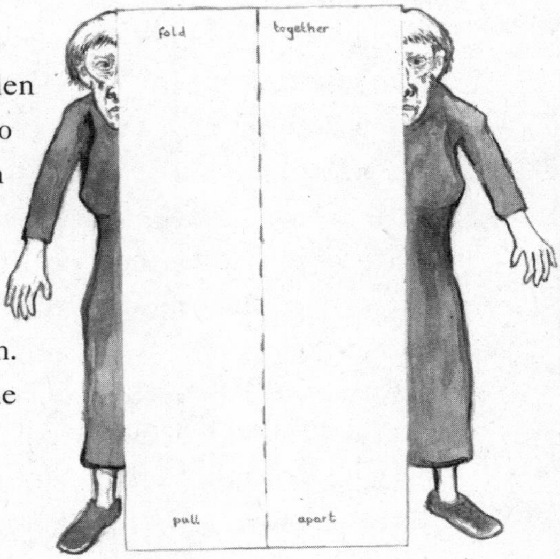

"DEAD SISTER!"

Mrs. Stead, in two halves, has fallen down. But there is no blood, only two halves of an old and rotten wooden thing. The spirit at last has abandoned it, given up its old shape.

"MRS. STEAD!" I cry.

"EDITH!" roars the giant woman.

By then I am downstage, near the pit, careful to avoid the trapdoor.

"I'll have you now!" giant Margaret hisses.

But just as she marches forward, someone else pushes me out of the way, forcing himself onto the knife.

It is Father! My own father, still in the clothes of Mr. Mealing's play. (And, indeed, how far we have come from that, in so short a time.)

Father now, stabbed, for me. Father, with blood all about him.

"Father!" I run into his arms. "Oh, my Father. You came for me!"

Until, right there before me, his nose falls off.

"Oh, Mr. Collin! Mr. Collin!"

"How was I?" asks Mr. Collin. "Was I good?"

"Oh, Mr. Collin, you were wonderful!"

"I may die happy now," he says, loud enough that those in the gods may hear. And then the poor sweet man slumps down, quite dead.

"You killed Mr. Collin!" I scream. "You killed Aunt Bleachy. You killed my own Aubrey. All that was ever dear to me!"

"You are dead, Edith!"

"*You* are dead, Margaret!" comes another voice.

But then—again!—it is Mr. Collin on the stage. Doubled up, I say. Mr. Collin twice over, and yet not Mr. Collin at all.

It is my own actual father, now, dressed as Mr. Collin. In his crumpled suit, in his simple shoes. With his hair parted like Mr. Collin. His skin pale like Mr. Collin's, using No. 1 greasepaint certainly.

"I hid as Collin, my own Edith. These many long days. Wounded I crept from my room and put in my place the dummy of Coriolanus."

"Father, you never came for me. Never once! I thought you were dead."

"I live yet, Edith. Frail, yet still alive. Look there, I see my audience!"

But Margaret—still onstage—swings at my father, and he topples instantly.

"I have lost my part," groans Father, his voice only just audible. "No more lines. Good-bye, Edith. You are on your own now. Ah, I always hoped to die upon the stage."

"Father!" And Father, in a great burst of red sawdust comes apart, smashing onto the floor.

"FATHER!" I cry. "A poor father, yet a father still. MY OWN FATHER!"

"Come to Mother, Edith. I'll have you now. Nothing between you and me anymore. There's no one left. Come now, come. You know you must. I own you. I've come to stop up all your stories forever. I will have this dull barn made proper use of: another factory for Norwich. That is all the theatre that is needed. So, Edith, it was always to be so, and now it shall be done: I AM HUNGRY."

By now Margaret has grown so large that she fills the stage and must stoop over or hurt her head. Such a massive size to her, larger than any giant we have ever mounted in our theatre. She opens her mouth, that huge mouth with those long and sharp teeth; she takes hold of me; and she lifts me high in the air, all the way up to her head. And then shoves me into her maw—and down and down I go, down the tunnel of her throat and into the depths of her.

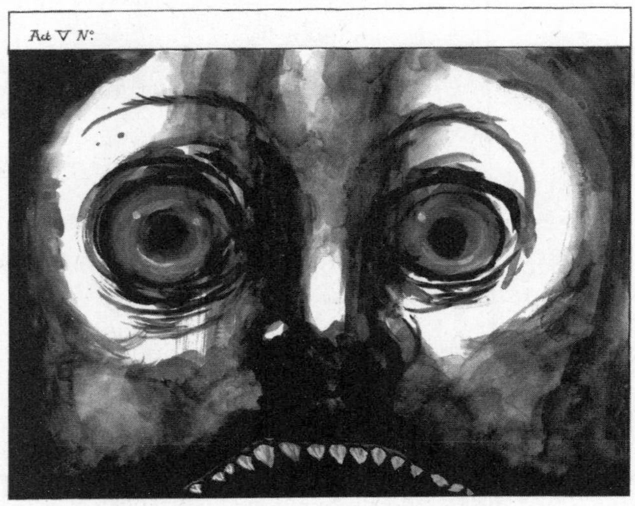

I am eaten.
It is done.
Over.

Huge Margaret walks forward. She sits on the edge of the stage, swallowing, licking her lips, smacking them in satisfaction. She swings her vast legs in the orchestra pit like a contented child.

Huge Margaret smiles.

The audience does not know what to do, for this ending is like none they have been traditionally served. In all previous productions, the hero or heroine has always prevailed. Why should a giant win now? How can it sit so vastly upon the stage, unchallenged, rubbing its tummy? There is a restlessness about them. They are unsure what to do. Is this the end? Should they applaud?

They do not applaud. Instead they sit and look at Margaret as she sits and looks at them. It is a true ancient devil woman they are watching. Then, from somewhere dark and deep, comes a loud click. A clack. A knock. We have heard this sound before, we know it well: it comes from that local toy, the death-bringer, the beetle rattle, the deathwatch dummy. It is well known, this toy, and has many names. Someone, somewhere, is playing on such a toy. Strange to hear it here. There it is again. A little louder. Everyone looks around, this way, that way. Who is playing with the beetle hammer?

Careful now, those heads were thinking, they do work, those toys.

Careful, you'll summon beetles.

Margaret looks confused. She holds her belly, scratches at it, but as she opens her great mouth, the noise of the beetle toy grows much louder. What's this? Can it be that the beetle clacker is inside Margaret? That someone is playing with the toy *inside* the enormous woman? And there it is again. Margaret puts her hands to her mouth; the noise is muffled, though still audible. Something shifts within the orchestra pit. Margaret stands up and staggers to the back of the stage.

Out of the pit, now, climbs another wave of beetles. Hundreds and thousands of them. Great Margaret retreats a few steps farther back, but

Mrs Margaret Holler
in the role of MAW MEG

the noise, the knocking, persists within her, and on the beetles come. Yet more and more, until the stage is a beetle land. And the knock it comes on and on and on. Beside the beetles come up the ghost children, every one of them, come to see what caused the beetles they were fighting to suddenly flee.

The beetles have reached Margaret. They are at her feet, at her ankles, and her calves, swarming up her dress now. And Margaret in her panic opens her mouth, but no scream comes. Only a:

Knock.

And through that opened gate, through that wide and panicked mouth, leap the beetles in a steady stream, all thousands of them, cramming themselves down her throat until there is no beetle to be seen. They've all gone in, rushed inside the belly of Margaret. The stage is as clean of beetles as if Aunt Bleachy had seen to it herself.

Only Margaret, looking rather bloated now, is alive upon the stage.

She holds her stomach. She has such a strange look about her, such an agony.

Her eyes, they roll in her head. She shakes her head in misery.

For a moment she stands still, a distillation of horror upon her face.

And then she explodes.

Dead beetles and gore burst out upon the audience in an enormous wave. Flesh and blood and liquid and insect and ooze. It all crashes out upon the audience, falls with such a force and in such profusion that even the little boy from Hellesdon is quite satisfied. There are noises of disgust, but then, too, a few nervous laughs. Everyone wiping themselves down, finding a rough camaraderie in the soaking—for the Holler Theatre has certainly outdone itself this night.

And with the dead Margaret and the dead beetles the dead children are gone now, too, just rags upon the stage. For their justice has been done at last, and the truth is known, and they are at rest, at peace, poor abused creatures. Yes, all the ghosts have gone now, no revenge no more.

It takes a little while for the audience to settle down.

When at last they do, they turn their eyes back to the stage.

There, among the corpses of Aubrey and Agnesia and Clarence and Mr. Jet and Mrs. Stead and Mr. Collin and Father, and the bits and pieces of enormous Margaret, stands a single woman. She is soaked—like the people of Norwich, only more so.

In her hands, the woman holds a wooden beetle hammer.

It is Edith Holler.

I am not smiling.

I have won.

Well, perhaps a very little smile. But it is gone in a moment.

I pick up a shred of torn worsted, once Aubrey's, and hold it in my hand.

I am going out.

I am free.

The curtain comes rushing down.

Exit Edith.

33.

Curtain call.

It took a long time for the audience to react. Most sat there in stunned silence.

The theatre had never been so quiet.

At last some person somewhere, we shall never know who, timidly slapped his sticky hands together—once, twice, a lonely sound—before he gave it up. Then another started somewhere else; he may have got as far as eight or even ten before stopping. There was a second silence, but not as long as the first. Then it picked up, the clapping did, and grew and grew in confidence. Soon it was very loud indeed, louder than anyone could remember. But it was not enough for them, the clapping. Soon the noise of the seats slapping into their backs was heard, but not because the audience was preparing to leave. No, the entire theatre was on its feet—many of them crunching fallen beetles beneath their soles. (The cleaning afterward would be historic.)

"Bravo!" some in the stalls cried. And many echoed this. "Bravo! Bravo!"

The audience clapped and clapped, for the dead children had finally been set free and full justice had been done. Clapped for the lost bodies of their small hometown. They clapped and they clapped.

They stayed clapping, waiting for the curtain to rise again, for the curtain call.

But it never came.

Instead, at last, their hands exhausted and their legs likewise tired, they gathered up their coats and children and went out into the night, for it had been a long evening and they were all ready to go home.

Edith Holler, authoress.

Acknowledgments

This fantasy came about during the bleak days of the pandemic. I had been working on another novel, but just then it seemed impossible. Sitting in a bungalow in Austin, Texas, with my beloved family, I was certainly very lucky; yet I longed for home, by which I mean England. I was brought up in a village outside Norwich, and Norwich, as a child, had always seemed to me the capital of the world. Whenever anyone mentioned London, I thought they really meant London Street. As a boy, whenever I had pocket money, I bought lead soldiers from the Games Room in Elm Hill and *Star Wars* figures from Jarrold's. The cathedral seemed both beautiful and forbidding, but its bishop, Maurice, was to me as close you could come to God. One day he actually visited my parents' house, and before going he left a postcard of Holman Hunt's *The Light of the World* on the pillow of each of us children. The next morning, upon waking up, we each had a message from Bishop Maurice blessing us, and we felt as though some saint had appeared among us. Norwich Castle was where I saw my first corpse, in the form of a partially undressed Egyptian mummy, an acquaintance I never forgot. Best of all were the occasions when my parents took us to the Theatre Royal, my first-ever visits to the theatre: pantomimes at Christmas—*Snow White and the Seven Dwarves*, *Jack and the Beanstalk*—and, if we were lucky, a straight play or a musical during the year.

During the pandemic, theatre came to seem the most wonderful, impossible thing. I would receive messages from my theatre friends back in England, sitting at home with little to do, hearing some members of the government suggest that they might think about retraining; some of them wondered if they would ever work again. All those theatres, all over the world—dark, empty caverns all.

I myself have spent memorable parts of my life working in theatre. Many years ago, when I lived in London (the city, not the street), I worked as a stage door keeper for a West End theatre—the Comedy Theatre on Panton Street, now known as the Pinter Theatre, because Harold Pinter worked there so often. I loved that theatre. The stage door keeper holds the keys to a theatre, and I unlocked ours in the morning as if it were my own place, no one there at that early hour but me. A few years later, for some weeks, I actually lived inside a theatre, while rehearsing a play I'd adapted in Craiova, Romania. Many of the actors actually lived inside the theatre, a huge, monstrous building built during the dictatorship of Nicolae Ceauşescu. Years after that, I worked with puppets both briefly with a shadow puppet master in Malaysia and with Faulty Optic, a theatre company in the UK. Just as the pandemic started, my last piece of outdoor sociability before fleeing back to Austin was with Clive Hicks-Jenkins, whose words and art have inspired me to use toy theatres as the principal illustrations in this novel. You may notice that many of the illustrations in this novel are designed as elements of an antique card theatre, and it is actually possible to cut the pages of this novel out and use them to construct a toy theatre—but if you'd rather not cut up your book, I've posted a full card theatre kit on my website, where it can be downloaded for free: www.edwardcareyauthor.com.

All of this, and all of these various theatres (not forgetting also the Theatre Royal Drury Lane, where I was a ticket-tearer one summer), have inspired the novel *Edith Holler*. So I would like to thank a few of the people I met at those theatres: Robert Coover, Lisa Creagh, Robert Delamare, Pak Dollah, Anca Dragomir, Pauline Fan, John Flint, Eddin Khoo, Michael Ginesi, Gavin Glover, Steve Harris, Clive Hicks-Jenkins, Pepsicola Pete, Terry Taylor, Liz Walker, Neil Wallace, Hugh Whitemore, Ed Wilson and Claudia Woolgar.

Enormous thanks as always to my wonderful and long-suffering agent, Isobel Dixon. I have been fortunate to have as my editor the very brilliant Calvert Morgan, whose advice, given with such grace and humor and insight, is always what I most need. Huge thanks to everyone else at Riverhead, especially Bianca Flores, Nora Alice Demick, Glory Plata, Jynne Martin, and Geoffrey Kloske. And thanks most of all to Elizabeth, Gus, Matilda, and Margaret Cat, with whom I was so fortunate to pandemic.

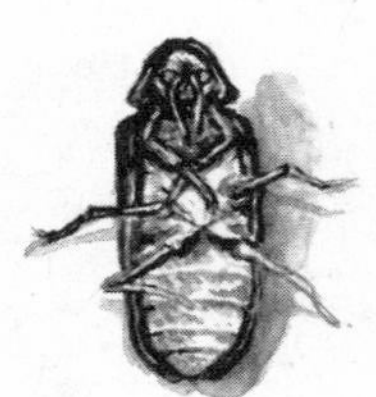